Praise for

THE
DANGEROUS
KIND

'Dark, uncompromising . . . I raced through it in a matter of days.
Highly recommended'
HOLLY SEDDON

'A dark subject but so relevant. Very cleverly employs our
obsession with true crime'
AMY LLOYD

'Great concept . . . originality oozing off every page'
EVA DOLAN

'A dark and unpredictable page-turner'
JENNY QUINTANA

'Searingly relevant'
GILLIAN MCALLISTER

'Brilliantly compelling'
T.M. LOGAN

'Powerful, timely and unnerving'
DAVID JACKSON

'Clever, unpredictable and beautifully done'
LIZ LOVES BOOKS

'Terrifyingly plausible . . . completely unputdownable'
MARTYN WAITES

'Absolutely brilliant . . . a really sophisticated, smart, engaging thriller'
JO SPAIN

Withdrawn
Dublin City Public Libraries
Stock
D0317016

Also by Deborah O'Connor

My Husband's Son

THE DANGEROUS KIND

DEBORAH O'CONNOR

ZAFFRE

First published in Great Britain in 2019 by

ZAFFRE
80–81 Wimpole St, London W1G 9RE

Copyright © Deborah O'Connor, 2019

All rights reserved.
No part of this publication may be reproduced,
stored or transmitted in any form by any means, electronic,
mechanical, photocopying or otherwise, without the
prior written permission of the publisher.

The right of Deborah O'Connor to be identified as Author of this
work has been asserted by her in accordance with the
Copyright, Designs and Patents Act, 1988.

This is a work of fiction. Names, places, events and
incidents are either the products of the author's
imagination or used fictitiously. Any resemblance to
actual persons, living or dead, or actual
events is purely coincidental.

A CIP catalogue record for this book is
available from the British Library.

Hardback ISBN: 978–1–78576–604–6
Trade paperback ISBN: 978–1–78576–827–9

Also available as an ebook

1 3 5 7 9 10 8 6 4 2

Typeset by IDSUK (Data Connection) Ltd
Printed and bound in Great Britain by Clays Ltd, Elcograf S.p.A.

MIX
Paper from
responsible sources
FSC® C018072

Zaffre is an imprint of Bonnier Books UK
www.bonnierbooks.co.uk

For my brother Danny

Potentially Dangerous Person (PDP): a person who has not been convicted of, or cautioned for any offence . . . but whose behaviour gives reasonable grounds for believing there is present a likelihood of them committing an offence or offences that will cause serious harm.

Association of Chief Police Officers (ACPO)

Friday 11 November

Present day

~ Pembroke Branch Tel. 6689575

I follow him across the garden and out through a gate in the wall. Away from the manor house it is dark, the night sky bloated with snow that has yet to make itself known.

We keep walking, and before long we reach the foot of a muddy hill. He tackles the incline at speed. I do the same. The hill is steep, and by the time we reach the top we're both panting. Ahead, a perimeter of ragged orange netting, held taut by iron posts, rings a copse. He lifts a damaged section of the netting into the air.

'The broadband in this part of the country is rubbish.' He nods towards the trees. 'They've been digging. New cables.'

I duck underneath and he joins me on the other side. The edge of the copse is overgrown with weeds and brambles. Thorns catch on my coat as we push our way into a small clearing.

'That's better.' He breathes in the cold air. 'I can think out here.'

The moon is full but the canopied criss-cross of branches means that large patches of the clearing are in shadow. I head for the carcass of a felled tree, covered with moss: the brightest available spot. I've been waiting thirteen years for this moment. I want to be sure to see the look on his face.

I don't notice the hole.

My ankle twists on the precipice. Unable to take my weight, the cliff ledge collapses beneath me and clods of earth crash into the puddles below. I scramble, trying to right myself, but the crumbling soil continues to give way. I am about to topple forwards, into the hole, when I feel his hand clamp my arm.

'Watch it.' He yanks me back to safety. 'That'll be the digging I warned you about.'

My legs are rickety. I stagger over to the mossy tree trunk and sit down, my breaths short and shallow. My bicep stings. I had forgotten about his hands. His grip. Strong enough to bruise.

He inspects the hole. 'This must be one of the sites they have yet to fill in.'

I wait until I've stopped shaking, then join him at the edge. This time I make sure to keep well back.

The hole is the diameter of a child's paddling pool and twenty feet deep, the bottom spotted with puddles. The walls are a sheer vertical drop, sliced clean where the machinery has dug down to the layers below, their surface punctuated by white knuckles, tree roots that have pushed out through the mud into thin air.

Now that my eyes have adjusted to the dark I see mounds of dirt lined up on the opposite side of the hole and that a trail of abandoned tools – spades, buckled plastic buckets and odd bits of metal – litters the ground all the way back to the edge of the copse.

'Come on, then. Out with it.' He steps forward into a square of moonlight. 'Why are you here?'

I look at him, standing there in his suit and tie. His brogues are ruined, the tiny holes and scalloped edges clogged with mud. He's in his late fifties, his features slacker than they once were, but overall he's aged well. He'd always dressed smartly: chinos and polo shirts, jeans with a crease pressed down the middle of each leg. But this suit looks expensive. Something about the cut and line of the shoulders, the way the material hangs flush against his shirt.

'Because it was wrong.' I try to sound braver than I feel. 'What you did. What you tried to do.'

He won't look at me. Instead he looks slightly to the left of my head, at the trees behind. 'Is it money? Is that what you want?'

I'd imagined this moment so often. How it would feel to see him again. Would I be angry? Scared? Now I'm here I feel something I had never anticipated. Disappointment.

'I told you what happened that night. You promised to help. You lied.'

He scoffs and waves his hand in the air. Filled with a new sense of purpose, he starts to pace up and down, as though he's dictating a letter and I'm his secretary, there to take notes.

'I saw you as a favour but now I think it best if you leave.'

'Times have changed. Back then, no one would listen. Now they're all ears.' The hole gapes blackly behind him. 'I'm going to tell them everything.' I pause. 'So are the others.'

He stops pacing. 'Others?'

'You passed us round like we were nothing. I don't care who you are now,' I gesture back towards the manor house, 'or who you're going to be. It's time you were brought to account.'

'Whatever it is you think you're talking about . . .' he lapses into silence, reaching for some memory, but it won't come, or he discards it '. . . you're mistaken.'

There is no sound. The temperature has dropped. A sudden hoar.

'Think about your family. That's why I'm here. To give you a chance to talk to them before it breaks.'

This was true, but it was more than that. Watching the after-effects on the news, him leaving a police station with his lawyer, harried and trying to cover his face with a newspaper, would not be enough. For my own sanity, I needed to be the one to confront him, to take back that bit of control.

He looks at his feet.

I relax a little. I've done what I came here to do. He reacted as I'd expected but now he seems to be taking me seriously. He is almost contrite.

He turns, and for the first time since I got here he looks me in the eye. I think he is going to apologise, to try and explain, but then he raises his hand and, whiplash fast, he slaps me.

I cradle my face. The skin under my eye is tight and hot.

He examines the hand he used to hit me. Adjusts his signet ring. 'I'll have Ennis drive you back.'

I flex my jaw, trying to disperse the pain.

He straightens his tie and it's then that he notices the state of his shoes. He tuts and uses his heel to scuff off the worst.

I step forward and, as he lifts his gaze, I give him a push towards the hole. He is confused more than surprised and only seems to understand what is happening to him at the last moment. He scrabbles with his feet and hands, but a little too late, and as he makes his descent, his head slams against one of the knuckled tree roots and bounces forward, cracking his chin into his chest. I fall to my knees and peer over the side, expecting to see him on his feet and angry, already trying to brush the dirt from his suit.

He is not moving. He's lying on his back, his head at an angle, eyes closed, mouth open.

The puddles surrounding him are now curdled with ice.

I get to my feet. Frightened. Guilty. Something inside me seems to loosen and come away from itself. I start to shiver.

The sky finally decides to release its load. Snowflakes thicken the air. They catch on his eyelashes.

A crackle in the undergrowth. Someone else is here. 'What have you done?' A figure appears and then, as they approach the hole, they ask again, louder than before: 'What have you done?'

Monday 28 November

Present day

Jessamine

The snow came on again around seven p.m. A band of white, for the third time in as many weeks, it quickly made its way from the bottom to the top of the British Isles, like a person pulling a duvet up and over themselves. On Oxford Street there was four inches and counting.

Inside Broadcasting House Jessamine Gooch was at work, preparing to go live on air. She usually liked to spend the hour before her radio show in the quiet of the studio on the second floor, going over the first few pages of the script. It contained a bust of Lord Reith, the founder of the BBC, and she found him a strangely calming presence. But there had been some technical issues of late and, while the sound engineers tinkered with faulty wires and widgets, she was stranded at her desk.

The change in routine was making it hard to concentrate. That and the cleaners who bustled about the place, vaccuming and emptying bins. No sooner would she read a line of text than it dissolved in her brain. To make matters worse, she could feel a hot flush blooming low in her chest. She fanned the sheets of A4 against her skin. Her instinct was to go outside to the cool air and do a lap around the block, reciting the script as she went. She'd done it once before during a fire drill. Somehow, walking had helped the words register.

But the snow.

It was deep and still falling.

Then there was the small matter of her footwear. As she'd left the flat tonight, Sarah, her daughter, had clocked the boots Jessamine was wearing and raised an eyebrow. 'Suede in this weather? Really?'

She wiped the sweat from her temples and looked to the small square windows that faced out onto Langham Place. The corner of each pane was webbed with ice. She'd have to make do.

Blocking out the nearby hum of a vacuum cleaner, she tried again to get the opening salvo clear in her head.

On 2 October 1998 Henry Manners raped and murdered Eloise Shaw. Last seen on the Thorne Road in Doncaster's notorious red-light district, Eloise's body was discovered many weeks later in a stretch of water called Swainby Beck. She had been asphyxiated and beaten with a crowbar. She would be the first of three women murdered by Manners in a killing spree that ended when he was apprehended nine weeks later.

Until that day, although Manners had had various brushes with the police, he had never been charged with a crime. Yet many experts believe that the deaths of Eloise Shaw and the two other victims, Natalie Rigden and Chanelle Roberts, were entirely preventable. They claim that Manners's actions did not come out of the blue, that throughout his life he left breadcrumbs, clear signs that, should someone have cared to pay attention to them, he could have been prevented from ever taking a person's life.

My name is Jessamine Gooch and you are listening to *Potentially Dangerous People*, the radio show that takes you inside the criminal mind and asks if it is ever possible to spot and stop the individuals who will one day go on to commit murder.

Mouthing the lines under her breath, she used a pencil to mark the points at which she might pause or when to emphasise a particular word in her delivery.

Tonight's guests were an ex-police officer, Charles O'Brien, and a criminologist, Professor Holly Humphries from Manchester University. O'Brien was a *PDP* regular and would be with her in the studio. Professor Humphries would contribute down the line, from a booth in Salford.

Mr O'Brien, even if the police had been able to identify Henry Manners as a potentially dangerous person, would they have ever had it in their power, realistically, to stop him committing these crimes?

O'Brien could have called in tonight's interview from home. The show's eleven p.m. start time meant guests often did – the listeners didn't care if the experts were in the studio or on the other side of the world. But the ex-detective superintendent always made the effort to be at Broadcasting House, regardless of the weather. He said it made for a better show, but Jessamine suspected there was more to it.

A giant of a man, O'Brien hailed from Cork and, although he had lived in Kilburn most of his adult life, he still spoke with a brogue that erupted into staccato 'Ha-ha-ha' laughter at the most unexpected moments. Once, in the early days of the show, he had asked Jessamine out on a date. She had turned him down, claiming it would be inappropriate (in truth, at that time, she had already been in a relationship of sorts) but O'Brien was undeterred. Even now he would bring her small gifts: a posy of jasmine (a reference to her name), which he produced, petals bruised, from the depths of his backpack, a pen that transformed at a touch into a knife or a torch ('It's a pen, a light *and* a weapon, all in one') and then just last week, most random of all, a leg of air-dried ham that he claimed to have picked up for a song in Lidl.

The cleaner reached Jessamine's group of desks and began hoovering under the desk opposite hers. It belonged to her producer, Mick, and as the woman pushed the nozzle into the hard-to-reach spot by the footrest, she banged the side of the desk a little too hard. A porcelain frame, containing a photo of Mick, his wife and their three children, wobbled and fell to the floor with a smash.

'Not again.' The cleaner picked up the broken frame. 'Last week I spilled some cold tea on his keyboard.' The top of the frame had 'FAMILY' moulded across it in pastel colours, and as she tried to join the two pieces back together the M crumbled to nothing.

Jessamine looked at Mick, thirty feet away in the glass-walled studio. Standing next to the bust of Lord Reith, he was supervising the sound engineers, oblivious to the fate of his family portrait.

Jessamine took the broken frame from the woman, then kicked at what remained of the M, dispersing the shards into the carpet. Returning to her desk, she opened her bottom drawer, placed the frame inside, winked and put her finger to her lips. The cleaner mouthed, 'Thank you,' unplugged the machine and made herself scarce.

Peace and quiet settled across the second floor. But the respite was brief. No sooner had the vacuuming stopped than the lift dinged and a man emerged. Wearing a navy wool coat, his shoulders were flecked with rapidly melting snowflakes, his glasses fogged. Jack Flagley, senior counsel to the topmost tier of BBC brass. He was headed towards the controller's office. In the past his presence there at this hour would have been a cause of concern. He would have brought with him an expectation that something big was about to break, something that couldn't wait till morning. But the corporation had experienced such a volume of controversy lately that seeing a lawyer convening an emergency midnight meeting was really quite commonplace.

Jessamine again looked towards Mick. He, too, had noticed the lawyer's arrival. He met her gaze and widened his eyes, as if to say, 'What's it going to be this time?' then knocked Lord Reith's head twice for luck, and went back to fixing the fault.

Jessamine was less blasé. Lining the wall next to where she sat was a series of framed photos of newsreaders, journalists, presenters and DJs who graced the BBC's airwaves. She sought out her own picture, sandwiched between a World Service veteran and a Radio 1 bright young thing. Taken not long after she'd won the first of three Sony Radio Academy awards, it showed her with brown hair pulled back into a low ponytail, her trademark fringe cut blunt to just above the eyebrows. She had what her father always described as a Very English Face, the jolt of her cheekbones like the curve in a teacup handle. At the time, she had been on the brink of forty, twinkly-eyed and smiley, unable to contain the pride she felt at being part of an organisation for which she had nothing but respect and admiration.

The eleven intervening years had changed her in more ways than one. Her jawline wasn't as tight as it had been, and although she had kept her fringe, she now preferred to colour her bob a pale ash blonde (better to hide the grey). As for that proud smile . . .

Recent events had brought to light a series of historic child sex-abuse cases, some involving the corporation's disc jockeys and presenters. Senior management's initial handling of the affair had left a stain she found hard to ignore and, these days, her feelings towards her employer were a little more complex. She was still in awe of its breadth and impartiality, but now when she walked around the studios and corridors she had once held so dear, she wondered what horrors had been perpetrated there and what secrets the walls might contain.

Back to the script.

Professor Humphries, you've studied the criminology of Henry Manners. In some ways his life story was a textbook case and echoes many of the patterns we have come across on this show before: domestic violence, petty theft, a chaotic employment history. In your opinion, was it inevitable that Manners would one day do this, that he would one day come to murder?

The professor would answer almost certainly in the affirmative. Then Jessamine would play an interview, recorded last week, with Manners's ex-wife. In it she described how during their courtship she had seen only the affable, considerate side of Manners but that when they had moved in together he had changed and several times had tried to strangle her. She would go on to explain how, although on numerous occasions she had been frightened enough to call the police, she had always decided not to press charges.

Whenever Holly laid out the forensic psychology of a case like this, Jessamine would find herself thinking of a car full of people, a brick weighting its accelerator. The car was driving fast towards a wall, a line of spectators watching its progress. Although they knew the car was going to crash they were powerless, forced to stand there and do nothing, even as it hurtled to its fate.

It was a good show. The story of Henry Manners was compelling and well-researched, with a set of moral and ethical questions at its heart. Yet she couldn't get any of it to stick. She tried not to panic. She didn't have to memorise the script. A hard copy would be in front of her throughout. But Jessamine knew that relying on it imparted a dull, stilted quality to her delivery.

Another bloom of heat in her chest.

She looked at the iced window panes, then down at her boots. The suede was supple against her calves. Sod it. It was only a bit of snow. She was going out.

Sarah

Sarah Gooch should have been asleep hours ago. Her mother was at work, and before she'd left their fifth-floor flat, Sarah had made her three promises: to feed the cat, to lock the door and to stay up no later than ten o'clock. Technically, she'd made good on all three. Munchie had had her supper and was now snuggled next to her on the duvet, the front door was secure, and she was in bed. Wide awake, but in bed.

Half listening to a podcast on her phone, she stared at the MacBook Air, willing something to happen. It had been fifteen minutes since her last message to him and still no response. The screen timed out and her room was cast into darkness. The podcast came to an end. She pulled out her earbuds and closed her eyes, the screen's blue after-image on the inside of the lids.

She tried to hold out for a few extra minutes. The longer she waited, the more likely there was to be a message from him next time she looked. To distract herself, she concentrated on the sounds of other people in the building.

On Commercial Road, the block had been built in the 1920s as a hostel for sailors when their ship was in dock, then converted into flats at the start of the Docklands boom. It was five floors high, and each flat was accessed by wooden walkways, safeguarded by waist-height metal railings. The building was triangular, with a smaller triangle cut out of the middle to accommodate the open courtyard. All the flats looked onto it and each other. The design gave the building an unusual acoustic, and on quiet days it was possible to pick out the jazz someone liked to listen to on a Sunday morning or to hear dinner being prepared through an open window, down to the sizzle and hiss of their chop in the pan.

Now was one of those quiet times. Sarah strained for something, anything, to make the seconds pass quicker, and was rewarded by mumbled conversation, the clickety-clack of heels, then a door opening and closing a floor or two below. Most likely the conclusion to a night out in the City or Canary Wharf. A truck rumbled by, the smack and clang of its loading bed travelling up through the walls. Her headboard vibrated dully against her neck.

How many minutes had passed since she'd last checked her screen? Two? Five?

Munchie nudged her hand, asking to be stroked. Sarah obliged, going straight to the velvet nap at the base of her ears. She smoothed them down and back, over and over, until the cat began to purr.

Sarah tried to hold out a bit longer but the urge to see if he had replied was overwhelming. She reached for the mouse, and as her finger made contact with it, the computer came back to life. Once more her room was lit by its swimming-pool glow.

Crunch time. Sarah held her breath and pushed her face close to the screen. Her last message sat there in its speech box, the space below it still empty. She checked the messenger bar. There was a green dot against his name. He was online, but he wasn't talking to her.

Trying not to cry, she read back through tonight's thread, looking for clues that might explain his silence. The exchange spanned two hours and was full of long, thoughtful sentences, funny GIFs and perfectly chosen emojis that had made her laugh. Each time her screen had made the new-message noise, like a bubble popping, she'd felt a tiny thrill. No, as far as she could tell, everything had been going brilliantly. There was no awkwardness, no tension, no hint of a problem, but mid-conversation he'd gone quiet, no explanation, no sign-off, nothing.

Maybe it wasn't that he didn't want to reply, just wasn't able to. He was always saying they had to keep their relationship a secret. That must be it.

She started to feel better but then another possibility occurred to her. What if he'd cut short their conversation because he was annoyed? What if it was because of the photos?

Not long after he'd first made contact he'd asked her to send him some pictures of herself, different from the ones she'd already posted on Facebook or Instagram. He'd told her what he wanted and she'd complied. She'd thought it would be enough to keep him satisfied, but the night before last he'd asked for others. This time his request was more specific.

Initially, Sarah had gone along with it, wanting to do as he asked. But when it came to putting them in an email and pressing send, she hadn't been able to follow through.

Her eyes began to droop. The flat was warm, her bed cloud soft. Another truck rumbled by, its vibrations rousing her briefly.

She'd been asleep for ten minutes, her head lolling sideways into the pillow, when the screen woke her with a bubble pop. He was back. She rubbed her eyes and pushed herself back up to sitting.

One new message.

Sorry about that.

Another four messages appeared in quick succession.

Miss me?

Gorgeous?

You still there?

Sarah?

I'm here, she typed, the rush of blood in her veins. *So, where were we?*

Jessamine

Jessamine emerged from Broadcasting House as the blizzard was starting to falter. She stood there for a moment, relishing the cold air against her hot face, then opened her script and began to walk.

The area directly out front had been gritted, but as she doubled back towards Great Portland Street her boots sank into snow up to the shins. Ignoring the wet already soaking through to her toes, she tramped in a loop around the block, reading, then reciting her lines. On any other day at this hour the city would still be all clatter and din, the pavements busy with people out drinking or on their way home post-dinner. Tonight, though, thanks to the weather, the streets were empty. Emboldened, Jessamine spoke her lines aloud, but the snow had muffled the acoustics and her words carried only a short way before dulling to nothing.

She soon had the first few pages lodged in her head. Happy, she decided to head back. Making her way down Margaret Street, she used the Church of All Souls' stepped incline to dodge up and around where the wind had formed a collection of thigh-high drifts in Langham Place, cleared the corner and there it was: Broadcasting House, *Prospero and Ariel* above the main entrance, its grey Portland stone curving out onto the street, like the hull of an ocean-liner.

She'd been on a year-long sabbatical from her job at *The Times* when she'd got the call to come in and try out for a new radio show. Mick had read the extended piece she'd written about a spate of suspicious deaths in Manchester and thought it demonstrated the qualities he was looking for in a presenter. Published before she had gone on leave, the feature had detailed her investigation into the theory, held by locals and police officers alike, that a serial killer had been at large for years in the city, and that the drownings, suicides or accidents attributed to the men they kept finding dead in the waterways were nothing of the kind, just a way to cover up something far more sinister.

Back then Mick was a relatively new producer. With a scrub of yellowy brown hair, and black-framed glasses, he was fresh from a stint on the *Today* programme and keen to make his mark with an idea of his own. Huddled in a meeting room on the second floor, he'd presented Jessamine with a milky coffee and explained how he wanted the show to be a twist on the true-crime genre. The Association of Chief Police Officers (ACPO) had recently coined a new category of offender in their multi-agency protection work: Potentially Dangerous People (PDPs). In other words, individuals who, they predicted, would one day commit a serious violent crime. Their plan was to identify them (often without their knowledge), then work with social services, education authorities and the NHS to try to prevent them from being able to commit such a crime. The term had caused a furore, with some experts arguing that it would lead to *Minority Report*-style policing, and human-rights infringements.

Mick, however, had seen an opportunity and had pitched a live, phone-in format that would turn the Potentially Dangerous People term on its head. His idea was simple. Instead of using the PDP diagnostic to look at future action, the show would use it to study the past behaviour of murderers, dissecting the historic signs and tendencies that all pointed to the fact this person would kill one day. His superiors had loved the idea and the series had been commissioned for an initial six-week run.

Jessamine had been flattered to be considered. Still, had Mick asked her to audition six months earlier she would have turned him down. She loved working on a newspaper. The pulse and stink of it. The way it drove her out into the most unlikely corners of the world in search of information and truth. But that was then. That day, as she'd sat across from him while he talked about his vision for the show, all she'd been able to think about was Sarah.

Before her daughter's arrival, Jessamine's plan had been to take a year's leave, after which she would settle her into appropriate child-care and return to her job at *The Times*. However, after a short while in

Sarah's company, she knew that that plan was untenable. Motherhood on paper, she'd discovered, was quite different from the reality. She'd been trying to come up with an alternative, maybe a little freelance work or teaching on one of the journalism courses at City University, when she'd got the call from Mick. The radio show was the answer. The job was part-time. It would allow her to keep her hand in, and to be with Sarah for the lion's share of the week. Not only that, many of the issues the show dealt with – violent patterns of behaviour and the apparent inability of government agencies to protect those most at risk – tapped into a subject that had recently become close to Jessamine's heart. Soon after their initial chat, when Mick had called to offer her the job, Jessamine had accepted.

She reached the gritted area outside Broadcasting House and was about to go inside when a young woman stepped in front of her, blocking the way. She was wearing a green parka, the fur-lined hood over her head.

'Jessamine? Jessamine Gooch?'

Her accent was pure Essex, all clipped vowels and pouty consonants.

She pushed the hood back onto her shoulders and laughed, as if she couldn't quite believe her luck. 'Sorry.' She retreated a step, gestured at herself and shrugged. 'I didn't know any other way.' In her late teens or early twenties, she had long brown hair, looped up into the kind of topknot currently favoured by Sarah and her friends. Beneath the parka Jessamine saw a flash of Breton stripe.

'Do we know each other?'

The woman shivered and blew on her hands to warm them. 'I listen to your show. Every week.'

Jessamine tilted her head discreetly and directed her gaze behind the woman, to where the security guards stood inside the main door. Her show had a big following and occasionally the families of the criminals she profiled, those who still believed in their innocence, would write angry letters after a programme had gone out. Was this young woman one of those people? Had she come here to confront Jessamine in person? She felt a ripple of fear.

'Don't worry, I'm not a weirdo,' said the woman, as if she had read Jessamine's thoughts. 'Although I would say that. It's not always clear who they are, the dangerous kind.' She reached into her pocket. 'It's about my friend, Cassie. Cassie Scolari.'

She pulled out a photo and thrust it into Jessamine's hand. It showed a young woman smiling widely at the camera. In her late twenties, she had blonde hair and was wearing a pink and white striped blouse. A turquoise jumper hung loose around her shoulders. She was attractive and had a cultivated, preppy, Boden-catalogue look, but something about the outfit wasn't quite right. Everything was cut a little too tight, the material thinner and a shade or two off its Jack Wills counterparts.

'I don't understand.' Jessamine tried to give it back but the woman refused to accept it and held up her hands, as if in surrender.

'Two and a half weeks ago Cassie went missing.' She pulled out another photo. 'Cassie's husband,' she said. 'Piece of shit. Knocks her around.'

'Ah.' Many of the cases Jessamine covered on her radio show involved domestic violence. When it came to murderous behaviour, hurting your partner was often the canary in the coal mine.

The woman tapped the photo with a neon-pink shellacked nail. 'He fits the pattern. I thought you'd be sympathetic.'

The woman was right, more so than she knew. Jessamine's interest in domestic violence might have found expression in her work, but the root of her preoccupation was intensely personal. Twice a week she volunteered as a support worker for Refuge, taking calls on the helpline.

'I presume the police are involved.'

'They were all over it in the beginning, now not so much.'

'If you're worried, maybe you should try a private investigator.' Jessamine was sympathetic but that didn't mean she was the right person for the job. It had been more than a decade since she'd worked in a newsroom, let alone got stuck into a police investigation.

'I don't want a private investigator. I want you.'

They were standing next to one of the bollards on the loop road used for BBC drop-offs and pick-ups. Jessamine noticed a black cab about to hook a left, directly towards them, and grabbed the woman's arm to pull her back onto the thin strip of pavement. 'My show is retrospective. We don't investigate ongoing criminal cases.'

The woman waited a beat, her eyes shining. 'But you used to.'

Jessamine stiffened. 'How do you – why would . . .?'

'I looked you up,' said the woman, shyly, sorry but not sorry. 'Seems you were quite the newshound in your day.'

Jessamine didn't know what to say.

The woman sensed an opportunity and took it. 'Eighteen days ago Cassie went missing. That Friday she went into work and just after one o'clock she got a call from her son's school to say he wasn't feeling well. She asked to leave early and they let her go. That was the last anyone saw of her. But the school never made that call. Her son was fine all day.'

In her pocket, Jessamine's phone buzzed. Probably Mick, wondering where she'd got to. 'I have to go.'

'There's more,' said the woman, speeding up. 'Five days ago I received a WhatsApp text from Cassie. I immediately tried to call her but it went straight to voicemail.'

'I feel for you, I really do,' said Jessamine. 'But I can't help.'

Again she tried to leave, but the woman grabbed her arm and placed herself between Jessamine and the building. 'Please.'

Jessamine looked down at the woman's hand, still on her arm. The woman released her grip and stepped back.

'Miss Gooch. I just want to know if she's dead or alive. Her son, Matteo, he's eight. Even if she'd wanted to run away, she would never have left him behind.' She held out her hands, pleading. 'His father is Italian. Since Cassie disappeared, he's been talking about moving back to Rome with Matteo.'

'They need me upstairs.' Jessamine handed back the picture, side-stepped her, and walked towards the entrance.

As she grasped the door's dulled gold handle the woman called after her, 'Can I at least send you some information?' The light had gone from her eyes, yet she'd decided to give it one last shot. 'You could take a quick look?'

'Sure,' said Jessamine, not wanting to give her false hope. 'But you're wasting your time.'

Inside Reception the mosaic floor rumbled underfoot: a Bakerloo or Victoria line train shuddering its way to the next station deep in the tunnels below. She searched for the pass hanging from a lanyard in the depths of her coat and glanced back as someone was leaving. The woman was still standing in the snow, clutching her friend's photo.

Upstairs the sound engineers were leaving the studio. The technical problem had been fixed. Mick waved at her and tapped his watch with a rolled-up script. Ten minutes to on air.

Weaving her way through the swathe of desks, she realised that the words she'd just memorised had gone. She'd have to rely on the script after all.

She took her place at the control desk, greeted O'Brien with a nod and was about to start her checks when she noticed a pair of knitted earmuffs lying next to the fader board. They were embroidered with fat red robins. She looked up to see O'Brien watching her expectantly. Another gift. Being careful to hide her smile, she put them to one side and Mick began to count her in to the start of the show, to the moment when her words would be broadcast live to the nation.

2002

Rowena

We sit in his car, the engine off. I press my face to the passenger window and look up. The flat is above a takeaway, a fried-chicken shop. Three sash windows mark its place in the row. The glass is grey with exhaust fumes and, instead of curtains, the windows are covered with blue and purple sheets, the seams trapped in the gap at the top of the frame. The entrance is around the corner, through a brown door.

'We should go in.' Sunny puts his hand on my leg.

'Please,' I say, and my throat tightens, as it does whenever I try not to cry.

Sunny smiles and cups my chin. His touch is soft. Then he leans forward and kisses me gently where my hair meets my forehead.

'One,' kiss, 'two,' kiss, 'three times for luck,' kiss.

He often does this. It's our thing. I let the tears come. He watches me for a few seconds, then shakes his head. He seems to be changing his mind. I feel relieved. He can't go through with it either. He loves me too much to share.

But then, making sure to keep one hand on my face, he reaches behind his seat with the other. He pats around on the floor until he finds whatever he's looking for, then brings forward a carrier bag. He releases my face and opens the bag. Inside is a small bottle of vodka.

'Have a drink.' He unscrews the cap and nods in the direction of the flat. 'Relax.'

I start to panic. 'But you're my boyfriend.'

'And I still will be. It's just this one time. Promise.'

I back away towards the passenger door. 'I don't want to. I won't.'

His eyes flash. 'Do you want me to get into trouble?'

He's about to go on when he stops, distracted by two minicabs pulling up on the opposite side of the street. Men get out of the cars and approach the door to the flat. They are laughing, caught in the aftermath of some joke. Before they go inside one man stops and, bending low, he peers into our car. He is fat and older than Sunny. He waves. Sunny waves back.

I start to shake.

'Drink.'

He offers me the bottle but I keep my hands in lap.

'I said, drink.'

He leans across and I think he's going to hit me but then he knocks twice on the glove box.

It takes me a moment to understand his meaning. I know what the compartment contains but until now I've only ever thought of the gun as something separate, nothing to do with me and him. Sunny runs the town's largest nightclub. He says it's a cut-throat business: he's often threatened and called upon to protect himself and his staff.

He pushes the vodka towards my mouth.

The alcohol reeks and I back away. Losing patience, he tuts and, without waiting for me to recover, he shoves the bottle forward. The glass bashes against my teeth and the liquid is on my tongue. I've only ever drunk the booze he buys mixed with something sweet, like Coke or Fanta, so the sting at the back of my throat comes as a surprise. I try to swallow but after a few mouthfuls I need to stop. He won't let me. I gag and splutter until, finally, he releases his grip. The vodka explodes out of my mouth into the car.

'Fuck.' He wipes his arm.

I cough and gulp at the air. My skirt and school bag are soaked.

I look at the car door. It's unlocked. I could get out and walk away. Catch a bus and go back to the home. I'd be there before curfew.

He seems to read my thoughts.

'You said you'd do anything for me.' He fiddles with his identity bracelet, adjusts it so that the silver nameplate lies dead centre on his wrist. 'You said you loved me.'

'I do!' I shout, angry my feelings should be called into question.

'Then what are we waiting for?'

He gets out, comes round to my side of the car, opens the door and offers his hand. Still, I hesitate. He waits a moment, then lets his gaze drift to the right of my shoulder, to the glove box.

Another mouthful of vodka and I place my hand in his. He leads me across the pavement and around the corner to the flat's entrance. Before he rings the doorbell he pulls me in close and, with his hand around my waist, he kisses the top of my head, one, two, three times for luck.

I am at another party. In a house on the edge of the Blackbird Leys estate. I'm not sure which of the men it belongs to but it's a lot nicer than some of the other places we've visited recently. There is carpet on the floor and curtains at the window. They were already drawn when we got here: protection against prying eyes and the bright end-of-day sun. Still, a bit of light has managed to sneak through where the fabric doesn't quite meet in the middle. It acts like a laser, showing the smoke and dust in the air.

I reach for my glass and top up the vodka with Fanta. I don't want it too watered down – I know now that it's best to drink as much as possible early on – but, try as I might, I can't get used to the taste of it neat. My hand shakes as I bring the glass to my mouth, my nerves more shot than usual.

Until now, Sunny collecting me from the home has been a simple process. At the agreed time he pulls up outside and I grab my coat and run to meet him. I get into trouble for returning after curfew but it's nothing I can't deal with. Tonight, though, it all went wrong.

I watched Sunny park, then headed out of the front door, not knowing that Raf, one of the youth workers, had followed me into the street. He grabbed my arm and asked where I was going. When I didn't answer he went and stood in the middle of the road, checking the cars. Then he marched over to where Sunny sat, his window down, music playing, and started asking him questions. Did he know how old I was? Where was he taking me? Why did he keep bringing me back so late?

I worried that Sunny would think I'd told and be angry. But he laughed in Raf's face, opened the car door and motioned for me to get in. Then he gave Raf a wave and drove off. He told me that normally he would have got *out of the car and given him what-for but he'd decided to let him off this once because he'd had such a good day. The planning application for his new club had been submitted and he'd had the nod from someone at the council to say it would get the green light. Then he'd turned the radio up loud and we'd sung along and things had felt like they used to, in the beginning.*

I look around the room. Some of the men are the same age as Sunny and work for him in his club, but the others are older – taxi drivers and takeaway owners, cousins and uncles. There are two other girls here. One looks about my age, the other a bit younger. The first has red hair braided tightly against her scalp. The younger one is wearing a clingy white T-shirt that rides up over her belly podge. From the way they keep jumping at every little thing, I'm guessing this is their first time.

Sunny catches me looking and winks.

Despite everything, I smile.

It might seem odd that I can love someone who scares me. But I love him – I do. More than I've ever loved anyone or anything.

We met at the Westgate shopping centre in Oxford. I often nick off school with my friends and we like to hang out near the benches by the fountain. A couple of months back these lads started talking to us. They were our age and went to a school on the other side of town. They were a laugh, and after that, whenever we bunked off, we'd knock around with them. Then one day a man came over to where we sat, good-looking with shiny black hair cut into Zac Efron-style layers and light brown skin. The boys seemed to know him and they talked and laughed together. Then he turned his attention to us. I was far from the prettiest in our group, in fact people often make fun of my baby-face, but still he made sure to talk to me more than the other girls. Before he went, he asked my name.

As he walked away, my friends and I fell about laughing. But secretly I was thrilled. No one had ever singled me out like that before, especially not an attractive man.

After that he kept turning up at the shopping centre whenever we were there. One day he asked if I wanted to go for a drive. I knew he was older but I didn't care. My friends were jealous. I said yes and followed him out to the multi-storey. That first time in his car we talked and talked. He told me about his work and his hopes for his business and asked me questions about myself, what I loved, what I hated, what I wanted to be when I grew up. Then he asked if I was hungry, drove me to the takeaway and bought everything I wanted. He dropped me outside the home before curfew, and, as I got out of the car, he told me I was beautiful.

I kissed him first.

He started to pick me up after school. He'd wait for me across the street, and all the other kids would look. I'd feel special and proud that he was there for me.

Then things started to change. Now when I'd get in the car I'd find him silent. He'd refuse to look at me, and whenever I asked him a question he'd reply in these horrible one-word answers. He owed money to a gang. They'd told him that if he didn't pay soon they'd hurt him, beat him up, maybe worse. He showed me the gun he kept in his glove box as protection.

The weeks went by. Sometimes he was in a bad mood and sometimes he was his old self, buying me anything I wanted. Takeaways, booze for me and my friends. Fags. For the first time in my life I felt safe, protected.

Then the gang decided to turn up the pressure. They wanted the cash they were owed and they wanted it by the end of the month. They threatened to torch his club. He said he'd begged for more time and that he'd almost given up hope when one of them had suggested a way he could pay off his debt. They'd noticed him around town with me and they thought I was pretty. They said that if I were to go with them just this once they would call it quits.

He said he didn't want to ask but he was scared, and even though he couldn't bear the thought of me with someone else, he had no choice.

I didn't hesitate. My answer was no. The thought disgusted me. Besides, he had a gun. If they tried to hurt him, he could soon see them off. We argued.

One of Sunny's cousins rolls a spliff and passes it around. I take a puff and hand it to the girl in the white T-shirt. She shakes her head and retreats back into the sofa. I offer it to her again. I want to tell her that she should take a drag, that it will make the time go faster, that, while they're taking their turn to come in and out, it will help her go outside of herself, up to a grey dent on the ceiling or down to a diamond-shaped stain on the carpet.

The men have been talking and laughing but now they're quiet. The sun has moved round and the light coming through the middle of the curtains has dimmed. There is a new crackle in the air. I recognise the shift. It means it's almost time. I finish my vodka, and Sunny takes my hand. He leads me and the younger girl upstairs. He'll set me up in one of the bedrooms and then the others will come. He prefers me afterwards, alone in his car.

There are three doors on the landing. One is a bathroom; the others lead into bedrooms. Sunny directs me to the nearest door and escorts the younger girl to another. Just before she goes inside we catch each other's eye. She looks at me, pleading. She seems to think I can help, that I can stop what is about to happen. I could try to reassure her, tell her I'll be in the next room if she needs me. But then I look at the way she's holding Sunny's hand, the way she stands close to his hip.

I lasted ten days without him. I never knew it was possible to miss a person so much. On the eleventh, when I couldn't take it any longer, I went and waited outside his club.

I make a point of looking the girl up and down and then I roll my eyes, flick my hair and push back my shoulders as though what is about to happen to her, to both of us, is no big deal, and that she, in her fear and shame, is nothing more than a silly kid. Then I press down on the door handle and, making sure to hold my head high, I go inside.

Tuesday 13 December

Present day

Jessamine

Midnight at the domestic-violence helpline. Jessamine had been on shift since ten p.m. So far, she'd spoken to five different women. She finished with her current caller, a first-timer named Hilary, and set to work logging the details on the system.

Until recently, Hilary had thought her relationship normal, her fiancé kind and gentle. But then, in the last week, they had celebrated their engagement with a party. It had been a wonderful night, and all their friends and family had been there. At the end of the evening they'd returned to their flat and had been about to go up to bed when her fiancé had noticed water dripping off the sill in the kitchen. The window had been left open and while they were out it had rained. It was Hilary's fault. She'd opened it earlier in the day and forgotten about it. They'd argued. Her fiancé had thrown her against the wall and punched her twice in the ribs. Hilary had yet to confide in anyone about what had happened and she was nowhere close to walking away from him or her impending marriage.

Jessamine often imagined the tone of a person's voice as a series of pictures. She supposed it was a by-product of spending so much time conversing with people she couldn't see, either here or on the radio. When Hilary had said goodbye her voice had lifted – the result of a joke Jessamine had made at her own expense: a regrettable incident involving her weak pelvic floor, Tena Lady pads and a trampoline – and Jessamine had been left with the image of a woman in a dress, holding up the outer corners of her skirt in a shy half-curtsy, the semi-circle of the hem like the beginning of a smile.

The log finished, she hit save, fanned herself with a newspaper and searched the room for Jackie, the supervisor on shift. In the corner, fiddling with a broken phone, she was wearing baggy jeans and a black-and-red lumberjack shirt. Jessamine waved to get her attention. 'Is the heating on?'

Jackie looked up from the splay of wires and plastic parts. 'It's December and minus five outside.' She turned her attention back to the broken phone. 'Yes, Jessie, the heating is on.'

Jessamine dabbed her sweating face with a tissue. She would have liked to get some air, but no – she checked the time – she'd be calling soon. Tasha. She didn't want to miss her. She'd have to settle for a quick trip to the loo instead.

Again, Jessamine waved at Jackie, signalling she was going to take her break. Jackie looked at her strangely, smirked, and gave her a nod in acknowledgement.

It wasn't until she was in front of the bathroom mirror, washing her hands, that Jessamine saw the source of Jackie's amusement. The tissue had disintegrated, leaving bits of itself on her skin. Jackie could have alerted her to this but instead had let her leave the room looking like she'd had a fight with a toilet roll. Jessamine wasn't surprised. Her supervisor took any chance she could to bring her down a peg. It had always been the same. When Jessamine had first applied to volunteer three years earlier, Jackie had conducted her interview. It had gone well and they'd been about to finish when Jessamine had mentioned her radio work. Jackie's eyes had widened. 'In my phone room, where you're from, what you do, how much money you earn, it doesn't matter. You could be the prime bloody minister, you still do as I say. Understood?' Jessamine had nodded meekly, then Jackie had got to her feet and adjusted her shirt sleeves. 'One more thing. Your name. It's a bit . . .' She'd screwed up her face.

Jessamine had decided to make it easy for her. 'Lots of people call me Jessie,' she'd said. 'Would that do?' Jackie had smiled, happy to be understood.

Back inside the helpline office, the air was full of the contralto hum of nine women talking into their headsets. With so many crises constantly bubbling just beneath the surface the atmosphere had a dense, charged quality that sometimes made it seem hard to breathe. There was some respite to the claustrophobia: a floor-to-ceiling window that filled one wall. It looked out onto the Tower of London, its moat packed with snow that had been there for weeks. The southern half of the country was caught in the grip of a freeze the likes of which had not been known for decades.

Jessamine retook her seat, put on her headset and scanned the desks. Every one of the other volunteers on shift was busy. That was good. It meant Tasha had a strong chance of getting through to her first time.

Twelve thirty a.m. came and went. Two more minutes passed and still nothing, from Tasha or anyone else. She was never late.

Jessamine's stomach grumbled. It had been a long time since supper. Her coat hung on the back of the chair. She reached into the pocket and grabbed a handful of pumpkin seeds – she'd bought some after reading that they could help with the symptoms of menopause. Although they tasted like wallpaper paste, she'd persevered.

Two more minutes passed.

Maybe Tasha had forgotten. Or maybe she'd called earlier than usual and was already talking to one of the other volunteers.

The first time Tasha had phoned the helpline Jessamine had taken her call. The conversation had gone well, and Tasha had wanted to know if she could ask for Jessamine in person, should she need to call again. Jessamine had given her her extension number, and from then on Tasha had called when she knew Jessamine was on shift. After a few weeks, Jessamine had found herself looking forward to their chats. They reminded her of the conversations she used to share with Sarah.

Sarah. They'd had an argument, another, just before she'd left for her shift tonight. Sarah had left a wet towel on the bathroom floor and Jessamine had asked her to pick it up. In the past she and her daughter had had what she would have described as a good relationship, great even, but recently it seemed like they couldn't spend any time together without a door being slammed, a voice raised, a dish thrown hard into the sink. Jessamine couldn't work out if Sarah's behaviour was to be expected – part of the normal, difficult stage of adolescence where you tried to shuck off your parents and forge your own way in the world – or if there was more to it.

Still nothing.

It seemed she wouldn't be speaking to Tasha tonight after all. She set to work on some admin and the phone rang. She punched the green flashing light, accepting the call.

'You're through to the domestic-violence helpline. Are you safe to talk?'

'Jessie?'

'Tasha?'

They laughed, happy to hear each other's voice, and Jessamine saw, in the corner, Jackie scanning the room for the source of the jollity.

When Jessamine next spoke she tempered her tone. 'How are you?'

'Fat, grumpy and I need to pee all the time. Also, in the last week I seem to have developed cankles.'

Tasha's accent was pure Brum, all singsong inflections and rounded vowels. Jessamine imagined her words as a rollercoaster, loop-the-looping their way towards the lower octave on which she ended every sentence. 'Not long now.'

Tasha groaned. 'The skin on my belly is itchy.'

'That's because it's so stretched. Rub it with olive oil.' She opened Tasha's log on the computer. 'How've things been since we last spoke?'

'Usual. It's like the more pregnant I get, the angrier he is.'

Tasha's boyfriend, Theo, worked nights, stacking shelves at Tesco. They lived on the outskirts of Birmingham and had been together for five years. What had begun as aggressive, controlling behaviour had soon escalated into physical abuse. Slapping and punching and then, since she'd been pregnant, kicking.

'Remember what I said. When the baby comes, it can make things worse.' Because it will make her braver, thought Jessamine. Because Theo knows the baby might give Tasha the courage to leave.

'Maybe. On the other hand, it could be the making of him.' There was a new barb in her voice. The rollercoaster stalled for a moment, held on the brink of a giant drop. 'Monday's my last day. The other girls are going to take me for tea. A baby shower.' And just like that the rollercoaster tipped over the edge, the potential energy turned kinetic, as it flew and lifted, round the rails. 'I'm going to wear this jumper dress I found on ASOS. It makes my bump look like a Christmas pudding.'

Tasha worked as a shop assistant with New Look in the Bull Ring shopping centre.

'Very festive,' said Jessamine, and smiled at the thought of Tasha, rotund behind the till. 'Have you talked to your midwife like we discussed?' she asked, trying to steer the conversation back to more difficult things. Anything the women did or didn't do was supposed to be their decision. Jessamine's job was to provide them with options. 'She might be able to help. If things take a turn for the worse.'

'You talk nice, Jessie,' said Tasha, after a little while. 'Posh, but not nasty posh.' She yawned. 'I should go.'

Jessamine sighed, conceding defeat. 'Same time next week?'

'Be there or be square,' said Tasha, her favourite sign-off.

Wednesday 14 December

Present day

Jessamine

At ten a.m. Jessamine strode across the second floor of Broadcasting House and dumped her coat and bag on her desk. She could see Mick and the show's researchers, Verity and Arshdeep, waiting for her in the meeting room. Mick clocked her arrival with a nod.

She adjusted her blouse. It was new, bought at the weekend during a dash round John Lewis. On the hanger it had seemed perfect: a V-shaped neckline that would expose the beginnings of her collarbone, a subtle yellow-and-pink rose pattern. Now, though, she suspected the blouse was almost certainly polyester, a material that tended to work against her constant battle to keep cool. Still, it looked nice, and with her first date in months booked for lunch, she tried to convince herself that was all that mattered.

They'd met online. His name was Robert. Good-looking in a crumpled, geography-teacher kind of way, he was recently divorced. In their online chats she'd found him to be nice, normal and occasionally funny. Not only that, he was self-sufficient: a vet with his own practice in Woking. However, the thing that had caught Jessamine's attention right off the bat was his age. At fifty-two Robert was a good ten to twenty years younger than most of the men who contacted her through the site. It was one of the brutal rules of internet dating. A man could be fifty, sixty or even seventy and still consider himself cock of the walk, able to take his pick of females aged thirty plus. But for a woman over fifty? She'd had a conversation about it with Abigail, one of the World Service producers. After Jessamine had bemoaned her latest online horror Abigail had told her that some men referred to mature single women as the last chickens on the shelf. In other words, the chickens left in the supermarket at the end of the day that no one wants. Even though there was nothing wrong with those chickens everyone assumed that, because they were still there, they must be defective and bought a microwave lasagne instead.

She grabbed her notebook and was about to join the team when the post guy appeared, pushing his metal trolley. He handed her an A3 padded envelope, her name written on it in black marker. She considered the handwriting and lack of postage, intrigued.

A series of bangs echoed across the second floor. Jessamine looked up to see Mick knocking on the glass wall. Unhappy at the continued delay, he motioned to his watch and beckoned her in with a flick of his wrist. Something about the gesture, like an owner summoning his dog, made her decide to keep him waiting a little longer. Verity and Arshdeep wouldn't mind. Besides, she wanted to see what was inside the envelope.

For such a large package the contents were slight. She pulled out a thin sheaf of papers, held together with an elastic band, and a small black diary. The sheaf had a handwritten note paper-clipped to the first page.

Jessamine,
    As promised, here is everything I have on the disappearance of my friend Cassie. It's not much but hopefully you and your team will find it interesting. I've also enclosed Cassie's pocket diary. Please help if you can.
    Yours, Marnie Clarke

Her contact details were written in the top right-hand corner.

Marnie. The woman who'd accosted her in the snow.

Jessamine spread the papers on the desk. At the top of the pile was a selection of news articles taken from local papers. The story, it seemed, had not been considered interesting enough for the nationals to pick up. They detailed the circumstances surrounding Cassie Scolari's disappearance. Jessamine skim-read the largest of the bunch. Dated four weeks earlier, it was written in the standard lifted-from-a-misper-press-release language journalists tended to use when the police suspected a person had taken their own life or run away.

APPEAL FOR HELP IN FINDING MISSING WOMAN

Police have appealed for help as they try to find a Loughton woman who has been missing since Friday. Cassie Scolari, 29, disappeared on her way home from work on the afternoon of Friday, 11 November. Last seen heading towards Embankment Tube station in central London, Mrs Scolari had told colleagues she had to leave early in order to take care of a family emergency but she never arrived home. Cassie is described as being of slim build, 5 feet 1 inch tall and has blonde shoulder-length hair. Officers are concerned for her welfare and have asked anyone with information to contact Loughton police station.

It might have been twelve years since she'd been in a newsroom but Jessamine could still read between the lines. The police knew something about Cassie Scolari they weren't saying, probably about her mental health. They clearly didn't believe it was likely she'd been murdered.

The article was dominated by a colour photograph of Cassie. In it her blonde hair was shorter than it had been in the one Marnie had shown her and parted in the middle, the right section tucked behind her ear. Her features were small, brown eyes framed by fair, almost translucent brows.

She put the articles to one side and examined the remaining papers: a series of CCTV images taken from a missing-persons website and the small black diary. Odd. How and why had Marnie come to have the diary in her possession? It could be a key piece of evidence. She must know that, surely. A skim through the weeks directly before Cassie's disappearance produced nothing of note. Doctor's appointments, parents' evening at her son's school, a friend's birthday. Going back further, to the start of the year, the only thing she saw of interest was a random address, 42 Colombia Street, Rochester, with a question mark next to it. She checked 11 November, the date Cassie had gone missing. The entry was blank, except for a single capital letter M with another question mark. M for Marnie?

She picked up the CCTV images and studied each in turn. A red circle picked out the figure of a woman leaving a building next to the Vaudeville Theatre on the Strand. Cassie. She was wearing a dark pea-coat, her hair tied back in a ponytail. Jessamine flicked through the next two pictures. They captured Cassie walking down the street past H&M, a shoulder bag clutched to her side. The next shot had her on the other side of the road, passing Superdrug, then turning left into Villiers Street. The last set of images showed her walking past a burger joint called Five Guys.

She looked again at the diary. There was something about the address she'd seen – 42 Colombia Street – that jarred.

Another knock on the meeting-room wall. She looked up to see Mick, hands on hips, mouthing angrily at her through the glass.

Jessamine took her time replacing the file inside the envelope. Then, making sure to keep a leisurely pace, she went to join him and the rest of the team.

Sarah

Canary Wharf. The start of the school holidays. Sarah ran a finger across the fan of ties arranged on the display table. A rainbow of silk, the selection ran from deep burgundy to the palest of pinks. Was he a tie man? If so, which colour would suit him best?

She picked one in a silvery grey and rubbed her thumb and forefinger against the material. She wanted the first gift she bought him to be special, something he'd keep for the rest of his life. She replaced the tie. It was too generic. Besides, everything in this shop cost a fortune. Her budget was forty quid. Earnings from the odd times she'd babysat for the McMurrays' kid, Isla, in flat 201. By her reckoning that meant she could stretch to nothing more than two pairs of the socks currently on sale by the till.

'Why are we even in here?' This from Sarah's best friend, Paris. 'I mean, who are we Christmas shopping for anyway?' Paris considered a mannequin in a tweed suit, a spotted handkerchief poking out of its breast pocket. 'Your granddad?'

Last night, asking Paris to come with her had seemed like a good idea. Sarah had figured that finding a gift would be simple, quickly dispatched at the start of their retail expedition, leaving them free to have lunch, wander around TopShop and see a film. Now, though, Sarah realised that choosing the right present would take time. Possibly all day. She was already fretting that she wouldn't be able to find anything. Trying to do this *and* pacify a bored Paris was only going to make things more stressful.

Maybe she should get him a photo album. Or a notebook.

'Let's go to Paperchase.'

'Okay, but be quick.' Paris got out her phone and started scrolling through her newsfeed. 'I'm hungry.'

Inside Paperchase Sarah left Paris by the Christmas decorations and went to the back of the shop, the shelves of photo albums. He'd yet to broach the subject of them meeting up in person. Sarah was glad, she didn't feel ready, but it meant she'd have to send his gift in the post. The only problem was she didn't know where he lived. The gift would be a good excuse to ask for his address.

She picked up the plainest option. The black canvas was simple and understated. Would he like it or would he prefer one patterned with coloured stripes? Again, she felt a rising sense of panic.

She looked over to where Paris was now busy Instagramming a reindeer tree ornament. Her plaited hair swished low on the back of her leather jacket, the ends tapering to a dry, bleached yellow. As with most things in life, Sarah's instinct was to ask her best friend's opinion. She usually told her everything so she knew she could be trusted. But every time she began to confide in Paris she chickened out. Probably because she knew her friend would say the same as anyone else looking in on her new relationship from the outside. Paris would warn her, tell her to be careful, say that he might not be everything he seemed. The internet was full of creeps and paedos.

Sarah didn't want to hear it. She'd already considered this and more. When he'd first made contact back in October, she'd told him to leave her alone. She was young, not stupid. But he wouldn't take no for an answer. He'd kept messaging her, telling her things, confiding in her about stuff he said he'd never told anyone. Gradually, over time, he'd managed to make her see things differently.

She examined the photo album's cardboard back. She was good at art and planned to take it for GCSE next year. She could customise the card with the swirling faces, leaves and tiny letters she liked to draw on her school files. Then she'd fill in the shapes with an explosion of colour. It would look cool, but would he like it or think it silly, childish even?

It was horrible, not knowing. Sarah tried to comfort herself with the fact that it was early days. Soon, things like choosing a gift or deciding what to cook him for dinner would be second nature.

Sarah hugged the photo album to her chest. She could populate the first few pages with snaps of herself, and the blank remainder would be like a symbol of the future and all the pictures they would take together.

The edges of the photo album began to cut into her forearms. She hugged it tighter.

Jessamine

The production meeting came to a close and, after gathering their things, Verity and Arshdeep left the room. Jessamine was about to do the same but Mick stopped her.

'I heard something,' he said, motioning for her to sit down. 'This morning. It's just a rumour.'

'Sounds serious.'

'They're going to put the show under review.'

'What? Why?'

'We've been on air eleven years.' He ran his hand through his hair and scratched at a spot just above his ear. 'The phrase "refreshing the brand" was used.'

'Bugger.'

'Quite,' said Mick.

'Who did you hear it from?'

'Amanda in Scheduling.'

'Should we put together a proposal, some new ideas, head them off at the pass?'

Mick shook his head. 'Best sit tight. It might blow over.'

'If it doesn't?'

'We'll cross that bridge when we come to it.'

Jessamine started to leave but again he stopped her. 'New blouse?'

She tugged it straight and nodded.

He smiled appreciatively. 'It suits you.'

'No,' she said, pushing past him. 'You don't get to say things like that. Not any more.'

Jessamine tried to put any worries about the show's future out of her head as she took the lift downstairs, then went out onto Langham Place. Her date was at one o'clock at the Riding House Café.

She'd chosen it partly for convenience – it was a five-minute walk from Broadcasting House – and partly because she thought it would make a good first-date location: quiet enough for them to chat without shouting but with enough hustle and bustle to mask any dips in conversation.

Inside the maître d' seemed to look right through her. Jessamine remembered something else Abigail had said in her dating talk of doom. She'd told her about an experiment Sainsbury's had tried in which they'd let someone in a gorilla suit walk around the fruit aisles for an hour. It was designed to demonstrate how hard it was to get customers to notice and buy a new product. As people went through the tills, they were asked if they'd seen anything unusual during their visit. No one mentioned the gorilla. It was as though it had been invisible. Women over forty, like themselves, Abigail had explained, were like that gorilla. It was as though they didn't exist.

Jessamine moved closer, until she was just inches from the maître d'. Next time he looked up he had no choice but to see her.

He tapped her name into a computer and smiled. 'The other person is already here.'

Jessamine straightened her blouse, tucked her hair behind her ears and followed him to the table.

When she'd first entered the online-matchmaking fray, she'd approached every encounter with a nervous excitement she hadn't felt since she was a teenager. It had almost certainly been the novelty of it, and that, back then, she still had a naive belief in the power of a computer algorithm to find her someone compatible, or, at the very least, a man with whom she could spend an afternoon at the pub without dying of boredom, halitosis fumes or both. But then, as she'd become more *au fait* with the reality of internet dating, that the men she met rarely corresponded with either their profile pictures or their purported personalities, the butterflies in her stomach had been replaced by the kind of pragmatic optimism more usually reserved for the moment you decided to order an exotic-sounding dish in a restaurant. You weren't expecting much from the meal but just this once you'd give the pineapple-infused halibut a try.

It took Robert a few seconds to notice her. Holding clear-rimmed glasses against his forehead, he was squinting at the drinks menu, which was pressed close to his face. In a navy jumper and jeans he had brown hair, silvery at the temples, and kind eyes. He was just as attractive as the pictures on his profile, perhaps even better-looking. Handsome, even. Things were looking up.

'Robert?'

He dropped the glasses back to the bridge of his nose. 'Jessamine?'

Jessamine was sure she saw him press his lips together: an involuntary flicker of resignation or, worse, disappointment? But it was such a tiny movement and it was there and gone so quickly that maybe she'd imagined it. He got up and she thought he was going to kiss her but then he offered his hand.

She shook it firmly and they sat down.

'So.'

'So.'

He poured her some water and they stared at each other for a few seconds.

'You said you work near here?' he said eventually.

She nodded. 'The BBC.' She took a sip of water. 'Radio.' In their online chats he'd never mentioned her show, even once he knew her full name, which meant he was probably oblivious to her job. Jessamine planned to keep it like that, for the time being anyway. 'And you're a vet?'

'I am.'

They'd covered all this online but she found that the first meeting with a person was often like this. Repeating the information seemed to work as an ice-breaker for a stretch of ice that had already been smashed and refrozen. All you had to do to break up the new, thinner layer was tap gently in a few key places.

His gaze drifted to somewhere behind where she sat. She couldn't be sure if he was trying to get the waiter's attention or if something more interesting had caught his eye.

All this uncertainty. All this wondering if someone liked you and if you liked them. Sometimes she felt her life would have been simpler if she'd just carried on having an affair. If it was easier to be the other woman.

Fucking someone from work. Worse, fucking your producer. It was such a cliché. Still, adultery had been fun. More than that, it had been hot. Mick lifting her skirt in a hotel hallway, unable to wait till they got to their room. Mick kissing her in the dark of Langham Place while she hailed a cab home after a show. Mick's mouth against her inner thigh while beside her, on the bedside table, his phone lit up. His wife, wondering where he'd got to.

They accepted food menus, then Robert removed the napkin from his lap and dropped it on the table. 'If you'll excuse me.' He got to his feet. 'Won't be long.'

Jessamine watched as he made his way to the toilets. Once he was out of sight she sank back in her seat and took a slow breath. Alone, her thoughts reverted to this morning's bombshell.

Her show might be under threat.

The prospect left her worried and angry: she'd won them numerous awards, after all, but then another part of her knew that after eleven years the format was getting stale. Still, if her superiors felt the programme needed shaking up, why not sit down and talk to them about it, like grown-ups? Muttering behind closed doors only created uncertainty and fear.

Her phone beeped. An email. Thinking it might be an update from Mick, she opened her inbox only to see a message from Jackie containing the Christmas helpline rota. She decided to look at it later and started to turn off her phone but something about the pink Refuge logo at the bottom of the email made her pause. She thought of the package she'd received that morning, Cassie Scolari's diary. She'd remembered what it was about that address – 42 Colombia Street – that bothered her. She'd seen it before, in the course of her volunteer work: 42 Colombia Street was a women's refuge.

Marnie had said Cassie's husband was violent. That address suggested things had got bad enough for her to put into play an escape plan. Refuge locations were highly confidential – you'd never find them on the internet or in any directory – and only ever released to the women being directed there on a specific date. The address had appeared in Cassie's diary at the start of the year. Had she been planning to leave, then decided against it at the last minute?

Jessamine grabbed the menu and was about to read it when she stopped. Someone was looking at her. She could sense it. She searched the room and soon locked eyes with a man sitting on a stool at the bar. Attractive, in a rangy, retired-footballer way, he was wearing a red polo shirt buttoned to the collar and had pale arms covered with thick black hair. He blinked and looked away.

She took an olive from the bowl on the table. The first few minutes with Robert had been underwhelming but she told herself it was always awkward at the beginning. She resolved to make more of an effort and ran through a list of all his plus points: smart, educated, attractive, her age, professional.

Not married to someone else.

Jessamine should have known Mick would never leave his wife. He and Natalie had been together since university and had three children, two dogs, a tortoise and a Victorian semi in Ealing. But every time she'd pressed against him beneath a hotel shower or felt his fingers brush hers as he'd reached for something on the studio control desk, she'd hoped, she'd wondered, and she'd believed him when he told her his marriage was over.

He'd promised it was just a question of time. That once his eldest was settled in secondary school, he'd ask Natalie for a divorce. Then he and Jessamine could be together. That was the worst part, the fact that, despite all evidence to the contrary from any man conducting an affair, she'd believed him when he'd said he'd leave his wife. Then, just after Easter, he'd broken the news over coffee in Caffè Nero next to Broadcasting House. At forty-three, Natalie was pregnant with their fourth child. Cleaning his glasses with the corner of his jumper, he'd told her he was terribly sorry and that she'd been lots of fun but the new baby meant he had to break things off and try to make a go of it at home.

She reached for another olive. Robert seemed to have been gone a long time.

Once more she became aware of the man at the bar. This time when she caught him staring, he waited a beat before looking away, the curl of a smile – or was it a smirk? – on his face.

The waiter appeared to take their order but Robert's chair was still empty. Jessamine peered toward the Gents. The restaurant had suddenly got very busy. Christmas office parties congregated around long tables, steam rising from their turkey and roast potatoes.

'My friend went to the toilets a while ago. Can you check he's okay?'

The waiter gave a nod and did as she asked. A minute later he was back. 'Sorry, madam, there is no sign of him.' He paused, not sure how to proceed. 'Would you like to order? Maybe a drink?'

The waiter had been in a rush, his manner so curt it was verging on rude, but now she noticed a new patience in his tone, a softening around the eyes. Pity.

Jessamine reached into her coat pocket for her phone. Her fingernails brushed against what felt like a collection of small beads. Pumpkin seeds. The packet must have split. She dug down, located it next to the now empty plastic wrapper and pulled it out.

No messages.

Maybe Robert had had to go off on some emergency – to deal with a diabetic poodle or a constipated Siamese. Nothing. His phone went straight to voicemail. She was angry more than sad, at the humiliation, at his cowardice.

That day in Caffè Nero, when Mick had told her about Natalie's pregnancy, she'd been heartbroken, then furious. First with him, for being so weak and full of shit, then with herself for having been taken in by a line that had fooled all mistresses since time immemorial. She'd thought more of herself than that.

The worst part was that now they had to keep on working together. She had to be civil to him in production meetings, to collaborate with him on air, to pretend not to notice when she came upon him at his desk, filling in his paternity-leave application.

Trying to keep her voice bright, she asked for the bill. She owed them for the water and the olives. Summoning her dignity she got to her feet. She'd delete her online profile.

She made her way along the bar towards the door.

'Going so soon?'

She stopped. This was too much. Had someone witnessed her being stood up?

'Buy you a drink?'

It was the man from before, the one she'd caught staring. He had a strange accent, Cockney with a Kentish twang, his vowels like those fairground mirrors that squished and compressed your reflection until you ended up wider than you were tall.

He motioned to the empty bar stool on his left. Up close, the cut and swoop of his jaw was even more pronounced, his skin weathered and coated with stubble that was at least a few days old. Looking at him, she was reminded of the feeling she got whenever she bumped into someone she'd gone to school with, the way that even though their face had changed over the years, she could still see their much younger features beneath the surface.

She began to decline but then she stopped. Robert's rejection had left her reckless.

'Why not?'

Slowly his mouth formed into a smile. He held her gaze for a second, as though some understanding had passed between them, and called the barman over.

His name was Dougie. She didn't ask his age but he looked to be in his late thirties or early forties. He lived in Crystal Palace and ran his own business, a garage that specialised in vintage cars. Today he'd been in town, dropping back a 1953 Porsche to a client in Marylebone, and had wandered into the restaurant for a quick drink before catching the Tube back south.

'Your name, I've not heard it before.' He moved a little closer, his eyes focused on her mouth.

'My dad chose it. It's a variation on Jasmine. A family name.'

'Lovely.' He was still looking at her mouth. Without realising, she moved ever so slightly in his direction, her head leaning towards his, as though for a kiss. He mirrored her movement.

She checked herself and pulled back, and as she did, she caught sight of the clock behind the bar. She had to go now or she'd be late back to work.

'Thank you for the drink.' She gestured at the table where she'd sat with Robert. 'And, well, you know.'

She got to her feet.

'My pleasure.' He raised his glass in a final toast. 'See you around.'

There it was again, that lazy smile.

'Unless,' he said, as she began to walk away, 'you'd like to do this again?'

Jessamine considered the question. He was at least a decade younger than her. He spoke like a barrow boy. In the last twenty minutes he had stared again and again, quite unashamedly, at her legs and breasts.

She thought of Mick in his Victorian semi, the pet tortoise hibernating in its cardboard box under the stairs, a new baby in Natalie's belly, and then she thought of Robert, the way he'd pursed his lips when he'd realised she was his date.

She pushed her hand into her coat pocket, her nails brushing against the spilled pumpkin seeds, pulled out her phone and prepared to exchange numbers.

2002

Rowena

We stop at the traffic lights and Sunny checks his tie in the rear-view mirror.

'There are going to be some important people here tonight,' he says proudly. 'I need you on your best behaviour.' He's had a haircut and smells different. Like lemons and mint from the garden. 'This could help the club. And you want that, don't you? You want me to be successful so that I have money to buy you nice things?'

The lights change and he pulls away. We leave Oxford's city centre behind and drive for a while. Soon he is turning left onto a country road. There are hedges to either side, and ahead I can see hills covered with trees, their leaves gold in the early-evening sun.

My mouth is dry. I swallow and clear my throat.

'I've been thinking.' I had planned on bringing it up as soon as I got into the car but then I saw him sitting there in his suit. I know I've left it too late. We're almost at the party. Still, I decide to try. 'I want things to go back to how they were. Before.' I've taken extra care with my hair and makeup in the hope that it will put him in a good mood. 'Just you and me.'

I figured out a long time ago that there was no gang, that the debt I was helping to repay didn't exist. That he knew the men he shared me with. But by then the reasons for stopping were too big and too many: the gun in his glove box, the fear of being cut from his life again, the worry I was damaged goods.

I put on my most encouraging smile. 'I wondered if, from now on, whenever there's a get-together, you could leave me out. Take someone else instead.' That's the other thing I've learned. Sunny has lots of girls. Girls just like me.

I let out a puff of air, relieved to have gone through with it, and wait for him to react. I know that my asking this will make him angry, that his face *will do that horrible thing where it goes completely still, his eyes slightly out of focus, as it prepares to twist and glare, that he might shout, that he might even open the glove box and threaten me with the gun. But then, after what happened last week, I feel I've got nothing to lose.*

There had been a party. Another. At the last minute a man had arrived I'd never seen before. His name was Imran. When we were downstairs he was nice. He made jokes, offered me drinks. But when we were alone he became a different person.

It's never pleasant, the things I have to do, the things I have to let them do. But that night was especially bad.

Afterwards, when Sunny came to get me from the bedroom he was shocked. He ran downstairs and I could hear him shouting at Imran. Then he took me home.

Later that night I was limping to my room when Raf appeared on the landing. He took one look at me and made me come to the kitchen to chat.

Maybe it was the shock of what had just happened or maybe it was that I'd finally had enough, but I decided I wasn't willing to do this any more. Whatever the reason, when Raf had asked what was going on, I'd decided to tell him the truth.

Raf came with me to the police station. We were taken into a room by two officers. I felt ashamed telling them what had been happening but they listened to what I had to say and wrote a few things down. Whenever I got upset, Raf held my hand and waited until I was ready to go on.

Afterwards I was drained but I also felt like a weight had been lifted. It was over. I signed my statement and they told us they'd look into it. As we reached the main exit I remembered my jacket and ran back to the inter-view room to get it. The officers we'd just been talking to were standing a way down the corridor next to a vending machine, their backs to me.

'What do you reckon?' said one. 'Anything in it?'

The other fed some coins into the machine. 'You heard her. She goes there of her own free will. So do the others.' He pressed a button and pulled a bag of crisps from the dispenser. 'If you ask me, they're just your regular garden-variety slags.' He opened the bag of crisps. 'She's probably had a fall-out with her boyfriend and wants to get him into trouble.'

The other nodded and they walked off.

After that I knew. The police weren't going to protect me. My only way out was to persuade Sunny it wasn't a good idea for me to do it any more.

Sunny leans forward over the steering wheel and studies a signpost. 'You can't let me down, Ro, not tonight.'

The signpost is made of wood painted white and has a collection of tiny carved arrows fixed to the top, the various place names printed on them in black.

'So stop whingeing.' He hooks a right and soon we're passing through a small village. It's pretty, like something from a film, and has a green, edged with white benches, a red post box and a war memorial. 'And get rid of the makeup.' He grabs the box of tissues from the dashboard and throws them at me. 'You're thirteen. You need to look it.'

Sunny marches up to the front door of the cottage, rings the bell and stands back to adjust his tie. I look at the iron knocker shaped like a lion's face and resist the urge to run my palm across the creature's mane.

'Remember what I said?' he says, fiddling with his silver bracelet. I notice that the nail on his index finger is bruised, purply black.

'Don't talk to anyone unless you say so,' I repeat. He worries at the nail with his thumb.

'And?'

'Stay by your side.'

He nods and, ignoring the lion knocker, presses again on the bell.

When he'd first pulled into the driveway that led down to this house I'd thought he must have made a mistake. With a thatched roof, nubbly white-washed walls and small square windows, it couldn't have been more different from the dumps we usually end up in

I lean back and look up to where the thatch overhangs the walls. In places, it has been cut back to show the windows beneath. It makes the cottage look like a person trying to peep out from a really long fringe.

Laughter, the chink of glasses and what sounds like a violin being tuned rise from the back of the cottage. Sunny is getting annoyed and is about to ring the bell again when the door opens a crack. An old man peers out.

'Yes?' he says, looking Sunny up and down. He is wearing a cream hat with a black stripe around the middle and has a shiny pink face.

'Leo said to come,' says Sunny, and puffs out his chest. 'Sunny – Sunny Ahmed.'

The man gives Sunny another once-over and then he looks at me. I think he's going to turn us away but then he opens the door wide. 'Come in.'

Inside we pass coats on hooks and mud-spattered wellington boots stored upside down, as we follow the cream hat down a low-ceilinged corridor. The walls are covered with paintings of people dressed in tweed sitting on horses or holding guns, a bunch of pheasants at their sides. The cream hat turns left into a living room and, after motioning to the open doors, disappears through them onto a terrace. Sunny follows in his wake but I've got a horrible feeling about where we're going and what might be about to happen, so, despite my promises, I dawdle behind.

I look around the living room. Beamed with black wood, the space is dominated by a brick fireplace and two sofas positioned opposite each other. The sofas are sandwiched inbetween small tables, their surfaces covered with photo frames. I move in close to the nearest. The pictures are all of the same family: a man with curly blond hair, combed back from his forehead, a ruddy-faced woman, presumably his wife, and a girl of around my age who looks to be their daughter. The largest picture on the table is of the daughter, contained in a silver frame. Here she is much younger than in the other snaps, maybe seven or eight, and she wears a green body-warmer, a yellow rosette pinned to her chest. In one hand she is resting a shotgun against her shoulder, in the other she holds a dead rabbit in the air, its white stomach fur damp with blood.

Sunny reappears and blinks, searching for me in the gloom. 'I told you not to leave my side.'

He grabs my arm and drags me over the threshold, down some steps and onto a lawn full of men and women, chatting and drinking. On the right edge of the lawn there's a group of people playing instruments – violins and cellos - and a long table covered with white cloths. Lines of glasses stand against silver buckets packed with green bottles on ice, and pinky-coloured jugs of liquid filled with orange segments and mint sweat in the setting sun.

The bottom of the garden is bordered by tall privet hedges, and beyond there are trees, their upper branches swaying in the breeze.

It seems like a normal party. For the first time tonight I relax. Maybe Sunny wants me here for no other reason than to keep him company while he does business. Like a real girlfriend.

A man comes striding over, wearing a blue polo shirt and chinos. I recognise him from the photo in the living room.

'Leo!' says Sunny, and puts out his hand, but Leo does not take it. He grabs Sunny by the elbow. After guiding him away from the other guests, he directs us both to the bottom of the garden, pushes us through a gap in the privet and over to a bench under the trees.

'What in God's name are you playing at?' he says, checking to make sure he hasn't been followed. In all the fuss a ringlet has fallen onto his forehead. He pushes it back and there is a flash of gold. A ring on his little finger.

'You invited me.' Sunny squares up to him. 'Remember?'

'Not you.' He gestures at me. 'Her.'

Sunny shrugs. 'I wanted to show you I'm good. For what we agreed.'

'Are you a total moron?' Leo drops his voice to a whispery hiss. 'My wife is here.' He looks back towards the privet hedge and the party beyond.

'The vote on my planning bid is next week. I wanted there to be no doubt I'd fulfil my side of the bargain.' Sunny sounds calm, jokey even, but as he talks he pushes his thumb against his bruised fingernail. I notice that the dead nail, thickened and black, has started to come away. 'In the same way I wanted to be certain you'd fulfil yours.'

Leo opens his mouth to say something but then he stops, thinking.

Sunny sees his chance and takes it. 'Introduce me to your friends, the ones on the council, and then we'll leave.'

I look at Sunny in his Burton's suit and shiny slip-on shoes and notice how different he looks, how shabby, compared to Leo and all of the other people here. I wonder if Sunny sees this too, if he knows he's not one of them and, if he does, whether this bothers him.

Leo's gaze slides down to where I stand and Sunny lets go of his grip on my arm, presses his hand into my lower back and pushes me forward. 'This is Rowena.'

Leo screws up his face and I think he's going to throw us out but then he seems to soften. 'Fine.' He sets off towards the gap in the privet. 'You've got one hour. But she waits here.'

I sit in the dark on a bench underneath the trees. It's been ages since I last saw Leo and Sunny, and I need the toilet. I'm trying to decide whether I should go in search of one or whether I could squat behind the trees when Leo appears through the gap in the privet. He is carrying two glasses of pale yellow liquid. He gives me one and sits down.

'Rowena.' He takes a sip and smacks his lips. 'It's an ancient name, did you know that?' He relaxes back and looks up at the night sky.

I bring the glass to my mouth. The fizz rises up and wets my nose.

'Rowena was the daughter of a Saxon chief and was considered one of the most accomplished beauties of that age. It comes from the Old English for joy, pleasure or bliss.'

No one has told me what my name means before. I feel a strange flush of pride.

'How do you know our friend Sunny?'

I look to the floor, my pride gone. 'He's my boyfriend.' I stop, not sure how to put the rest into words.

'Is he kind to you?'

I hesitate, not sure whether this man is to be trusted.

On the other side of the privet the sounds of the party have all but disappeared. He glances around to make sure no one is looking, then reaches across and strokes my hair. One side has fallen forward and covers my face but now he tucks it gently behind my ear. The action is so tender and unexpected that, for reasons I can't explain, I start to cry.

'There now.' He pulls me in for a hug and my tears blot his shirt. Underneath the material I can feel the warmth of his body.

'Time to go.'

I look up to see Sunny. He tries to grab me, but before he can get close Leo stands, blocking his way.

Sunny thinks it's some kind of mistake. He steps around Leo and tries again to grab me. This time I step back and place myself at Leo's side.

Sunny stops, confused. 'Seriously?'

'Leave the girl,' says Leo. 'I'll make sure she gets home safely.'

Sunny laughs. 'Sure you will.' He shoulders Leo out of the way and grips my wrist. 'Come on, Ro.' But then he flinches and lets me go. 'Fuck.' He brings his hand up to his face and examines it. The index finger has a white space where the bruised nail used to be, the newly exposed skin puckered and dry.

'Your bid will be approved,' says Leo, once more positioning himself between me and Sunny. 'I guarantee it.'

Sunny sucks his finger. 'Fine. You're welcome to her.' He starts to walk away, but after a few steps he stops and returns to where we are. He bends in close so that his face is almost touching mine. 'You think I'm bad,' he says, his lemon and mint smell from earlier now replaced by a meaty stink, 'but these people . . .' he gestures to Leo and the fading party '. . . what you're getting yourself into, you have no idea.'

With that he's gone, back through the privet and away, into the night.

Wednesday 14 December

Present day

Jitesh

Evening prayers at the Mandir, and Jitesh Ganguly couldn't breathe. He tried to calm himself with the exercise his therapist had taught him. Inhale, hold for five seconds, then exhale for ten. Repeat. But the air in the temple was warm and cloyed with burned ghee and every time he took a breath he felt as if he was being choked. He tugged at the neck of his *kurta*. If he couldn't relax soon he'd have to make a bolt for the exit or, worse, risk hyperventilating and passing out on the floor. Not for the first time, Jitesh wondered if physics would ever come up with a device to teleport him instantly from situations like this.

The source of his breathing difficulties was Kishor Patel, Kish to his friends. Jitesh usually tried to avoid him, but a few minutes earlier he'd spotted him sitting four rows in front. Kishor was eighteen, six feet tall and broad of chest. Jitesh had last seen him on the final day of their A levels. Now in his first year of a geography degree at Cambridge, Kishor must have come home for the Christmas holidays. Jitesh's parents said Kishor was a nice boy, polite, clever – 'He rows for his college.' Jitesh knew otherwise.

He studied the back of Kishor's head. Unlike the coarse thicket that curled from his own scalp, Kishor's hair was a shiny oiled black and fell from his crown in neat lines that ended in a naped curve, just above his *kurta*. The pillared hall was packed with devotees hunched forward, arms wrapped around their knees, all trying to take up as little space as possible. Kishor, though, had stretched his legs across the under-heated floor as if there was room to spare.

Jitesh switched his gaze to the monks at the front of the congregation and focused on counting the seconds as he breathed slowly in and out. Gradually, the tightness in his chest began to loosen.

His breathing stabilised, Jitesh checked back on Kishor. His head was turned towards the women's side of the temple where Jitesh's younger sister, Anisha, was sitting with his mother, aunts and cousins. Anisha was barely sixteen but she sat with the poise of a *grande dame*: legs crossed, spine erect, her purple sari edged with gold. Once more, Jitesh felt his heart jump and twitch. Was Kishor looking at her or some other girl?

His thoughts were interrupted by a sharp pain in his ribs. An elbow. He turned to see his father, next to him, clapping and singing. He nodded, urging Jitesh to join in. Jitesh heeded his prompt.

This part of the ceremony was supposed to be a meditation, a chance to clear your mind. He had always enjoyed the ritual and the still, centred feeling it gave him, but now, with Kishor there, it had the opposite effect. Emptying his brain made space for thoughts he wouldn't otherwise allow, thoughts he usually worked hard to keep at bay.

January, and the gentle *thwap* of post landing on the doormat.

His mother's scream when he'd ripped open the envelope and read what was inside.

The day Jitesh had received an offer to study at Cambridge was supposed to have been one of the best of his life. Instead it had marked the beginning of a chain of events he'd much rather forget.

After a morning at home with his overexcited parents (at one point his father had picked him up and jigged him around the living room like he was a little kid), he'd gone to school. There he'd learned that he and Kishor had been the only two boys in their year group to be offered a place, both at the same Cambridge college, Kishor to read geography, Jitesh natural sciences. Word spread, and that lunchtime Kishor had approached him in the common room and volunteered his congratulations. His face had darkened a little when he'd discovered that Jitesh's offer was unconditional (he could totally balls up his exams and they'd still let him in), but he'd been nice, friendly. He was having a house party that weekend – his parents would be away – and wondered if Jitesh would like to come. Jitesh had been delighted.

On Saturday night Jitesh had put on his best jeans and T-shirt and shown up on Kishor's doorstep at eight p.m. sharp. At first it had been okay. The door opened and he was swept into a living room full of teenagers. Some were slouched on sofas, others dancing and drinking. He grabbed a Coke and stood in a corner, watching, not sure what to do next. He soon spotted Shanae Roberts, also alone in a corner but on the other side of the room. Shanae was in the lower sixth and had recently moved to the area. Small, with curly brown hair, she was on the school fencing team, and Jitesh often saw her lugging an enormous kitbag on and off the bus. He thought she was cute but had yet to say hello.

Now the music in the temple rose in a crescendo, the Mandir's marble cupola vibrating with the sound of four hundred voices united in song. Jitesh watched Kishor clap along in time, his shoulder-blades pumping up and down beneath his lilac *kurta*. As the monks began to circulate their lamps around the deities, he noticed Kishor shift on his haunches and sneak another look at Anisha. He cocked his head to the side, predatory, like a tiger assessing a kill. Jitesh tensed. Anisha, sensing she was being watched, tilted her head slightly, and for a moment, she met Kishor's gaze . . .

At the party Jitesh had just plucked up the courage to go over and talk to Shanae when Kishor appeared. Jitesh watched as he offered her a drink. She accepted and they stood chatting, Kishor leaning towards her, his right hand planted high on the wall just above her head. The stance had cast Shanae's face and upper body into shadow. It made her look like a half-person, nothing more than skinny jeans and a pair of fluorescent pink and yellow Nikes . . .

The ritual was almost at a close. The saffron robes of the monks blurred with the moving flames. Jitesh watched the corner of his sister's mouth lift. A faint smile. She was flattered that Kishor was looking at her. It was the tiniest movement but Jitesh saw it and so did Kishor.

For the second time that evening, Jitesh's chest was being squeezed. He tried to restart his breathing exercises but it was impossible. The air was too thick, his lungs too small. Light-headed, he lurched to his feet and staggered towards the exit. He made it outside just in time and crouched on the ground. There, with his head between his knees, he gulped at the cold night until his throat hurt and his eyes watered.

He recovered in time to see his parents emerge from the temple. They joined him at the bottom of the marble staircase.

'You okay?' asked his mother.

Jitesh nodded and pushed his scarf up to cover the lower half of his face.

Somewhere during the process of collecting their shoes and coats his parents had lost sight of his sister so they stood to one side of the path to wait. There was always a sense of release after prayers, and as the crowd streamed past, laughter and chatter mixed with the thump and wail of music from departing cars in the street. In the near distance, Wembley's latticed steel arch curved into the night, its shape picked out in lights. There was a sudden roar from the football fans, a surprise goal, and as the sound rippled out of the stadium, the lights turned red.

His parents were soon approached by another couple, friends of theirs. A girl trailed in their wake. She was tall and slim, her hair cut into a short bob. A ruby studded her left nostril. He'd never seen her at temple before but she seemed familiar.

While his mum and dad exchanged greetings, Jitesh hovered in the background and scanned the steps, waiting for Anisha. He searched the mouth of the building for any sign of her purple sari but she was nowhere to be seen. He was just starting to wonder if she had stayed behind deliberately, to chat to Kishor, when he felt his father's hand on his shoulder. He guided him forward, into the conversation. 'Jitesh, this is Mr and Mrs Desai.' He gestured at the thin man in a suit and tie and the woman, currently preoccupied with positioning a pair of furry pink earmuffs on her head. 'Mr Desai is an old friend.' At the mention of the name he grinned, revealing the bright white teeth that had earned him the nickname 'Smiler'. People often speculated that it wasn't possible for a man of his age to have such perfect teeth and would enquire as to his secret. Bleaching? Dentures? Implants? His father would put them straight: 'No coffee, no smoking, and I floss and brush twice a day.'

'Your dad says you have an internship,' said Mr Desai.

'The BBC,' said his father, squeezing Jitesh's shoulder.

'Impressive. Doing what?'

Jitesh looked to his father, waiting to see if he was going to answer for him. He often did, whether Jitesh wanted him to or not. It was easier that way. At other times his dad would hold back, as though he'd decided that his son should learn to speak for himself. This was one of those times.

Jitesh dropped his scarf away from his mouth and took a breath to prepare. 'S-s-s-s-s—' He tensed. If he wasn't careful he'd seize up, like the Tin Man in *The Wizard of Oz*. He stopped, took another breath, a single shallow sip, and tried again. 'S-s-s-sound engineer.'

'We thought it would be good for him to take a gap year,' said his father. 'Get some life experience. Before he goes up to Cambridge.'

Desai reached for the girl with the ruby nose-stud and pulled her near. 'My youngest, Meera. Medicine at Durham. Just finished her first term.'

Meera caught Jitesh's eye and pulled a face, making fun of their parents' bragging. The collusion was unexpected and he blushed.

He retreated back into his scarf and then, once he was certain she'd looked away, he braved a glance at her face. Heart-shaped with high, sharp cheekbones, her eyes were ringed with thick black liner.

'Ganguly! Long time no see!'

Jitesh turned to see Kishor, Anisha by his side. His breath huffed white on the cold air and Jitesh noticed how, instead of dispersing, it seemed to linger by his mouth, like a cloud.

'Kishor,' said his father, 'how is college? How is the rowing? Will we see you in the boat race?'

'Maybe,' said Kishor. He lifted his arm and clenched his biceps. 'I'm training hard.' He offered it to Anisha. She patted it and giggled.

That night at Kishor's party, Jitesh hadn't lingered in the living room. Venturing out to the relative quiet of the kitchen, he'd been headed for the conservatory when he'd heard a strange noise. It was coming from a cardboard box on the floor next to the bin. He lifted the flap and peered inside. Huddled in the corner was a frog. A dirty brown colour, it was perfectly still, the underside of its mouth ballooning in and out.

A boy passing through paused and peered over Jitesh's shoulder. 'Kish found it in the garden earlier.' Jitesh could smell the boy's breath. Weed mixed with whisky. 'Said he's going to keep it as a pet.'

Jitesh studied the creature for another minute before closing the flap and continuing on his way.

In the conservatory he edged around the weed-and-whisky boy, now locked in a kiss so vigorous it looked like his and the girl's jaw might dislocate, and carried on through to the garden. There he settled on a bench and sat listening to the sounds of the party. He was delighted to have been invited but he felt out of place. He'd use the bathroom and then he'd leave.

He returned inside and went upstairs. On the landing he was faced with five identical doors, all closed. The one to his left was in roughly the same position as the bathroom in his own home. He pressed down on the handle . . .

Now, outside the temple, Kishor had turned his attention to Meera. Nudging Anisha out of the way he stepped forward and offered his hand. 'Kishor Patel.' He smiled. 'Everyone calls me Kish. And you are?'

Jitesh remembered how he knew her. They'd been at primary school together. Meera was one of the few other Bangladeshis in a class of largely Gujarati children.

'It's a relief to have seen you all,' said Mr Desai to his father. 'We'd heard . . .' He trailed off, clearly unsure how to continue. 'People had said . . .' He was trying to find a way to put what he knew into words. He seemed to be going for a third attempt but shrugged his shoulders in defeat. He turned to Jitesh. 'It's good to see you looking well.'

Jitesh's father blew on his hands and rubbed them together. 'We'd better be going.' He guided his family to the stone arch. There was another roar from Wembley. They felt the sound come towards them, then ricochet off the walls of the Mandir. His father waited for the noise to subside, then gave the Desais another flash of that toothy white grin. 'Take care.'

Jessamine

Jessamine leaned against the roof-garden wall, breathed in the freezing night air and stared out at the London skyline. To her right were the Gherkin, Tower 42 and St Paul's. The outline of the buildings was like the ECG dip and spike of a patient about to go into cardiac arrest. To her left, much closer to home, was Canary Wharf's triumvirate of towers, her preferred view, the blocks of metal and glass, with the Hawksmoor spire of St Anne's just across the road from where she stood.

She came up here whenever she had something to muddle through. Tonight it was Cassie Scolari. More specifically, that Cassie's friend had asked her to look into her disappearance. After her disastrous lunch-date at the Riding House Café Jessamine had returned to work and spent the rest of the afternoon with the package containing Cassie's file beside her on the desk. She must have looked at the contents of that envelope another three or four times.

In theory, the women's refuge address in Cassie's diary shouldn't have made any difference to her interest in the case. Her friend had already told her that Cassie was in an abusive relationship. But there was something about seeing it written in black and white that she found utterly heartbreaking. That, and the fact that trying to leave was the single most dangerous thing an abused woman could do.

She thought of a recent story they'd covered on her radio show: the murder of Alice Dunford and her two children. Alice had been in a violent marriage for years when she'd finally decided to leave. Afraid for her life, she had asked for a police officer to escort her to the refuge and been refused. Her husband had stabbed her, their five-year-old daughter and seven-year-old son before they had reached the garden gate.

Although it was less high profile than most of the stories they featured on *Potentially Dangerous People*, it had got under her skin. At one point in the show she'd pushed O'Brien so hard on the question of police culpability that Mick had stood up and made a slicing motion across his neck, his way of telling her to reel it in. She usually prided herself on her ability to remain impartial but that night she'd been surprised by the anger she'd felt – the rage. Afterwards she'd apologised to a cowed O'Brien and had tried to figure out what it was about the case that had thrown her so off kilter. She guessed it was, in part, because the murder was so very ordinary – Alice Dunford was one of the two women killed every week by their partner – but there was more to it. It had got to her because it reminded her of something else, something much closer to home.

A squeak. Someone had pressed down on the door handle that led to the roof. The door was swollen with moisture and the person had to give it a shove to get it open. Sarah emerged. Shivering in her favourite oversize purple fleece, she was talking to someone on the phone, her voice high and giggly.

A boy. That was Jessamine's first thought. Sarah was talking to a boy she liked.

'Sarah.' Jessamine stepped forward into the light. Sarah said something quietly into the phone and hung up. It was too dark to see her expression.

'I wanted some fresh air.'

Jessamine was sure this was a lie. Sarah had almost certainly come up here because she'd thought her mother was in the flat and hadn't wanted to risk being overheard. 'Who were you talking to?'

'Nobody.'

Sarah moved in close to where her mother stood and put an arm around her waist. They stared at the flashing pinnacle of No.1 Canada Square. On cold days a chimney of steam flowed out of the tower's pyramid roof. 'Remember when I used to think that was smoke?'

Jessamine laughed. 'You saw it out of the living-room window and started shouting, "Fire!" You even tried calling nine-nine-nine once. I got to the phone just in time.'

Sarah sighed and snuggled closer to her mother. She often got her to recount stories like this, Jessamine mused, stories she'd heard a hundred times before.

'What else?'

'You were two years old the day I brought you home. This was one of the first things I did. I carried you up here to show you the city.'

'What did I do?' Sarah knew the answer, but this was all part of it. The parry back and forth was like the gradual deposit of silt along a floodplain. Each layer was minuscule but eventually the grains of sediment had the power to change an entire landscape. The retelling and re-remembering of tiny moments forged a bond, a cartography, all their own.

'You pointed at the tower and you giggled.' Jessamine remembered marvelling at the beauty of her new daughter's face bathed in the flashing white light. 'Then you turned to me, delighted, and said, "Lighthouse!"'

Sarah laughed and pulled her mother close. Jessamine buried her face in her daughter's hair and kissed the top of her head. The smell of her scalp – loamy and sweet – triggered an unexpected, almost painful rush of feeling. The sensation was bizarre and Jessamine struggled to find a word for it.

Jessamine had always wanted children and, until life threw her a curve-ball, she'd assumed they'd come to her in the usual way. Her thirties had been spent in a relationship with a paramedic called Finn. They'd met in the A and E department of King's Hospital while Jessamine was there researching a story on the prevalence of knife crime in the capital. She'd noticed Finn on the first morning. Australian with gingery blond hair, he had a scar above his right eyebrow, the remnants of a teenage surfing accident. At the end of her third and final day at the hospital Jessamine had asked him out.

Despite his initial enthusiasm, it soon transpired that Finn was terrified of commitment. It took him four years to agree to them moving in together, but they eventually rented a flat in Balham and things were good. Time passed, and occasionally Jessamine would broach the subject of children, only to have Finn laugh it off. Then, a month before her thirty-eighth birthday, he'd told her it was over. There was someone else. Melissa. A nurse. He moved out, and within six months, Finn the commitment-phobe had proposed. Not long after that he and Melissa had had a child.

A year later Jessamine had still been reeling – from the loss of her relationship and the loss of the life she'd thought was hers – when she'd bumped into Finn on Clapham Common, a chubby baby strapped to his chest.

After that she decided to take matters into her own hands.

Friends in a similar situation had gone down the sperm-donor route but Jessamine knew from the off that she wanted to adopt. She'd thought the biology unimportant, that she'd love her child however they came to her and, besides, there were so many kids in care. Giving one a home where they would be loved and nurtured had felt good. More than that, it had felt right.

She'd thought adopting as a single parent might be more difficult, but the process – intense and stressful as it was – had been exactly the same as if she had been in a couple. It took a year and culminated in a month in which she got to meet and know Sarah for a few hours each day at her foster-parents' home. When the time came for Sarah to say her final goodbyes she had been distraught. It wasn't that Sarah understood the significance of what was happening, the finality of it (she was too young for that) but rather that she hated being separated from her foster parents, even for a short time. After Jessamine had brought her back to the flat, she'd spent the rest of the afternoon mute, ignoring the hugs, food and toys her new mum had offered to try to coax her from her shell. Increasingly desperate, Jessamine had hitched Sarah onto her hip and carried her up to the roof to show her the lights. It was the first time the little girl had smiled all day.

She thought again of Cassie Scolari. Maybe she should look into it. Just some cursory research. Jessamine knew of too many cases in which it had been assumed the woman had committed suicide or left of her own accord when in fact her husband had buried her in the front garden or hidden her body in the septic tank.

Besides, if the rumours were true and the show was under threat, it might be good to have something different up her sleeve. As soon as she got back downstairs she'd call O'Brien, ask if he could put her in touch with someone from the case. Then she'd arrange a meet with Cassie's friend, Marnie. Depending on what she uncovered, she could go for it. Pitch it to Mick as a *PDP* special. It could be the start of something fresh, more forward-looking.

Arms linked, she and Sarah moved towards the door. They were about to head down the steps when Jessamine stopped, remembering Sarah's laughter when she'd first appeared on the roof. 'Are you seeing someone?'

'Mum,' groaned Sarah.

Jessamine took that as a yes. 'Are you being careful? Just tell me you are.'

Sarah removed her arm from Jessamine's waist. It was replaced by a cold stripe of air. 'There's nothing to tell.'

Sarah took to the steps without her. Jessamine watched her go, Canada Square's flashing white light faint against her purple fleece.

Jitesh

At home, his parents went into the kitchen. Anisha sloped into the lounge to watch TV. Jitesh retreated upstairs. His was the smallest room, the box room. It contained only one item of furniture: a bunk bed accessed via a ladder, with a desk and wardrobe fitted into the void underneath. Some years earlier the room's walls had been painted blue but were now covered with posters of Jitesh's hero, the theoretical physicist Richard Feynman.

He sat down at the desk and opened his laptop.

All he'd thought about on the drive back was the girl from outside the Mandir, Meera. Her dad had said she was home for the holidays. That meant she might be at prayers next week. As might Kishor. He wanted to see her again almost as much as he didn't want to see Kishor.

He clicked on the Safari icon at the bottom of the screen. If he were to bump into her again, he wanted to be prepared. He started with the obvious things, the stuff Meera had available for public consumption. Neither her Instagram nor her Facebook account was set to private. He did a quick skim through her timelines. The most recent entries showed her at university in Durham, goofing around in a dinosaur onesie for rag week or posed outside a formal dinner, perfect in a cream silk dress. He noticed that in every shot, even the ones of her eating cereal, rumpled in pyjamas, she was wearing the black eyeliner he'd seen tonight, its thick stripe ending in a neat sixties flick at the corner of each lid.

He scrolled back a little further. There she was, ecstatic in the sunshine after getting her A-level results, then covered with mud at Glastonbury, and later revising in the sixth-form common room. He noted with some satisfaction that there was no boyfriend in any of the pictures.

He clicked on the red cross in the top left-hand corner of the screen and the page disappeared. After checking that the door was shut he crossed to the window and closed the curtains. Before he went any further he wanted to be sure of his privacy. He knew his precautions were pointless. If he were ever to be caught it would be through his IP address, not someone spying on him through his bedroom window. Still, the seclusion seemed to help his concentration and he liked how it made him feel: battened down, cocooned from the world.

He was about to return to his desk when he stopped. In the corner by the window two cardboard boxes were stacked one on top of the other. They had been bound for his room at Jesus College, Cambridge. The same college as Kishor. Inside were books, tea towels, a tin opener, cutlery and a toaster. Brown packing tape seamed the middle of the top box. Left in the spot where it had been at the start of the summer, it was covered with dust. He used his finger to sketch his favourite Feynman diagram: a wiggly line with inverted arrows at either side. It looked like a drunken H and showed what happens when an electron and a positron annihilate each other. Jitesh traced a small arrow on the bottom left leg of the H to indicate time going backwards. The ability to turn back the clock was taken for granted in quantum physics. If only the same could be said of everyday life. He wiped the diagram from the box. Dust clumped against the heel of his hand. He dislodged it with a shake and watched the air carry it slowly to the carpet.

Back to Meera.

A bit more mooching online and he should have everything he needed. Then he'd start his hack into her email, into her life.

It wasn't that Jitesh was a tech genius. Far from it. He wanted to specialise in physics, not computer science, and, like most people, until he'd watched that documentary on YouTube, he'd assumed that to be a good hacker you had to be as they were in the movies: code-breaking supremos who could type binary really fast. It was only once he'd found himself in a desperate situation, in which he'd had to find his way into someone's inbox, that he'd learned differently. That it was actually more effective to infiltrate a person than any mainframe, that if you could tap into someone's humanity – their foibles, friends and favourites – you could unlock their online world and all its secrets, every last one.

It was called social engineering. Far more prevalent than the major tech corporations liked to admit, it involved harvesting the personal details people had sloshing around on the internet, then using them to snoop on or defraud them in some way. 'People put so much information about themselves out there, more than they know,' said the expert in the documentary. 'All you have to do is join the dots.' Once you'd done that you had a good chance of breaking into someone's accounts, either by outsmarting password-reset questions or by calling up their service provider helpline, convincing them you were that individual and getting them to change the password for you.

His fingers hovered over the keyboard. He could usually assuage any guilt he felt about snooping in people's private accounts by promising himself that he would do something good, some later act of kindness, to restore the karmic balance. Now, though, he found that the mere thought of looking at Meera's cloud made his insides squirm.

A knock at his bedroom door and, before he could answer, his father was there, peering into the darkened room.

'You're up late.' He considered Jitesh, sitting at his desk. 'Everything okay?'

Jitesh flipped his laptop shut and turned to face him. 'F-f-f-fine.'

His father edged over the threshold, his gaze flicking to the back of the door. There was nothing on it, except Jitesh's blue towelling dressing-gown, suspended from a single brass hook. 'Aren't you tired?'

Jitesh let the question hang.

'Okay then.' He gave Jitesh one of his blindingly white smiles. 'Goodnight, son.'

Jitesh waited until he heard his father's footsteps on the stairs, then reopened his laptop and brought up the Apple log-in page. Meera's email address had been listed on her Facebook account for all to see. He thought of her ruby nose stud, the neat black flick at the corner of her eyelid. He typed the address into the first box, then clicked on 'Forgotten password?' A series of three reset questions appeared. All he needed to do was figure out the answers and he'd be in.

He reopened Meera's Facebook page and gazed again at the picture of her in the cream silk dress. She looked happy. People often did. He waited until his breathing had steadied, then rubbed his forefinger on the mouse pad. The search engine reappeared and he set to work. Guilt stuck to him, like glue.

Thursday 15 December

Present day

Jessamine

Nine a.m., Thursday, and Jessamine was in the car, headed down the A12 towards Loughton on her way to meet Cassie's friend, Marnie. The verges on either side of the dual carriageway were heaped with snow, by-products of the freeze that had yet to release its grip on the country. The further she got out of the city, the higher the piles became, until eventually they merged into deep, ice-crusted drifts pushed there by the ploughs. Beyond, as far as the eye could see, were fields of white, their edges striped black by hedgerows and the odd bare-branched oak.

The satnav instructed her to pull off the A12. She continued to follow the directions and before long she came to a stop outside the address Marnie had given her, a shabby 1930s semi. She was about to get out of the car when her mobile rang. O'Brien.

'That was quick. You have something for me?'

'And a good morning to you too,' he said, chuckling.

'Sorry. Morning, O'Brien.' She gave it another beat, then jumped back in. 'So?'

'I talked to a mate. Used to work out of Paddington Green before he moved to the sticks, near where your misper is from.'

Charles O'Brien had been forty years old, at the peak of his career, when he'd decided to leave the force. Jessamine had once asked why and he had given her some platitude about wanting a better work-life balance. She suspected there was more to it. The last case he'd worked had been a high-profile child abduction. They'd got the guy but it had been too late. O'Brien had found the victim, a three-year-old boy, encased in bin bags in the loft. That had been five years ago. He now did consultancy for various private security firms, and although he said the money was good, Jessamine got the feeling he missed the grit and scratch of real police-work.

'And?'

'Standard stuff. Cassie had a history of depression and anxiety, and in the weeks building up to her disappearance, various people had noticed her behaving oddly.'

'They think she committed suicide?'

'Consensus is she jumped in the Thames.'

'Her friend said her husband was violent.'

'There are some documented domestic-violence call-outs. But he was at work at the time she was last seen. His alibi is solid.'

'Do they think there's any possibility she might have run away? An affair?'

'They don't believe she'd leave her son behind. By all accounts she was a devoted mother. Almost too devoted.'

'How do you mean?'

'Teachers at the kid's school say that during his first year in Reception she called the office every day at lunch to find out what kind of a morning he'd had. If he came home with so much as a grazed knee she was in the headmistress's office, demanding an explanation about why her kid wasn't being supervised properly at playtime.'

'Maybe she planned to take him with her but something went wrong.'

'Maybe.'

'Anything else?'

'Her friend got a WhatsApp message from her nearly a fortnight after she disappeared but they think it was composed earlier, held in a queue, then sent automatically when the phone was turned on by who-ever stole it. Other than that, she didn't take any clothes, her debit and credit cards haven't been used, there's been no activity on her mobile and her voicemail hasn't been listened to. They'll put out an appeal every now and again but, to be honest, they're just waiting for the body to surface.'

'Thank you. This is really useful.'

'Why the interest?'

The net curtains twitched in the 1930s semi. A moment later the front door opened. Marnie peered out into the street. Her hair was tied into the same topknot it had been that first night outside Broadcasting House. In a black jumper dress that came to just above her knees, a black quilted jacket and opaque black tights, the only splash of colour was a red, fat-beaded necklace that looped down past her bust.

'Her friend asked for my help. She thinks there might be more to it.'

When she'd called Marnie last night and told her she was willing to do some preliminary research, the young woman had been delighted, and although Jessamine had been careful to manage her expectations, Marnie had insisted they meet first thing today.

'I guess I'll see you next week,' said O'Brien. 'Last show before the holidays.' He paused. 'Or we could meet up beforehand. A Christmas drink?'

'Thanks again, O'Brien.'

'Understood.' He laughed. 'Take care, Jessamine.'

Marnie was joined on the doorstep by an older woman and a little boy in school uniform. She came over to Jessamine in the car and, once she was inside, gave them both a wave.

'My mum and my son, Jayden.' She shifted in her seat and the friction of her jacket's arms against her body made a high-pitched, swishy sound.

'You live at home?'

'I had Jayden when I was fourteen,' she said, giving them one last wave. 'Getting a flat-share with your mates is a lot trickier with a kid in tow. Plus, I don't earn that much.'

Jessamine did the maths. Jayden looked to be eight or nine, the same age as Matteo. That made Marnie twenty-two or -three. She seemed younger.

'Thanks for coming,' she said. Her fingers danced around the lower part of her necklace. 'For helping.' She brought the beads up to just below her mouth and pressed them against her bottom lip. 'The police seem to have given up. I've felt so much better since I got your call.'

Up close, Jessamine could see that Marnie's foundation stopped just short of her jaw-line. The fine blonde hairs that grew on the sides of her cheeks emphasised where the makeup had clumped on her skin. 'Like I said, I can't promise anything. It's likely I won't get any further than they already have.'

Jessamine placed her phone in its window holster and tapped the Voice Memo app. Last night, on the phone, they'd agreed they'd begin with Marnie showing Jessamine where Cassie lived. 'I can't take notes while I'm driving so I'm going to record our conversation. You okay with that?'

Marnie nodded and pointed at the road ahead. 'Aim for the high street. Back out the cul-de-sac and turn right.'

Jessamine did as instructed. 'I've read the things you sent me but I'd like to hear the story from you.' She guided the car onto the main road. 'From the beginning. I want all the details, no matter how small.'

Marnie took a breath to prepare and grabbed her necklace again, its beads like a loop of red lifebuoys against her chest. 'The first I knew something was wrong was when I got a call from the after-school club. I'd picked up Jayden at five forty-five. Matteo, Cassie's little boy, was still there. But that wasn't unusual. Cassie often cut it fine. She couldn't help it, rushing there after work. She was always at the mercy of the Tube.'

Her words and the order in which she chose to reveal things felt prac-tised. No doubt she'd had to give this same account many times before.

'The club closes every day at six on the dot. They're pretty strict. When it got to five past and there was still no sign of Cassie they called her. But they couldn't track her down at work or on her mobile and tried her husband, Luca. He didn't answer his phone either so finally they rang me. I'm on her in-case-of-emergency list.' Jessamine noted the hint of pride in this last piece of information. 'I wasn't worried. I figured Cassie must have got stuck in a tunnel and that any second I'd get a call from her in a panic. Jayden and I put our coats back on and returned to the school for Matteo. He was a bit upset at being the last one there but other than that he seemed fine. I sent Cassie a text to let her know Matteo was at our house and then I made the boys a snack.' She stopped at the memory and smiled, wistful. 'They're so cute together.' She continued, 'It was going on for nearly seven o'clock and I still hadn't heard anything from her when I got a call from Luca.' She rolled her eyes. 'He'd been at Army Cadets – he's a volunteer – and had only just picked up the voicemail from the school. He hadn't heard from Cassie either and said he'd be right over.'

The residential road they had been driving on started to widen and Jessamine soon found herself at the mouth of Loughton high street. A mix of coffee shops and chain stores, the street was punctuated by the odd flash of Essex sparkle: a glitzy baby shop called Ba-Ba-Boom, the chrome and black of a nightclub called Minx, and a furniture store called Bella Sorella.

'And how was Luca when he arrived?'

'His hair was wet and he smelt fresh, as though he'd just showered.' She shook her head as though that disappointed her. 'He'd stopped to change.' She stalled, lost in thought.

'Then what happened?'

'He arrived, we exchanged pleasantries.' She paused, apologetic. 'Knowing what he does to Cassie, I find it hard to be in the same room. He said there'd be a simple explanation, told me not to worry and took Matteo home.'

'And did you, not worry?'

'I still hoped she was stuck on a broken-down Tube in a tunnel somewhere but when I checked the TfL website there were no reported delays or breakdowns. Then I wondered if maybe she'd been in a road accident. She was always in a hurry. I kept calling her phone but it remained turned off. Later that night I called Luca for an update but he didn't answer. I went to bed and hoped I'd hear from her in the morning. When I didn't, I tried Luca again. There was still no answer so I decided to go round. The police were just leaving. Luca told me that Cassie still hadn't come home so he'd reported her as missing. I got upset and asked if he'd hurt her. He got nasty, accused Cassie of having an affair.'

'Was she having an affair?'

'No. At least, not that I know of.'

'You think she would have told you, if she was?'

Marnie shrugged. 'Cassie was secretive about lots of things. Private. It's possible.'

Jessamine wondered about the nature of Cassie and Marnie's friendship. Marnie obviously cared about Cassie or she wouldn't have sought out Jessamine's help, but for someone who had gone to such great lengths she seemed to know little about the woman she purported to be so close to. Was the friendship more one-sided than Marnie understood or was Cassie a genuinely secretive person?

'How was Cassie in the weeks building up to her disappearance?'

'Up and down. She seemed distracted, but also excited. It's hard to describe, but it felt like she was preparing for something.'

'To run away?'

'No. Oh, look, I don't know. It was just a feeling.'

'In the file you sent me there was a diary. Cassie's date diary.'

Marnie shifted in her seat. 'The day before she disappeared I saw her in the playground. We were waiting for the bell when Matteo complained of being thirsty. She got him a juice-box out of her bag but he took one sip and said he didn't want it. Instead of giving it to her he shoved it into her bag. It went everywhere. We tried to get the worst of it off with some wet wipes but her bag was light brown suede and the blackcurrant drink had left purple stains all over the outside. She had no time to rush back home and swap it for a dry one so I offered her mine. She emptied her stuff into my bag and promised to return it later. I thought nothing more of it. Then, a few days after she'd gone missing, I came across her bag at home. I was about to take it round to Luca and that's when I felt something hard. There was a small zip pocket that Cassie hadn't remembered to empty. Inside was the date diary.'

Jessamine thought the story odd. Would Cassie have been so concerned about a few stains that she'd feel the need to swap bags with someone in a playground? But, then, who knew what Cassie had planned that day? Maybe she'd been especially concerned about her appearance. Still, it jarred.

'On the date Cassie went missing there's a single entry, the letter M, with a question mark next to it. I thought it might refer to you. Was it your birthday or had you guys maybe made plans for that night?'

'No plans, and my birthday is in January.'

'Has she got any other friends with that initial?'

'She doesn't have many.'

Again, Jessamine wondered if this was true or if Marnie just wished that were the case. 'We need to hand the diary in to the police. It could be important.'

'I know. It's just I don't trust them to do anything with it. It's obvious they've given up on her, that they think she killed herself.'

They reached the end of the high street. Jessamine stopped at the traffic lights and looked to Marnie for a prompt.

'Turn right at the roundabout, then take the first left.' Jessamine did as she said. 'Stop over there,' said Marnie, once they were halfway down the street, 'next to that tree.'

Jessamine pulled up outside a new-build block of four maisonettes. Tall and thin, each maisonette was two storeys high and had a front door that opened onto its own drive.

'They've lived here how long?'

'Since just before Matteo was born.' There it was again, that smile. Bittersweet. 'A little over nine years.'

'And before that?'

'Cassie had a flat-share in Buckhurst Hill. Luca had a place in Leyton-stone. I only got to know Cassie once the boys started school. We were the youngest mums at the school gates by miles so we sort of gravitated towards each other.'

Jessamine squinted at the window on the ground floor, trying to see if any lights were on. 'Do you think Luca will talk to me?'

'Doubt it.'

'Let's see.' Jessamine got out of the car and knocked on the door. No answer. She peered through the letterbox. A week or so's worth of post was piled on the floor.

Marnie joined her.

'They gone away?'

'Not that I know of.'

Jessamine cupped her hands over her face and peered through the living-room window. There was no tree or Christmas decoration to speak of. 'What kind of mum was Cassie?'

For the first time since they'd started talking, Marnie hesitated before answering. It was a tiny moment, maybe half a second or so, but Jessamine clocked it. For some reason Marnie was trying to decide how best to censor her response, to convert it into something other than what she really thought and felt.

'You have to remember, Matteo is an only child. It was only natural she spoil him every now and again.'

'Spoil him how?'

'He got whatever he wanted whenever he wanted it. Sweets, toys, you name it. It was like she didn't know how to say no.' Marnie fiddled with her necklace obviously uncomfortable. Did she think that, by saying these things, she was betraying her friend? 'He could do no wrong. Last year he bit another boy in the playground and Cassie was called into the school. Matteo denied the whole thing and, although a teacher had seen him do it, Cassie wouldn't accept it and took Matteo's side.'

Marnie's picture of Cassie as a parent echoed what O'Brien had said. Jessamine tried to imagine going against the teachers and other parents like that, how it would feel to believe and then defend your child so resolutely. 'Why do you think she's like that?'

'I guess a lot of it is to do with feeling guilty about staying with Luca, about what Matteo sees and hears, so she tries to make up for it in other ways.'

'Did Cassie tell you Luca was violent?'

The women Jessamine spoke to in her volunteer work rarely confided in others about the abuse they experienced. They were too ashamed.

Marnie shifted from foot to foot. 'Not exactly. She'd say the odd thing and I'd see the bruises. I put two and two together.'

'So what do you think happened? You know her, you know her husband, what's your theory?'

At this Marnie perked up: the question she'd been waiting for all along, perhaps. 'I think Luca was worried that Cassie had had enough and that she was going to leave him. He wanted to make sure it didn't happen. You said on your show that seventy-five per cent of domestic-violence homicides happen at the point of separation or after the victim has already left her abuser.'

'That's right.'

She nodded, vindicated. 'I think he found out what she was up to, that she was planning to leave. I think he was the one who called her at work that day, that he came to pick her up and then maybe he took her somewhere, they argued and he killed her.'

'Did Cassie ever tell you she was planning to leave?' asked Jessamine, thinking of the Colombia Street address she'd recognised in Cassie's diary. 'Maybe go to a refuge?'

Marnie shook her head, unhappy that her theory should be called into question.

'You said you're worried Luca might flee the country?'

'With Matteo. He's Italian. Cassie has no family – she's an only child and her mum and dad are dead. I think he wants to get away before they can find Cassie's body.' She looked at the empty maisonette. 'That is, if he hasn't left already.'

Jessamine went back to the car and got out the CCTV images of Cassie walking down the Strand. She held one up in front of her, looking from it to the front door, trying to imagine her here. What type of a woman was she? What type of employee, friend, wife, mother?

'That's why I don't think she was going to meet someone,' said Marnie, peering over her shoulder. She motioned to the CCTV printouts. 'You don't look like that if you're off to meet your lover.'

Jessamine stopped. 'She didn't normally look like this?'

'Cassie's the kind of woman who contours just to go to the shop for a pint of milk. She's always immaculate.'

Jessamine couldn't decide if that filled Marnie with envy or pride. 'But not that day?'

'Not a scrap of makeup, not even lip-gloss. And look at her hair.' She tapped at the picture with her nail. 'Scraped back. It was almost as though she was deliberately trying to make herself as unattractive as possible.'

Or, thought Jessamine, she was having some kind of breakdown and had gone past the point of caring.

Marnie got out her phone and pulled up what seemed to be one of many pictures of Cassie. 'This is her usual look.'

Jessamine studied the photo. Marnie was right. Cassie was perfectly put together. With smooth hair, tonged into soft waves that framed her face, her lipstick and mascara were expertly applied, her foundation flawless. In the picture she wore a navy V-neck over a crisp white shirt. A delicate gold chain rested against her collarbone.

'What do you think?' asked Marnie. 'Can you help? Can you find out what happened to my friend?'

On the face of it, Cassie's disappearance was as the police had said, a simple but tragic case of suicide. It was an entirely plausible scenario, yet the more Jessamine learned about Cassie and the people who surrounded her, the longer her list of questions grew about how and why she'd got up and walked away from her desk that day. 'Leave it with me,' she said, motioning for Marnie to get back into the car. 'I'll see what I can do.'

2003

Rowena

I lie hidden under a picnic rug in the back seat of the car, a pile of papers slipping around beneath my head. It's always the same. Leo makes sure of it. 'Just in case,' he says, every time he gets the rug out of the boot. I don't mind but it does mean that all I can see is the sky and tall buildings going by and that whenever he turns a corner I'm poked by one of the random bits of crap that clutter his car.

We turn right and stop. Leo reaches inside his trouser pocket for a slip of paper, opens the window and taps whatever code is written there into something outside I can't see. Ahead, the barrier lifts and, with a grunt of satisfaction, he drives down into an underground car park.

A few minutes of circling under strip lights and he finds a space, parks and comes round to open my door.

'Out you get. Come on, Shortie.'

That's his nickname for me. He thinks it's funny. He once asked if everyone else in my family was my height. I laughed and made some joke about the Seven Dwarfs. I didn't want to tell him the truth. That my social worker said I'd stopped growing a while back, before I went into care.

We walk over to the lift. The car park is lined with row upon row of neatly arranged cars. They are all like Leo's. Shiny. Big. Expensive.

Inside the lift he checks the scrap of paper again, then chooses which button to press. Floor Six. He seems nervous and keeps twisting the ring on his little finger and checking to make sure his cufflinks haven't come loose.

It's been nearly a year since we first met. A year since he promised to protect me from Sunny and his friends. And he has stayed true to that promise, kind of. I no longer worry about Sunny even though, whenever I see him around town, he does this pretend gun thing. Holding his finger up in my direction, his thumb cocked, he squints, as though he's taking aim. And then he fires. Bang.

In exchange, though, Leo wants things.

At first it was just me and him, either at his house or in some country lay-by. Then we started with the parties. Now it's much the same as it was before. The houses are nicer, true, and the beds. With Leo there are always beds. Although that seems to be more about the comfort of the men involved than me.

The lift opens and we walk down a corridor past a series of numbered doors until we reach Flat 673. Leo knocks and we go inside.

The flat is small. A kitchen leads off the living room and there seem to be two, maybe three bedrooms branching away from the hall. The decor is plain: a glass coffee-table, beige sofa and armchairs. Two of those wheelie suitcases, one large and one small, are lined up next to each other in the corner. A number of other girls are already here and, for the first time since I've started going places with Leo, a selection of boys.

He leaves me in the living room and goes to greet the men in the kitchen.

The others are looking at me. I ignore them and go over to the open window. I see a huge garden square, almost as big as a park, filled with trees and flowers. Directly below is a pond. In the middle of it three bronze dolphins are arranged one on top of another, as though they're playing together in the ocean. A fountain pushes up through the middle of them, covering their backs with pretend sea-spray. On the grass next to the fountain, people drink wine and laze around in the evening sun. I look around. There must be hundreds of flats in the complex, maybe thousands. All the windows cut into the reddy-brown brick are the same design as the one I look out of: white frames divided into waffle-like squares of glass.

In theory I could have refused Leo. Used the handover from Sunny to walk away and try to become a normal girl again. One who goes to school and spends her days worrying about what to wear to the Christmas disco, who snogs boys and spends her nights hanging around bus stops drinking cider or carving her name into park benches. But without Leo I'd be at the mercy of Sunny. And it's not as if I can go to the police. If they didn't believe me the first time, there's no way they'd trust what I had to say about Leo. I don't know what he does exactly but I do know he's important. Besides, whenever I think of all the things I've done and the sort of people I've done them with, who'd want me now? It's just like those police officers said: I'm not dragged to these places kicking and screaming.

I wait another minute, then go and sit between two girls on the sofa. They tut and huff, but eventually they shuffle aside to make room.

'Like what you see?' says the girl to my right. She motions at the window.

'That fountain always makes me need the toilet,' says the girl to my left. 'All that rushing water. They turn it off at night, but until then, it's just there in the background, making me need a wee.'

They giggle.

The girl on my right is beautiful. About my age, her skin is toffee-coloured, her hair a mass of brown spiral curls. She reminds me of Scary Spice. The girl on my left seems younger, but that might just be because she's small like me. The upper sides of her cheeks are covered with acne and she holds her head at this strange tipped angle, which means her hair swings forward, hiding the spots.

A knock at the front door and another man appears. Sweaty and out of breath, he's really fat, so fat that he struggles to walk. At his side is a boy who looks to be eight or nine. He gives the child a Game Boy and settles him on the floor in the living room, then waddles into the kitchen to where the other men are laughing at some joke.

My stomach turns. This isn't right. The girls at either side of me are also sitting up a little straighter. I call the kid over to where we are but he won't look up from his game.

'My one brought a camera with him tonight,' whispers the girl who looks like Scary Spice.

'A camera?' says acne girl.

'A video camera. Dirty bugger.'

'What? Why?'

'Why do you think?'

They pause. Then the one to my right turns to me. 'This your first time?'

'In London, yes. We normally go other places.'

'We?'

'What are you – his girlfriend?'

They fall about laughing.

'What's your name?' asks the one to my left.

'Rowena.'

'I'm Queenie and this,' she reaches behind me and gives the smaller girl a tickle under the armpit, 'is Erin.'

The little boy is still focused on his Game Boy. It gives off a stream of beeps and dings. The electronic noise mingles with the sound of the water from outside.

'Who's he?'

Queenie shrugs. 'The fatty likes them young.'

'But he's a child.'

She grabs the back of my head. Then, gently, as though she is a ventriloquist and I am her dummy, she turns my gaze towards the kitchen.

'See those blokes in the corner?' She drops her voice to a whisper. 'Judge, police officer, cabinet minister.' Every time she moves on to a different person in the line, she moves my head ever so slightly. 'The judge has the worst bad breath. Total toilet. Avoid at all costs.' Done with her lesson, she removes her hand. 'Sometimes there's a few celebrities here, pop stars, even.'

'What's that got to do with anything? He's a kid, just a baby.'

'What's it got to do with anything?' Queenie and Erin roll their eyes. 'They're all rich. Powerful. If they want to bring little kids in from children's homes, they can. No one cares about those children and these guys know it. They can do what they like.'

Two of the men break away from the crowd and stand at the entrance to the living room. They look at us like they're on the other side of a disco, working up the courage to come and ask for a dance. As if we could ever say no.

Leo hasn't noticed, he's too busy talking to the man pouring the drinks. Every now and then a snatch of what he's saying travels up and out of the din. The talk is the same everywhere we go, all council seats and parties.

Queenie gets to her feet. There seems to have been some cue, a prompt that only she registered. A man in a dressing-gown takes her hand and she follows him down the hall.

I watch her go and it's then I realise I can no longer hear the shush of the fountain outside. In the short time I've been here I've already got so used to the constant slap and patter of the water hitting the dolphins' backs that I'd stopped hearing it, only noticing it once it was gone.

Monday 19 December

Present day

Jessamine

Monday morning, and Jessamine was on the top deck of the number 15 on her way to work. She usually relished the journey. The bus route took her past the Tower of London and St Paul's Cathedral. Today, though, her enjoyment was marred by the bus being grossly overheated.

She unbuttoned her coat, reached for the long, thin window to her right and yanked it open. Air streamed in onto her face, cold and sweet. The man next to her tutted and pulled his scarf tight. She gave him her best fuck-you smile and settled back into her seat.

Today she was going to moot the idea of a *PDP* special to Mick. She was excited and had spent most of last night awake, running through the details of Cassie Scolari's case in her head. A present-tense investigation would give the show a new lease on life. If the rumours were true and the show was under threat, a fresh approach might make the powers that be reconsider or, at the very least, keep them at bay for a while. She was about to go over the case's key points again when her phone rang.

She answered as soon as she saw the caller ID. 'Ellen?'

'Jessamine, hello. Is now a good time to talk?'

'It's always a good time to talk with you, Ellen, you know that.'

Ellen laughed.

Ellen Griksaitis was Sarah's social worker, assigned to her when she'd first entered the care system at eighteen months old. Jessamine had got to know her when she'd applied to adopt Sarah, then aged two. Ordinarily, once an adoption had been finalised, the family fell out of touch with the social worker. Ellen was different. Not long after Sarah's adoption had gone through, Jessamine had gone to her for help. They'd stayed in contact ever since.

'I thought you'd want to know. I had a call from your daughter yesterday.'

When Ellen spoke she tended to emphasise those words in a sentence that usually went unnoticed. 'To', 'had', 'from'. It gave her voice a rocky, jolting cadence that made Jessamine think of a rapidly deflating balloon, jerking from wall to wall as it descended to the floor.

'Really? She didn't mention it.'

'The tinker.' Ellen laughed again. 'I guessed as much.'

A prickle of worry. Sarah also remained in regular contact with her social worker but she usually told Jessamine whenever she was planning to check in.

'She was asking about her file. She wanted to know if she could see it.' Ellen paused, waiting for Jessamine to speak. When she didn't, she carried on. Her tone was still light but there was a new tinge to it, an edge of concern. 'Has something happened?'

'No.' Jessamine thought of Sarah on the sofa at home before she'd left for work this morning. She'd been swaddled in her dressing-gown, her hair damp from the shower. 'At least, I don't think so.'

'It often happens at this age,' said Ellen. 'They get that bit older and they start to think things through. They have questions they didn't have before.'

Jessamine considered this as a possibility, then discarded it. It made no sense for Sarah to ask Ellen for her file. She knew perfectly well that Ellen wouldn't be able to give it to her and would almost certainly mention the request to her mum.

Jessamine used her coat sleeve to wipe the fogged glass and fanned herself with a newspaper. Even with the window open, her forehead was sheened with sweat. Peering out, she saw that the bus was now on Fleet Street, headed towards the Strand: the street where CCTV had captured Cassie Scolari coming out of her office on the day she'd gone missing.

'What did you tell her? About the file.'

'The same thing I tell any of my kids. As stated by the law of this land she will be able to see it when she reaches the age of eighteen and not a day before.'

Since Sarah had first come to the attention of social services her life had been meticulously documented and collated by a variety of state-run agencies. A secret history of sorts, her Child Placement Report contained details of every police call-out, hospital note and foster-family, and every court order made in relation to her care. Sarah had been told the rough story of how and why she had come to be removed from her birth family – she knew, for example, that her mother had been in abusive relationship with her father and that, after an altercation with him, her mother had died. The details were vague and it was up to Jessamine, with Ellen, to decide how and when Sarah should be exposed to the uncensored and distressing truth that surrounded her adoption.

The bus inched past the Royal Courts of Justice. In the distance Jessamine could see the signage for the Vaudeville Theatre and, next to it, the door to Ticketmaster's headquarters, Cassie's place of work.

'Look,' said Ellen, yawning, 'it's your right as her mother to keep her file sealed, but that as a strategy has a limited shelf life. My advice? Talk to her. I know you're worried about how she'll react when she sees what's written there, but it will be so much better if she hears it all now, from you, voluntarily. And I mean all of it.' She softened. 'Jessie, what happened back then, I see it more often than you might think. She'll understand.'

'I'll talk to her, I promise. But in the meantime, if she calls again, will you let me know?'

Ellen agreed, and Jessamine put the phone in her bag. Sarah's Child Placement Report was a series of A4 ring-binders stacked on a dusty shelf in some office, but Jessamine thought of it as a kind of Pandora's Box: for years its contents had been no more than a speck on the horizon, but now its dark hulk was drawing closer, its lock and key coming into terrible focus.

The heat on the bus was unbearable. Her inner thermostat seemed to have given up completely, her back and underarms drenched with sweat. She checked the time, an idea forming. Her production meeting wasn't for another two hours. Cassie's office was literally over the road from where she now sat. She could swing by, see if anyone was willing to talk.

A first-hand account of Cassie's behaviour in the hours before she disappeared might strengthen her pitch.

She pressed the stop button and was about to make her way down to the lower deck when she noticed the man she'd been sitting next to was still huddled underneath his scarf. She reached back to flip the window shut, then noticed a woman in the seat behind. Her coat was in her lap, her cheeks and neck flushed, her face raised to the breeze, eyes closed. Jessamine recognised the signs.

The bus was pulling into its stop. She'd need to get a move on if she was going to make it down the narrow stairs. Instead of closing the vent she reached across and opened a second window, increasing the flow of cool air. Her eyes still closed, the woman smiled. The man grimaced, deep in his scarf.

Jessamine gave him a finger-waggle wave, then lunged for the stairs. She only just made it through the doors in time.

Jitesh

There was a problem with the microphones. The sound kept cutting out. The last time it had happened was this morning, during a live show. There had been complaints. Jitesh Ganguly placed the screwdriver between his teeth, got down on all fours and crawled underneath the control desk.

'That's it,' said Malcolm, from above. He tugged at the red wire so Jitesh would know which one to isolate. 'Follow the cable to the breaker circuit, then check to see if it's loose.'

Jitesh did as he was told and traced the wire's origin to a square metal panel in the floor. He unscrewed the panel and shone his pocket torch inside. The wire looked fine. 'C-can't s-s-s-see a problem.'

'Shit.' Malcolm let go of the red wire and it fell back into the tangle. 'Okay, out you come.'

When Jitesh stood up, Malcolm was already surveying the nearby walls and floors. He replaced the screwdriver in his tool-belt and made sure to keep very still. Malcolm had an uncanny ability to map in his head the thousands of hidden wires and fuses that snaked under and behind the building's carpets and plasterboard, but to complete his inventory he needed absolute silence.

Malcolm was the radio division's chief electrician. Jitesh had been assigned to him at the start of his internship and, although he had the option to be seconded to at least three other specialities, he'd long ago decided to stick with him for the duration. The reasons for this were two-fold. One, Malcolm was a decent, kind person (a cursory trawl through his email had shown him to be a straightforward family man with an interest bordering on obsession in old Land Rovers). Two, he wasn't fazed by Jitesh's stutter. Whenever he struggled to articulate something,

Malcolm never did the awful encouraging-smile thing, and he never grew so impatient for Jitesh to finish that he said the words himself.

Their job was to maintain and repair the electrics in all twenty-two of the radio studios spread across old and new Broadcasting House. Problems happened, people reported them, then he and Malcolm fixed them. And, boy, were there a lot of problems. Especially in the last month or so. Today's issue with the microphones was the tip of the iceberg. In the last week alone entire control desks had randomly lost all power, an editing suite had fizzled out for no apparent reason, and switches in the voice booths had refused to work. The faults were clustered around three or four studios and meeting rooms on the second floor of old Broadcasting House. It was a mystery, and being unable to determine the root of the problem was driving Malcolm crazy.

A minute or so more of staring at the wall, and Malcolm thought he might have located the source of this particular issue. 'The problem is that this floor was never meant to be organised like this. When they renovated BH all the studios and offices were laid out differently. Then someone made them add in all these weird partitions at the last minute. It makes it harder to figure out the electrics.'

He approached a seemingly anonymous section of plasterboard and, reaching to just above head height, used his finger to trace a horizontal line from one side of the studio to the other. It mirrored the journey of the wire beneath and came to a halt at the divider that sectioned the studio from the glass-walled meeting room next door.

'Oh, Lord.' Malcolm left his finger in place as a marker and nodded. 'The breaker we need to check is in there.'

Jitesh appraised the group of people on the other side of the glass. A man with black-rimmed glasses was pacing up and down on his phone while two women sat at a table drinking coffee. One woman wore a bobbled cardigan over a Jean-Michel Basquiat T-shirt; the other had a gold nose-stud and wore a striped Oxford shirt, buttoned to the collar. In the middle of the table was a pile of scripts, the Radio 4 logo in the bottom right corner.

The woman with the nose-stud made him think of Meera. His stomach lurched. It had been five days since he'd hacked her account and he'd yet to do anything good to make up for that, never mind his plan to act on what he'd learned (an email exchange in which Meera had arranged to meet a friend called Katy this coming Tuesday). Eager to see her again, Jitesh had made a note of the date and was aiming to be in the vicinity at the same time. He resolved to do something soon, within the next forty-eight hours, and if he couldn't he'd make a donation to charity.

'We're going to have to interrupt their production meeting.' Malcolm grabbed the stepladder and went back out into the corridor. 'Brace yourself.' He rapped on the door and, without waiting for them to acknowledge him, barged in. 'Don't mind us,' he said, marching over to the wall in question. 'Won't be long.'

Jessamine

Up two flights of stairs, Ticketmaster's London HQ was all high ceilings and walls hung with posters advertising pop concerts and West End shows.

Cassie's boss showed Jessamine into his office and told her to wait while he removed a pile of cardboard boxes from the sofa. One had split, a perforated length of blank tickets spilling over its sides, and as he lifted it to the floor it collapsed, the tickets splaying out across the carpet.

'Thanks again for seeing me at such short notice,' she said, as he attempted to manoeuvre the mess into the corner with his foot. She took a seat on the newly exposed sofa.

'Anything to help,' he said, abandoning his strategy for the even less effective technique of trying to scoop up the ticket loops in his arms. 'It's so awful about Cassie, the whole thing.'

His name was Stuart Coombes and he wore black trousers and a white shirt, underneath which Jessamine could see the faint outline of a vest. He had granted her an audience without much fuss. Rocking up at Reception, she'd explained that she was looking into Cassie's disappearance. The receptionist had been predictably suspicious. Jessamine wasn't police and she didn't have an appointment. But then Jessamine had said the three magic letters that opened doors for her and thousands of other journalists all over the world: BBC. As soon as the receptionist had seen her work ID, she'd made a call. Moments later Stuart had appeared.

A knock at the door and a gawky boy, a few years older than Sarah, peered into the room. 'Can I get you a drink? Tea? Coffee?'

'Tea, white, two sugars,' said Stuart, still preoccupied by the tickets.

The boy looked to Jessamine. 'Coffee, black. Thank you,' she said, then got out her phone and notebook. When she looked up again, the boy was still there.

'That will be all, Jamie,' said Stuart, loudly. Jamie startled and, after fumbling with the handle, closed the door.

'Intern,' said Stuart, as if that were explanation enough. He picked up a plastic ruler from his desk and began bending it back against the heel of his palm. 'Tell me, how can I help?'

'I'm investigating Cassie's disappearance. Depending on how it goes we might do a programme about her on Radio 4.'

He raised his eyebrows and nodded approvingly. Radio 4 was serious, respectable. 'What would you like to know?'

'I'm trying to build a picture of what she was like and how she was on the day she went missing.' Jessamine placed her phone on the table in front of her. 'Mind if I record our conversation?'

He waved the ruler in agreement.

'Let's start with the basics. How long had Cassie worked here?'

'Four years, give or take. If I remember correctly, she'd been a stay-at-home mum, came back to work once her son started school. She dealt with accounts admin, invoices, that sort of thing.'

'What kind of employee was she?'

'Until recently? Reliable, hardworking, friendly, although she kept herself to herself. She never came out for drinks on a Friday or anything like that, but she had a kid, had to get back for him.'

His responses were quick. Like Marnie, he'd been primed by his conversations with the police.

'Until recently?'

'In her time here she'd taken maybe all of two days off sick. But then in the last few months she was off loads.'

'How many days exactly?'

'Let me see.' He brought up something on his computer. 'In total she called in . . .' he counted the list of columns on his screen '. . . eleven times.'

'Did you have cause to talk to her about it?'

'There's been a lot of bugs going round and everyone's been off. Plus it wasn't like her. I believed her absences to be genuine.'

Jessamine wondered if Cassie had been ill or if she had stayed away from work for some other reason. Maybe the violence at home had escalated in recent months. Bruises in the wrong places might have raised awkward questions from her colleagues. Alternatively, if she had been headed towards a breakdown, maybe her absences were linked to her depression, a run of days when she hadn't been able to face the office.

'Could I have a printout of that?' She motioned to the document he had open on the screen.

'Sure.' He hit return, and from under his desk she heard the click and whirr of a printer.

There was a knock at the door and Jamie entered with their drinks. They thanked him and he left them to it.

'Tell me about the day she went missing.'

'Everything that morning was normal. She was normal. Talk to the people who sit near her and they'll tell you the same thing.' He reached down to the printer and handed her a sheet of A4 listing the dates of Cassie's absences. 'Then just after lunch she came into my office. She said she'd had a call from her son's school, he wasn't well, and she needed to leave to collect him. I told her that was fine, wished her son well and she left.'

'Do you have a log of her incoming landline calls?'

'I can give you the same thing we gave the police.'

'I don't know how far back the police went but could I get the last two months' worth?'

Stuart hesitated slightly. It seemed his goodwill had limits. 'Leave me your details. I'll have them sent on.' He got to his feet. 'If that's everything?'

'Of course. Thank you for your time.' Jessamine stopped the recording.

Stuart saw her to Reception and was about to say goodbye when Jessamine turned to him. 'Can I see Cassie's desk?'

'The police have already gone through it.' Jessamine held her silence. He sighed and shook his head in defeat. 'This way.'

She followed him through the office and over to an empty desk in the corner. Apart from one or two people, the place was deserted, most staff having cleared out for the Christmas holidays.

Jessamine motioned to the chair. 'May I?'

'Sure.' He checked his watch. 'Is it okay if you see yourself out?'

'Of course.'

She sat down and surveyed the desk. It was unremarkable and contained only a screen, a keyboard and a small picture of Matteo. A few members of staff stopped what they were doing, distracted by her presence. Jessamine waited for their curious glances to abate, then she leaned down and opened the drawer pedestal. The contents were paltry. A stapler, a few packets of ketchup, two stray paperclips and a tin of lip balm.

She leaned back in the chair, looked out of the window and tried to imagine herself as Cassie that day. The right edge of the window was fringed by what looked like purple tinsel, overhanging from the hoarding on the Vaudeville Theatre next door. Beyond that, on the Strand, she could see the top deck of buses going past.

Jessamine stood up and pushed Cassie's chair back under the desk. Cassie was an elusive figure. Aside from Matteo and Luca she had no family, few friends, and although she had worked in the same place for the last four years, her boss seemed to know virtually nothing about her, except that she was a mum.

She headed for Reception and had just reached the bottom of the stairs when she heard footsteps.

'Wait.'

She looked back.

It was Jamie, the intern. He stood there blushing, a pack of padded envelopes under one arm. 'You're here about Cassie, right?'

'Yes.'

He looked back towards Reception, as though he was worried about being overheard. 'I used to get her coffee. I get everyone coffee. Or at least I try to.' He fiddled with the corner edges of the envelopes.

'Jamie, is there something you wanted to say?'

'I might have imagined it.'

'Go on.'

'Once or twice, when I was near her desk, I thought I heard another phone.'

Jessamine felt her neck tense. It used to happen all the time when she worked in news and stumbled across a new lead. She shrugged her shoulders, trying to shuck off the muscle memory. 'Another mobile?'

'Yes. There'd be one mobile on her desk, the one with the picture of her son on the back, and another ringing in her bag on the floor.'

'Ever see her answer it?'

'This one time I think she was going to but then she saw me watching and left it to ring out.'

If what Jamie was saying was true, Cassie had had a second phone. Why? Because her husband monitored her usual mobile use and she wanted to make and receive calls without him knowing? Because she was having an affair? Or because she was trying to plan her escape?

'Mention any of this to the police?'

Jamie's face mottled red. 'I didn't want to send them on a wild-goose chase. I'm not completely sure.' He shifted the padded envelopes to the other arm, then back again. 'But I keep worrying, what if it's important?' Once more he shifted the envelopes from one arm to the other but he misjudged and they fell to the floor. Jessamine watched as they slid down the stairs and landed in a pile at her feet.

Jitesh

Jitesh positioned the stepladder beneath the TV bracketed to the wall and held it steady while Malcolm climbed to the top. Every meeting room, studio and corridor had a television. Tuned to various BBC channels they were all kept on mute so as not to distract the people working below. This screen displayed twenty-four-hour rolling news.

Jitesh had just passed Malcolm a screwdriver when, through the glass, he noticed a woman hustling out of the lift. Jessamine Gooch. He'd seen her picture on the wall. She was one of the presenters and, although she wasn't famous-famous, he knew from the trophy cabinet next to the controller's office that she'd won awards, lots of them. She wore a brown wrap dress that complemented her figure and there were sweat marks under her arms. He watched as she barrelled into the meeting room where he stood and took a seat next to the man with the glasses.

'Morning, all,' she said, grabbing a script from the pile in the middle of the table.

Jitesh noticed the man register the cut of her dress. Jessamine met his gaze, defiant, and held it. Then she stared down at the man's wedding ring. He seemed to shrink in on himself. Only then did she look away.

'Before we talk about tonight's show, I've been wondering,' she said, rummaging in her bag, 'what if we were to investigate a live case?'

Her accent was brittle, her delivery brisk. She enunciated every syllable. Jitesh was reminded of Mary Poppins, carpet bag in hand.

'What – you mean like an unsolved?' chipped in the younger woman in the striped shirt.

'Exactly. Something the police weren't able to solve. There's a story I've been looking into. A missing woman. We could do it as a special.'

The man sucked in his cheeks. 'Those things are a bloody minefield.' He shook his head. 'Contempt of court issues, libel issues . . .'

Jessamine slapped her script on the table. 'Or maybe it's exactly what this show needs,' she said meaningfully. 'A breath of fresh air?'

'Maybe we should talk about this later,' said the man, signalling the presence of the two other women with his eyes.

At the top of the stepladder Malcolm was busy adjusting the wires that fed into the TV. For a moment the screen went dark, then flickered back to life, but it seemed the action of turning it off and on again had switched off the mute function. Sound leaked into the room: a scream of sirens and the sombre cadence of a reporter halfway through a piece to camera.

The production team stopped what they were doing and glared at Malcolm.

'My apologies,' he said, muting the TV. 'Won't be much longer.' He gave Jitesh a wink. Malcolm thought the producers and presenters were silly and relished any opportunity to puncture what he thought of as their up-their-own-arse importance.

The production team went back to marking up their scripts but Jessamine's attention seemed to have been caught by something on the TV. Jitesh followed her gaze and saw a reporter, microphone in hand, in front of a blue and white police cordon that whipped and bucked against the breeze. To the reporter's right, scattered across the pavement, were blood-stained clothes and abandoned bits of gauze. Meanwhile, in the background, people in forensics suits were taking photos.

There was a cough and Jitesh looked up. Malcolm was done. Jitesh held the stepladder steady while he descended, then followed him out into the corridor.

'I've replaced the fuse but I've got a feeling there's something bigger at play. I'm thinking mice. There could be a nest. They get behind the walls and destroy the wires. I'll get Facilities to look into it.'

While Malcolm went off in search of lunch, Jitesh found a nearby hot desk and set to work logging the fix.

From where he sat he had a clear view of the meeting room. Jessamine was still staring at the TV. She had a strange expression on her face, as though what she was seeing frightened her. She kept craning her head to one side, as if she was trying to see something just out of shot. The man with the glasses stopped what he was doing and said something to her. She replied and refocused her attention on her script, but within a few seconds she was back to looking at the screen.

Jitesh submitted his log and then, with a bit of time to spare, he opened Facebook and went to Shanae Roberts's page. He liked to keep an eye on the comments people posted there: it made him feel he was protecting her somehow, keeping watch. He scanned her wall. No one had posted anything since yesterday. He clicked on her profile pic. Lying on a sofa with her legs crossed, arms behind her head, she looked like the girl he'd seen chatting to Kishor at the party: eyes shining, neon pink and orange Nikes catching the light. Even in repose, her posture had an *en garde* tension, as though at any moment she might produce a fencing foil from behind her back and pounce.

He felt his breathing quicken. A tightening in his chest. If he wasn't careful, he'd have a panic attack, right here at work. He closed the tab and looked around, searching for distraction. In the meeting room Jessamine was still fixated on the TV. What was it about the news report that had caught her attention?

Curious, he got rid of Facebook and brought up the BBC news site.

It didn't take long to match up the images he'd seen on the TV screen with the stills on the homepage. The story was time-stamped to an hour or so earlier.

Breaking News: Pregnant Woman Stabbed Seven Times

A pregnant woman is dead after she was found with stab wounds to her neck, back and abdomen. The victim was heard screaming after she was attacked outside the Bullring Shopping Centre in Birmingham this morning at around 9 a.m. Officers were flagged down by passers-by at around 9.10 a.m. after the woman was stabbed multiple times with what is thought to have been a knife. A 29-year-old man has been arrested by West Midlands police on suspicion of murder. The woman was cared for by local people until an ambulance arrived and took her to Birmingham City Hospital where she was pronounced dead on arrival. The baby has been born and is 'doing well', police have said.

Jitesh had just finished reading the article when the glass door of the meeting room opened. The production team filed out and over to a bank of desks in front of where he sat. The two younger women deposited their notebooks, then wandered off in the direction of the staff kitchen. Jessamine took a seat in front of her computer and called up the news story that was on his screen. She pushed her face close, scanning the text, and then, apparently unable to find what she was looking for, picked up the phone and tapped in a three-digit extension.

'Elaine. It's Jessamine . . . Yes, yes. How are you?' She waited a beat. 'Listen, I saw a story on the news.' She stopped again. Jitesh got the impression that while she wanted to get straight down to business she had to be polite and let the other person shoot the breeze. Finally, she got her chance: 'The one about that murder in Birmingham, the pregnant woman. Do you have any details on the names of the people involved?' She sat up in anticipation. 'You don't.' She slumped. 'I understand,' she said, her voice wavering. She hung up. 'Bloody hell.' She seemed to be on the verge of tears.

She picked up the phone and was busy searching the directory when the man from the meeting approached. 'What just happened in there? I told you about the show being under threat in confidence, then you swan into a meeting alluding, not very subtly, to the need for a whole new format.' He softened, his anger spent. 'Verity and Arshdeep are just kids. They shouldn't have to worry about this stuff, that they might lose their jobs. Not until we have something more concrete.'

Jessamine shrugged.

'Look,' he said, dropping his voice to a whisper, 'I know you're upset. About us. But you've got to stop acting out. What with the way you were during the Alice Dunford show the other week,' he said, 'and now this.' He placed a tentative hand on her arm. 'We've got to find a way to work together.'

Jessamine stared at his hand until he removed it. 'Mick, not everything is about you.'

He waited a second, unconvinced. 'We'll make those changes to the script you wanted,' he said, when nothing more was forthcoming. His posture was one of exhausted defeat. 'Get it back to you this afternoon.'

She nodded, and as soon as he was gone she dialled another number.

Jitesh looked back at the news article. Why was she so interested in the story? If she thought she knew the people involved, why couldn't she just call a friend or family member? It didn't make sense. Maybe the local paper would have more information. He brought up the *Birmingham Mail*. It had dedicated its entire homepage to the murder but it too was missing any names of the people involved. Jitesh checked the by-line. The piece had been written by a journalist who claimed to have been first on the scene. Sam Gardiner. Judging by her phone call, Jessamine seemed to think the reporters knew more than they were letting on. That they had information they weren't yet able or willing to broadcast.

Jessamine was now on the phone while simultaneously trawling the internet. The sweat patches under her arms were expanding and her face was flushed. Once more she seemed on the brink of tears.

What if he were to put her out of her misery? This could be his post-Meera-hack act of kindness. It would set things straight.

After a quick check to make sure no one was looking, he typed the journalist's name and the title of her newspaper into the search box. He decided to focus on the journalist's Apple account. To access it he'd need three things: her email address, her date of birth, and the answers to two out of her three security questions. If he answered all of those correctly, he'd be able to reset her password, and once he'd done that, he'd be able to see everything, her emails, photos, iMessages.

Locating Sam Gardiner's date of birth and email address turned out to be easy. Her gmail address was provided by a quick Google search and her birthday was on Facebook. That got him past the first two steps of the password reset. Then it was time for her security questions. What was the name of her first boss? What was the name of her favourite sports team? What was the name of the street where she grew up?

These were a little trickier to crack. Tricky, but far from impossible.

Sam's LinkedIn profile told Jitesh where she'd started her career, as a parliamentary researcher for her local MP, Chris Woolfson. Jitesh typed the politician's name into the first box and was rewarded with a blue tick. Next up was Sam's favourite sports team. This was simple. She'd declared her love for Manchester United in many of her Facebook likes and groups. Another blue tick. An empty box asking him to create a new password appeared on the screen.

A tiny thrill. He was in.

Jitesh reset the journalist's password, then logged in and scrolled through her most recent sent messages. There were three from this morning, all to a guy named Josh Genower, all marked 'Urgent'.

The first two were broken sentences confirming the key facts as they'd emerged from the murder scene. Josh seemed to be Sam's editor, based at the newspaper's Fort Dunlop HQ. The third and final email had been sent an hour later.

Josh. Tried calling just now but you were on the other line. Have confirmed the name and age of the murder victim. Natasha Alleyne, 24. My source tells me the lad they've arrested for it is Natasha's boyfriend, Theo Kendrick. The names are embargoed until they can notify the next of kin. Can you get the team on to it while I finish off here – social media, etc., etc. – so that once we get the green light we'll be ready to go? I'll be back at the office in half an hour or so. S x

Natasha Alleyne and Theo Kendrick.

He wrote the names on a Post-it and went over to Jessamine's desk. Still busy scanning news sites, she took a few seconds to notice him.

'Yes?' She blinked, struggling to refocus after staring at the screen for so long. 'Can I help?'

'Here.' He handed her the scrap of paper. 'I th-think th-this is what you're looking for.'

She peered at the paper and, for a moment, she seemed confused. Jitesh worried that he'd made a horrible mistake. Maybe she didn't care about the names after all. Then her hand flew to her mouth. She looked back at the screen, comparing the names on the Post-it with what she saw there. 'I don't understand. How did you find this?'

But Jitesh was already gone, his conscience absolved, on to his next job with Malcolm, a new spring in his step.

Sarah

Sarah sat cross-legged on her bedroom floor, a series of photographs spread out in front of her. The man had asked her to send him more pictures of herself. This time he wanted some from when she was younger, as a small child.

Wanting to please him, Sarah had waited until her mum was out of the flat, then gone into the living room and the shelves where the photo albums were kept. She hadn't looked through them in years and it had been nice to see them again, to revel in the retro creaking noise the spine made whenever you turned a page. Some of the clear plastic film that covered the pictures had come loose, sticking the edges of the gluey cardboard together. She had adjusted them carefully, trying to prevent any further damage.

It had taken her ages to choose but in the end Sarah had selected some pictures that seemed to match up with what he'd asked for.

The first was of her when she was really little. Maybe three years old. Her hair was fairer then. Strawberry blonde. In it she was on a swing at the park, her hands clinging to the safety bar. Her expression was scared and uncertain, and Sarah wondered if it was because she had been frightened of the swing going too high or something else, some residue of her life before.

He'd wanted as many as possible so she'd chosen another three: one of her at the beach, one of her in the garden at her granddad's house in Somerset and one of her in the school play.

Spacing them evenly on the floor, she got out her iPhone ready to make digital copies she could send via email, but then she stopped to watch the afternoon sun travel across each of the photographs in turn. She wanted to do as he asked, to show off this part of herself and, in doing so, help him get to know her better, but she also wanted to protect the pictures and the three-year-old girl gripping the swing.

In the end she didn't send them. But she didn't return them to their albums either. Instead she scooped them into a shallow pile and placed them in an envelope in her desk. Tomorrow she would arrange them on the carpet again and wait for the sun to glide past.

Jessamine

Tasha's murder dominated the six o'clock news. The baby, they said, was in intensive care, Tasha's mother, the baby's grandmother, by the infant's side.

Jessamine had spent the afternoon torturing herself as to whether she could or should have done more to intervene. She'd been speaking to Tasha on the helpline for months. If only she'd been more forceful, perhaps she could have persuaded her to go to a refuge. Tasha would still be alive now, safe from harm.

All things considered, going on air when she was feeling like this was not the smartest decision. She should have cried off, feigned illness, given herself time to process what had happened. But she'd thought she was okay. She'd thought she could handle it.

She was wrong.

Halfway through her radio show, things started to go awry.

They'd been discussing the criminology of a man named Victor Lambert. Lambert, upon discovering his wife was going to leave him for another man, had murdered his four children and arranged their bodies on chairs around the kitchen table for his wife to discover when she returned from work. Until that day, Lambert had apparently led an uneventful, law-abiding life, without so much as a parking ticket.

In the studio to discuss the case was Luke Scratcher, a criminal psychologist who specialized in filicide, and O'Brien. They'd reached the point where they opened the discussion to listeners. Jessamine took a call from a woman who wanted to talk about her theories on why the last decade had seen a marked increase in family annihilation cases and an elderly gentleman who came on to point out gently that, when it came to men like Lambert, he would very much like the death penalty to be reinstated.

Then Jessamine took a call from Ian in Lyme Regis.

Jessamine Gooch
What are your thoughts on Victor Lambert? Were the signs always there?

Ian
His wife has to take some responsibility for what happened. She could have left him at any point in the years preceding the murders. She knew what kind of man he was, what he was capable of. These deaths are on him *and* her. End of.

Jessamine looked through the glass to Mick. It was his job to vet the callers, partly to find people with the most interesting things to say but also to weed out the weirdos or those who were just plain offensive. Still, sometimes, despite his best efforts, the odd one managed to slip through.

Jessamine Gooch
The mother could have done more to prevent the deaths of her children. Luke Scratcher, what would you say to that?

The psychologist parried Ian's comments with grace and professionalism, citing the complex reasons women stay with abusive partners. Jessamine went to move on to the next caller but it seemed Ian from Lyme Regis wasn't done.

Ian
Doesn't change the fact that their blood is on her hands. It's like that woman on the news today. The one that got stabbed.

Jessamine felt her diaphragm tighten. In the corner of her vision, the red light of the 'On Air' box seemed to flicker and flare.

Ian

By all accounts her boyfriend, the one that did it, was knocking her around for years. But she stayed and now that baby is going to grow up without a mother.

She tried to take a breath but the air seemed to stall near her sternum. She tried again, but with every breath she took the less space there seemed to be in her lungs until, finally, she felt as if she could breathe into only a tiny gap near her collarbone.

Jessamine Gooch

Let me get this straight.

She worked hard to keep her voice neutral. She was here to moderate, not take sides. Callers were often antagonistic. It was her job to steer and deflect the conversation away from inappropriate or nasty exchanges or, if they became too much, to cut them off completely. But she couldn't help it. Her vocal cords tightened. When she spoke next her voice was clipped, her tone an octave higher.

Jessamine Gooch

You're saying that being stabbed, being murdered was her own fault?

Mick caught the new edge to her tone. Through the glass, his eyes widened and he shook his head, a warning.

Ian

She should have been out that door the first time he raised his hand. She chose to stay.

O'Brien

Ian, I'm sure you don't mean that.

But O'Brien's attempt to defuse the situation was no good.

Jessamine tried to focus but her head was too full of stuff. Of what Tasha must have looked like this morning, all ready for her last shift at work in her silly Christmas pudding dress. Of the white sheet in the middle of the pavement, Tasha's blood pooling on the ground.

The best thing to do with callers like Ian was to get rid of them politely and move on to something else.

Jessamine Gooch

Ian, you're a horrible, horrible person.

Mick got to his feet and made a 'quit it' slicing motion across his throat. But it was too late. Jessamine's heart was racing. Finally, the cloud of air near her sternum seemed to disperse. It rushed down into her lungs, filling them with oxygen.

Jessamine Gooch

Go fuck yourself.

2003

Rowena

Another party in London. The end of the evening.

Queenie and Erin are here, along with some of the other regular girls. We sit around, waiting to be taken home. Billy, the kid with the Game Boy, lies asleep on the floor at our feet. His knees are tucked into his chest and he is sucking his thumb.

For the first time tonight there was a celebrity there, an older man with shaggy black hair who I recognised from the telly, and his brother, who is not famous at all. Queenie got all excited when they walked in but I found them both repulsive.

Before things got started, the one with the black hair made a point of going around the room and kissing the hand of every girl, as though he was a knight in shining armour. His hair was coated with a mousse that made it look wet and when he kissed my hand I saw his roots were grey.

I want to go now. I feel sore and outside of myself. It's a long drive back to Oxford and I have school tomorrow but Leo is in the kitchen, talking to one of the men. I notice that every time the other man makes a joke Leo laughs that bit too easily. It reminds me of a new kid arriving at the home. Sometimes they can be so desperate to make friends, to make everyone like them. It's hard to watch.

The man drains his drink and, before he can refuse another, Leo rushes to fill it. He starts talking about his wife and her love of tennis. The man is not interested but Leo doesn't seem to realise this and keeps going.

'Every afternoon, like clockwork. She eats lunch and then she grabs her racquet and she's off to the club for her lesson with Raoul, her coach.' He says the coach's name in this high-pitched drawn-out way that I think is supposed to sound like his wife. 'She never misses a game. Sometimes I wonder if I should be worried, if it's not the tennis she's in love with but Raoul.'

His wife.

Just lately, I've found myself wondering more and more about his family and the pictures I saw, that first night at the garden party. I think it's because I keep finding things in the back seat of the car that must belong to them. A stray hair-slide, a lipstick, a well-thumbed Judy Blume. I try to imagine what he's like as a father and husband, if they have any clue as to what he gets up to in his spare time.

I feel my eyes start to close and place my head in Queenie's lap. She smoothes my hair away from my ears, then does it again and again, her nails trailing across my scalp. My mum used to do the exact same thing every night, just before she went out. I'd told Queenie about it once, how much I'd loved it when she did that for me but also how hard I'd fight to keep my eyes open, even when I was exhausted, as I so didn't want her to go.

Before long I'm asleep, but I know that, even once my breathing starts to slow, Queenie will continue to stroke my hair. Even when my eyes close, she will still be there.

Tuesday 20 December

Present day

Jitesh

Jitesh wandered around the café, a mug of hot chocolate in one hand, an almond croissant in the other, and tried to work out which seat would afford him the clearest view of the door. Meera had arranged to meet her friend Katy there at eight thirty and he wanted advance warning of her arrival.

He settled on one of the tables in the raised section at the back. Parallel to the toilets and obscured by a wooden barrier it was the perfect vantage-point and would allow him to see without being seen. His plan was to wait until they had taken their seats and walk slowly past their table on his way out. He'd catch Meera's eye and say hello.

He sat back to wait and tried to ignore the feelings of disgust that had plagued him all morning. He knew that engineering a meeting like this was creepy, but he told himself it was a one-time thing. He'd been locked out of Meera's email within twenty-four hours of breaking into her account (this was standard, his hacking methodology had a limited time-span: as soon as people realised what had happened, they tended to up the ante on their security questions and change their password) so after today any meetings would have to come about through conventional means.

He'd just taken his first bite of croissant when someone he recognised entered the café.

Kishor Patel.

He startled and the croissant slipped down his gullet and lodged there. Coughing and spluttering, Jitesh ducked behind the barrier and gulped his hot chocolate, trying to clear the blockage.

Once he was sufficiently recovered he ventured a peek.

Wearing a hoody, Kishor had a black and red striped college scarf tied around his neck. He bought a coffee and, after sorting himself out with milk and sugar, went to sit at a table by the window.

Seeing him in person was less shocking than it had been that night at the Mandir, but still Jitesh had to concentrate on his breathing until his heart rate returned to normal. Was this how it would be when he took up his place at Cambridge next year? At the same college, it would be impossible to avoid each other. Would he fall apart every time he saw Kishor in the bar or walking to lectures on the other side of the quad?

Back in January he'd imagined things differently. As soon as Kishor had invited him to his party, Jitesh had developed notions of the two of them spending the remainder of their upper-sixth year becoming best pals, a friendship that would continue when they went up to college in October. It wouldn't be long before they were known as the Neasden boys. Maybe they'd even share a set in Chapel Court in their second year.

But then he'd attended the party. He'd gone in search of the bathroom and, in an instant, everything had changed.

He'd pushed a door open into a dark room, then stepped inside, trying to gauge whether it contained a toilet, then had seen his mistake. A desk in the corner, an open laptop and a wall of Arsenal posters had identified it as a bedroom or study.

Jitesh used a napkin to wipe the croissant grease from his hands and finished the last of his hot chocolate. There was still another ten minutes before Meera was due to arrive but he didn't care. He couldn't risk another encounter with Kishor. He gathered his things and peered over the wooden divider. Kishor was engrossed in his phone. He put on his coat, kept his head down and left the café unnoticed.

He hadn't gone far down the street when he barrelled into someone coming from the opposite direction.

'Watch it.'

He looked up, about to apologise and stopped.

Meera.

'You?' she said, smiling.

Up close he could see the neat swoop of black liner on her eyelid. Her ruby nose stud twinkled in the sunshine.

'Jitesh, right?'

He nodded.

'Where are you off to in such a hurry?'

'W-w-w-work.'

'That's right. You're some BBC big shot.'

'H-h-hardly.'

She nodded at the café. 'I'm meeting a friend.'

Katy. He already knew this from her email. It was, after all, the reason he was there.

She blushed. 'You two were at school together.'

Jitesh stopped. He hadn't gone to school with anyone called Katy.

'Kishor.' She said his name proudly, like she was announcing the results of a prize draw. 'He was there the other day, outside the Mandir.'

That night at the party, standing in the bedroom, Jitesh had noticed a shape on the bed. Too big to be a person, it spanned the length of the mattress. A pile of coats? He'd opened the door a little wider. Then he'd seen them. Kishor and Shanae. Kishor's jeans were around his thighs and Shanae was underneath him. They were kissing, Shanae's hands around the back of Kishor's neck.

'Busy here,' shouted Kishor, his hand up Shanae's T-shirt.

Jitesh had backed out of the room. Not fast enough.

Kishor had turned to the door.

'You some kind of perv?' He'd squinted against the light. 'I said, we're busy.'

Now Meera leaned in conspiratorially. 'It's all a bit random.' She nodded at the café. 'A girlfriend cancelled on me at the last minute so I asked Kishor if he wanted to be my breakfast date instead.'

Jitesh felt like he'd taken a punch to the gut.

After a few more seconds had passed, when he'd still failed to respond, Meera smiled awkwardly. 'Best be on my way, then,' she said.

Jitesh moved to block her. 'N-n-n-no.'

She paused. There was still a smile on her face but it was close to collapse. She waited for him to say something else. When he didn't she patted him carefully on the arm and stepped around him. 'Nice seeing you, Jitesh.'

He wanted to say something to keep her there on the pavement, away from Kishor, a little while longer, but what?

He let her go.

Jessamine

Jessamine entered Broadcasting House, pressed her pass against the barrier and joined the crowd waiting for the lift. Judging by the whispers that greeted her, word of last night's show had already done the rounds. She pretended not to notice the curious stares and focused instead on the statue situated in the small alcove just behind Reception. Sculpted by Eric Gill, the artist responsible for the *Prospero and Ariel* above the main entrance, it was called *The Sower* and showed a roman-nosed man in a loincloth, his hand thrust into a bag of seed. Above the statue was a gilded inscription, placed there at the opening of the building. Jessamine used her O-level Latin to translate:

THIS TEMPLE OF THE ARTS AND MUSES IS DEDICATED TO ALMIGHTY GOD BY THE FIRST GOVERNORS IN THE YEAR OF OUR LORD 1931, JOHN REITH BEING DIRECTOR-GENERAL. AND THEY PRAY THAT GOOD SEED SOWN MAY BRING FORTH GOOD HARVEST, AND THAT ALL THINGS FOUL OR HOSTILE TO PEACE MAY BE BANISHED THENCE, AND THAT THE PEOPLE INCLINING THEIR EAR TO WHATSOEVER THINGS ARE LOVELY AND HONEST, WHATSOEVER THINGS ARE OF GOOD REPORT, MAY TREAD THE PATH OF VIRTUE AND WISDOM.

She plunged her hand into the pile of spilled pumpkin seeds in her pocket and held one between her thumb and forefinger. We reap what we sow.

Mick had called first thing. The controller wanted to see them both at nine sharp. Until then neither he nor Jessamine were to talk to or email anyone – press, colleagues, friends – about what had happened.

It didn't bode well.

She reached the front of the crowd, and when the next lift opened, she stuffed herself inside. As she stepped out onto the second floor she was met by Mick and a woman in an ill-fitting suit. 'Faye Williams,' said the woman, offering her hand. 'Union rep.'

In all the drama, she'd never once thought of calling BECTU. Mick had treated her badly at the end of their affair but on this he seemed to have her back. She gave him a grateful smile.

'How bad?' asked Jessamine, as they navigated the edge of the open-plan.

'Best-case scenario?' said Mick. 'We get a rap on the knuckles and the Trust and Compliance watch us very carefully for the next few months. Worst case . . .' He tailed off and looked to Faye.

'Second-guessing is not useful at this stage,' said Faye, refusing to meet his eye.

Jessamine felt a new wave of dread. This was all her fault. To have put her own career in jeopardy was one thing, but Mick's too. The show was already on shaky ground. How could she have been so stupid?

They took a seat outside the controller's office. Kimmy Sorenson had been appointed to the role of Controller of Radio seven years earlier: in that time she had had to weather a number of storms, many relating to abuse or events that had happened decades before she was in post. Tall, thin and elegantly dressed, it was rumoured that as a teenager she had modelled for *Vogue* before taking up a place to study philosophy at the Sorbonne.

An assistant appeared and shuffled them inside. Kimmy was sitting at her desk, typing on a laptop. 'Jessamine, Mick,' she said. Her words were squished, as if she didn't have enough space in her mouth to sound them properly. She gave Faye a quick nod and gestured at a man on a sofa in the corner. 'This is Giles from HR.' A glass wall stretched the length of the room behind her, through which it was possible to see across the road to the Langham Hotel and its stone ledges and curlicues, iced with snow. She closed the laptop and got to her feet. 'I've now listened to the show in full and I've got lots of questions, but first I'd like you two to explain.'

'As producer, I take full responsibility,' said Mick.

Before he could go any further Jessamine placed a hand on his arm. 'It's okay,' she said quietly. She turned to Kimmy. 'It was my fault. I'd had some bad news earlier in the day. I let my emotions get the better of me.'

Jessamine still couldn't figure out how that sound-engineer kid had got hold of Tasha and Theo's names before they were released to the press or how he'd known to give them to her. He must have overheard someone talking in News – that was the most likely explanation. 'I know that doesn't excuse what happened. What I said. I lost control.'

'I see.' Kimmy turned to face the window. 'The show's been on for what, ten years?'

'Eleven,' said Mick.

'We've been thinking of shaking up the schedule for a while now. We want to pilot some new things, move time-slots around.' She turned back to them. 'Rest a few of the more tired brands.'

Jessamine felt Mick tense at this slight on the show he had created.

'Christmas feels like a natural break. Maybe it would be good if you took a breather. Give us all time to take a step back, re-evaluate.'

'Just to be clear,' said Faye, 'what exactly is happening here?'

Kimmy looked to Giles from HR. Giles sat forward, his red BBC lanyard bright against the check of his shirt. Absenting herself from the next part of the conversation, Kimmy went back to studying the snow on the Langham.

'We're suspending Jessamine on full pay until further notice. She needs to issue a formal apology to the caller in question and last night's show will not be uploaded onto the iPlayer.'

'What?' Mick was indignant. 'Faye, can they do this? Tell me they can't do this.'

Kimmy strolled round to the opposite side of the desk, stopping once she was standing over them. 'Look,' she said, 'I'm sure you both understand how vulnerable we are right now, how vulnerable we've been for some time. We can't do anything that might poke the tiger in the eye – we can't be seen to be letting things go.'

'This is a joke,' said Mick, standing up. 'It never ends. We pussy-foot around in the build-up to Charter Renewal. Charter Renewal happens, everyone breathes a big sigh of relief – and now what? We have to keep on creeping about just in case. Look, we all know that Jessie fucked up last night but that doesn't mean she deserves to be suspended, that you need to cancel the entire bloody show.'

'To reiterate, we're not cancelling the show, we're merely resting it until further notice,' said Kimmy, her mouth set firm.

'An investigation will be launched into your conduct,' said Giles from HR. 'Until then, Mick will be reassigned and Jessamine should go home.'

They were shown out.

Jessamine found an empty cardboard box and started to clear her desk.

'About last night,' said Mick. 'I know you weren't happy when I broke things off. Was it – is it – are you . . .' He faltered, and tried again. 'I'm worried about you.'

Jessamine placed the padded envelope containing Cassie Scolari's file on top of her things. 'The way you treated me, the way you lied was atrocious.' At this he flinched. 'But last night, that was my own shit.'

He waited a second, unconvinced. 'Really?'

'Really.'

He watched her gather her things. When she was ready he grabbed hold of the box. 'Shall I walk you out?'

'I'm good, thanks.' Jessamine was touched by the offer but she felt she might burst into tears the minute she got into the lift and she didn't want Mick to see.

He looked at the floor.

'What?'

'You have to give in your pass. Giles said I have to make sure of it.'

She cringed. Even now, after everything, she'd thought he'd wanted to walk her out because of the feelings he still had, because he wanted to stay by her side as long as possible.

She was such a fool.

'That's ridiculous. What do they think I'm going to do? Come back and rob the place?' She almost launched into a rant, then thought better of it. 'Fine.'

They were about to leave when the post guy appeared pushing his trolley. He handed Jessamine an A4 envelope that she shoved into the box on top of everything else and they went down in the lift to Reception. At the door she hooked her lanyard over her head and held it out. Mick took it from her, and as he did so, she leaned in and kissed him softly on the cheek. So what if she was foolish? This morning with Kimmy he'd defended her as much as he'd been able to and for that she was grateful. She held her mouth there a second too long and as she pulled away her lips brushed his.

As though in a trance, his mouth followed hers, but then he seemed to come to and stood back with a jolt.

'You know we can't.' He seemed surprised at himself, confused by what he'd been about to do.

'Have a good Christmas,' said Jessamine.

'We'll have you back on the air in no time,' he said, trying to regain control. 'You wait and see.'

Jessamine smiled as if she believed him, then pushed her way out through the doors and into the winter sunshine.

Jitesh

Jitesh took a seat in the waiting area, unwound his scarf and shucked off his coat. He usually arrived late on purpose – avoiding talking about the precise thing you were there to talk about for a whole hour was exhausting – but today, glad to have someone he could ask for advice, he'd got there five minutes early.

At exactly one o'clock the door opened. Jitesh kept his eyes on the floor and only looked up once he was sure the other person had gone.

'Jitesh.' Marty said his name like it was both a question and an invitation. Jitesh got to his feet and Marty stepped back to allow him inside.

For the last three months Marty had been Jitesh's therapist. Sessions with him cost an eye-watering £120 an hour and took place on the third floor of a grand Harley Street mansion. Jitesh's parents had tried to get him referred through the NHS but the waiting list had been eighteen months. When their GP had delivered the news and offered a prescription for citalopram instead, Jitesh's father had been outraged. He had dragged his son to his feet, then marched him out of the surgery and into the car. There he'd sat staring straight ahead, his hands gripping the steering wheel.

'We'll go private,' he'd said eventually, his hand shaking as he reached for the key in the ignition. 'Get you seen now, tomorrow. A year and a half's wait. Don't they know what you did?'

'How was your week?' asked Marty, once Jitesh was settled into his chair.

'G-g-good and b-b-bad.'

Marty smiled kindly. 'Which would you like to start with?'

Marty's therapy room was small and simple. The only furniture was two armchairs facing each other, and a desk under the window. A generic shot of Ayers Rock that looked like it had been bought as part of an Ikea job-lot hung on the wall. Jitesh knew the lack of decor was deliberate. That therapists weren't supposed to tell or show any part of themselves to their patients. But that was okay. Jitesh didn't need to see Marty's paperback collection to know who he was. He'd read his email. From everything he'd seen, Marty was a good man. Recently single after a two-year relationship with a flautist named Theresa, he was pretty broken up about the split and had collected all of Theresa's old emails into a special folder in his inbox marked T.

'I-I-I-I met a girl.'

'Oh?' Marty failed to hide his surprise. Jitesh rarely volunteered information, especially so early on in a session.

'She-she has a nose stud. A ruby.'

'You like her?'

Jitesh remembered standing outside the café with Meera that morning. Seeing her face again, he had felt he was stepping from shadows into warm sunshine. But on hearing that she was on her way to meet Kishor that feeling had been replaced by the cold snip of fear.

Jitesh tried to figure out a way to explain this fear to Marty. He wanted to ask what to do about Meera, about how he might keep her safe – but he couldn't figure out how to do that without also revealing something he considered strictly off limits.

That night at the party, after walking in on Shanae and Kishor, Jitesh had returned downstairs to the relative quiet of the kitchen. He was embarrassed at what he'd just seen but he was also jealous. He liked Shanae and had hoped to ask her out. He decided to go home and was about to leave when he heard a muffled croak. The frog. It was still in the box on the floor next to the bin.

He lifted the flap and peered inside. The frog's skin seemed drier than before. Surely it needed water or food of some kind. He went through the cupboards until he found a small pan and filled it with water. He was about to lower it into the box when Kishor appeared.

'You.'

Jitesh cringed.

'S-s-sorry.' He gestured to the ceiling. 'I was looking for the b-b-bathroom.'

Kishor laughed and waved his hand in the air, as though Jitesh had made a joke that didn't quite deliver. He began to walk away but then he clocked the pan in Jitesh's hand. 'What are you doing?'

'The f-frog,' he said, pointing at the box. 'It's c-c-cruel.'

Kishor stopped and cocked his head, thinking. He looked from Jitesh to the box, a smirk forming. 'You're quite the pervy party pooper, Ganguly, you know that?' He took the pan from Jitesh and placed it on the hob. 'You're going to read science, right? An unc-c-conditional offer,' he said, mocking Jitesh's stammer. 'Unlike me. Four As or I'm toast.' He went over to the box, removed the frog and placed it in the pan, just as Jitesh had intended. Jitesh felt a surge of relief. The frog was going to be okay. But then Kishor bent down and, after locating the correct dial on the cooker, he turned on the heat.

'Being such a clever little shit you must know about the boiling frog experiment.' He didn't wait for Jitesh to respond. 'It goes like this. If a frog is put suddenly into boiling water, it will jump out, but if the frog is put into tepid water, which is then brought slowly to the boil, it will not perceive the danger and will stay there, until it is eventually cooked to death.'

Marty coughed twice, a prompt. He often did this when Jitesh went quiet for too long.

'In our last session we talked about October,' said Marty. 'Starting university. How are you feeling about that?'

'F-f-fine.' He thought of the boxes collecting dust in the corner of his bedroom. Of Kishor, already installed in his college quad. 'Though I'm no l-longer sure I want to go to C-Cambridge.'

'You think the pressure might be too much?'

'I had an offer from UCL. I could go there.'

'You don't sound terribly happy about that either.'

He wasn't. He wanted more than anything to go to Cambridge, to Newton and Hawking, to Jesus College with its lawns and the people playing cricket on summer afternoons.

'If I went to UCL I could live at home. I wouldn't have to pay r-r-rent.'
I wouldn't have to see Kishor, thought Jitesh, have to breathe the same air.

In the pan the frog had sat perfectly still, the underside of its neck inflating and deflating. Jitesh tried to calculate how long it would take for the water to heat up. One minute, two?

'In actual fact,' said Kishor, searching the drawer for a pan lid. 'The experiment is a myth. Studies into the thermal relations of amphibians have found that, once the temperature of the water reaches a certain point, the frog will jump out.'

Bubbles started to form at the bottom of the pan. Jitesh watched, horrified, as Kishor placed the lid on top, sealing the creature inside.

'So how about we do a little experiment of our own?' said Kishor. 'If you can tell me to stop I'll let the frog go.' Kishor got out his phone, pointed it at Jitesh and pressed record. 'Say the word,' said Kishor. 'One word, that's all.'

Jitesh looked from Kishor to the pan, trying to understand what was going on.

Kishor moved his phone between Jitesh and the creature. The glass lid was fast becoming obscured by steam. After a little while he started humming the jingle from *Countdown*. Soon it was no longer possible to see the frog inside. The water must have been close to scalding.

'Say it!' shouted Kishor. 'Why can't you just say it?'

Jitesh remembered trying his hardest to form the word in his mouth. He'd taken breath after breath, but no matter how hard he'd concentrated he couldn't do it, couldn't get the word out.

The rest of Jitesh's time with Marty was spent in the usual way, with chat about his supposed perfectionism and the need he felt to excel academically. It was all fiction. Academic achievement had nothing to do with what he'd done. Still, it was plausible and more palatable than the truth, so he let him keep thinking it.

Marty went to see him out but when they reached the door Jitesh hesitated. When it came to knowing what to do about Meera and Kishor, he was no further forward.

Marty looked over Jitesh's shoulder, to the person in the waiting room.

'H-h-how do you protect someone that doesn't know they need p-p-protecting?'

Marty smiled kindly. 'We're out of time today.' He put his hand on Jitesh's shoulder and squeezed. 'Let's explore that next week.'

Jitesh nodded and, making sure not to catch the eye of the waiting patient, he wound his scarf tight and headed for the lift.

Jessamine

Jessamine dumped her box on the kitchen table, took a deep breath and tried to ignore the constant buzz of her phone. Sarah was still in bed. In the holidays she liked to sleep in till at least noon. Jessamine was glad. The last thing she needed right now was another set-to.

She went to the fridge and took a bottle of Sancerre from the bottom shelf. The cork came loose with a pop and she poured a slug into a glass. She brought it close to her face, considered it for a moment, then swallowed it in one.

Her phone buzzed again. Word of her suspension had spread quickly, and during the cab ride home, she'd been barraged with messages. At first she'd read the texts and listened to the voicemails. Half were from concerned friends wanting to know if she was okay. The other half were from journalists, on the hunt for a comment. It was clear from the tone of her friends' messages, bright but sombre, that they weren't sure whether to offer comfort or outrage at the unfairness. They were also wary. Their messages tap-danced around the elephant in the room: why had she spoken to the caller like that? Was she having a breakdown? Had she lost the plot? Jessamine's instinct had been to call them back one by one, but then she'd realised the first thing they'd ask was how she was feeling and the truth was that she wasn't sure.

She was definitely angry with herself, at her lack of control. That was a given. But she was also confused. She had never felt at once so inside and outside herself. Sure, the news about Tasha had been upsetting, but to have behaved so unprofessionally . . .

In the end she'd decided it best not to talk to anyone, friend or foe, and had turned her phone on to silent. Now, though, she found the buzzing just as stressful as any bleep or ringtone. She was about to turn it off altogether when she saw the caller ID. It was a text from Dougie. The guy who'd bought her a drink in the Riding House Café. Although they'd exchanged numbers she'd figured he was just being kind. Not for one second had she expected him to get in touch.

She opened the message. It was a photo of a jasmine flower. Its petals were white, its stamen like a fat green nipple. Underneath it was a caption and a flower emoji: *Saw this and thought of you.*

She smiled. The message was sweet, romantic even, but for some reason, probably the stamen, it felt loaded with innuendo. She had no idea how to respond so she returned the phone to her bag, poured herself another glass of wine, necked it and poured herself a third.

Not wanting to look at this reminder of her suspension any longer than she had to, she grabbed the box by both handles. She'd stuff it away, in the cupboard next to the boiler. But as she went to lift it from the table the flimsy cardboard lid fell to one side and onto the floor. She tutted, picked it up and was about to put it back when the envelopes at the top caught her eye. The padded one contained Cassie Scolari's file, the one she'd been sent by Cassie's friend; the other had arrived that morning as she was leaving. She opened it and emptied the contents onto the table.

Inside was a sheaf of A4: the phone logs she'd requested from Cassie's boss at Ticketmaster. A cursory glance at the printouts revealed he'd made a mistake. As well as all Cassie's incoming calls for the two months leading up to her disappearance, he had also sent a list of every outgoing call. She picked up the padded envelope, slid the contents of Cassie's file onto the table and placed them alongside the logs. Cassie's face stared out from one of the newspaper articles.

A click in the hall. A door opening. Sarah.

She emerged blinking into the living room, her pyjamas creased, her dressing-gown half on, half off. When she saw her mother her face crumpled, preparing to assume the scowl Jessamine had become so familiar with over the last few weeks. Then she registered the wine and the fact that Jessamine was standing there, drinking, still in her coat. The scowl collapsed. 'Starting early?'

Jessamine raised her glass in a toast. 'I've had a bit of a morning.'

Sarah hoicked her dressing-gown around herself and took a tentative step forward, reminding Jessamine of a game they used to play when Sarah was small: What Time Is It, Mr Wolf? 'What happened?'

'Last night ...' she faltered, '... I said some things I shouldn't. On air.' She didn't want to go into the whys and wherefores with Sarah. That would prompt too many questions about what had caused her outburst, and the last thing Jessamine wanted to talk about was what had happened to Tasha. There were too many grim parallels with the fate of Sarah's own birth mother.

Jessamine had not been made privy to the identity of her daughter's biological parents – it had been a closed adoption – so their name and the town they had lived in had been deliberately withheld – but she did know the horrific sequence of events that had led to Sarah being placed in the care of the state. Sarah's birth mother had been in an abusive relationship. She'd been planning to leave, to take herself and her daughter to a refuge, but somehow her husband had got wind of it. That night while thirteen-month-old Sarah was asleep upstairs in her cot, her father had subjected her mother to an especially vicious attack and left her unconscious on the living-room floor. As well as breaking three of her ribs, her wrist and her cheekbone, he had ruptured her spleen, causing massive internal bleeding. The next morning he came down to find her dead. Ellen, Sarah's social worker, told her that, although they couldn't make it stand up in court, the police believed he had sat down to a leisurely breakfast of cornflakes and coffee before he called 999. He'd been found guilty of manslaughter and sent to prison.

Sarah took another two steps forward. 'You okay?'

One more step. She was almost in touching distance.

'I will be.'

Jessamine sat down at the table with her back to her daughter and took another sip of wine. Sarah gathered her dressing-gown close and took the final two steps forward so that she was now standing directly behind her mother. When they used to play the game, this was the point at which Jessamine turned and shouted, 'Dinner-time!' Sarah and her friends would scatter, shrieking with delight.

'So, what, you're out of a job?'

Jessamine stared at her glass. 'The union is on it but, yes, for the time being I'm what you might call a free agent.'

At least she didn't have to worry about money, not immediately anyway. They'd suspended her on full pay. If and when it came to the worst and she found herself unemployed, she had savings she could fall back on.

Sarah wrapped her arms around her mother and rested her cheek against her upper back. Jessamine met her embrace and pushed her face into Sarah's dressing-gown sleeve.

'It'll be all right, Mum.' Sarah hugged her tighter. 'I'm sure.'

'I had a call from Ellen yesterday,' said Jessamine, making sure to keep her tone casual. 'She said you'd asked to see your Child Placement Report.' Sarah didn't respond. 'Is there something you're worried about? Something you want to know?' Again Sarah said nothing. Jessamine was about to try another tack when Munchie appeared from where she'd been sleeping behind the sofa and jumped up on the table. She landed with a thud, her paws skidding slightly on the smooth surface. Discovering the envelopes on the table she pushed the edge of her mouth against the nearest corner, marking it with her scent.

Sarah reached forward and picked up one of the news articles from Cassie's file. 'What happened to her?' she asked, changing the subject.

'I don't know. No one does.'

'It's not from one of your shows?'

'It's an open case. A member of the public sent it to me. Her friend is missing.' Jessamine took another slug of wine. 'She wanted me to help. Or perhaps I should say she wanted the show to help.' Again she faltered, trying to decide whether or not to share the next piece of information. 'Her friend had a violent partner.' At this she felt Sarah tense. 'She thinks he's like one of the people we profile.'

Sarah stayed like that for a few seconds more, leaning over her mother while she read through the article. When she tried to straighten, Jessamine did not relinquish her grip. It had been so long since her daughter had cuddled her and longer still since she had allowed herself to be cuddled. She'd broach the subject of Sarah requesting her Child Placement Report again later, see if she couldn't get to the bottom of it.

Sarah laughed. 'Mum.' She wriggled. 'Enough. I need to shower.'

Jessamine gave Sarah's forearm a final kiss and let her go. She sat there for a moment, happy with the brief truce that had just taken place and then she got up, took off her coat and went to hang it in the hall. She hadn't been able to face breakfast, and an empty stomach plus wine had left her a little unsteady on her feet. Not that it mattered. She stopped by the bathroom door and listened to the rush of the shower. Sarah was humming her favourite song from the Michael Bublé Christmas album. Maybe they could have a movie afternoon on the sofa. It used to be one of their favourite things to do together – huddling under blankets and eating microwave popcorn.

Back in the kitchen Cassie Scolari's face stared up from the press cutting on the table where Sarah had left it. Cassie had been in an abusive relationship. If she could find out what had had happened to Cassie, it might help assuage some of the guilt she felt at not having been able to protect Tasha, to keep her alive.

She pushed the file to one side. For the time being, her radio show was on hold. She couldn't help now, even if she wanted to. She poured herself the last of the wine.

2003

Rowena

I wait out of sight, across the road from Leo's house, and hope all the things I've heard him say about his wife's love of tennis are true. It's hot and the three different buses I took to get here have left me sick and light-headed. I'm wearing an oversized black and white Adidas T-shirt I borrowed from Bianca in the next room to mine at the home and my purple velour trackie bottoms. I don't look my best – before I left this morning Bianca told me I looked like a homeless person – but I'm comfortable and, besides, today isn't about trying to look pretty.

I waft the T-shirt against my belly, trying to cool myself. I know Leo will be angry with me for coming to the cottage like this, but I had no choice. There isn't any credit left on my pay-as-you-go and this can't wait until the next time he decides to invite me to a party.

Twenty minutes later a black Range Rover appears at the mouth of the drive. A woman at the wheel. Leo's wife. It has to be. She pulls out into the road, turns left and accelerates.

I wait two more minutes, just to be sure, and then I come out from my hiding place, cross the road and make my way down the drive. I lift the lion-shaped door-knocker and rap it twice. Silence, and then, somewhere in the house, I hear footsteps. I take a breath. I've decided it's probably best if I come straight out with it, that as soon as he hears the reason I'm here he'll forgive my turning up unannounced.

But when the door opens I'm not faced with Leo but with a girl. About my age, she is wearing jodhpurs and a white polo shirt streaked with grass stains, a pink jumper tied around her shoulders. She is older and heavier than she is in any of the photographs I've seen but I recognise her immediately. Leo's daughter.

She looks at me, confused, then peers behind where I stand, as though that will offer some explanation for my presence. 'Yes?'

'I think I have the wrong house.' I start to back away.

Her eyes take in my T-shirt and fake Juicy Couture tracksuit bottoms. Something in her face changes. 'Wait, are you from Redbridge Hollow?'

I have no idea what she's talking about and am about to put her straight when she speaks again. 'Look, I'm sorry about the damage to the fences. Pablo can get a bit tetchy when the cars race past on the road down there. I'll pay for any damage caused.'

Pablo?

She mistakes my silence for anger. 'It won't happen again, I promise. It's just if Mum and Dad find out I've been down there, I'm done for.' She sighs dramatically. 'I wouldn't be allowed to ride any more and the rest of the school holidays would be an epically disastrous bore.'

I'm still none the wiser but I go along with her. If she thinks she knows who I am then she won't ask any difficult questions.

'I won't tell them,' I say. 'Promise.'

I go to walk away but she stops me. 'Do you want a cold drink? It's such a hot day.'

The thought of trekking back to the bus-stop in this sunshine makes me feel sick. I look behind her, into the house. From the way she's been talking it sounds like she's alone. I decide to risk it. I'll have a drink and a rest, then be on my way. I'll come back and talk to Leo tomorrow. 'Sounds lovely.'

'Super.' She claps her hands and I follow her into the house. 'I made lemonade.'

I've never heard of anyone making lemonade before and am even more puzzled when, instead of the clear Sprite or 7Up I buy from the shop, she presents me with a cloudy glass of something pale green that isn't even fizzy. I sip at it suspiciously but I soon discover that it's delicious, and gulp it down.

The girl laughs and pours me another glass. 'I'm Millie.' She offers her hand.

'Rowena.' We shake.

'I've got to say, I'm glad you came by. All my friends have gone to Walberswick or Perugia or wherever the hell else they've decamped for the summer.' She dresses differently from any other girl I've met. It's not just the jodhpurs. There's something about the cut and colour of the material, the way she wears her hair in a messy high bun. She's covered with grass stains but, still, she seems clean, special. 'I've been going to the stables and riding Pablo every day but I'm already bored. Plus, the shooting season doesn't start till August.' I remember the picture of her with the gun and the dead rabbit. 'We're usually away but this year Daddy says we need to be here while he prepares his bid.'

Daddy.

The word wakes me up to the fact that I'm sitting at Leo's kitchen table drinking lemonade with his daughter. I know I should go. That I've chanced my arm here long enough. But I realise I want to stay. I want to know more about her and her life with her father.

The table is piled with different things. Newspapers, bills, a box of wine. My eye catches an open DVD case. Bend It Like Beckham. 'Have you seen it?' She picks it up and wiggles it in the air. 'Our dorm must have watched it a hundred times.'

I quote one of my favourite lines from the film and we both laugh. We fall into a brief silence, but then we look at each other again and once more burst out laughing.

Eventually our giggles fizzle to nothing and suddenly we're shy, both of us unable to meet the other's eye. The sound of a door slamming somewhere at the side of the cottage. I freeze. Is her mum back from tennis already?

And then there he is. Leo. Wearing shorts and a white linen shirt rolled up to his elbows, he is carrying a basket of tomatoes, his fingernails caked with mud.

'Daddy,' says Millie, brightly, 'this is Rowena.' Still worried about the thing with Pablo and the fences, she falters, not sure how to explain my being here.

'I was just passing when I started to feel unwell,' I say, jumping to her rescue. 'I knocked at the door and asked for a glass of water.' Millie smiles at me gratefully.

Until the mention of my name Leo had been more focused on his tomatoes than on either of us, but now he looks up. At first he's confused. That soon changes to anger. He dumps the tomatoes in the sink.

'I should be going.' I get to my feet. 'Thanks for the lemonade.'

'Can't you stay a little while?' Millie looks to her father and pouts. 'I've been so bored.' She turns back to me. 'We could go swimming?'

'I'll see you out,' says Leo already guiding me away from the kitchen.

He waits until we're out of sight, halfway up the drive, before he says another word. 'What are you doing here?' He locks his hand tight around my upper arm. 'Talking to my daughter. Sitting at my table.'

He is shaking with rage and also, I think, a little bit frightened. My being here has rattled him.

My arm is starting to hurt so I try to twist away, out of his grasp. But the movement only makes him squeeze harder. I say the one thing that will make him let me go, the thing I came here to tell him.

'I'm pregnant.'

It works. He lets go and I rub at my bicep.

He looks at my stomach. 'You said you were on the the Pill.'

'I am. I was.' I cross my arms over my belly. 'Sometimes I get my days mixed up.'

When I told Queenie and Erin that my period was late they took me to the chemist's to buy a test. They sat with me while I peed on a stick and they said I should tell Leo. They said that whenever it had happened to other girls it had been up to their bloke to sort it out.

He runs his hands through his blond curls. He smells of grass and the earth. 'I'll get you an appointment. Until then you talk to no one.'

I nod.

'And never come back to my house. No matter what.' His eyes flash. 'Or I'll throw you back to Sunny and his mates. Understand?'

I try not to cry.

'Go.'

I do as he says and have almost reached the end of the drive when I hear someone behind me on the tarmac. Thinking it's Leo, back to see me off, I speed up and turn onto the road towards the bus-stop.

'Wait, Rowena.'

Millie.

She runs to catch up with me.

'Look, we don't really know each other but this summer is going to be so boring and you seem fun and, well,' she gestures up the road, 'you live so nearby.' She retrieves a purple Nokia 8210 from the back of her jodhpurs. 'We should hang out.'

I look to the drive, checking for Leo.

'I don't know.' I try to think of an excuse, something polite but effective.

A car appears in the distance and we press ourselves into the prickly hedge to let it pass.

'Oh, come on, silly,' she says, once the car has gone. She opens her contacts, ready. 'What's your number?'

I'm terrified Leo is going to come out and catch us. Giving her my details seems like the quickest way to get rid of her. I tell her my number and warn her I have no credit. She promises to be in touch. I say goodbye and begin the long walk to the bus-stop. I haven't gone far when my phone beeps.

'Hi.'

Millie.

She's sent me another quote from the film.

I stand and flex the part of my arm where Leo gripped me, and even though the bruise is already starting to form, I hear myself laugh. The sound carries through the warm country air, light and clear.

Jessamine

Jessamine woke up in bed, fully clothed. For a brief, blissful moment she was confused. How and why had she got there? Then she remembered. Her suspension. Once more awash with shame and embarrassment, she hid her face in the pillow.

Outside the winter sun was fading. Inside, Munchie was curled asleep on her abdomen, a warm pressure that would have been pleasurable if it weren't for the fact that she had a sudden need to go to the toilet. She pushed herself up to sitting and winced. Her head felt as if it was being squeezed and her mouth was dry. She needed the bathroom, water and paracetamol in that order. Gingerly, she moved her legs to the side of the mattress. Munchie huff-miaowed in protest, then quickly took up a position near her pillow, basking in the residual heat.

Sarah had not, as it turned out, been interested in a lazy afternoon on the sofa watching movies. When Jessamine had suggested it she had screwed up her face and told her she had other plans, specifically to go and hang out at Paris's house. Jessamine had been hurt. She'd thought that, after the morning's events, Sarah might decide to keep her company. Still, not wanting to rock the boat, she hadn't made a thing of it and waved her off with a smile. Then she had finished the last of the wine and gone for a lie-down.

That had been when? Around midday? Now, as she emerged into the living room, she found that, at some point while she'd been asleep, Sarah had returned. Sitting at the kitchen table, she was hunched over a piece of paper, reading. Totally focused on whatever it contained, she would look up occasionally, apparently cross-checking what was there against her open laptop. At first Jessamine thought Sarah was doing homework but then she saw it was Cassie Scolari's file.

Breathing through the pain at her temples, Jessamine came and stood behind her daughter. She saw that she had carefully arranged the contents into some kind of sequence and that she was currently focused on the CCTV images.

It took Sarah a few seconds to notice her mother's presence. She got to her feet and motioned for Jessamine to take her place. 'Sit. Look. I'll make tea and toast.'

Jessamine did as she said and tried to focus on the papers immediately in front of her. The flat had a clean pine tang, thanks to the Christmas tree in the corner, and while she'd been asleep, Sarah had turned on the fairy lights and closed the blinds.

'I've spent the last hour reading through this stuff,' said Sarah, as she set the kettle to boil in the small kitchen that led off the living-dining area. 'Once I started I couldn't stop. It's just so weird, don't you think?' She put two slices of sourdough in the toaster and the smell of the warming bread made Jessamine's stomach growl.

A few minutes later Sarah presented her with a mug of tea, and toast saturated with butter and honey. Then she dropped two painkillers into Jessamine's hand and drew up a chair.

'Look.' Sarah pushed the CCTV stills towards her.

Jessamine looked from her daughter to the photographs. The pounding in her head made it hard to think.

'Tell me this. How does a woman vanish from the street in this day and age?' Sarah tapped each photograph in turn. 'Look at the pictures. She comes out of the door, she's walking down the street towards the river and then, poof, just like that, she disappears.'

Interested to hear Sarah's thoughts, Jessamine decided to play devil's advocate. 'The key piece of information there is "towards the river",' she said, through a mouthful of toast. She swallowed. 'The police think she committed suicide.'

Sarah dismissed this with a shake of her head. 'I've been cross-checking the pictures against this.' She motioned to the laptop. It featured a map of central London. There were hundreds if not thousands of red spots dotted across the heart of the city. Jessamine squinted at the name of the website. It declared itself as a non-profit blog that existed to provide an unofficial database of the location of every private and public CCTV camera in London.

'Vanishing into thin air like she did, it doesn't happen. It can't. Not any more. I mean, hello? GCHQ, surveillance state. Snowden.' Sarah was getting excited, her voice climbing half an octave at the end of every sentence. 'It's not like she was in some village backwater.' She tapped at a coordinate on the map. 'She was in town. The Strand.' She angled the computer so it was easier to see. 'You don't just disappear in central London without your movements being tracked. It's not possible.'

Jessamine finished a triangle of toast, sucked honey off her fingers and picked up a photograph.

'She leaves work and five minutes later she vanishes. See what I mean?'

Jessamine shook her head. The paracetamol hadn't touched her hangover: maybe she should double up with ibuprofen. 'There'll be an explanation. A blind spot. A faulty camera, a power cut.'

'Maybe,' said Sarah, 'maybe not. But aren't you just a little bit curious? You could look into it. It's not like you've got anything better to do.' Jessamine gave her a look. 'Sorry, but you know what I mean. It'll keep you ticking over.' She nodded at the empty Sancerre bottle on the side, waiting to go into the recycling. 'And keep you off the sauce.'

'Hey,' said Jessamine.

Sarah smirked. 'Too soon?'

Jessamine grimaced and Sarah took the photo from her hand.

'Look, I thought it was interesting, but whatever . . .' Her face was now a mask, her voice small and hard. She did this sometimes. Turned suddenly. It was like a switch flicking.

'I agree with you – it's intriguing. I'm intrigued,' said Jessamine, trying to talk her down. She'd taken the devil's advocate thing too far. 'I had been looking into it. But now I have to ask myself, to what end? As of today I don't have a team, I don't have a job.'

'The BBC? Please. They're dinosaurs.' Sarah stopped, struck by some thought, and clicked her fingers. 'Do it as a podcast.'

'Sarah, my love, I barely know how to access my voicemail.'

'It's simple. Anyone could do it.' She paused, a smile sneaking into open ground. 'Even you.' And there she was again, the real Sarah. Funny, cheeky, brilliant. 'Give me your phone.' Puzzled, Jessamine did so. Sarah opened the Amazon app and typed some words into the search box. A selection of microphones appeared on the screen. Sarah scrolled through them, reading reviews and comparing price brackets, then settled on one and hit 'add to basket'. 'It should arrive in the next few days,' she said, handing back the phone.

'It's a lovely idea,' said Jessamine, trying to be supportive, 'but even with a microphone, I wouldn't know where to start.'

The mask was back. 'You give up very easily, you know that?'

'What? No, I don't.' Jessamine was suddenly paranoid.

Sarah spun on her heels. 'I'm going out.'

Jessamine got to her feet. 'Again? Wait.' In her haste to get to Sarah she knocked the empty plate off the table. It smashed on the floor. Barefoot, she picked her way through the ceramic shards and toast crumbs into the hall – too late: Sarah was already out of the door, gone into the night.

Friday 23 December

Present day

Jessamine

Black Eye Friday. The last Friday before Christmas. The domestic-violence helpline's busiest night of the year. The phones hadn't stopped since Jessamine had arrived and she was glad of the distraction. The last few days had seen the fallout from her suspension rumble on, internally at the BBC and in odd news articles, and while she tried hard to ignore most of it, she had little else to fill her time now she had no job to go to. At least here she was still of use.

She finished a call and tried to relieve the stiffness in her neck with a few side-to-side head rolls. The latter part of her day had been fraught, never mind the hours she'd spent since on shift, and every tendon in her upper body was strung tight.

The problem was Sarah.

Tonight the argument had been over their plans for Christmas. They were going to spend it, as always, with her father, Sarah's granddad, in Somerset. Sarah was usually happy to go. She liked the cobbled streets of Wells and the carols in the cathedral at midnight. But this year the prospect had incensed her. Why couldn't they stay in London just this once? she'd asked. Why did they have to drive all that way, to the middle of nowhere?

At first Jessamine had tried to pacify her, to explain coolly and rationally why three days out of the city wouldn't be that bad and why the alternative, leaving her elderly father to fend for himself over the holiday period, was neither festive nor humane. Her case had fallen on deaf ears and Sarah had become even more agitated. Jessamine had put her foot down: they were going whether Sarah liked it or not.

She thought of the look on Sarah's face before she'd had to leave the flat tonight. Sarah had had time to calm down and had accepted a hug, but when Jessamine had looked at her daughter's expression she was sure something was still bothering her.

She gave her head one last roll and pushed away her keyboard. She was due a break. She should take it now, before she got caught up in the post-pub rush.

Just as she stood up the phone rang. She scanned the room but the other volunteers were already engaged, talking quietly into their headsets. It was her or the answering machine.

She moved towards the bank of square buttons next to the phone. The top one was flashing red. She pressed it and the light turned green. 'You're through to the domestic-violence helpline. My name is Jessie. Are you safe to talk?'

Her headphones crackled. The rasp of someone struggling to breathe in and out.

'Please help me. You have to help me.' The woman's voice was adenoidal. It sounded like she had a bad cold. 'I'm in the bathroom. I've locked the door.'

In the background Jessamine could hear whimpering. A child.

'It's okay, Ethan.' The woman's voice grew distant. She had moved her mouth away from the phone. 'Don't worry, baby.'

Jessamine adjusted the microphone on her headset, manoeuvring its foam nub to within kissing distance. 'Are you safe to talk? You say the door is locked. If your partner is still in the property I cannot speak to you.' She hated saying this, but it was the drill. Sometimes the caller tried to reassure her it would be fine, that their abuser was asleep or in another part of the house. Jessamine's trained response was always the same: it's too much of a risk. Phone back once you're alone.

But these women were desperate and sometimes they refused. In that case she had no option but to hang up.

'He's gone. I think he broke my nose.' A rustling and, for a second, everything was muffled. 'There's a lot of blood.' She sounded surprised, as though she was only now examining the damage in a mirror. 'It looks worse than it is. I've tried to clean myself up but it's upsetting my youngest.'

The pubs had been full since early afternoon, everyone giddy at the prospect of the holidays. Jessamine had walked past the Hung Drawn & Quartered earlier, on her way here. Men and women had spilled onto the pavement and huddled under the orange glow of umbrella heaters, beer glasses smeary in their hands. The ground they stood on was compacted with dirty snow, the road lined with grimy drifts. Now it was almost midnight, half an hour past throwing-out time, and the men were starting to come home.

'Do you want to tell me your name?' She held her fingers in the air over the keyboard, ready.

'Nicky.' She huffed hard into the receiver. This small confidence had cost her. 'My name is Nicky.'

'This next question is going to seem odd after everything you've already said, but I have to ask, what prompted you to call us today?' She kept her words slow and steady and stuck to the script they'd been taught to follow. Ask questions; give them options; never offer advice. 'Keep to the script,' Jackie always said, in her sternest supervisor voice. 'Keep to the script and nothing can go wrong. It's there to protect them and you.'

The woman at the other end of the line sniffed. The action must have hurt as it was followed by a wince-sharp intake of breath. 'My friend, she said you have places we can go.'

Jessamine's pulse quickened. 'You'd like to go to a refuge?'

'Only if I can take the kids.' She was suddenly fierce, emboldened by the need to protect her children. 'I'm not leaving them.'

This instinct, like blinking or breathing, was standard among the mothers who called the helpline. It had a ferocity that startled and fascinated Jessamine in equal measure. On the way tonight she had seen a woman trying to navigate the icy pavement outside Tower Gateway DLR station with a boy in tow. At one point he had lost his footing and the woman had scrambled to keep him upright. Her efforts were successful and he had regained his balance, but his safety had come at a price. To help him the woman had had to jeopardise her own precarious stability and had fallen. Unthinking, she had put herself in harm's way. Jessamine had flinched as she watched the woman smack shoulder first into the pavement. As she recovered herself, Jessamine had expected to see her grimace in pain, but when she cleared the hair from her face, she was smiling. Her son was unhurt.

'You can take your kids but to help you with that I need you to tell me where you live.'

Silence.

'You don't have to give me your address. Your local authority is enough.' The helpline had a policy. Never send a woman to a shelter in the same area as that in which she currently resided. The aim was to get her to safety, as far away from her abuser as possible.

'Cambridgeshire.' She conceded the information with a sigh.

Jessamine brought up the relevant hub, excluded Cambridgeshire from the search, selected the two neighbouring counties and hit return. The results appeared on the screen. There were no available spaces in any of the listed shelters. She expanded the search to the entire south-east region. Nicky would have to travel some distance, but needs must. The next set of results filled the screen. A thin line of zeros. Everywhere was at capacity.

At the other end of the line, the child's whimper turned into a sob.

'Do you have any friends or family you could stay with?' Jessamine was frustrated but she made sure to keep her voice bright. 'Every refuge is full. If you can stay with someone else, just for tonight, and call back tomorrow at ten a.m., there's a chance that a space might have opened up.'

'He knows where my friends live, he knows my family. If I leave and he finds me he'll kill me.' Her voice dropped to a whisper. 'He'll kill all of us.'

Keep to the script.

'Can you give me your number? That way, if we get cut off I can call you back.'

'I'm not sure, I—' Nicky was interrupted by a thud. Someone banged on a door. A man shouted. Swear words.

'Nicky? Nicky, what's happening?' Protocol said Jessamine should hang up. That by continuing with the call she was putting her at further risk. 'Nicky?'

It could have been the routine horror of the evening so far, and the routine horrors she knew were still to come, or maybe it was nothing more than sheer impulse, but in that moment Jessamine decided, just this once, that she was going to stay listening, acting as witness.

Her infraction was futile. She watched as the square button on her phone turned from green to red. The line was dead.

2003

Rowena

I finish my milkshake and then, even though the cup is empty, I keep sucking the straw for a few more seconds, making a loud, slurpy echo that I hope will make Millie laugh.

She smiles.

'Aaah,' I say, once the dregs are gone. I pat my belly. 'That was good.'

A few people at the next table to us in the diner tut. Her smile breaks wide. Nearly there.

I flick a curly fry at her head. She ducks and it sails over her shoulder, landing in the middle of the table where the tutters sit.

Her smile drops, a sudden intake of breath, as though she's preparing to dive underwater, and then she does it: she giggles.

Success.

I join in and soon we're laughing so hard that our sides hurt and we have to grip them in the same way I do after cross-country in PE.

It's been two weeks since my termination. Two weeks since Raf agreed to come and collect me from the clinic. In that time I have neither seen nor heard from Leo. It's almost as though, for him, I no longer exist. The same can't be said of his daughter, Millie.

I ignored her first text but that didn't put her off. If anything, it seemed to make her keener.

'You want dessert?' Millie offers me the menu.

I look at it and hand it back. 'I'd like to order some ice-cream but I can't think straight because my mind is still too full of images of Orlando-oh-oh-oh!' I say his name with my eyes closed. At the end I mix in a few of the moans the women make on the mucky videos that are sometimes on in the background at parties.

Millie's smile disappears. She busies herself with the menu, her face red.

After that first text she sent me two more. I didn't reply because I knew that if Leo were to find out he'd throw me straight to the wolves. But then I realised I liked her. I wanted to see her again.

I texted her back.

Soon we were texting all day every day.

We discovered we were both desperate to see Pirates of the Caribbean. *She suggested meeting outside the Odeon in town. I agreed.*

'You got any brothers or sisters?' she asks, once her blush has gone.

'Mum and Dad reckon I'm enough of a handful,' I say, enjoying the fantasy.

She stops and looks at me like she's embarrassed to ask the next question. 'What's it like, going to school and then coming back at the end of every day?'

Millie goes to boarding school, and has done ever since she was seven years old. Earlier she told me how her school has these really long holidays, much longer than the state schools. She broke up for the summer four weeks ago.

'It's okay.' I think of the TV room at the home. The ripped sofas and the mouldy carpet on the floor. 'Mum always has the fire on for me if it's cold and on Mondays she makes my favourite thing for tea, lasagne and chips.'

'You have a fire?'

Millie still thinks I live on the Redbridge Hollow traveller site a few miles from her cottage.

'The caravans have gas fires, toilets and showers. Everything a normal house has,' I say, not sure if any of that is true.

Millie considers this, a dreamy look in her eye. 'We always have games or homework till at least six. Then it's supper.'

'Don't you miss them, your mum and dad?'

'When I first went away I cried every day. Wet the bed. But they have a policy where you aren't allowed to go home or to see your parents for the entire first half term. When it eventually came time for them to pick me up I was so overwhelmed that I hugged Mum and threw up my breakfast, right there on the lawn.'

I wonder if Leo has ever tried anything with Millie. Or if he does the things he does with me so that he doesn't do them with her.

'So let's talk about more interesting things,' I say. 'Boys. What's your type?' I look around the diner. 'Is there anyone in here you like?'

'What?' She blushes again.

'Go on. It's just a bit of fun.'

She takes a sneaky look around. 'Maybe.'

'Interesting.' I start checking each table in turn, trying to guess her choice.

'Rowena, don't,' she says, worried. 'You're embarrassing me.'

I grab a napkin and lay it flat on the table.

'Okay, show me where he's sitting on here.' I sketch the rough layout of the room. 'Go on, just like in the film.' I hand her the pen. 'Show me where the treasure is buried. X marks the spot.'

She takes the pen and marks an X in the corner by the door. I wait a beat, then turn to look. I see a boy sitting with his parents. He has short black hair, parted to one side, and is pretty in a DiCaprio kind of way. I wolf-whistle under my breath.

'Stop. You're too obvious.' She starts to slide low in her seat. 'I mean it.'

'Okay, okay,' I say, holding up my hands in surrender.

'What about you?' asks Millie, once she's recovered. 'Anyone in here to your taste?'

'I kind of already have a boyfriend,' I say, without thinking.

'Oh?'

'He's a bit older.' I don't know why I'm telling her this. The words seem to fall from my mouth.

'So have you, you know?' she asks, suddenly eager.

I think of Leo's face, the way it hovers above me, his breathing quick. The fries I've just eaten rise to the back of my throat. 'Did you tell your mum and dad you were seeing me today?' I ask, changing the subject. The question has been on my mind all day. If Leo is going to find out about us I want some kind of warning.

She hesitates, wrong-footed by my change of subject. 'I told Mum. She's glad I've got a new friend.' She stops as though she's only now remembered she has a message to pass on. When she next speaks, her voice is brighter, higher, like she's delivering a line in a play. 'She said you're to come for tea, *any time you like.' Her message delivered, she returns to normal. 'Dad's in London a lot at the moment. It's supposed to be this big secret but everybody knows. He's standing to be an MP. Bo-ring.' She splits the last word into a two-part singsong.*

I relax. For the time being, it seems, I'm safe. 'So,' I say, putting on a pretend-serious voice. 'We're obviously going to go and see it again, right?'

Millie draws her eyebrows down into a V-shaped frown. 'Obviously,' she says, copying my tone. 'At least twice.'

'Orlando-oh-oh-oh.' This time Millie joins in. Our voices ring out across the diner and the woman serving behind the counter gives us a look. We burst into laughter and then we bite down on our milkshake straws, teeth bared, as we try in vain to stifle our giggles.

Jessamine

Jessamine pulled off her headset. Her mouth was dry, her hands twitchy. She knew she'd spend the rest of the night wondering what had happened to Nicky and her kids and that, come morning, she'd still be wondering. She said a little prayer that, if and when Nicky did call back, a refuge space would have opened up and they'd be able to get themselves to safety, without incident.

She took another call and had just hung up when the phone rang again. 'You're through to the domestic-violence helpline . . .'

'I was talking to someone. Before. I got cut off.'

Jessamine recognised the thick, bunged-up consonants. The sound of someone struggling to breathe through their nose.

'Nicky.' She failed to disguise her relief. 'Are you safe to talk?'

Jessamine could hear crying. There were now at least two children in the background.

'He's gone out.'

It was highly unlikely but Jessamine checked the computer to see if any refuge spaces had opened up in the last half-hour. The search came back the same. Everywhere was full. 'If you're worried for your safety, you should call the police, or do you want me to call them for you?'

'No police. They do nothing and it just makes it worse.'

Jessamine didn't push her: Nicky was right. 'Are you sure there's no one you can stay with? Or maybe you could check into a bed-and-breakfast?'

'I haven't got a job. I have no money. He doesn't let me have a debit card.'

The children's wails were getting louder. One of them was doing that hiccupy, panicked crying that happens when a person can't get their breath.

'Nicky, can you bear with me a second?'

Jessamine put Nicky on mute, half stood and waved until she caught Jackie's eye. 'I have a lady who's been assaulted once already this evening. She needs out. Tonight. I've done a search but everywhere is full.'

'Again?' Jackie shook her head. 'The police?'

'Not keen.'

She shrugged. 'Then there's nothing we can do.' She paused. 'You know that.' Her reprimand needled, small and questioning. 'Ask her to call and check in again first thing.'

Jessamine bridled. She wanted to tell Jackie that she wasn't sure the woman would last the night and she was frightened for her. But there was no point. Whatever she said, Jackie's answer would remain the same. Keep to the script.

She returned to Nicky. 'You said you live in Cambridgeshire.' She lowered her voice. 'Can you be more specific?'

'Huntingdon.' She took a quick breath. 'Near the hospital.'

Jessamine checked Jackie was out of earshot. She had retreated to the other side of the room and was helping one of the volunteers with a faulty wire on her headset. 'I've explained your situation to my supervisor. Sometimes, in exceptional circumstances, we can place women in a hotel.' Jessamine thought of her helpline conversations with Tasha, of all the missed chances she'd had to urge her to get away to safety. And then she thought of Tasha dead on the pavement outside the Bullring Shopping Centre, the white gauze pads stained with her blood, flip-flopping in the wind, and her baby, in the neo-natal intensive care unit at Birmingham City Hospital. She reached down into her bag and fished out her purse. 'While you wait for a refuge space to come free.'

She slid her credit card onto the desk and brought up Google. The rules be damned.

She found a reasonable hotel, selected a family room for the next seven nights and inputted her credit-card details.

'Pack a few things, get the kids together and leave. Only the basics. Do you understand? You can charge food and drink to the room.' She relayed the hotel details. Jackie had fixed the headset and was now moving back in her direction.

'The room is yours for the next week.' She gave Nicky her extension and told her the next day she'd be on shift. 'Call back then and I should be able to find you something more permanent. I promise.'

They weren't supposed to make promises.

'I will. Thank you.'

Jackie was within a few feet of her desk. Jessamine reduced the booking on the screen and replaced it with an innocuous database window.

Then she started to say goodbye to Nicky, to wish her luck.

But, for the second time, the line was dead.

Monday 26 December

Present day

Jessamine

Boxing Day in Somerset, and Jessamine was up early, her father and Sarah still asleep. Kneeling on the living-room floor at the cottage, she drew her dressing-gown tight and huddled close to the embers of last night's fire. The contents of Cassie Scolari's file were spread on the rug. At the last minute she'd decided to bring it away with her to appease Sarah's interest in the case, but also because she couldn't stop thinking about it. Whether she'd have a show to broadcast her findings on or not, she wanted to know what had happened.

She looked again at the CCTV stills of Cassie walking down the Strand towards the Thames. In the pictures her mouth was pursed, her brow pinched – but that could have been down to anything: a cold wind nipping at her ears, the worry that she didn't have enough spuds in for dinner. Jessamine selected the clearest shot and studied it up close. Cassie looked concerned, yes, but suicidal?

Outside, Wells Cathedral rang the hour, its *dong* muffled by the inches of snow that carpeted the ground. She reached for her coffee, steaming on the hearth, and took a gulp. Usually the lack of Wi-Fi and inability to get more than one bar of signal in her father's cottage drove her crazy but this year she had found the lack of connection a blessed relief.

Grabbing her pen and notebook she wrote down a list of what she considered the biggest questions about Cassie's disappearance. First was the phone call Cassie had said she'd received from Matteo's school. If the school hadn't called Cassie that day, who had? Or had Cassie lied about the call? Next up was why, when she'd left work, she had headed towards Embankment Tube. Was that her usual route home? How had she managed to disappear so completely from CCTV? Were there more images in the sequence not included here or was the group of cameras near the station not working that day? Who had sent the WhatsApp to Marnie? Cassie, a thief, or someone else? Why had she taken so many sick days from work of late? And finally, most critical of all, did she have a secret second phone and, if so, why?

Putting the CCTV to one side, she picked up the date diary she'd found among the papers. She had planned to return it to Marnie so that she could hand it in to the police, but after her suspension she'd forgotten about it. She made a note to give it back as soon as possible. In the meantime she decided to make a copy of every page. She turned on the camera, laid the diary flat and took a picture, then turned the page and did the same thing, until she had worked her way through the whole year. All done, she was about to return it to the padded envelope in which it had arrived when her finger felt a small lump on the inside of the diary's back cover. A cream storage pocket. She hadn't noticed it before. She opened the diary wide. The pocket seemed unused but when she poked her finger under the cardboard flap she could feel something. Carefully she pulled out a piece of white paper, folded into quarters, and set it on the rug. She was about to open it when she heard footsteps on the stairs. Her father.

'Good morning, darling.'

The stairs curved slightly into the living room, and as he tried to follow them round, he stumbled and grabbed for the banister. Jessamine jumped to her feet and ran to help. He accepted her arm and let her guide him to the sofa.

Her parents had downsized to the cottage from their terrace in Twickenham not long after Jessamine had left home for university. Mum had grown up in Wells and had always wanted to return to the place of her birth so it had seemed like the natural spot in which to retire. She'd fallen in love with the house as soon as she'd laid eyes on it, delighted that you could see the cathedral from every window on the north side. But she'd only got to enjoy it for a short time. Within a month of moving in she'd become ill. Bone cancer. Stage four. She'd been dead within the year.

'Tea? Breakfast?' asked Jessamine, keen to get her father sorted out so that she could return to her find.

'In a minute.' He patted the space next to him. 'Come, sit.'

She did as he asked. Up close his dressing-gown was rough, the coarse check bobbled at the elbows.

'I wanted to ask. Is Sarah okay? Are you two okay?'

He was alluding to Christmas Day. In the morning Sarah had been her usual self, laughing and joking and full of hugs as she'd opened her presents. But then, as the day had progressed, she'd become more and more twitchy, snapping at her mother and grandfather, until finally after lunch she'd gone for a walk alone only to return an hour later, distraught. Jessamine had asked her what was wrong but she had refused to talk and dashed upstairs, where she'd remained for the rest of the day. After the last few months Jessamine had grown used to such erratic behaviour and so, not wanting to worry him, she tried to shrug it off. 'She's a teenager.'

He'd thought for a moment. 'It feels like more than that.'

Sarah was his only grandchild – Jessamine had no siblings – and she had adored him from day one. Jessamine had first brought Sarah to stay at the cottage six months after her adoption. On the way Sarah had suffered terribly with car sickness and she'd had to stop several times. When they'd reached Wells it had been way past Sarah's bedtime and the then two-year-old had been fractious and grumpy. But as soon as she'd seen her new grandfather, Sarah had transformed and, having allowed herself to be scooped into his arms, was soon giggling and standing on his slippered feet while he walked her around the kitchen, like a penguin.

'Boyfriend trouble?'

'Maybe. Even if it was, she wouldn't tell me. She never tells me anything any more.'

'Talk to her.'

'I will.'

She made him some tea and toast, turned on the TV news and then, once he was settled, she returned to the piece of paper she'd found at the back of the diary. Carefully, she opened it and spread it flat.

A5 in size, it was yellowing in places and had the buckled, uneven texture paper acquired after it had been exposed to water, then dried.

There was no writing. Instead there was a single sketch: a collection of lines and shapes outlined in blue biro. It seemed to be a diagram. One of the lines was bisected with a cross, and the only other vaguely identifiable thing in the picture was a crudely drawn face: a circle with two eyes, a nose and a straight line for a mouth.

Jessamine turned it on its side, then upside down, trying to make sense of the image. It was the only thing Cassie had stored in the pocket of her diary so it must have been significant. A drawing from her son? No. Jessamine remembered the type of thing Sarah used to scribble at that age. It was too abstract. She took a picture of it on her phone and was about to return it to the diary when she noticed a black mark running along the top edge of the paper. She moved to the lamp next to the sofa and turned it on. The light illuminated a line of text. The water damage seemed to have washed away the surface ink but under the light you could just make out the sequence of printed letters and numbers. It was a postcode. Somewhere in Oxfordshire, by the look of it. It could be nothing or it could be a lead, her strongest yet.

Her father came to stand behind her where she crouched and placed a hand on her shoulder. His dressing-gown sleeve smelt of Olbas oil and toast. 'Sarah will be fine. She loves you and you love her.' He kissed the top of her head lightly. 'You're a good mother, Jessamine. Know that.'

Sarah

Sarah stalked through the cobbled streets towards the archway at the end of Vicars' Close. Beyond was Cathedral Green, the most private place she could think of. Her route was clear of snow, the main walkways having been gritted with a soft brown salt that left malty smears on the sides of her new Vans. Still, now and then she'd find herself blind-sided by a hidden patch of ice and have to grab for one of the stone walls, her feet doing a kind of cartoon caper slip and slide.

He was supposed to have called the day before, on Christmas Day. He'd promised. Cross his heart and hope to die. It was to have been their first actual conversation. But the call hadn't happened. This despite Sarah having done everything she was supposed to: going out to the Green at the allotted time, having her phone turned on and fully charged, keeping it a secret from her mum.

She'd waited an hour in a temperature of minus four before finally giving up and returning blue with cold to her granddad's cottage. There she'd retreated to her room and, after messaging him to find out what had gone wrong – he had yet to give her his number – had spent the rest of the day crying quietly into her pillow.

He'd eventually messaged her this lunchtime. He'd told her he hadn't been able to get away like he'd planned and it had made talking to her impossible. He'd asked if they could rearrange their call for later that day. Of course she had agreed.

She reached the edge of the snow-covered Green and was about to march into its mix of slush and ice when the clock struck four. The cathedral's bells boomed the hour and with each clang Sarah felt her ribcage vibrate, the sound rippling through her body like a series of tiny earthquakes. She thought of the science experiment they'd conducted during the last week of term. The teacher had dropped a bowl of sand onto a metal plate and then, using a violin bow, she had strummed the side of the plate, one simple movement in which she had drawn the bow from top to bottom. The action had created a beautiful, completely symmetrical pattern in the sand that had made the class gasp. Then the teacher had strummed a slightly different part of the metal plate, creating a different frequency, and an entirely new pattern had appeared in the grains. The teacher had explained that the movement of the sand made visible the otherwise invisible effects of the vibration.

Sarah liked to think of the man's mouth as that bow. He might be hundreds of miles away but today, when he got to speak to her for the first time, the vibration of his voice would travel across the surface of the earth, and when it reached her, she would feel the shiver of his words against her skin.

Silence returned to the Green. The lamps that lined the edges of the grass picked out the shapes of people walking dogs, their breath white on the air.

In a way, being sequestered upstairs after her disappointment yesterday had been a kind of relief. She'd always loved coming to stay at Granddad's cottage but as she'd got older she'd found the cascade of framed family photographs on the wall next to the stairs hard to stomach. It wasn't as though she didn't feature in any of them, she did, more than any other family member. No, the thing that bothered her was how all she could see when she looked at them was lack. The physical resemblances, so obvious between everyone else, were not there when it came to her.

She checked and double-checked the screen on her phone, paranoid it had stopped working or that in her nervousness she had turned it to silent. It was fine.

When he'd first suggested a phone call she'd been reluctant. The thought of hearing his voice, and him hearing hers, had scared and delighted her in equal measure. She was desperate for their relationship to move on to the next level but she was also worried that once she got talking she wouldn't be able to stop. Online, with the distance between them, it was easy. She had time to think and compose her replies, to make sure they hit just the right note: friendly, happy, not too keen. But to have an actual human conversation? She worried she'd frighten him off, perhaps for good.

Gradually, though, she'd got used to the idea and started to look forward to it. Soon she was counting down the hours till the moment they'd finally get to speak and worrying about what tone of voice she should use in her first 'Hello'. She'd practised by recording different versions on her phone, then listening back to herself over and over until she felt she had the intonation – happy and relaxed – just right.

Five minutes passed. Then another five. He'd said he would call at dead on four. This was like yesterday all over again.

Tears blotting the outer edges of her lashes, she began to walk away, back towards the arch from which she had come. She thrust her Vans deep into the snowy mush, not caring if they were ruined, and had almost reached the green perimeter when her phone rang, its tone brash against the still air.

It gave her such a shock that in her scramble to answer she dropped it and had to search for it in the snow. Terrified he might ring off, when she finally got to speak her practised nuances were forgotten, replaced by a panicky breathlessness.

'Hello?'

'Sarah?'

She laughed, relieved.

'Happy Christmas, sweetheart.' His tone had a smooth, rolling quality. It was like a magic key, able to access a part of her she hadn't known existed.

And then, even though she knew she shouldn't, the words came tumbling out of her mouth, still tight with the tears she'd been about to cry. 'You didn't call. Yesterday. You promised.'

'We're talking now, aren't we?' There was an edge to his voice, as though he was annoyed at being reprimanded. He paused, and when he next spoke it had returned to normal. 'That's all that matters.'

'We are.' Even though he couldn't see her she covered her mouth to hide her smile.

'Santa bring you anything nice?'

'This and that.' Her mum had bought her an Apple watch. She'd been campaigning for it since August but had never seriously thought she'd get one: they were so expensive. When she'd pulled away the wrapping paper and found it, she'd squealed and rushed over to her mum with a hug that made her spill her tea.

'I got you a Christmas present.'

'You did?' He sounded pleased.

'I wanted to post it but I don't have your address.'

A beat.

Her comment hung, like unpicked fruit.

'You thought any more about what I said, about us meeting up?'

Sarah looked at the towers of the cathedral. He'd been driving at this in their online chats for a while. She wanted to see him but she was also scared. What if she messed it up? What if, when he met her, he decided he didn't like her after all? That she was just a silly little girl?

'We could meet in a café or maybe somewhere more private, somewhere we can talk. My flat?'

She shivered. The slush on the ground had soaked through to her socks.

'I want us to be together. Don't you?'

'More than anything.'

She knew that if she were to meet him she'd be consenting, by default, to something else. Something unsaid. Her mum had always told her to wait, that if and when the day came it was important she was mature enough to handle it, that she be ready.

'I'll bring it with me. Your Christmas present.'

'So that means you'll do it, you'll meet?'

She'd heard the smile in his words. 'Yes.' She headed back towards the cobbles of Vicars' Close. Her feet were sodden but there was a new lightness to her step. 'I think I will.'

Thursday 29 December

Present day

Jessamine

Jessamine hunched over the last of her miso soup and tried not to make eye contact with any of the other customers. Set across the road from Broadcasting House, this particular Pret A Manger was frequented by BBC staff, which meant that, the longer she stayed, the more chance there was of her bumping into a colleague and having to engage in an awkward conversation about if or when she might be coming back to work. The location had been Mick's idea, of course, and as she'd been the one who'd requested the meeting, she'd had to go along with it.

Her phone rang. Thinking it Mick calling to cry off, she checked the screen. But it wasn't Mick, it was Jackie, her supervisor at the domestic-violence helpline. It was unusual for her to call. Any changes to the rota were usually agreed via email.

Jackie didn't say hello. 'I want to ask you something and I want you to tell me the truth.' Her voice was tight. She was angry but trying not to be. 'The last time you were on shift, Friday before Christmas, did you pay for a woman and her kids to stay in a hotel?'

Jessamine's stomach dropped. Instead of calling back on her own extension Nicky must have called the general number. 'She and her kids were in danger. I did what I thought was right.'

'It's not your job to think. The protocols are in place for a reason. They're there to protect the callers and you.' Jackie paused, readying for the ultimate purpose of her call. 'Your volunteer contract is now terminated. You'll receive formal confirmation in the post.'

Despite everything, Jessamine had to admire Jackie's straight talk. It made a refreshing change to BBC HR double-speak.

'I'm sorry.'

Jackie humphed. 'Shoulda, woulda, coulda,' and then she was gone.

Jessamine used a plastic spoon to scrape at the dregs of soy paste in the bottom of her cup. She waited for the feelings of shame and guilt to wash over her but they didn't come. She'd miss her work at the helpline but she stood by her decision to help Nicky and her kids that night. If anything, she felt defiant.

Mick was now twenty minutes late. She was just debating whether or not to give up on him when he knocked on the window and waved. He wasn't wearing a coat and his red BBC lanyard swayed against the front of his jumper.

He came inside and took a seat. 'So, how've you been?' he asked brightly, as if she was a distant aunt he hadn't seen in a while. 'Nice Christmas?'

'Really?' she said, motioning to his fake smile and chirpy posture. 'Are we going to do this?'

He kept the act going a moment longer, then let his shoulders drop. 'Fair enough.' He put up his hands in surrender, his voice back to normal. 'You said there was something you wanted to talk about.'

Since her suspension Jessamine had sent Mick a variety of emails and texts asking about the word on the grapevine. Had anyone heard any murmurings about their show? Did people think it likely she would be reinstated? After his fourth one-word reply, she'd figured out the only way she'd get the information she was looking for was if she saw him in person. It was hard to evade someone when they were sitting directly in front of you.

'How's it going?' She nodded in the direction of Broadcasting House.

He rolled his eyes. 'I've been reassigned. *Big Fat Facts*.'

'Oh.'

Big Fat Facts was a dull, archive-led show about the stories behind unusual statistics. It played out in the early hours of the morning, and being made to work on it was usually seen as a punishment of sorts, the place they put staff they didn't know what else to do with.

'What's the chatter, about our show?'

'*PDP* might come back. As for you . . .' He couldn't meet her eye. 'I'll be honest, Jessie, it's not looking good.'

Jessamine bit her lip. It was as she'd suspected, but hearing it said out loud was like a punch to the gut.

'Maybe it's for the best.' He placed a hand on hers. 'Eleven years on the same show. You said yourself it needed a bit of a refresh.'

Jessamine stiffened. 'A content refresh. Not a new me.'

He fiddled with his laminate.

She hated being pitied. She wanted to retaliate. 'As it happens I've been working on something new.'

'Oh?' He smiled benignly.

She'd been mulling the idea of turning her Cassie Scolari investigation into a written piece since Boxing Day. She still had contacts at the broadsheets: she could pitch it to them as a feature. Now, though, she saw that to Mick it would seem like a step backwards. She thought about the microphone Sarah had ordered her from Amazon, still unopened in its box. If she was going to stick two fingers up at the BBC, she'd need to ramp up her ambitions.

'A podcast.'

'You?' The idea seemed to amuse him.

'Something in the crime genre,' she said, trying to sound more confident than she felt. 'Should have it up and running by next week. Just finalising the script.'

'Really? Wow.' He sat back, clearly impressed and also, maybe, even a little envious.

Jessamine felt a rush of victory but this was soon replaced by dread. A podcast, available next week? She had no idea how the technical side of things worked. Maybe Sarah would know, or she could watch a YouTube tutorial.

He looked across the road to Broadcasting House. A kid who'd played out past his curfew. 'I'd better get back.'

'But you've only just got here?'

He got up and moved to give her a hug, but seemed to think better of it. He waved awkwardly instead, his hand up near his shoulder, and then he was gone.

Jessamine stuffed her napkin into the empty miso cup and crushed the cardboard tight. She gathered her things and was about to go when she noticed someone queuing at the till. A young man with coarse black hair. He seemed familiar.

He finished paying for his sandwich and turned to leave. It was the kid who had given her Tasha and Theo's names that day. Jessamine got up and, as he headed out, she followed him onto the street. She tapped him on the shoulder. 'Remember me?'

He blushed furiously and looked around as if for an escape route.

She wanted to ask him about the names, how he'd come upon them. 'You're a sound engineer, right?'

He opened and closed his mouth, sipping the air. He looked terrified. 'Int-t-t-tern.'

She considered this a moment. Asking him about Tasha and Theo could wait. 'Know anything about podcasts?'

Sarah

Sarah ran down the two flights of stairs and out through the front door. On the street she paused, disoriented by the bright sun, then turned right and, with no particular destination in mind, began to walk.

It had finally happened. They'd met. And although it hadn't felt anything like she'd expected, it had been good . . . or, at least, she'd thought it had.

His flat had been ordinary. Not much furniture. No pictures on the walls. She'd been shy at first, unable to meet his eye, let alone speak. That hadn't lasted long. He'd cracked a joke and she'd laughed. After that there'd been no stopping her. She'd asked question after question. What was his job? What was his favourite food? Did he support a football team? Then she'd asked him about all the other things. The important stuff. The things she really wanted to know.

She tried to pick over the best parts of the encounter in her head. He'd talked loads but now, when she thought about it, his answers had been like those phone calls where the signal keeps dropping out. You can try to keep up, to fill in the gaps with guesswork and common sense, but in the end you find you have so little to go on that you might as well have been in conversation with yourself.

A building site reared up on her left. All dust and piles of sand. A gust of wind swept grit into the air. She closed her eyes but she couldn't stop it catching in her lip-gloss. She paused to pick clear the tiny particles and, for the first time since she'd started walking, she took in her wider surroundings. She didn't know this part of London. All dirty white terraces and crumbling front walls, it had a drab, down-at-heel vibe.

They'd spent two wonderful hours together. But then, as it came time for her to leave, his behaviour had changed. He became quieter, maybe even a little offhand. She'd worried that she'd done something wrong, that she hadn't lived up to expectation. The notion had left her on the verge of tears.

She picked up the pace and tried to put aside her unease.

So what if he hadn't answered her questions? The other things he'd said, about them being together, about how much he loved her and how special she was, were all that mattered. That and the way she'd felt when he'd hugged her just before she'd left, her head on his chest, listening to the *whump* of his heart.

Warm, safe, happy.

Home.

Jessamine

Propelled by her fib to Mick, Jessamine returned home and spent the rest of the afternoon contacting key people connected to Cassie's case. Jitesh, the sound-engineer kid she'd accosted in Pret, had agreed to help her with the initial podcast record, edit and upload to iTunes. Still, if she was going to get a script together in a week she had a lot of work to do.

First on her list had been Cassie's husband Luca – Marnie had supplied her with his number. His phone had been switched off so she'd left him a voicemail asking him to get in touch. Then there was Matteo's school. Jessamine had also looked up the postcode she'd found on the slip of paper in the back of Cassie's diary. It corresponded to an Oxfordshire bed-and-breakfast. She'd called to ask if they had any record of Cassie staying there but she'd been out of luck. The phone had rung twice before defaulting to a recorded message, which informed her that the hosts were away for the holidays: any booking enquiries should be directed via their website.

Now sitting cross-legged in bed, she'd moved on from calls to transcribing her chat with Marnie. Her fingers flew across the keyboard and before long she reached the part of the recording in which Marnie had explained how she and Cassie had come to swap handbags in the playground. Hearing it again, Jessamine was even more aware of the pride in Marnie's voice whenever she said her friend's name. She scrolled the recording back thirty seconds. This time she made sure to listen extra carefully. Marnie's tone was proud, yes, but also possessive. When she spoke Cassie's name her mouth seemed to close around the word, as though she was reluctant to share even this small part of her with the world. Jessamine made a note to dig a little deeper into the exact nature of their friendship and was about to continue with the recording when she noticed Sarah hovering in the doorway. She smiled and lowered the screen. 'Hello, darling.'

Sarah approached the foot of the bed, lifted the covers and snuggled underneath, stopping only once she lay perpendicular to her mother. Jessamine felt a twinge of nostalgia. Sarah had done this all the time when she was little and had had a bad dream. Back then she had been so stealthy that Jessamine would be unaware of her presence until the morning when she'd wake to find her daughter's knees pressed into the soles of her feet.

Sarah pulled the duvet down, away from her mouth.

'Everything okay?' Jessamine knew she had to disguise her pleasure at Sarah coming into her room. In recent months, to acknowledge or draw attention to positive behaviour in any way was to scare her off or, worse, to start a fight.

'I just want to lie here for a bit.' She bunched the duvet up around her chin. 'Go back to whatever it is you were doing.'

Desperate to keep her close, Jessamine did as she asked. At first she found it hard to concentrate. There was an energy coming off Sarah, as though she wanted to tell her something, if only Jessamine could ask the right question. But after a little while she started to relax. Having Sarah nearby was comforting, and after the disaster of the Christmas holidays it felt like a reconciliation of sorts.

She enlarged the document at the bottom of the screen and went over the list of questions she'd compiled on Boxing Day. Lots could be answered quickly and cleanly by the police, but for that she'd need access to someone on the case.

She picked up the phone and dialled O'Brien.

'Jessamine. How are you?' There was a crackling noise that sounded as if he'd pressed the phone into his jacket. Through the muffle she could hear him talking to someone. His tone was placatory. Another crackle and he was back. His voice had dropped to a whisper that was as conspiratorial as it was apologetic. 'I'm in the middle of something.'

'I can call back.'

He hesitated. 'Give me a second.'

More crackling and muffled chatter, then footsteps. When he spoke next his voice was back to normal. 'What can I do for you?'

'I wanted to thank you for my Christmas present.' O'Brien had sent her a pair of slippers that doubled as a floor mop. Each sole was covered with knobbly Microfiber, which the accompanying leaflet explained you could use wet or dry.

'Ha-ha-ha! Glad you liked them!'

She gave it a beat. 'Also, I need your help. That misper case I told you about. I need to talk to someone direct.'

He whistled. 'I'll ask, but you know what they're like. They all march to the beat of the press office, these days.'

In the background she heard giggling. A woman.

'O'Brien, are you on a date?' Jessamine's tone was light.

'Ha-ha-ha.' His staccato was more uncertain than usual. 'I'll do my best to get you someone that can help. Glad you liked the present. Talk soon, Jessie.' And with that he was gone.

As she put down her phone she caught Sarah's eye. 'What?' she said, going back to her laptop.

Sarah smiled.

'What is it?' Jessamine was torn between annoyance at being mocked and delight that Sarah was behaving like her old self.

She ignored the question and nodded at the open laptop. 'You're looking into it, then? That missing woman?'

'I'm going to do it as a podcast.'

'That was my idea.' She smiled.

'It was.' She remembered the look on Mick's face when she'd told him her plans. 'A very good one.'

Sarah's smile grew wider. 'Have you found out why she disappeared from the CCTV?'

'Not yet, but I did find this.' She brought up the picture she'd taken of the diagram she'd discovered at the back of Cassie's diary and showed it to Sarah.

'What is it?'

'No clue. It could be everything or nothing.'

'Have you checked her social media?'

'Not yet.'

Sarah scooched up the bed until she was lying next to Jessamine. 'Give me the computer.' Jessamine did as she asked. 'Let's see.'

Sarah began searching for Cassie on a variety of sites, some of which Jessamine recognised and some of which she'd never heard of. 'That's strange,' she said, after a few minutes.

'What?'

'Most people are at least on Facebook. Not your woman, though. When it comes to the internet she's a ghost. Almost like she's made a point of it.'

'That doesn't mean anything. I'm not on social media.'

Sarah shrugged and started skim-reading the Marnie transcription. Next to her, Jessamine could feel the warmth coming through her pyjamas. She uncrossed her legs and stretched out under the covers so that she lay alongside Sarah and propped herself up on one elbow. 'We still haven't talked about that call you made to Ellen before Christmas. You asked to see your file.' Jessamine waited for Sarah to respond. 'Is everything okay?' She reached for her hand. 'Whatever it is, you can talk to me.'

Up close Jessamine could smell Sarah's breath. Sweet with a tang of stale garlic, it was unpleasant and she wanted to move her head back, but she worried that that would alert Sarah to her distaste.

She'd once read an article in which a journalist had described her surprise at the lack of revulsion she felt for her offspring's piss, shit and vomit. The journalist had theorised it was primal, that because the children were a biological extension of her, everything they did or produced, no matter how rank, was the same as if she had done or produced it herself. Jessamine loved Sarah, deeply and keenly, but she often worried that, because they weren't blood-related, she would never experience the connection the woman had described.

'Why did you lose it on air?' Sarah shook off her hand. 'The real reason, not the rubbish one you gave the Beeb.'

Jessamine considered telling her the truth, about what had happened to Tasha, how it had thrown her totally off kilter. But that would lead to more questions, about how and why Tasha had died, which in turn would lead to inevitable parallels with Sarah's birth mother.

'The caller said some horrible things. I lost my temper.'

Sarah shut the laptop and faced her. She held her gaze without blinking. Jessamine was the first to look away. Sarah nodded, vindicated, then got out of bed and left the room.

Jessamine reached out and pressed the spot where Sarah had just been. The mattress was already cold.

Saturday 31 December

Present day

Jessamine

New Year's Eve, and Jessamine was busy emptying bed sheets from the washing-machine. She patted inside the drum, checking she'd got everything, then separated the duvet cover from the pillowcases and arranged them on the airer.

The thirty-first of December: 'Should auld acquaintance be forgot'. Clocks striking midnight. When it came to Jessamine's least favourite day this was right up there in the number-one spot, closely followed by her birthday. It was the expectation that surrounded it, the forced jollity, the way it seemed to expose the parts of your life – relationships, family, friendships or lack thereof – that weren't quite up to scratch. Parts that, in the normal day-to-day routine, you could ignore.

That and the fact that it marked an anniversary she'd rather forget.

By the time her first New Year with Sarah rolled around they'd been a family for two months, during which Sarah had pined continuously for her old foster-mum. She took out her feelings on Jessamine, kicking and shouting and, worse, withdrawing quietly to the corner of the room. Jessamine had been prepared for this, but still she had struggled to see her daughter in distress. She'd started to lose faith in the adoption and in her own abilities as a mother. Then she'd done something terrible, and even though Ellen had reassured her it was just a blip, something she and the other social workers had come across countless times before, Jessamine had never been able to forgive herself.

The duvet was now arranged across the top of the airer but some of the edges were stuck on the lower rungs. She set to work freeing the snags and stood back to admire her handiwork.

She usually spent New Year's Eve on the sofa, eating a takeaway and watching movies with Sarah. Tonight, though, she'd be alone: Sarah was going to a party at Paris's house.

Her eye caught on the leg of air-dried ham, wrapped in foil on the kitchen counter. O'Brien had given it to her nearly a month ago and, although she'd never imagined that she and Sarah would ever be able to get through that amount of meat, it was almost gone.

She picked up her phone and dialled.

He answered after two rings. 'Jessamine?'

'O'Brien.'

'Ha-ha-ha. To what do I owe the pleasure?'

'Short notice, but I wondered what you're up to. Tonight, I mean.'

A pause.

'Me?'

She cringed.

'Sounds lovely and you know I never miss a chance to see you, but . . .' Again he went quiet. 'It's just I've already got plans.' His tone was apologetic. 'Susan. It's early days but she's nice. An optometrist.'

'Of course.' She remembered his awkwardness on the phone the other day. 'I wanted to talk to you about this case. The missing woman,' she lied. 'To tell you where I'm at with it.'

'Another time?' he said kindly.

She said goodbye, hung up and returned to the washing basket. Reaching for a pillow case she shook it out, snapping the fabric straight. This day. This bloody day. She didn't want to be this person. She wasn't this person. She resolved to treat it like any other night. To embrace the chance for a little solitude. She'd order her favourite Szechuan chicken and sticky rice, indulge in a Hitchcock movie marathon.

Her phone beeped. She thought it might be a text from O'Brien, telling her he'd changed his mind and wanted to meet up after all. But instead she was greeted by a message from Dougie, the guy she'd met that day in the Riding House Café: *I'd like to see you again. Tonight? You and me? What do you say?*

She scrolled back up his message history to the sweet but also weirdly sexual picture of the jasmine flower he'd sent a week or so earlier. She'd received it on the morning of her suspension. Distracted by everything she'd had going on at the time, she'd never replied.

She reread his most recent message. She couldn't take seriously the prospect of any kind of relationship with him but maybe that didn't matter. Maybe she should think of him as a 'for one night only' experience. Someone she could hang out and have fun with. What was the expression – living in the now? *You're on. But no standing in the cold watching fireworks, no crowded pubs where it's impossible to get a drink and/or use the loo, and absolutely no Auld Lang Syne.*

He replied instantly: *Deal.*

She smiled and reached for the last of the pillowcases. Before she hung it up to dry she brought the material close to her face and breathed in its fresh, newly washed smell. Szechuan chicken and sticky rice would have to wait

Eight fifty, and Jessamine stood outside Farringdon Tube station, waiting for Dougie. She wasn't sure where they were headed. He'd said he wanted to keep the details of their final destination a surprise.

Around her, the streets were full of women wearing winter coats over sparkly dresses and vertiginous heels. They moved in packs, chattering and whooping as they contended with the bumpy stretch of cobbles to Jessamine's left. Across the road from where she stood there was a pub, its windows vibrating with the bassline of old Christmas hits. Whenever the door opened she'd hear a snatch of Wizzard or Cliff Richard over the roar of the crowd inside.

At nine o'clock exactly, Dougie appeared around the corner.

He looked her up and down, nodded appreciatively and offered her his arm. 'Shall we?'

Dressed in a camel coat and navy scarf, his hair was slick with product, pushed back from his forehead.

She linked her arm through his. 'Where are we going?'

'You'll see,' he said, as they set off towards Cowcross Street.

They walked in silence. Now and again Jessamine sneaked a glance at his profile. His jaw was clean, a neat line that ran from his earlobe to his chin. He was freshly shaved but she could already see tiny black buds, new bristles, pushing their way up through the surface of his skin.

They were almost at Smithfield Market when he guided her to the right, into a small side-street. 'Here we are.'

Jessamine scanned the row of Georgian houses, puzzled. All the windows were shuttered and, apart from a small light over the third door down, the place seemed deserted.

Dougie stopped outside the house with the light, knocked twice and stood back to wait.

A few moments later the door opened. A young woman wearing a white shirt and black skirt ushered them inside. After taking their coats she motioned for them to climb the stairs.

'What is this place?'

The walls were bare, the stairs painted white.

'My dad was a butcher,' said Dougie, as they followed the landing round to the next flight up. 'The pubs opposite the meat market open at dawn but those places have been ruined by tourists. Here, we're off the radar and the trade likes to keep it that way. It stays open all night every night.' He winked. 'Even New Year's Eve.'

On the next landing there was an open door. Jessamine wavered on the threshold so Dougie took her hand. Pulling her close, he led her inside.

A large high-ceilinged room, where candles and a dim electric bulb over the small bar in the corner were the only source of light, the air smelt of blood and the floor was covered with sawdust. An array of tables, dining chairs, sofas and armchairs were occupied by people, mainly men, talking and drinking.

Dougie settled her at a table in the corner and went to get a round in.

She looked around the room intrigued. She'd expected a pub or maybe a table at a restaurant. Something obvious. This was a genuinely original first-date location. Maybe there was more to Dougie than she'd thought.

As he returned with their drinks he caught her sending a text to Sarah. 'Everything okay?'

'My daughter. She's at a party.'

'How old is she?'

'Fourteen. It's at her friend's house. The parents are there to supervise, but still.'

'You two close?'

'As close as anyone can get to a hormonal teenage girl.'

'They grow up so quickly.'

'They do.'

Her earlier flash of optimism started to fade. Five minutes in and they'd already lapsed into platitudes and small-talk. She gulped her white wine and was trying to think of something else to say when a man in bloodied white overalls approached. 'Dougie? Dougie Winston? As I live and breathe.'

Dougie's face dropped. Not wanting to get involved in their conversation, Jessamine got up to go to the loo. 'If you'll excuse me.'

In the Ladies she steadied herself at the washbasin and tried to remind herself why she was there. So what if the conversation wasn't up to much? Tonight was a one-off, a chance to have fun with someone she'd never planned on seeing again.

Back at the table Dougie was alone with another round of drinks. She retook her seat and sipped at her wine. They sat there in silence, both of them apparently at a loss as to what to say next.

'Any new-year resolutions?' he asked eventually.

Jessamine hesitated. She could carry on with the small-talk and give him some pat cliché or she could tell him the truth. 'I'm going to try to be braver and do something I've been avoiding for years.'

'Sounds serious.'

Jessamine considered him, sitting there in this strange bar. Once tonight was over they'd never see each other again. It would be a relief to tell someone, to say it out loud.

'My daughter Sarah, she's adopted. When she first came to live with me . . .' she faltered, not sure how to put those first few months into words '. . . it was hard. Harder than I'd ever imagined. I persevered, of course. You can't expect to bond overnight. It takes time. But in the end it got so bad I called the social worker. Told her I wasn't sure I could continue. Sarah had already been through so much. I suggested that maybe, as she'd obviously had such a close relationship with her foster-family, it might make sense and be fairer to Sarah if they were to bring her into their family on a more permanent basis. I didn't tell Sarah but I packed her things and arranged for them to collect her the next morning.'

Dougie reached for her hand and squeezed it, encouraging her to go on.

'But then that night, for the first time, I felt this little person crawl into the bed. Sarah. She didn't lie next to me, instead she curled up near my feet and hugged one of my legs close. She needed me . . . and I needed her. It would be hard but we could do it, we could make it work. I called the social worker first thing. Told her I'd changed my mind.'

'Does your daughter know any of this?'

'No, but she needs to. The whole sorry incident was logged in her file. It's standard protocol. When she reaches the age of eighteen she'll be given access to it. Whether I like it or not, she'll see how close I came to letting her down, how easily I almost gave up on her and us. Next year I'm going to tell her. I want her to hear it from me.'

As soon as she finished speaking she felt as if a weight had been lifted but the admission had cost her. She tried to pick up her wine glass but her hands were shaking too much to get a proper grip. Her whole body felt febrile, her insides drained. She wanted to go home.

'I'm sorry but I'm not feeling well.' She got to her feet. 'I need to leave.'

Dougie looked concerned and went to accompany her but she waved him off. 'Stay.' She motioned to the guy who had come over to say hello at the start of the night. 'Hang out with your friends. I'll get an Uber.'

Stumbling towards the stairs she asked the girl for her coat and made her way out into the night.

Wednesday 4 January

Present day

Jessamine

Jessamine poured herself another coffee from the Thermos, returned the flask to the footwell and went back to staring at the front door of Cassie Scolari's house. The maisonette was dark, curtains closed, a white van branded with the DPD home delivery logo, presumably belonging to Luca, parked outside. She'd been here since six. It was now almost seven o'clock and, although the sun had yet to rise, the other buildings in the cul-de-sac were slowly coming to life.

She was there because Luca had yet to respond to any of her voicemails. His account of what had happened the day Cassie went missing was key and so, tired of waiting, she'd decided to try approaching him in person.

At home the script for her first ever podcast sat waiting on her laptop. She'd finished writing it last night, and although she'd found it tricky – it had been so long since she'd worked solo on a project – she'd started to enjoy herself. She'd realised that the number of unanswered questions that still surrounded Cassie's disappearance was the case's strength, not its weakness, and so, at various points during the show, she had made sure to solicit the help of listeners. Of course, those inclusions presumed that somebody would download the podcast. She'd find out soon enough. Tomorrow she'd arranged for Jitesh to come to the flat and help with the recording. He'd promised it would be only a matter of days before it was edited and available on iTunes.

Her phone beeped. A text from Dougie. She'd messaged him the morning after their disastrous New Year's Eve date and apologised for having run off but had heard nothing since. Now she saw that he'd sent her a stock picture of a candle-lit dinner for two and his address in south London: *Saturday night. You, me and a bottle wine? I'll cook. xx*

She was about to decline – they weren't suited, even in the short term – when across the street, the door to Cassie's maisonette opened. A rectangle of yellow light. She dumped her coffee dregs out of the window, put her phone away and sat up a little straighter. It was too early for Luca to be taking Matteo to school. Maybe he went to the breakfast club. But it wasn't Luca or Matteo who appeared in the doorway. It was a young girl. A teenager. She stooped down to tuck her jogging bottoms into the sides of her Uggs, zipped up her coat and stepped out into the morning. She ambled down the street, turned the corner and was gone. Jessamine looked back to the maisonette. There was now a light on upstairs and in the living room.

Who was she? A relative? A babysitter? Five minutes later, she reappeared at the mouth of the cul-de-sac carrying a pint of milk and a loaf of bread. She headed back towards the maisonette and was admitted.

Jessamine got out of the car and knocked on the door. It opened almost immediately and she found herself face to face with the girl. Jessamine saw that what she'd thought were jogging bottoms were pyjamas.

'I'm looking for Luca.' She peered over the girl's shoulder. 'Is he home?' In the living room she could hear the zap and crash of a kid's cartoon.

'Luca,' shouted the girl, without taking her eyes off Jessamine. 'There's someone here wants to talk to you.'

Footsteps on the stairs and Luca appeared, hair wet. He had golden, biscuit-coloured skin, and his dressing-gown was loosely tied around his waist, the two sides falling apart to expose a red and orange Roma tattoo on his right pec.

'Go check on Matteo,' he said to the girl, as soon as he saw Jessamine.

'Mr Scolari?' She held out her hand. 'My name is Jessamine Gooch. I tried calling. It's about your wife.'

He looked at her proffered hand and sneered. 'I know who you are.'

Despite the cold he moved forward onto the step as if to guard against Jessamine making a sudden bolt for his living room. 'I already told the police everything.'

Luca's voice bore only the trace of an Italian accent. He uttered every vowel separately, as if the *e* and the *a* in 'already' were distant cousins rather than enmeshed partners in crime.

A face appeared around Luca's hip. Matteo. Jessamine recognised him from the newspaper articles. 'Dad?' His brown eyes were still crusted with sleep, his hair askew.

'Go eat your breakfast.'

Matteo stole one last look at Jessamine, then did as he was told.

'Ten minutes of your time. It might help . . .'

'Not going to happen.'

He took a step back, ready to close the door, but Jessamine wasn't going to let him get away that easily. She wedged her foot next to the frame, and just before the corner of the door hit the side of her toes she asked the one thing she thought might give him pause. 'Who's the girl?'

The door stopped centimetres from her foot, and he reopened it halfway. The question seemed to rattle him but then the right side of his face lifted into a smirk. It was as though he'd suddenly remembered something, some talisman that meant he no longer needed to feel worried by Jessamine and her questions.

'After you called the first time I looked you up. You were fired for going off on one on the radio.'

'Suspended.'

'My wife has disappeared. I don't want to talk to any journalists, and even if I did, do you really think I'm going to talk to you?'

'Mr Scolari, if I could just explain—'

'If you don't stop harassing me I'll call back one of the reporters that have pushed their number through my door, the ones that still have a job, and when I do I'll tell them about you and how you keep bothering me.'

His eyes glittered at the prospect and she knew he wasn't bluffing. She hated to retreat but she couldn't take the risk. If Luca were to make a fuss, it could become a story, and if it did, it would undermine her chances of being reinstated.

'I'll go,' she said, cowed. 'But if you change your mind . . .'

'I won't.'

'. . . you have my number.'

'I got your number all right.'

He looked down to where her foot remained wedged in the corner of the doorway. A prompt. She pulled it back, just in time for Luca to slam the door, and tried not to flinch as the frame rattled and shook inches from her face.

Ruffled by her encounter with Luca, Jessamine spent the rest of the morning at home. It was one thing to have him refuse an interview, quite another to have him threaten her reputation. What little was left of it. Still, she wasn't easily deterred. Luca was a bully and, from now on, when it came to any dealings with the man, she'd need to tread that bit more carefully, but that didn't mean she would give up. If anything, she was even more determined to find out what had happened to Cassie and if he was somehow responsible.

She decided to return to Loughton, this time to Matteo's primary school.

Marnie had said that her son, Jayden, and Matteo attended an after-school club. That meant neither she nor Luca would be there at picking-up time. It would allow Jessamine to talk unsupervised to the other parents and see if she could glean anything useful about the weeks building up to Cassie's disappearance.

A quick Google of Matteo's school told her that it finished at ten past three. She made sure to get there five minutes early and headed for the playground. Essex, like the rest of the south, was still in a battle with the persistent freeze and the tarmac was covered with salt. The grit was abrasive, and as she strode towards the parents and childminders clustered by the climbing frame, she felt the scratch of the granules underfoot.

The school was a single-storey, flat-roofed design. Every doorway was adorned with brightly coloured lengths of twisted plastic that twirled on the air, the brick walls decorated with mosaics of children holding hands and smiling, WE SHARE and WE LISTEN TO EACH OTHER printed above them. She tried to imagine Cassie there with Matteo on that last morning. Had she left her son behind on purpose? Or was she hiding somewhere, even now, missing him terribly and trying to work out how to steal him to safety and a new life far from here?

Her phone beeped. Another text from Dougie: *Hello???*

Jessamine bristled. She'd received his first message only that morning and he was already chasing her for a response. She had planned to decline his offer of a second date with a now-isn't-a-great-time-for-me type text but now, irritated at being hassled, she decided to ignore him altogether.

She approached two women and a man in the playground. Chatting in the low, jokey voices she remembered from when she used to collect Sarah from school, they had the easy body language that comes from being around each other day in day out. One of the women was trying to deter a snow-suited toddler from scaling the climbing frame while the man stood guard over a double buggy containing twin baby girls. From time to time one of the babies would toss something onto the ground and, without missing a beat, the man would stoop to pick it up.

'I wonder if you can help.' They stopped talking and turned to her with polite smiles. Smiles that meant although they had yet to recognise her as part of the usual pick-up crowd, they were willing to give her the benefit of the doubt in case she was a nanny collecting for the first time or a family member not used to the drill.

'I'm investigating the disappearance of Cassie Scolari, Matteo Scolari's mum.'

At this, their faces changed. The woman wrestling with the renegade toddler lifted him to the ground and took a step forward. 'Are you police?'

'I'm a journalist.'

The toddler screamed in protest but the woman ignored him and hoisted him under her arm, like a rugby ball, where he continued to wriggle and squirm. 'We can't talk to you.' She was about to continue when the bell rang out across the playground. The two women scrambled into action and moved towards the building. But the man with the buggy was slow off the mark. 'Don't mind them,' he said, retrieving a ragged rabbit from the ground. 'They're just doing as they're told. The head has asked everyone to stay away from the press.' He stuffed the rabbit underneath the buggy and headed towards one of the classroom doors.

Jessamine looked down. A Sophie Giraffe teether lay on the ground. She picked it up and ran after him. 'You forgot this.'

He accepted it gratefully. 'Why are you here now? It's been weeks,' he said, giving it a cursory wipe. 'Is it because of the fees?' He handed the giraffe to the baby on the right and there was an immediate squeak as she started to gnaw at one of its rubber feet.

A teacher appeared at the classroom door and began searching out relevant parents, then shouting the corresponding child's name into the cloakroom behind her. Seconds later identical twin girls ran to the man, clutching wilting paintings, scarves, hats and gloves. The man bent down to embrace them and pulled two bananas out of his coat pocket.

Jessamine looked from the grown twins to the babies.

'IVF,' he said, offering the fruit to the older pair. 'Then we fell pregnant naturally with these two.' He patted the babies' heads. 'Go figure.'

With a flick of his foot he released the buggy brake and joined the crowd shuffling towards the exit.

'What fees?' asked Jessamine again, falling into step beside him. This was a state school.

'Matteo's after-school-club fees.' His older daughters had run on ahead. 'Rumour is they hadn't paid them in months. They're something like five hundred quid in arrears.'

He navigated the buggy expertly through the crowd, taking care not to ram anyone's shins while keeping one eye on the whereabouts of his two other children.

'Do you know Cassie?'

'I'd see her at drop-off on a morning and at the odd kid's party but that was about it. Oh, and a little while ago she came as a volunteer on a school trip.'

They reached the gates that led out onto the road and he steered the buggy right, onto the pavement that led up the hill.

'What was she like on the trip?'

'She'd never volunteered before, probably because she works full time. She seemed normal at first, made an effort to talk to everyone, was nice to the kids. But halfway through the tour things got a bit weird.'

'Tour?'

'The BBC. The kids get to do a pretend weather report, then they show you where they do the news, the studios, that kind of thing.'

Jessamine resisted telling him her connection to the place.

'When we crossed into the other part of the building she started behaving oddly. Distracted.'

'You went into Broadcasting House?'

'The radio bit. A few of the kids in Cassie's care wandered off into one of the studios without her noticing. Then they did it again. In the end the teacher had to have a word, told her to keep a better eye on them. She broke down in tears, said she wasn't feeling well and left.'

'When was this trip?'

'Just before the October half-term.' He stopped at a black SUV. 'This is me.' He opened the doors and the older twins scrambled inside. He removed the first baby from the buggy and started strapping her into the car seat.

'Do you know Cassie's friend Marnie, one of the other mums?'

He smiled knowingly. 'She's the one that dresses like her, right?'

Jessamine stalled, surprised.

'It happened after the first term, when the kids were in Reception. She started wearing her hair the same, same clothes. My wife would talk about it with the other mums. It was a bit like . . . What was that film?'

'*Single White Female*?'

'That's the one.'

Both babies now strapped in, he collapsed the buggy and stored it in the boot. He got into the driver's seat and started the car.

'Thank you for talking to me.'

He didn't return her smile. 'My advice? Don't come back. Not without permission from the head.'

She watched him pull away, and for the second time that day, she found herself marooned on a pavement.

2003

Rowena

We are at the flat by the river, my first party in months, and everything feels strange. Tonight before I left the care home I went into the office to say good-bye to Raf. I don't sneak out any more. I don't need to. He barely looked up from the computer. It's been like this ever since he came to collect me from the clinic. He used to try to talk to me about what was going on. He said he'd heard that what happened to me had happened to other girls, and that if I ever wanted to go back to the police he'd come with me. But now he seems to have given up. Tonight he said that if I don't want to help myself there's nothing he can do.

I didn't know whether to feel sad or relieved.

I go into the living room to find Queenie and Erin already here. As usual, they're sitting together on the sofa. I expect them to be happy to see me, to get up, maybe, for a welcome-back hug. But after a glance in my direction they look away.

The place seems smaller than the last time we were here. So does Leo. Maybe it's because I've grown or, these days, I'm walking that bit taller.

He called yesterday. It was the first I'd heard from him since my termination.

My first thought was that he'd found out about my meet-ups with Millie. But no. He was calling to say that, although he was still angry at my mistake, if I promised to be more careful with my contraception, he was willing to move on.

I go and stand in front of Queenie and Erin. Queenie is wearing a red spaghetti-strap dress. She looks tired and thin. Erin's acne is worse than ever.

'Miss me?'

They share a look.

'How are you both?' I say. 'How are things?'

Again, they look at each other. A secret seems to pass between them.

'Sorry I haven't been in touch. I didn't have any credit on my phone.'

That is a lie. I have credit but I want to save it all for my chats with Millie. Since that first outing to the cinema we've been meeting up at least twice a week. I like her. More than that, I like the person she thinks I am.

Finally, Queenie shuffles to one side, creating a space for me to sit down. Once I'm settled she peers at the jumper tied around my shoulders. Erin fingers the plait in my hair. 'You seem different,' she says.

My hand goes to where the knotted sleeves rest on my collarbone. I've been trying out a new look. Millie says it's pretty, that I look like Audrey Hepburn in Roman Holiday.

'Why are you like this?' I ask, on the defensive. 'Are you in a sulk because I've not been around? Because if you are . . .'

'It's not that.'

'Then what? Tell me.'

Again, they look at each other. A beat, and Queenie nods at Erin. Permission to speak.

'While you were away things got a bit weird,' says Erin, carefully.

'Weird how? Weirder than this?' I point at the men and children in the room.

She grabs my hand and brings it back down to my knee. It's as though she wants to draw as little attention to us, to our conversation, as possible.

'Remember that celebrity?' She says it so quietly that, to hear her, I have to lean in close. 'The one with the brother.'

I say his name and they both hush me while checking to make sure the men in the kitchen haven't heard. All at once I realise something. Queenie and Erin aren't behaving oddly because they're annoyed but because they're scared.

'At the last party the brother went with Queenie.' Erin checks back on the men in the kitchen. 'Everything was fine and then halfway through he tried to put a pillow over her face.'

'When you can do what you like, you do what you like,' says Queenie. She tries to sound like she's not that bothered but her voice breaks a little. I look at her, trying to understand her meaning. She chooses not to go on.

Instead, she reaches for the jumper around my shoulders, unties the sleeves and places it gently in my lap. Then she pulls the bobble from my hair and runs her fingers through the plait until it sits loose around my shoulders.

'That's better,' she says, looking me up and down. 'It's good to have you back, Rowena.'

Thursday 5 January

Present day

Jitesh

Jitesh tapped his finger against the microphone and watched the screen for a reaction. The needle in the corner lifted and fell. 'You're g-g-g-good to go.'

He handed Jessamine the headphones and gestured for her to take his place at the kitchen table.

'Testing, one two, one two.' She watched the needle flicker in response and smiled. 'It works.'

Thursday, early evening, and Jitesh was at Jessamine's flat in Limehouse prepping her laptop for her first podcast. The plan was for her to record the script at her leisure, then send the long version to him. He would edit out any gaps or pauses and upload it onto iTunes. He'd also offered to set up a dedicated email address people could use to get in touch with information they might have about Cassie's case.

He'd fretted all day about coming here. On the one hand he was excited and honoured at having been asked to work on a project with a serious (albeit disgraced) presenter, like Jessamine Gooch, but on the other he didn't know what to expect. A quick mooch around her email in the hours beforehand had produced little of use and she wasn't on social media.

He needn't have worried. As soon as he'd arrived she'd put him at ease with scones and tea and explained the story behind the podcast. Before long any nervousness he'd felt was gone, replaced with intrigue about Cassie Scolari and what might have happened to her. Jitesh had read Richard Feynman's biography countless times. The physicist's investigative approach into the Challenger disaster was well documented. With his meticulous detective work, he had figured out what had gone wrong with the space shuttle. Now, sitting at Jessamine's kitchen table, Jitesh daydreamed: maybe with this podcast he'd get to be like his hero, finding answers where others had found none.

He felt something brush past the bottom of his legs and jumped.

Jessamine laughed, reached under the table and reappeared with a large ginger cat. 'Don't mind Munchie,' she said, nuzzling the creature's neck. 'She's just saying hello.'

'Munchie?' he said, not sure he'd heard the name right.

'I wanted to call her Valentine,' she pointed to a patch of heart-shaped white fur on the creature's hind leg, 'but Sarah overruled me.'

'What is it I've done now?' A girl emerged into the living room and went straight to the fridge. Wearing tartan pyjama bottoms and a hoody, she had long brown hair, tied in a bun on top of her head.

'Sarah, this is Jitesh,' said Jessamine. 'He's helping with my podcast.'

Sarah emerged from the fridge with a bottle of water, grabbed a croissant from an open packet on the side, then disappeared back the way she had come.

'I'll l-l-leave you to it,' he said, putting on his coat.

'Thanks again for all your help.'

'N-no problem.'

Jessamine saw him out. He'd opened the door no more than a crack when Munchie darted past him, making a break for freedom.

'Shit,' said Jessamine, grabbing the cat just in time. She scolded her, then put her back in the living room and shut the door. 'We try not to let her out. We're five floors up and she's such a daredevil.'

A beat.

'How did you get those names that day?'

Jitesh felt his stomach drop. She'd probably spent the whole time he'd been here building up to this.

'Tasha and Theo. How did you know?'

'I-I-I-I-I . . .' He couldn't get past the first syllable. Panic overwhelmed him. Did she know? Was she about to report him to the police?

'Did you overhear something in News?'

'I-I-I-I . . .' He tried again.

'For the life of me, I can't figure it out.'

'S-s-send me the file when its r-ready.' His panic subsided a little. She genuinely seemed to have no clue as to how he'd accessed those names, but the exchange had rattled him. Wanting to get away before she could ask any more questions, he sloped off towards the lift 'I'll get to w-work as s-s-soon as I can.'

Friday 6 January

Present day

Jessamine

Pellicci's in Bethnal Green. Jessamine pushed her way through the stained-glass door, took off her hoody and searched the café for O'Brien. He stood up from a table in the back corner and waved. Solid in a blue shirt and jeans, he looked trimmer than usual.

She'd been at the gym, trying to work off the nervous energy created by her impending podcast debut when he'd called to tell her he'd found someone willing to talk about Cassie's case, but only if she came now, within the hour. Otherwise she risked the guy changing his mind. Not wanting to miss her chance she hadn't bothered to change or shower and had jumped straight into an Uber. Now, as she wove her way over to him, she caught sight of herself in one of the mirrors on the wall. Her fringe was plastered to her forehead and the sweat patches under her sports bra had leaked through to her T-shirt, creating two dark half-moons under her breasts.

O'Brien took in her Lycra-clad legs and, blushing, averted his gaze. 'Jessamine, this is Jimmy Laird,' he said, gesturing to the man sitting opposite. 'He's an old friend.'

Jimmy had black hair, flecked with white, cut close to his scalp. Overweight, he was wearing a charcoal suit, the jacket pinioned across his belly by a single button.

The air was rich with the smell of fried food, and as Jessamine took a seat opposite Jimmy, her stomach growled. Her post-workout body wanted calories. She caught the waitress's eye and ordered a sausage sandwich and a coffee.

'Charlie said this is off the record,' said Jimmy, shifting in his chair.

'That's right.' The waitress placed the coffee in front of Jessamine and she took a sip. 'I want to talk to someone close to the case, make sure I'm on the right track.'

Jimmy nodded.

'Shall we start at the beginning?' said Jessamine. 'The first you heard of Cassie was when her husband reported her missing. Is that right?'

'Luca Scolari. Thirty-one years old. He called it in around nine p.m. Said his wife had yet to come home from work and he was worried.' Reciting the facts seemed to relax him a little. 'Normally we wouldn't get involved so early on, it had only been a couple of hours, but he said his wife had a history of mental-health issues and that he was concerned for her safety. That changed things.'

The waitress returned, this time with the sausage sandwich. Jessamine doused the inside with tomato ketchup and took a bite.

'We put out alerts with her description and then we set about trying to work out the last time she'd been seen. We soon discovered she'd left her office early to go and collect her son from school.' Jimmy had an odd voice. Every time he spoke it was accompanied by a strange clicking sound, like a metal flipper on a pinball machine. It seemed to catch and push the words up and out of his mouth. 'This was confirmed by CCTV. She walks down Villiers Street towards Embankment and then, a little before she gets there, she disappears. After that we have no idea where she went or what she did.'

'But?' said Jessamine, already finished with the first half of her sandwich.

'But the school said they never made any such call. A fact confirmed by Cassie's incoming landline and mobile logs. She lied.'

Jessamine thought of the second phone the intern thought he'd seen Cassie with. What if someone had called her on it and tricked her into leaving her office by impersonating the school?

'Cassie's friend, Marnie,' said Jessamine. 'She said Luca was violent.'

'Ah, yes, Marnie.' Jimmy rolled his eyes.

Jessamine wondered what it was about Cassie's friend that seemed to bother people so. Was it because she was a busybody or was there something more?

'So, the domestic violence?' said Jessamine, getting him back on track.

Jimmy hesitated. He seemed to be trying to find the right words. 'That, alongside her mental-health history, was another reason we upgraded her investigation to high risk. There are a number of documented call-outs spanning a period of years, but on every occasion she decided not to press charges.'

Jessamine held her silence. Let him squirm, like a fish on a hook. Behind the counter in the corner, the espresso machine hissed and gurgled.

'We checked out her husband's alibi,' he went on. 'It's solid. He was at work all day, then at Army Cadets. He's a volunteer.'

'Did Marnie hand in the date diary?'

'She did.' He smiled grimly. 'Eventually.'

'And?'

'And what?'

On this it seemed he wasn't going to be drawn. Either the police had not found anything of significance in the diary and the piece of paper in the pocket at the back or he wasn't willing to share.

'What about Cassie's Oyster card?' she asked, trying to make sure he didn't shut down completely.

'Aside from her journey into town that morning, it hadn't been used.'

'How about her card history? Was that her usual route home, via Embankment?'

'Typically, she caught a bus to Bank, then got on the Central Line. But we don't think that's significant because we don't think she was headed for the Tube.'

'The river?'

'She'd been on antidepressants for years. Once, in the past, she tried to commit suicide.'

Jessamine was surprised. So far no one had mentioned that. Maybe because they hadn't known.

'She could easily have jumped in the Thames without anyone seeing,' said Jimmy. 'It happens more often than you might think.'

'In a busy spot like that?'

'Even there. And at this time of year, with the river at that temperature, she would only survive a few minutes. We're waiting for a body to surface but sometimes they get caught on or under things. Those never reappear.'

'What about her phone?'

'It was last active at around two p.m. that day on Villiers Street so she had it with her. The only rub is that in the CCTV images she looks to be holding a mobile up to her ear but when we checked her phone log to find out who she was talking to there was no call that corresponded with that time-stamp. So either she was holding some other object against her face – a hairbrush or makeup maybe, the CCTV isn't that clear so it's possible – or she was very confused and thought she was talking to someone, when in fact no such call had been made.'

Jessamine thought of the second phone. The one the work-experience kid thought he'd seen. 'Marnie mentioned getting a WhatsApp from Cassie nearly two weeks later. Did you cell-site that?'

'We think Cassie composed it just before she disappeared but that she didn't have any signal. In it she says she's running late and asks Marnie to pick up Matteo. The message was held in a queue and sent when the phone was turned back on thirteen days later. It came from somewhere in the Berkshire Downs, near the M4. Then it was turned off. I can get you the rough coordinates.'

'You don't think that's significant?'

He sighed. He was starting to lose his patience. 'I think it means that before she jumped she left her bag on the Embankment and someone stole it.'

'I spoke to an intern at her office, who thought he might have seen Cassie with a second phone.'

This surprised him but, after considering it a moment, he dismissed it out of hand. 'That would explain the phone she's using on the CCTV but no other mobile accounts have turned up in her name, which meant it wasn't registered to her, most likely a pay-as-you-go. Those we can't trace.'

'Is it possible she ran away? She could have been headed for Waterloo, across the footbridge.'

'Of course. But we haven't picked her up anywhere on CCTV and in that station we'd expect to.'

'Isn't it a little bit odd for her to just vanish?'

'She didn't vanish. A few of the cameras were faulty. It happens. We're pretty sure she continued on, just wasn't filmed doing so. She could have slipped down one of the many alleys that run off that street, or out through Victoria Embankment Gardens, the small park that leads off from there.'

Jimmy sat back in his chair and crossed his arms. He was done.

O'Brien coughed: a prompt. 'Haven't you forgotten something?'

The two men shared a look. Whatever he was alluding to Jimmy was reluctant to share. O'Brien held his gaze, staring him down until finally Jimmy shook his head. Surrender.

'This is highly confidential,' he said, leaning in close. 'We haven't told her husband this piece of information and we certainly haven't released it to the press.'

He sat back again, as if he was having second thoughts.

'Jimmy,' said O'Brien, in a voice Jessamine had never heard him use before. A threat.

'Fine.' Jimmy held his hands up in defeat. 'When Cassie went missing we sent out an alert, along with her photo, to every police station in the country. Standard procedure. Usually we never hear anything back but a few days ago we had a call from Kent Police. Vice. Turns out Cassie was picked up for soliciting there in broad daylight at the start of October. At the time she didn't give her real name, which is why her caution never showed up on our system. But then the officer who brought her in recognised her from the picture we'd sent through. Says he remembers her because she was dressed so differently from any of the other women she was with.'

Jessamine thought again about the fact that Cassie might have had a second phone. Was it to facilitate some secret second life as a prostitute?

Jimmy looked at his watch.

'One more question. Was Cassie in debt?'

He shrugged.

'Minimal stuff on the credit cards, car loan.'

'They were in arrears with her son's after-school-club fees. Might she have turned to prostitution as a way of earning cash, to help fund her escape from her husband?'

He smiled sadly. 'In my experience people seek out money for the things you'd expect. Drugs, gambling, extortion.' He got up and pulled his jacket taut over the mound of his belly. 'If that's everything.'

O'Brien gave him another look.

Jimmy sighed and reached into his pocket. He brought out a USB stick and placed it on the table.

'Thank you, Jimmy,' O'Brien said, palming the USB, 'for this and for coming here today.' He offered his hand but Jimmy refused to take it.

'You didn't give me much choice.'

Jessamine scribbled her number on a napkin. 'In case anything else comes up,' she said, and handed it to him, waiting until he'd gone before she turned to O'Brien. 'Thank you.' She finished the last of her sausage sandwich and licked the ketchup from her fingers. 'I don't know how you got him to talk but I appreciate it.'

'Aw, now, you know I'm always only delighted to help.'

Somehow Jessamine sensed that this chat with Jimmy had cost O'Brien more than he was willing to admit. She was touched. 'Not the cheeriest bloke, is he?'

'He's on the defensive because of the domestic violence.'

'How so?'

'You know how it is. They're supposed to risk-assess any women they come across in a DV situation but it's mostly a tick-box exercise. It's not their fault – they don't have the resources. My guess, your woman Cassie had been assessed as at high risk but nothing had been done to help her. If the husband did do it, they'd be found culpable.'

Jessie considered this. 'So,' she said, nodding at his right hand, 'are you going to tell me?'

'What?' He smirked, pretending not to know what she was talking about.

'The USB?' She thumped his arm. 'Put me out of my misery.'

He reached under the table for his bag and slid a laptop onto the table. 'The police released the CCTV stills of Cassie to the press. You've seen those.' He plugged in the USB and waited for the file to appear on the screen. 'But they also have video. Jimmy said they've been through it a hundred times and that there's nothing significant. He's probably right, but I thought it might help for you to see it.' He turned the laptop to face her and came round to her side of table. 'In case you notice something they didn't.'

Jessamine pressed play and fixed her eyes on the screen. The video was jerky, the images grainy. She watched as Cassie emerged from the door next to the Vaudeville Theatre and made her way down the Strand, towards Villiers Street. Everything was much as it was in the still images, except for one thing. In the video it was clear that she had been walking at speed: she was obviously on her way somewhere in a hurry.

'Well,' said O'Brien, once she'd looked through the footage a few times. 'Any use?'

'Yes.' She squeezed his arm in thanks. Under the cotton shirt she could feel the heft of his biceps. Dense, with a little flex, it reminded her of the crash mats at the gym this morning. She left her hand there a beat too long and O'Brien turned to look at her. When she still didn't remove it, he smiled. A question. She removed her hand and sniffed at her armpits. 'I must stink.'

'You smell just fine,' he said, returning to his side of the table. He gave her the USB and put the laptop away.

They sat there in silence. Jessamine noticed he'd had his hair trimmed, exposing an area of pink skin at the nape of his neck. A few seconds more and O'Brien startled. He reached down to his bag. 'Almost forgot. I got you these.' He placed two ceramic salt and pepper shakers on the table. One was in the shape of a small fat nun, the other a small fat vicar. Built into the section near their feet was a digital display containing the date, time and temperature.

'They're salt and pepper shakers *and* a clock, calendar and thermometer all in one.'

She laughed and thanked him. 'How was your date?' she asked, peering at the detail on the vicar's face. 'Susan. Going to see her again?'

'Maybe. I'd like to think so.' He moved his hands away from the salt and pepper shakers and the side of his wrist caught the nun, knocking it onto its side. A pile of salt spilled from her wimple onto the table. He tutted and gestured at the mess. 'You know why it's unlucky?' Jessamine shook her head. He righted the shaker and grabbed a pinch between his fingers. 'Judas Iscariot spilt some at the Last Supper. It's supposed to symbolise lies and treachery. But if you throw some over your left shoulder it will blind the devil waiting there.' He smiled at Jessamine and winked. 'For luck,' he said, and tossed the tiny white granules into the air.

Jitesh

Jitesh sat at his desk, headphones in. He wanted to check through the podcast one last time and then he'd upload it to iTunes. But, first, a quick scan through Meera's social media.

Ever since he'd bumped into her outside the café he'd been checking on her daily, sometimes twice, searching her posts and photos for clues. He wanted to know if she had met up with Kishor again, if he needed to worry. But when he looked he saw that she still hadn't updated her Facebook or Instagram. Jitesh wondered if he should send her a message, warning her against his old classmate, just in case. But how could he do that without sounding weird? It wasn't like he could tell her the reason for his concern. He couldn't tell anyone.

He was too ashamed.

Trying to put all thoughts of Meera and Kishor out of his head, he replaced his headphones and pressed play. Jessamine's voice filled his ears, softer and more measured than it sounded in everyday conversation, but her brisk vowels and strict Mary Poppins enunciation meant it was still unmistakably her.

A Friday afternoon in late November. Central London. A woman leaves work early to go and collect her son, who has been taken ill at school. She makes her way down the Strand, towards the Tube, and then, just before she reaches Embankment, she disappears. Her name is Cassie Scolari and even now, months later, no one knows what happened to her. Did she vanish of her own accord or did something else happen? My name is Jessamine Gooch and you are listening to *Went/Gone*.

Jessamine had told Jitesh that she'd decided on this as the title of the series because of something she'd noticed in the articles that had been written about Cassie's disappearance. Some of the journalists had said that Cassie 'went' missing while others had described her as having 'gone' missing. Jessamine said that 'went' implied that Cassie had had some control over the event – in other words, she had chosen to disappear of her own volition. Describing her as having 'gone missing' implied she had been removed against her will. As far as Jessamine was concerned, the dichotomy between the two turns of phrase encapsulated the crux of the case.

Once Jessamine had established the facts of Cassie's disappearance she moved on to her initial theories about what might or might not have happened. Finally, she threw the case open to the listeners.

When it comes to the disappearance of Cassie Scolari, I have lots of questions. Too many to list now. But here are some of the more pressing ones. Why were her son's after-school-club fees in such arrears? What was she using that money for? Was it her only way to accrue cash secretly, cash she then used to run away? Or did she need the money for something else? How and why did she manage to vanish so completely from CCTV that day? And finally why, nearly two weeks after she first disappeared, did her phone send that WhatsApp message to Marnie? Most likely she composed it just before she went missing and the message was held in a queue until the phone was switched back on and found a signal. But who turned on the phone and why? This is where I turn the case over to you, the listeners. If you think you can help, please, get in touch. Maybe you took a picture or a video in or around the Embankment area on the day Cassie was last seen. Send it to us. Maybe you have information or even just a theory that hasn't occurred to us yet. Either way, I'd love to hear from you.

She finished with the email address Jitesh had set up for her and then, after a quick trail for episode two, the recording ended.

Jitesh sat back in his chair and considered the audio file on the screen in front of him. It was a little rough around the edges – next time he'd suggest they do the main recording in a smaller, less echoey part of her flat – but the content was great. He cut and pasted the link into the white text box on the iTunes site and hit 'submit'. *Went/Gone* was now live. He sent Jessamine a text to let her know, then reopened Meera's Facebook. He'd check on her one more time, just to be sure.

Monday 9 January

Present day

Jessamine

Jessamine navigated the car carefully down the narrow drive. The tarmac looked recently gritted but she wasn't taking any chances. Her journey had been full of country lanes covered with black ice.

She parked and peered out at the bed-and-breakfast's grand Georgian façade. It was three storeys high, with a low, snow-covered hedge, a window peacocked above the front door, and a sign cut into the brick announcing the B-and-B's name – Wolsy Lodge – in a tasteful font.

Room rates started at £110 a night. Not cheap. But that was hardly surprising. The nearby village and surrounding area were drowning in cash, populated by those who wanted their second home picture-postcard perfect.

She looked up to see someone opening the curtains in one of the first-floor rooms. This was the address that corresponded with the postcode she'd found on the scrap of paper in the back of Cassie's diary. Had Cassie once stayed there?

The people who ran the place thought not. Jessamine had finally got through to them yesterday. They'd been away for Christmas, to the Maldives for some winter sun. She'd explained the nature of her interest and waited on the phone while they'd checked their records but they'd been unable to find any evidence of Cassie having been a guest. Jessamine had been disappointed but undeterred. Just because Cassie hadn't turned up in their log didn't mean she hadn't been there. She could have stayed under a different name, or maybe the room had been registered to whomever she had been with at the time. O'Brien's friend had said that Cassie had been caught soliciting. If she was working as a prostitute, perhaps she'd been brought here by a client.

Jessamine asked the guys who ran the place if she could pay them a visit. She said it was to show them Cassie's photo and see if her face jogged any memories. In truth that was a task easily accomplished over email, but she knew that, when it came to getting to the bottom of a story, there was no substitute for going somewhere in person.

They'd been more than willing to oblige.

Her phone beeped with a text from Jitesh: *Forty-two and counting!*

She smiled. The podcast had appeared on iTunes last night and, as expected, had yet to make much of a splash. Still, Jitesh was obsessed with monitoring the paltry numbers and every time there was a tiny spike he'd messaged her to let her know. She wondered how long it would take her BBC colleagues to pick up on her new endeavour. Would they think it interesting or amateurish? She didn't care. For the first time in years she'd created something new. She felt proud.

She zipped up her coat and stepped out into the cold. The change in temperature made her wince. Studying the ground so that she didn't slip on the rogue patches of ice, she made her way to the front door, rang the bell and waited. The smell of breakfast, bacon and coffee, hung thick on the air.

The door opened and she was greeted by a tanned man wearing a V-neck jumper over a shirt and tie. A checked pinny was tied around his waist.

'Mr Honeybourne?'

'That's my other half,' said the man, and shouted down the hall. 'Hugh. There's someone here to see you.'

An older man appeared. Wearing burgundy cords and a green polo-neck, his face was also lightly tanned. 'Yes?' He lowered his glasses and searched the ground near her feet for suitcases.

'We spoke on the phone.' She offered her hand. 'Jessamine Gooch.'

'The missing woman.' He stepped back. 'Come in. You must be freezing.'

Jessamine followed the men into a side room, their reception area. A mahogany desk and chair sat next to a fireplace, a leather-bound visitors' book and piles of leaflets advertising local attractions arranged next to the computer.

'I won't take up much of your time.' She passed Hugh Honeybourne a photocopy of the newspaper report. 'This is Cassie Scolari. Nearly two months ago she disappeared. In her diary was a sketch. Printed at the top of the paper on which she drew the sketch, it's possible to make out a partial letterhead. That letterhead contained your postcode.'

They studied Cassie's picture carefully, the man in the apron peering over his partner's shoulder.

'Never seen her before.' Hugh passed the picture to the man in the pinny. 'Malcolm?'

'Sorry.' He shook his head. 'We've been here for over ten years.' He gave the photocopy back. 'We don't remember every single person who comes through our doors.'

'Does Wolsy Lodge have branded stationery?'

'We do.' Malcolm reached into one of the desk drawers and presented her with a piece of A4. In the top right was the B-and-B's logo, a tiny line drawing that depicted the front of the house. The address and phone number sat alongside it and ran the top width of the page. 'The design has remained the same the whole time.'

Jessie compared it with the close-up photo she'd taken of the paper from Cassie's diary. Postcode aside, it in no way matched the font.

'It seems like you came here for nothing,' said Malcolm. 'Cup of tea before you go?'

Jessamine declined – the roads were treacherous enough as it was and she didn't want to risk the temperature dropping any lower – and headed back outside. She was almost at her car when she heard a crunch on the grit.

'Miss Gooch.' It was Malcolm, the one in the pinny. He was clutching a piece of paper.

'We don't live here on site at the B-and-B, we're next door.' He gestured to the right but all Jessamine could see were trees. 'It occurred to us as soon as you left. The two properties share the same postcode.' He handed her the scrap of paper. 'This is the forwarding address of the people who lived in our house before us.' He shivered and hugged himself against the cold. 'We never got their name and it's been over a decade but they might be worth a try.'

Jessamine studied the piece of paper. It was a central London address. Kensington. 'Thank you. Really, I appreciate it.' She put the paper into her bag and strode the last two steps to her car. As she reached for the driver's door her foot made contact with a sheet of black ice and her boot went out from under her. She scrambled for traction, but it was no good. She hit the ground with a thud and lay there, trying to catch her breath. Above, the pale winter sky sailed by, oblivious.

Jitesh

Monday night. The open-air skating rink at Somerset House. Jitesh edged onto the ice and then, keeping hold of the barrier, moved to a spot by the Christmas tree where the crowds were biggest. Five minutes later Meera and Kishor skated past. Smiling and holding hands, their cheeks were pink with cold. It was unlikely they could see him, but as they got close he turned away, to the tree and the grand façade of the house beyond.

His continued vigilance of Meera and her various social-media platforms had finally paid off. Checking her Facebook page this morning, he'd seen a post in which she described how much she was looking forward to going out that night and had tagged Somerset House and Kishor. Again, Jitesh had considered trying to warn her off. Again, he had discarded the idea. In the end he'd decided that the next best thing would be for him to go along and keep an eye on her. He hadn't accounted for how hard it would be to see her and Kishor together having fun.

Jitesh watched as they performed lap after lap of the ice. Then the music changed and Kishor let go of Meera's hand. He wove in front of and behind her in an elaborate figure-of-eight loop, his arms crossed in a pose of faux-relaxation. Then he tried to do it again but this time he misjudged it, or maybe he did it on purpose, and cut in front of her at such high speed he almost knocked her off balance. Meera let out a high-pitched scream, delight mixed with fear.

Jitesh shuddered.

That night at the party, after the incident with the frog, Jitesh had gone home. He'd been upset and humiliated, and every time he thought about the fate of that poor creature he'd felt sick but what was he supposed to do? Kishor was obviously a lot more weird and nastier than he'd thought. He told himself it was good to have found that out now, before they got to Cambridge.

Then he went into school on Monday morning.

It started at break time: looking at phones followed by glances his way. The laughing. It seemed Kishor had shown the video of Jitesh and the frog to his friends. Terrified it was all over the internet, Jitesh checked Kishor's social media, but it turned out he was too smart to share something like that publicly. It would infringe the school's anti-bullying policy and might even jeopardise Kishor's place at Cambridge. That left one other possibility. Kishor was sharing the video privately, by email or WhatsApp.

Meera and Kishor rejoined hands, and after completing another few loops together, Kishor motioned to the drinks cabin. Meera nodded, and at the next juncture, he left the rink. The next time she skated by, Jitesh forgot to hide his face. She did a double-take and slowed her pace. Jitesh panicked. She'd seen him, he was sure of it. He was right. She broke away from the throng and skated over to where he stood.

'I thought it was you.' Her ruby nose stud twinkled in the light. 'Here by yourself?'

'I'm m-m-meeting s-s-someone. Y-you?'

'I'm on a date.' She grinned. 'Kishor, your friend from school. We decided to meet up before we both go back to uni in a few days' time. He's gone to get us hot chocolate.'

She took in Jitesh's grip on the barrier.

'Come on,' she said, offering him a gloved hand. 'We'll do a lap while you wait for your friend.' Jitesh shook his head. The thought of being able to touch her was tempting but it was far outweighed by his fear of landing flat on his face.

'Trust me.' Slowly, she removed his hand from the barrier, slid her fingers through his and led him forward into the fray. 'Push your feet out to the side,' she said, demonstrating for him. 'One two, one two.'

He tried not to look down. The ice rink was covered with giant blue snowflakes, beautiful but disorienting light projections that moved and shifted in time to the music.

'There you go,' said Meera, 'you're doing it.'

He didn't dare turn to look at her for fear of losing his flow, but it didn't matter, he could hear the smile in her voice.

They completed their first circuit and Jitesh was just starting to relax when he saw Kishor emerging from the cabin clutching two cups heavy with whipped cream. He was suddenly conscious of how his feet felt inside his skates. The blade seemed to be hitting the ice all wrong and the more he thought about the mechanics of the action, the harder it became.

'You okay?' said Meera, sensing his discomfort.

The first time one of Kishor's friends came up behind him at school and made a frog-like, 'R-r-r-r-ribbit,' noise in his ear, Jitesh had had to run to the toilet to be sick. The second time it happened he'd been in the lunch queue and had been so upset he'd dropped his entire tray of food on the floor. The taunts continued in class, in study time, on the bus. It went on for weeks. He thought they'd lose interest and that, given enough time, they'd find someone else to pick on, but it came to the end of term and the comments, the nicknames showed no sign of abating. He considered reporting it to the head-teacher, but what good would that do? Kishor would deny it and Jitesh had no proof. Besides, the thought of having to recount the incident to someone else made him cringe with shame. No, the only way he could put a stop to it was by destroying the video, removing it completely from existence.

Jitesh watched as Kishor scanned the ice for Meera.

'I think my friend is here,' he said, wanting to extricate himself. 'I should go.'

Having located Meera, Kishor smiled. But then his gaze moved left, to Jitesh. He was confused at first and then his eyes narrowed.

Jitesh needed to get off the rink. He let go of Meera's hand and tried to move back to the safety of the barrier but he couldn't get through – there were too many people. After scrabbling around on the ice for a few seconds, he lost his footing. His skates flew out from underneath him and he fell. He slid across the rink on his back, surface water collecting inside his collar, until finally he came to rest against the barrier. A dull hard thump.

Jessamine

Jessamine sat at the kitchen table, fluorescent marker held aloft. Spread out in front of her were Cassie Scolari's landline phone logs. She'd spent the last hour working her way through every call made to Cassie's work extension in the two months leading up to her disappearance. So far there had been no great surprises. A mix of office-supply companies, theatres and HMRC, each had been connected to her job in some way. She processed the final three numbers on the list. The calls Cassie had taken during the day she disappeared. Just as the police had said, there was nothing from Matteo's school or from anyone else of any note. All done, she gathered up the sheets of A4 and put them to one side. Now for the list of outgoing calls. The batch Cassie's boss had sent to her by mistake.

There were far fewer, no more than two sheets' worth. Jessamine was glad: her shoulders were still sore from the drive back from Oxfordshire, and hunching over the kitchen table wasn't helping matters any.

Her laptop pinged. New email. She opened her inbox and saw three messages, all from Jitesh, all of them forwards from the *Went/Gone* inbox. In the last few days the number of people downloading the podcast had started to increase, so much so that yesterday, for the first time, it had charted in iTunes' 'Crime' category. And with the downloads came the emails from listeners eager to help. Most were from well-meaning people who wanted to posit their own theories about what had happened to Cassie; others were from weirdos, who said all kinds of strange and unpleasant stuff. Still, she and Jitesh made sure to read them all. The latest lot seemed to be more of the same. One was from a woman in Cardiff, who was certain she'd seen Cassie in the dairy aisle while doing her weekly shop in Sainsburys; another came from a man claiming Cassie was actually an undercover Mossad agent, who had finished her mission and had now returned home to Israel; and a third from a guy who called himself Linus85 and had an image of Snoopy asleep on his kennel as his signature. He introduced himself as a builder from Norwich: although he had no theories or information to offer, he had wanted to get in touch to say how much he'd enjoyed the first episode and thought it a travesty Jessamine was no longer on Radio 4.

She brought up the iTunes app on her phone. It was hard not to keep checking all the time, but the constant feedback was addictive. She punched the air. In the last half-hour they'd climbed another two spots in the Crime chart. She returned her phone to her bag. The response to the podcast was exciting but she needed to focus.

Back to the outgoing phone logs. Looking at the list in front of her, she decided on a simple approach. Every time a new number appeared she would input it into her phone and dial. Then she'd ask the person at the other end who they were and where they worked.

The first people she spoke to were obviously connected to Cassie's work for the ticketing company. Then Jessamine dialled the twelfth number. Cassie had called it twenty-five days before she had disappeared, at eleven fifteen a.m. The call had lasted one minute and fifty-four seconds.

'Miguel Hampson's office.'

Jessamine hesitated. 'Is it possible to speak to Miguel?'

'He's in Shanghai on a project, back next week. I can take a message?'

'Don't worry,' said Jessamine, already reaching for her laptop. She typed in the number she had just dialled, with Miguel Hampson's name. The first hit was for a high-end architecture firm called Mai, Hampson & Oakes. Based in Shoreditch, it specialised in chi-chi office complexes and buildings of national or historical significance. Miguel Hampson was a partner.

She clicked on his thumbnail and was greeted with a picture of Miguel, handsome in a three-piece suit. In his late fifties or early sixties, he had white hair and eyebrows to match. His profile said he had been a partner at the firm for the last twenty years.

What reason had Cassie to call an architect, especially one like Miguel? Even if she and Luca had been thinking of having some work done to their maisonette, Mai, Hampson & Oakes was hardly the kind of company that dealt in loft conversions and side returns.

Jessamine moved onto the next number on the list. An office-supply company. She crossed it off and was about to move on when her eye caught on a number she recognised three entries down. Miguel Hampson's. Cassie had called him again, the very next day. Jessamine did a quick skim through the remaining pages. Miguel's number kept appearing. A rough tally had Cassie calling the man on at least ten different occasions over a twenty-day period.

Jessamine looked at his picture. Was it possible he and Cassie were having an affair? If she was working as a prostitute, was he one of her clients? She checked the duration of each call. They all lasted for no more than a few minutes. Too short for any meaningful exchange. Then Jessamine considered another possibility. Had they been having an affair and Miguel had called the relationship off? Were these the calls of a spurned lover, trying to pursue him by phone?

She clicked on Miguel's email address and sent him a message asking to meet as soon as he returned from Shanghai, then continued with the rest of the log, but there was nothing else of interest.

She got up and was stretching her arms, trying to release the tension in her shoulders, when her phone rang. It wasn't a number she recognised.

'Hello?'

'Jessamine. It's Jimmy.'

Jessamine paused. The name didn't mean anything.

'Charlie's friend.' Then she heard it, the clicking at the back of this throat. Like a flipper on a pinball machine. Jimmy Laird. The detective on Cassie's case.

'Has something happened? Have you found her?'

'Still nothing.' Ping, ping, ping at the back of his throat. 'You wanted the coordinates. From the WhatsApp.'

Jessamine noted them down.

'The message will have originated from somewhere within a two-mile radius of that point. Most likely it came from the person who stole the phone or whoever they sold it on to, in a car travelling down the M4.'

She wanted to ask him about Miguel Hampson, to see if he'd come across the name before, but she didn't get a chance.

'Next time you see Charlie, you tell him this makes us square.' Each word fired from his mouth at speed, ping, ping, ping. 'You got that?'

'Got it,' said Jessamine, but the line was already dead.

2003

Rowena

Millie holds her hair behind her ears, leans forward and in one quick huff, blows out the fourteen candles on her cake. We all clap and start a chorus of 'Hip hip hooray' while her mum hands her the knife. 'Make a wish, darling,' she whispers, as Millie slices through the strawberries to the sponge below. When the knife meets the foil-covered base Millie closes her eyes and mouths something under her breath.

It's Saturday night and I'm one of the ten friends Millie has invited to her birthday sleepover. So far this evening we've watched Bring It On while eating pizza and now, after cake, the plan is to watch another movie – probably Titanic if the DiCaprio chat from her mates is anything to go by – then go and settle into our sleeping bags on Millie's bedroom floor.

I'm happy to be here – more than that, I'm proud. When Millie was told she was allowed to choose ten friends to come and celebrate her birthday, I was on the list. Still, when she'd first handed me an invite I'd been far from keen. Meeting up with her at the cinema or wandering round Abercrombie & Fitch was one thing, but going to her home, to where Leo would be, was strictly off limits. Not that I could tell her so. Then there was the thought of meeting her other friends. They all had names like Cecily and Amelia. One was even called Plum. Like the fruit.

When I told her I was sorry but I had other plans she got upset. Said that her birthday was already going to be rubbish on account of her dad having to be away that weekend.

I thought about it a while. Maybe I could go. Leo wouldn't be there. All I had to do was make sure to keep out of any photographs that might be taken and he'd be none the wiser.

Her mum starts cutting the cake into neat squares and transfers them onto plates. I queue up for a slice, and as she hands it to me I study her face, *trying to imagine her and Leo together. Her forehead is smooth and freckled, her hair the same frizz of ash and ginger as Millie's. She smiles at me but as I continue to stare her smile wavers. I'm making her uncomfortable.*

I back away towards the breakfast bar and am halfway through my cake when Millie's mum goes up behind her and places her hands over her eyes. 'I have one last surprise,' she says, and Millie gasps in delight. Millie's friends titter and stand by the Aga. They seem to know what's coming. Gently, Millie's mum turns her around until she is facing the back door. Through the glass I can see a shadow, the outline of a person. Her mum removes her hands just as the door opens. Millie blinks, trying to focus, and then, as she sees who it is, she shrieks.

'Daddy!'

Leo.

'Happy birthday, darling.' He steps forward and sweeps her into a hug. The cake I'm eating sticks in my throat.

Millie presses her face into his chest. 'I thought you were in London.'

My first instinct is to run. But that would be pointless. Where would I go?

'I couldn't miss your birthday.' His focus is still on his daughter. 'Thought I might take you out hunting tomorrow, just you and me. What do you say?' He mimes cocking a shotgun up against his shoulder, then surveys the room, pretending to look at us all through his crosshairs. He reaches me and stops. His arms drop back to his sides.

Without letting me out of his sight, he accepts a glass of champagne from his wife, necks it and slams the glass down on the side.

Millie opens a gift he has brought with him. A fat golden locket in the shape of a heart. She squeals and kisses him in thanks.

The other girls have drifted back into the living room. I hear the opening bars of Titanic. *Maybe I could just slip away now without anyone noticing. When they ask later I'll tell them I felt ill and decided to go home.*

I take my chance and break off from the group, towards the front door. I'm in the boot room, putting on my trainers, when he grabs my arm. 'What are you playing at?'

'Let me go.'

'Are you two friends now, is that it?' He tightens his grip.

My arm hurts. 'I said, let me go.'

'Daddy?'

He releases me and I tumble forwards.

'I think I left something in the car.' He opens the front door and marches off, the crunch-crunch of the gravel marking his steps.

Millie comes closer, confused. 'Rowena?'

I replace my trainers next to Plum's Nikes and rub my bruised arm. Millie stands there, waiting. I can't meet her eye. In the moonlight her new birthday locket flashes, fat and gold.

Tuesday 10 January

Present day

Jessamine

Loughton Army Reserve Centre. A modern red-brick building with a car park out front, a field, climbing wall and AstroTurf pitch at the back; this was Luca Scolari's detachment. On the day Cassie had disappeared, Luca had said he'd come here after work, just as he did every Friday, to volunteer with the young cadets.

Jessamine stood on the field's floodlit sideline and waited for Officer Martin Cooper to finish issuing instructions to the twenty or so teenagers in his care. The field was frozen solid and she had to stamp her feet to keep warm.

'Thanks for agreeing to talk,' she said, when he returned to her side.

He shrugged, his eyes fixed on the cadets now engaged in a set of gruelling press-ups. 'I've already told the police everything I know.' Dressed in camouflage trousers and a white short-sleeve T-shirt, Officer Cooper didn't seem to feel the cold. 'Luca was here that night, just like he said.'

Jessamine nodded. She wasn't here to check out his alibi. 'I'm trying to get a sense of his behaviour these last few months. Notice anything out of the ordinary?'

The officer's response was instant. 'Nope.' He reached for the silver whistle on a string around his neck and blew it twice. The cadets switched from press-ups to star jumps.

'Are you guys friends?'

'Nope.'

Again, his response was instant.

Jessamine decided to try a different tack. 'How long has Luca volunteered?'

'At Loughton?' He kept his focus on the cadets while he talked, his face twitching in displeasure whenever he spotted any waver in form or effort. 'Nine years.'

'Do you need an army background to volunteer?'

'Some do, but most, myself and Luca included, are civvies. You start as an AI, an adult instructor, and go from there.' The warm-up complete, he blew his whistle and pointed at the cones arranged on the floor by the climbing wall. 'Bleep test!' The group jogged into position. 'Luca is a good instructor. Better than good, actually. He cares about the kids, takes a proper interest. Some of them have issues at home or school or whatever, and when that happens he's there for them.' He started to walk away. 'Look, it's awful about his wife, but you're wasting your time.' He bent down and righted a cone that had toppled onto its side. 'Luca had nothing to do with it – he couldn't have.'

Back in the car, Jessamine saw that while she'd been inside the centre her windscreen had become obscured with a thin coating of ice. She turned on the heater and waited for the glass to clear. Officer Cooper hadn't told her much but she was intrigued by his description of Luca: kind, caring, adept at pastoral care. It was at odds with everything she'd seen and heard about the man so far.

The screen cleared, revealing the entrance to the Army Reserve Centre, its double doors picked out in orange light. Jessamine was about to leave when she saw a woman who gave her pause. In a padded black jacket, she approached the building, then stood to one side, as though she was waiting for someone. There was something familiar about her. The woman shifted slightly on her feet and the orange light hit her face.

Marnie.

What was she doing here?

Jessamine beeped her horn, trying to get her attention, but Marnie was focused on a group of teenage girls now emerging from the entrance. She stepped in front of them and said something. The girls stopped briefly, laughed and continued on their way. Again Marnie said something. This time one peeled off from the group and came over to where she stood. The girl was in army fatigues and a hoody, a backpack on her shoulder.

They hadn't talked long when Marnie's body language changed. She started jabbing her finger close to the girl's face and then back, towards the Centre. The girl went to walk away but Marnie wasn't done. She grabbed her shoulder and the girl twisted, trying to shake her off. As she turned towards the car park Jessamine realised she'd seen the girl once before, last week, at Luca's house. The babysitter.

The teenager finally extricated herself from Marnie's grip, rearranged her backpack on her shoulder and walked away. This time Marnie let her go.

Jessamine guided the car to the double doors, towards Marnie. She'd offer her a lift, ask what had just happened. But in the short time it took to get there Marnie had already disappeared down a footpath cut into the woods at the side of the Centre.

Jessamine was wondering what to do next when Officer Cooper emerged from the building, a giant pack strapped to his back. Seeing Jessamine, he stopped and raised his hand in salute, then jogged off, his breath huffing white on the night air.

2003

Rowena

I wake up just after three a.m. in my sleeping bag on Millie's bedroom floor. I'm thirsty, my throat dry from too much salted popcorn and party food. All I can think about is water. Everyone around me is asleep. In her bed, Millie snores gently. There is no way I can wait till morning, and the bathroom is right next to the one place I want to avoid: Millie's mum and dad's room. I'll have to go downstairs.

I still don't know what the fallout of my being here will be, but I do know that, whatever it is, it won't be good. After Millie caught me and Leo arguing I lied and told Millie her dad was angry because he'd thought I was going outside to smoke. She knows I like a cigarette and I think she bought it. In the morning Millie's mum has promised to make us all pancakes before Millie leaves to go out shooting with her dad. I'm planning to be gone way before that, as soon as it's light.

I unzip my sleeping bag and, taking care not to step on anyone, slowly pick my way over to the door. Millie stirs. Worried I may have woken her, I stop. She snuffles, grinds her teeth and turns onto her side. I wait a few seconds more, just to be sure, then venture out onto the landing.

The cottage is cold and soon I'm shivering in my pyjama shorts and vest.

I creep down the hall and am almost at the kitchen when I hear a noise. It's coming from the living room. Someone is in there, watching TV. I peer round the door and see Leo sprawled asleep on an armchair, a half-drunk bottle of Scotch at his side. I consider going back up the stairs, to the safety of Millie's room and the others, but I'm so thirsty. I'm just about to cross the threshold into the kitchen when I step on a warped floorboard. Yarrrp. It's not that loud but in the still of the cottage it feels deafening. There is no sign of any movement in the living room so I go to the sink and run a glass of water. I gulp it down greedily, some of the water splashing out of the sides of my mouth and onto my cheeks. Feeling better, I refill the glass and head back upstairs.

I'm just making my way back past the living room when he appears in the doorway.

'*Rowena?*'

I pretend not to have heard and keep going.

'*Come in here a moment.*'

Reluctantly, I do as he says, and follow him into the living room. The news is on low and balloons, streamers and empty Coke cans – rubbish from the party – litter the floor.

'*I suppose you think you've got one over on me?*'

I shrug.

'*Inveigling your way into my daughter's life.*'

'*Millie is nice. She's my friend.*'

He laughs. 'You think she's your friend?' He shakes his head. 'She feels sorry for you. That's all. You're her charity case. Those other girls who were here tonight, they're her friends.'

I go to leave but he comes and stands in front of me, blocking the way. His shirt is undone, his eyes red.

He takes the bottom hem of my pyjama vest between his thumb and forefinger and, testing the fabric, he sneers. I try to step around him but he grabs me by the hair, turns me around and pushes me against the back of the sofa. Some of the water I'm carrying sloshes over the side of the glass onto my wrist. As he pulls down my pyjama shorts, I try to focus on a picture of Millie on the mantelpiece. The one of her in her school uniform, a gap in her front teeth. She looks shy, as though she's not quite sure of the person behind the camera. In the hall I think I hear the floorboard and ask him to stop but he won't listen. I try to hold the water steady but eventually it starts to spill. Beneath me, the water blots the cushions and sofa. The stain spreads across the fabric, dark and wide.

Thursday 12 January

Present day

Jessamine

Jessamine ran her finger down the line of buzzers until she found the one she was looking for: Flat 4a. Some of the residents had written their names on the thin strips of cardboard alongside the buttons. She checked the cardboard next to Flat 4a but it had been left blank.

No matter. She'd find out who they were soon enough. She pressed the buzzer and, behind the door, somewhere deep inside the building, she heard a corresponding bell ring.

No answer.

She tried again. Again, there was no response.

The door was sheltered by a stone porch, ballasted by fat stone pillars. Jessamine retreated a few steps, onto the pavement, and looked up, searching the windows in the mansion block for any signs of life. But the net curtains remained still, the front door locked.

She crossed to the small garden square on the other side of the street, took a seat on a bench, and tried to work out her next move. This was the forwarding address that had been given to the bed-and-breakfast proprietors, Hugh and Malcolm, by the previous occupants of their house. Situated in a grand crescent just off Gloucester Road, it was accessed by communal front doors skirted by black and white tiles. Whether the same occupants were still living there nearly ten years later remained to be seen. A Google search had told her that the flats inside were worth millions. It hadn't been able to tell her who lived in Flat 4a as the owners had set their names to private on the electoral roll.

At a loss as to what to do next, she decided to give Marnie another call. Puzzled by the encounter she'd witnessed between her and the babysitter outside the Army Reserve Centre, Jessamine had spent the last two days trying repeatedly to get in touch. But, for the third time today, Marnie's phone rang out to voicemail. She'd try again later.

She looked back at the mansion block. It seemed she wouldn't be talking to the inhabitants of Flat 4a either, at least not today. She was about to leave when, across the street, she saw a man with a number of tiny dogs approach the building. A mixture of Bichon Frise, Pugs and Chihuahuas, the dogs and their leads kept getting tangled round the man's ankles, almost tripping him. Sensing an opportunity, Jessamine crossed the street, and watched as the man herded his charges towards the block.

He fumbled with his keys and was about to open the door when he seemed to become aware of Jessamine's presence. He turned briefly and scanned the pavement. Jessamine braced herself for some kind of confrontation about why she was loitering in the street for no apparent reason, but it was as though she was invisible, and the man, either not seeing her or not considering her a threat, turned back to the door and wrestled his dogs over the threshold.

Being a gorilla in a supermarket had its advantages, after all.

Jessamine waited till the man was out of sight and then, just as the door was about to click shut, she leaped forward, caught it and slipped inside.

The man with the dogs was already gone, disappeared into one of the ground-floor flats. Jessamine assessed the grand staircase that looped up to the top of the building. The banister was broad, carved from smooth oak, the stairs marked by brass spindles, there to keep the carpet in place. She made her way up to the third floor and soon found the door for Flat 4a, tucked into a mini-vestibule at the back of the building.

She knocked and waited, listening for signs of life. Silence. She sniffed. The air around the door and in the small vestibule was scented with bleach and something else, almost medicinal, that seemed to emanate from inside the flat.

She knocked once more. Still nothing. No one was at home. She reached into her bag for her pad, about to scribble a note, when on the other side of the door, she heard a metallic rasp. Someone had opened the spy-hole cover.

She smiled into the fish-eye lens, and a moment later a woman peered out from behind the door. 'Yes?'

In her late twenties, her face was long and angular, her hair pulled back into a severe bun. She looked tired, her skin grey.

'My name is Jessamine Gooch. I'm investigating the disappearance of a woman and I think she may somehow be connected to this address. I wondered if I could ask you a few questions?'

'Are you the police?' She looked behind where Jessamine stood, as though a team of detectives might be there, waiting to talk.

'I'm a journalist.'

'It's not a good time.' She went to close the door.

'Please,' said Jessamine, taking a step forward. 'This woman. She has a son. Two minutes, that's all I ask.'

Cassie's being a mother seemed to hit some kind of a nerve. The woman bit her lip and looked at the floor. She reopened the door. The medicinal smell was getting stronger.

'Maybe I could show you a picture?' She handed her the news article. 'Her name is Cassie Scolari.'

The woman studied the picture, an expression on her face Jessamine couldn't quite read. Her eyes softened and Jessamine was sure she saw a hint of a smile. But then, shaking her head, she handed it back. 'Sorry.'

Again, she went to close the door.

'One last thing.'

The woman sighed.

'Do you live here alone?' It was unlikely a single person could afford the rent on a place like this. 'Maybe keep the picture and show it to your flatmates?'

'I come here to look after Mrs Wiles.' She pulled a tube of pills out of her pocket and gave it a shake. 'She is very sick.' The woman had an odd, drawn-out way of pronouncing 'I'. It was as though she had reached deep at the back of her throat and brought the sound up slowly. Like a bucket being drawn from a well. She looked over her shoulder, into the depths of the flat. 'Even if she wanted to, she wouldn't be able to help you. The medication.' She laughed bitterly. 'Most days she struggles to recognise her own daughter.'

'Of course. I'm sorry.'

'If you'll excuse me.' She checked her watch. 'I need to get back to my patient.'

The door closed and Jessamine was left clutching the picture of Cassie Scolari. Downstairs, on the ground floor, she could hear the tiny dogs behind the closed door, yapping for their supper.

Jitesh

Jitesh got into the lift and pressed the button for the fifth floor. Jessamine's flat. He was there to help with the recording of the second podcast and also to go through the latest batch of emails from *Went/Gone*. The first episode had been climbing slowly up the charts, and the higher it got, the more messages came in. Until now he'd been forwarding them to Jessamine as and when they appeared, but with so many arriving in the last twenty-four hours they'd decided on a new plan. He would weed out the oddballs, then he and Jessamine would go through the credible emails together and decide how best to follow up on those with the most promise.

He was grateful for the distraction. Since embarrassing himself on the ice at Somerset House, all he'd been able to think about was the look on Meera's face as he'd scrabbled away, wet and bruised, to the safety of dry land. She'd been concerned, yes, but she'd also been amused. She'd thought his tumble funny.

He stepped out of the lift and turned right, through the door that led onto the wooden walkway. There he paused, taking in the view of the city skyline beyond. The skyscrapers glittered gold and blue against the night. If he half closed his eyes the sequence of tiny lights looked almost like code. A series of ones and zeros that, arranged in the right way, could be used to do anything: send an email, start a car, launch a rocket. He withdrew his gaze back, to the building before him. It was quiet this evening, the tree in the courtyard lit by spotlights sunk into the ground. It was because of this, because the building was so peaceful, that he became aware of someone talking a few floors below. It sounded like Sarah, Jessamine's daughter.

'Course I do. You know that . . . Don't say that.' She seemed to be talking to someone on the phone. Not wanting to alert her to his presence he made sure to stand perfectly still. 'I'm babysitting. A kid in my block, Isla.' She paused. 'I've asked Mum to renew it.' Another pause. 'I told her I need it for a school trip. She said she'll take it into the Passport Office. If you pay a bit more you get it back the same day.' She paused, presumably listening to the person at the other end. When she spoke again there was desperation in her tone. 'She doesn't know . . . Yes, I'm sure. Of course I still want to . . . Don't say that. I love you, you know I do.'

Her pleading was interrupted by the shrill bleat of his phone. No doubt his father, wondering why he wasn't at the Mandir tonight. He fumbled for it in his pocket and turned it to silent. But it was too late. From below there was silence, then footsteps: Sarah searching for the source of the noise.

'I'd better get back to Isla,' she said, lowering her voice. 'Talk later.' He heard the sound of a door shutting and that was it. She was gone.

He looked at the city skyline. This time he opened his eyes wide. The lights shone out of the windows in each tower: small, neat, uniform.

Monday 16 January

Present day

Jessamine

The reception area at Mai, Hampson & Oakes was as imposing as you might expect for a firm of its stature. A giant glass cube fixed to the front of a converted Victorian hospital, the space was dominated by a swoop of white marble in the shape of a cresting wave. Behind it sat the receptionist, formidable in a black roll-neck, Capri pants and ballet flats.

Jessamine checked herself in and took a seat on one of the brown velveteen sofas dotted around the waiting area. She was there to meet architect Miguel Hampson. Newly returned from his Shanghai sabbatical, he had replied to her email yesterday, inviting her to come in and see him at the earliest opportunity. Jessamine hoped this was a good sign. The last few leads she'd had had fizzled to nothing.

Ten minutes early, she decided to kill time by working her way through the latest batch of emails from *Went/Gone*. Jitesh had uploaded the second episode onto iTunes last night and they'd already had a huge response. She scanned the first three or four. They were now starting to get messages from people who genuinely thought they could help. Most notable were the listeners who had heeded her request for photos or videos shot in or around Embankment on that day. Jessamine studied each of the images in turn, trying to spot Cassie in the back of the shot. One selfie, taken at the bottom of Villiers Street around the same time Cassie would have been there, looked promising. She enlarged the image and scrutinised the faces of everyone in the back of the picture. Her hopes were briefly raised by a woman with blonde hair passing alongside EAT, but up close her facial features were completely different. The last email in the list was from the man whose email signature was Linus85. Again he had nothing of note to impart and had got in touch just to say how much he was enjoying the series.

Behind the desk, the receptionist was taking a message. While she typed she kept her shoulders back, her head erect, her voice polite but firm. Presumably she had fielded Cassie's calls to Miguel.

Jessamine got up and approached where she sat.

A flicker of irritation crossed the young woman's face. Her hand went to the top of her roll-neck, her fingers kneading the soft black material. 'Mr Hampson will be out in a minute.'

'Actually, it's you I wanted to talk to.'

'Me?' She pushed her headset back, her mouth a prim twist.

'Last year around October time a woman kept calling here for Mr Hampson. Ever deal with her?'

She huffed and rolled her eyes at the memory. 'Cassie something? That the one?'

Jessamine nodded.

'Every day I'd tell her he wasn't here, but she wouldn't take no for an answer.' She tutted at the memory. 'Nuisance.'

'Did she ever say why she was calling? Or give any clue about what she wanted to speak to him about?'

'That was just it. She wouldn't leave a message or a number he could call her back on. She was insistent that she speak directly with Miguel.' She leaned conspiratorially towards the marble barrier. 'After a little while I started to wonder.' She checked back in the direction of the main building. 'Her behaviour.' She leaned a little closer. 'Miguel. He has a certain reputation.' She was about to go on when she caught sight of something or someone and retreated behind her computer.

'Jessamine Gooch?'

She turned to see a man standing there. She recognised him from his profile picture. Impeccably dressed in a three-piece tailored suit, he pronounced her name with a slight accent, the syllables seeming to twist and turn on his tongue. Jessamine imagined each letter lengthening and spiralling onto the air, like a collection of mini tornadoes.

'Miguel Hampson.' He offered his hand. 'So happy to meet you. I used to listen to you on Radio 4 every week without fail.'

So that was why he had been so eager to meet. He was a fan.

He motioned to the corridor. 'Shall we?

Jessamine followed him into the Victorian section of the building, then into an office with his name on the door. A vast high-ceilinged room punctuated by a series of round clerestory windows, it looked as if it had once been one of the hospital's wards. A desk, chair and sofa were the only pieces of furniture. The walls were covered with a combination of bookshelves and huge, framed technical drawings of buildings large and small that ranged from jaunty skyscrapers and futuristic sports stadia to Oxbridge quads, brought up to date by sympathetic additions of glass and steel.

She examined a particularly large before and after sketch of an office wing that had had its insides transformed without apparently compromising the historic integrity of the building. The text at the bottom of the drawing identified it as the V&A.

'These all yours?'

'Every one.'

He took a seat on the sofa and patted the space next to him. 'How can I help?' he asked, as she came to join him. He crossed his legs neatly and stretched his arm towards her, along the back of the sofa.

'I'm investigating the disappearance of a woman. Cassie Scolari.' She handed him a picture of Cassie and studied his face for any change in expression. 'I wondered if you knew her.'

'The name isn't familiar.' His reaction seemed genuine. He looked briefly at the photo and shook his head. 'Is she a client of ours?'

'You tell me. In the month leading up to her disappearance she called this company, specifically your office, on ten different occasions. Any idea why?'

'No clue.'

He held her gaze a moment too long and then, slowly, he smiled. The upper line of his teeth was perfect but the lower ones were crowded and collapsing in on each other, their roots tinged with brown coffee stains.

She thought about the receptionist's earlier comment. Had she meant that Miguel was a bit of a ladies' man, or something else?

He leaned in a little closer. This sofa was too small for the pair of them.

'You sure you don't recognise her? Please, take another look.' Again, she handed him the photocopy. As he took it, he let his fingers brush against hers.

This time he studied it properly but again he shook his head. 'I have a photographic memory. If I'd met her, I'd remember.'

Thinking he was teasing, she laughed.

'The technical term is eidetic,' he said, dead serious. 'Although, admittedly, I'm better with architectural plans than faces. I can remember every version of every technical plan I've ever worked on.' He tapped the side of his head with his finger. 'This woman you're looking for, she may not be one of those plans, but I can assure you I've never seen her before.'

He seemed to be telling the truth. But if that was the case, why had Cassie called here so many times? And why specifically Miguel? Did she have some random stalker fixation with the man, something he was totally oblivious to? Or was there something more to it, something he wasn't telling her? Perhaps something connected to Cassie's work as a prostitute.

Jessamine thanked Miguel for his time, and as she got up to leave, her phone rang.

She didn't recognise the caller ID. 'Hello.'

'I heard your podcast.'

She recognised his voice immediately. Luca.

'I want to talk.'

Friday 20 January

Present day

Jitesh

Friday night, and Jitesh was sitting on a wall across the street from Kishor's house. It was Kishor's nineteenth birthday and, although it was only a week into a new term, Kishor had come home from university to celebrate with one of his famous parties.

Jitesh watched as another two boys approached the front door. According to Meera's Facebook page, she was making the two-and-a-half-hour train journey back from Durham to attend but he'd yet to see her arrive. Maybe she was already inside.

Jitesh waited until a largish crowd of kids appeared, then crossed the road and hovered on their periphery. When the door opened he huddled in close and followed them into the hall.

Being back in Kishor's house for the first time since that night last year was dizzying. Very quickly it became difficult to breathe. He steadied himself against the wall and tried to distract himself from his racing heart by focusing on the task in hand. Finding Meera. Once he'd located her he wouldn't let her out of his sight until she went home at the end of the evening. That way he could make sure she came to no harm.

The party was packed with people. Some were old school friends but they were mostly new faces. No doubt Kishor had made a fresh set of pals at college. Jitesh went from the living room, to the kitchen, to the conservatory. She was nowhere to be seen. He'd check the garden, then have a look upstairs.

Outside he moved slowly along the path that ran parallel to the fence, searching the dark. Again, there was no sign of her – or anyone else, for that matter. The grass was packed with old snow, the air freezing. He hugged himself to keep warm and was about to return to the house when he saw an orange light at the bottom of the garden next to the shed.

A cigarette. He sniffed the air. Or a spliff. He crept a little closer. There, underneath a lean-to, two people were sharing a joint. Meera and Kishor.

Once he'd set his mind on destroying the frog video, Jitesh had been like a man possessed. He'd spent hours researching and thinking up possible ways he might go about it. He'd considered sneaking into the changing room while Kishor was playing rugby, then finding and deleting the file from his phone. But to do that he'd need Kishor's passcode. He'd considered breaking into Kishor's house and trying to access his computer while he wasn't there. But that was fraught with difficulty. Even if he'd found the courage to smash a window or force a door he'd have had to log into his computer, to figure out his password. In the end a YouTube documentary on social engineering decided it. Hacking into Kishor's cloud would be the easiest and cleanest way to delete the video that was slowly ruining Jitesh's life.

He set to work late one night. He was nervous but took his time, and before long he had access to Kishor's cloud. He searched iPhoto by date and soon found the offending video. He might not be able to do anything about the people to whom Kishor had already disseminated the footage but he could remove the source and that, at least, gave him back some sense of control. All done, he'd been about to log off when he'd noticed another video, taken on the same date. Time-stamped to forty minutes before the incident with the frog, there was something familiar about the image that marked the start of the clip. Intrigued, he pressed play.

In the garden Kishor had just said something to make Meera giggle. Jitesh moved a little closer, just in time to see Kishor bring Meera in for a kiss.

He shifted on his feet and Meera's eyes shot open.

She pulled back from Kishor and whispered something in his ear.

Jitesh retreated towards the house and was almost at the patio when Kishor caught up with him. He grabbed his arm and turned him around. 'What the fuck, Ganguly?'

Again, Jitesh tried to retreat but Kishor had him held fast.

'First the ice rink and now this. What are you? Some kind of stalker?'

'Leave him, Kish,' said Meera. 'It's okay.'

'No, it's not. He creeps me out. He's mental, everyone knows. Tried to off himself, didn't he, last day of A levels?'

That second video Jitesh had found on Kishor's computer changed everything.

Judging by the angle and the distance of the shot, it had been filmed on a webcam, most likely the computer he'd seen on the desk in the corner of Kishor's bedroom. It captured Kishor and Shanae having sex, without, it seemed, her knowledge that she was being filmed. That was disturbing enough but the worst part was at one point, halfway through, when Kishor looked up to the camera. Without breaking stride, he winked and gave his soon-to-be-audience a thumbs-up. Jitesh didn't hesitate. He deleted the video immediately. But then he thought of the thumbs-up. He searched Kishor's email. He'd shared the video with his friends. Their comments – about Shanae's body, her performance – made him feel sick.

Now Jitesh turned to Meera.

'K-K-K-Kishor is a bad per-person. You sh-should stay away from him.'

Kishor laughed and shoved him to the ground. The snow blotted his shirt.

'Come on.' Kishor took Meera's hand and started to lead her back inside.

'Ask him about Sh-Shanae, Sh-Shanae Roberts. Ask him what he did,' he shouted after them.

Meera looked back briefly, but Kishor pulled her into the house.

Jitesh lay in the snow and breathed deep. The cold air filled his lungs.

Saturday 21 January

Present day

Jessamine

Saturday morning, and Jessamine was back at Cassie's Loughton maisonette. This time, Luca let her in without a fuss.

She followed him into the living room where a boy was sprawled on a beanbag in front of the TV. Matteo, Cassie's son. His hair was almost Scandi-blond, buzz-cut close to his head, his skin the same golden biscuit colour as his father's. He gave Jessamine a passing glance and went back to his cartoon.

'Let's go in the kitchen,' said Luca. As he closed the door he dropped his voice. 'It upsets him, hearing people talk about his mum.'

The house was warm, and as Jessamine took a seat at the table next to the fridge she felt her face flush. She took off her coat and wafted her shirt, trying to cool herself with the moving air. It was no good. Within seconds sweat had started to collect around her temples and in the hollow of her collarbone.

'Tea?' asked Luca, turning on the kettle.

'A glass of water would be lovely,' she said, fanning herself with her notepad.

He drew one from the tap, placed it on the table, then stood by the cooker while he waited for the kettle to boil. Reaching forward with fingernails bitten to the quick, he tapped out a beat on the hob's cold surface. The action produced a dull, scuddy sound.

'So you listened to the podcast,' she said, trying to break the ice.

He stopped tapping. 'I know we got off to a bad start and I'm still not sure how I feel about you, about how you're using what happened, but the police . . .' He stopped, not wanting or unable to finish the thought. 'At least you're trying.' He was like a different man from the one she'd first encountered. Gentle, sensitive, thoughtful. Jessamine wasn't taken in by any of it. She knew from her volunteer work at the helpline how these men could turn it on and off at will. It was how they got the women to stay after they'd hurt them, how they persuaded them that, from now on, things would be different.

Jessamine let his comments settle, and while he busied himself with the tea, she took the opportunity to have a proper look at the kitchen. The cooker, washing-machine and units formed an L on one side of the room. Opposite them were the round table and the chair on which she sat. Jessamine sniffed the air. Plates were piled in the sink, their surfaces scummed with old food, hard and brown, and the bin was overflowing, a banana skin and soggy Rice Krispies spilling over the side. She wondered if the kitchen was always like this or if Luca had failed to stay on top of things since Cassie had been gone.

'Okay if I record our conversation?'

He looked at her phone, not sure.

'It's easier than taking notes. It doesn't have to go in the podcast.'

'Fine,' he said eventually, coming to join her at the table.

She turned on her Voice Memo app and hit record. 'Tell me about the day she went missing.'

'I left the house at seven a.m. for work as usual and was back to back with deliveries all day.' His answer was rote. The construction of the sentence, his tone. 'I headed for home around four, got changed, went to Cadets and finished there around six.'

'Then what?'

'Cassie normally picks up Matteo from the after-school club. But I had all these messages. She hadn't turned up.'

'Marnie said that when you got to her house you'd showered.' At the mention of Marnie's name his body language changed. It was a slight action, a drawing up of the shoulders towards the ears that was part flinch, part shudder. 'You always do that at the end of the day?'

'Cadets can get a bit physical. Muddy.'

'So, your wife has failed to pick up your son, it's getting late, and you decide that instead of going to get him you'll freshen up?'

'He was at a friend's,' he said, a new barb to his voice. He caught himself and when he next spoke he'd curbed his tone. 'He was safe. An extra hour wasn't going to make much difference.'

'Okay,' she said, deciding to leave that for now. 'Can we talk about your relationship with Cassie? How you met?'

'Usual story. I was out one Friday night with my mates in a pub in Buckhurst Hill. She was there with her mates. I thought she was a tidy sort and asked if I could buy her a drink. It went on from there.'

'And how long had you been together before you first hit her?'

At this he flinched. Then he smiled and shook his head, wagging his finger at her, as if she was a naughty schoolgirl.

Jessamine kept her voice neutral. He wasn't getting off the hook that easily. 'It's documented fact, Luca. You have in the past been violent towards your wife.'

'What's that got to do with anything?'

'I went into Cassie's work. Talked to her boss. He said she'd been off work ill a lot these last few months. I want to know why. Was she catching more colds than usual, was her depression getting worse or was she staying away because she had bruises she didn't want people to see?'

'I don't know anything about her being off work.' He seemed genuinely flummoxed. 'I honestly can't remember the last time she called in sick.'

Jessamine wanted to go on, to push him harder on the domestic violence, but she was now sweating so profusely that it had started to drip down her forehead into her eyes.

She got to her feet. 'Can I use your bathroom?'

Distracted by her last revelation he barely looked up from his tea. 'Up the stairs, first on the left.'

At the sink she threw palmfuls of cold water on her face until she felt the flush start to pass. As she was drying her face on the towel, her eye caught on shelf above the sink. It was lined with makeup. Presumably Cassie's, left there in case she ever came back.

She was about to return downstairs when she noticed the door to the bedroom across the hall was open. She ventured a quick peek inside.

It looked like the master bedroom, Cassie and Luca's room. The double bed was unmade, the curtains still closed. On the right side of the bed, abandoned on the floor, there was a bra and a pair of knickers. A black lace thong. It seemed odd for Cassie's underwear still to be there more than ten weeks after she'd disappeared. Then she thought of the dirty kitchen and the overflowing bin. Maybe he was just extremely lazy.

Back in the kitchen she retook her seat at the table. 'Tell me more about Cassie. What was she like?'

'She was devoted to Matteo. She said her mother wasn't so great when she was growing up and felt it important to raise her own kids differently. She could have put him in nursery but she felt very strongly that she should be the one to take care of him while he was small. She would only go back to work once he started school and even then she wasn't happy.'

'Were you and Cassie having any money troubles?'

'You heard about the after-school-club fees.'

Jessamine nodded.

'We have a joint account. The same money was going in. I've checked. Cassie hasn't been paying them for some reason. I don't know why, or what she was doing with the cash.'

Luca was earnest but Jessamine wasn't convinced. If Cassie had been trying to amass a secret fund – perhaps so she and Matteo could run away – and Luca had found out, who knew what he might have done? Especially if he'd discovered she was on the game. Pocketing the after-school-club fees was one thing, but prostituting herself?

'This may seem like an odd question, but were you two planning on having any building work done?' She knew Miguel's architecture firm wasn't likely to be involved in small-fry domestic work but she wanted to be sure.

He gestured at the modest kitchen. 'There's not much scope for that kind of thing.'

She handed him a copy of the picture she'd found at the back of Cassie's diary. 'Do you know what this is?'

He looked at it and shook his head. 'No idea.'

'How about Wolsy Lodge? It's a bed-and-breakfast in Oxfordshire. Ever been to stay there?' she asked, deliberately barraging him with questions. She wanted answers to all of them but she also wanted to build up enough momentum to push him off-guard, unbalance him, to get him to reveal something he might be trying to hide.

'No.'

'And, as far as you know, did Cassie just have the one phone?'

That did it.

'I knew it!' He slammed his hand against the table. 'She was having an affair.'

'I didn't say that.'

'Bed-and-breakfasts I've never heard of, secret phones, what am I supposed to think?'

'Those things aside, did you get any sense that she might have been seeing someone?'

'Nothing I can put my finger on. But these last few months, this last year even . . .' He tailed off.

'What is it?"

'It seemed like she was carrying something around inside her, something precious that no one else knew about. She was the same when she first got pregnant with Matteo. She kept it to herself for ages.'

'So, just to confirm, as far as you're concerned she only had the one phone?'

The doorbell rang but Luca made no attempt to answer it. 'She'd had the same one for years. She never upgraded it.' He nodded at the fridge. 'That one there.' He pulled a photo out from under a magnet and handed it to her. It was one of Matteo as a toddler. He had a phone squished against his cheek as though he was talking to someone. The casing on the back of the phone was customised, a large C picked out in white 'diamonds'. Some of the stones had come away, leaving small black holes in their wake.

Matteo poked his head around the door. 'Daddy, Jayden's here.'

Luca smirked. 'Let him in, then.' He smiled at Jessamine. 'Playdate.'

Jessamine gathered her things and went into the living room.

There, helping a small boy out of his coat and scarf was someone she knew.

'Marnie?'

The younger woman blushed and gave her son a quick kiss. She told Luca she'd be back to collect him in a few hours and ushered Jessamine outside. 'Before you say anything, I know this is weird.' She gestured towards the maisonette. 'But Jayden said that none of the other kids will come to play at Matteo's house now. All this business with Cassie. I felt sorry for him.'

Marnie's explanation was plausible but she wasn't just any random school mum: she claimed to hate Luca, whom she knew to be a violent and dangerous man. Not someone you'd leave in charge of your son.

Jessamine decided to let it slide, for now. 'Actually, I'm glad we bumped into each other. The other night I saw you at the Army Reserve Centre.'

Marnie's face had been twisted into a sheepish grimace but now that expression disappeared, to be replaced by something else. Fear?

'You were there?'

'Investigating Luca, like you asked me to.'

Marnie looked to the floor, thinking.

'So?' Jessamine prompted.

'I pick up a neighbour as a favour sometimes. A girl who lives on my street. The centre's on my way home.'

A flimsy lie.

'I need to update you on where I've got to with the case. Maybe we should get together for a catch-up.' In truth Jessamine wanted more time to find out what was really going on with Marnie and the babysitter.

That perked her up. 'Wednesday night? I'm usually back from work around seven. Come to the house?'

'Perfect.'

Jessamine was halfway down the A12, almost home, when her phone rang. Jitesh.

She put it on speaker. 'I've just finished with Luca,' she said. 'He was incredibly candid, although I still think he's hiding something. And you won't believe who arrived as I was leaving – our friend Marnie.'

'Ch-ch-check your email. Now,' said Jitesh. 'S-s-s-someone with information just got in touch.'

'Great. Did they know her, Cassie?'

'Th-that's just it,' he said. 'Cassie Sc-scolari isn't her real name.'

Monday 23 January

Present day

Jessamine

Jessamine stood at the front of the Chancery Lane Costa and searched the room for a woman wearing a cream coat and purple scarf. She soon spotted her sitting in a corner on a low sofa.

Her name was Erin Cohen. A PA at a law firm in Lincoln's Inn Fields, Erin claimed to have known Cassie as a teenager and had dropped the bombshell that Cassie was not her real name.

The two women shook hands and sat down opposite each other.

'Thanks for meeting,' said Jessamine, getting out her notepad.

'I'm here on my lunch hour.' Erin scanned the coffee shop, left to right, as if she was expecting someone else to come and join them. 'I can't stay long.' She wore a thick layer of foundation and beige iridescent lipstick. The skin tone on her face did not match that of her neck.

'So, you listened to the podcast?' said Jessamine.

'I did.' Erin's eyes flicked towards the entrance and Jessamine saw that her makeup thinned a little where her cheek met her ear. Just beneath the surface there was a smattering of acne scars. 'Someone was going on about it in the break room at work. I like listening to that sort of stuff on my commute so I downloaded it. After the first episode I wanted to put a face to the name so I googled her, Cassie. One of the news articles had a picture. I recognised her straight away. But not as Cassie, as Rowena.'

'Rowena? What was her surname?'

'Garbutt.'

Jessamine had called Luca as soon as she'd got home on Saturday night with the news that someone had come forward claiming Cassie was not his wife's real name. Luca had been genuinely shocked and had said that it was probably a hoax and that he wouldn't believe it, not until he saw proof.

'Look, I know I contacted you but I can't go on record with this. I won't.' Again, Erin's eyes flicked around the room. 'Nobody knows about my life back then, not my husband, not my friends, not my work. And I don't want them to know.' So, Jessamine thought, Erin was constantly checking the café because she was worried about being overheard. 'But in the podcast you mentioned Rowena, I mean Cassie, has a little boy so I thought you should know, her family too. In case it was of any help.'

'When was the last time you saw Rowena?'

'That's just it. I hadn't seen her in years, not since we were kids. But a few months ago she called me at work. She found me on the company website.'

Jessamine felt a flutter of excitement. 'Why?'

'I didn't speak to her, she left a message. She said something about wanting my help. She asked me to call her back.'

'And did you?'

Erin reached for the empty sachet of sugar next to her coffee cup and crumpled it in her palm. 'I've worked really hard to leave behind who I was. I've got a good job, a family.'

'Erin, how did you know her?'

Again, she checked the nearby tables for potential eavesdroppers. 'Growing up I was a bit wild. I lived with my mum, but she wasn't around much. I got into some stuff I shouldn't. Parties with older men.' She shuddered. 'That's where I met Rowena.'

'Who were the men?'

'They were all rich, powerful. Some were famous. I still see some of them on the telly. Gives me the creeps. Most of the girls they brought along were like Rowena, from care homes.'

'Rowena grew up in care?'

'From the age of four. Her mum was on the game, kept leaving her alone at night. One night while her mum was gone Rowena woke up and went looking for her. Ended up out in the street in her pyjamas.'

Jessamine showed her the sketch she'd found at the back of Cassie's diary. 'Does this mean anything to you?'

Erin studied it and shook her head.

'How about this address?' She showed her the Oxfordshire postcode and the name of the nearby village. 'Did you ever go to parties there, or at a flat in Gloucester Road?'

'No, they were always in the same place. By the river. Dolphin Square.'

Jessamine's eyes widened. The press had speculated about Dolphin Square and the rumoured goings-on there for years, but as yet, the police had been unable to prove anything.

'I have to get back.' Erin retrieved her bag from the floor and wound her scarf a little tighter around her neck. 'The person you need to talk to is Queenie O'Leary. She and Ro were close.'

'Any idea how I might find her?'

Erin shrugged. 'She lived in Brixton. Grew up there. But that was years ago.'

As soon as she was gone Jessamine emailed Jitesh with an update and asked him to see what he could find on Queenie O'Leary. Then she messaged Ellen, Sarah's social worker, and asked how she might go about tracking down the record of a child who had once been in care.

Why had Cassie changed her name? Because, like Erin, she wanted to leave that part of her life behind? Odd that the police hadn't clocked it. Surely it would have shown up on the system? And why had Cassie got in touch with Erin after all this time? What had she needed her help with? Whatever the answers, Jessamine now had the feeling that the key to Cassie's disappearance lay not in her present, but in her past.

Wednesday 25 January

Present day

Jessamine

Wednesday night, rush-hour. There was surprisingly little traffic and Jessamine arrived at Marnie's house half an hour early. She parked and turned off the engine. The hall light was on but she decided to give it another ten minutes before she went in. She'd use the time to go through her inbox.

There were three new emails, all from Jitesh. Since her meeting with Erin he'd been hard at work trying to track down Queenie O'Leary online. He said that he was now almost certain he'd found her on Facebook. She hadn't updated her profile page for two years but she was around the right age and she'd named her hometown as Brixton. It had her down as working in a pub on Coldharbour Lane. Jessamine would go over there tomorrow and ask around. He'd forwarded the other two emails from the *Went/Gone* inbox: he thought they were worth a closer look.

The first was from a woman who thought she might have seen Cassie walking across Hungerford Bridge, headed towards Waterloo, on the day she'd gone missing. The second was from their old friend Linus85. She wondered why Jitesh would bother to forward it. The emails were always nice and supportive but that was all they were, fan-mail. She was about to delete it when she saw Jitesh's note at the top of the message: 'Take a look at his theory about the sketch from Cassie's diary. He might be on to something.'

Jessamine did as he asked and then, feeling excited, she read it again.

From: Linus85@gmail.com
To: wentgonepodcast@wentgone.com

Still totally addicted to the show – keep up the good work! After listening to the last episode I went and looked at the mystery drawing you put up online. This might sound a bit bonkers but I've been in the building trade for twenty years and that sketch looks a lot like the room plans my clients give to me when they're trying to explain how they want their new kitchen or living room. My guess, your woman Cassie was planning on having some work done on her house and this was the sketch she did to show the builder how she wanted it.

Jessamine brought up the photo of the sketch on her phone and turned it this way and that. Linus85 was right: the lines and demarcations could be a room plan. But what about the face Cassie had drawn and the X? Taken on its own, Linus85's interpretation was just as he said, a bit bonkers, but Cassie had repeatedly called an architect in the month before she disappeared. She fired off an email to Miguel Hampson, asking to see him again, then got out of the car and made her way down the path to Marnie's house.

Marnie's mum opened the door.

'Is Marnie home?'

She peered out into the dark and pulled her cardigan close. 'You're the one helping Marnie with her friend. Janine?'

'Jessamine. That's right. I'm a bit early.'

'I'm Sandra. Come in. She won't be long.'

Upstairs Jessamine could hear the thump and crash and 'Pew-pew-pew!' sound effects of a child at play. Presumably Jayden.

While Sandra went to make tea Jessamine took a seat in the living room. The gas fire was on full, the TV on low, the mantelpiece crowded with photos of Jayden as a baby. A cosy family home.

'Did you know Cassie?' she asked, when Sandra returned with the tea.

'Marnie talked about her all the time, but I only met her once or twice at pick-up.'

Jessamine looked again at the pictures on the fireplace. 'Is Jayden your only grandchild?'

'He is.' She got up, retrieved a picture off the mantelpiece and handed it to Jessamine. 'His new school photo,' she said proudly. 'Got it last week.'

Jessamine looked at the little boy in the cardboard frame. He had a shy smile and a smattering of freckles across the top of his nose and cheeks. 'Beautiful child.' She got up to replace it on the mantelpiece but stopped at the sight of another large photo. A group shot of teenage girls and boys in uniform. Cadets.

She studied the picture more closely. There, in the second row, was a much younger Marnie. 'Your daughter was in the Cadets?'

'For years. She loved it. Then she got pregnant with Jay.'

Jessamine looked at the picture again. Sitting front and centre in a slightly different uniform from all the others was someone else she recognised. A man.

The metal *shunk* of a key in a door, followed by a blast of cold air. Marnie was home.

'You're here,' said Marnie, taking off her coat. 'Hope Mum's been taking good care of you?'

Jessamine raised her mug of tea in proof.

'I need to go and run Jay's bath,' said Sandra. 'I'll leave you to it.'

'What's going on?' asked Jessamine, once Sandra was gone.

Marnie's smile wavered briefly. 'What do you mean?'

'See that?' She pointed at the picture on the mantelpiece. 'The man at the front of that picture is Luca.'

Marnie managed to maintain her smile for a few seconds more but then she gave up and, after checking her mum was still upstairs, closed the living-room door. 'I can explain.'

'Why have you been lying to me?' said Jessamine.

Marnie went over to the picture and squinted at her younger self. 'I was thirteen when this was taken. I was three months pregnant with Jayden but I didn't know it yet.'

'And Luca?'

'Is Jayden's father. We were in love – at least, I thought we were. He dumped me not long after I told him about the baby. But I still loved him and I didn't want him to get into trouble so I never told anyone, not even Mum. We lost all contact, years went by and then Jayden started school.'

'Matteo was in his class?'

'It didn't take me to long to work out who he and Cassie were. Scolari.' She laughed bitterly. 'It's a distinctive surname.'

'Did Cassie know about your connection to her husband?'

'She had no idea and I made sure to keep it that way. At first I was jealous that Luca had married her and they had a family, but then I started noticing things.' She rubbed at her wrist, as if to soothe a bruise. 'Luca would sometimes get a bit physical when we were together. Cassie tried to cover it up with clothes or makeup but now and again I'd see it, a blue tinge by her jaw, a flash of purple on her arm. He was hurting her, just like he used to hurt me.'

'And Cassie's diary?'

'I was always curious about her, about her life. Then one day, the day before she went missing, she put her bag down on the floor during pick-up. It was right there so I took it. I was going to put it back but I never got the chance.'

'What about the girl outside the cadets centre?'

'Turns out me and him weren't a one-off. He has a thing for teenage girls. She's his latest. I was there to warn her but she wouldn't listen. She thinks they're in love.'

'You could have reported him.'

'And leave Matteo without a mother *or* a father? No, thanks.'

Jessamine considered this. Cassie had grown up in care. There would be a horrible irony if Matteo ended up the same way. Still. 'It's up to you whether you want to come forward about what happened to you. But, just to be clear, you were a child. He groomed you. You were a victim. The new girl, the babysitter, this is going on right now and if you don't do something about it I will.'

Marnie nodded, defeated.

Jessamine got to her feet. 'I should go.'

'I'm sorry I lied,' said Marnie, following her out into the hall. 'But this shouldn't change anything. Cassie is still missing and I still think Luca had something to do with it. Please, don't let this put you off.'

'I've no intention of stopping the investigation, but after I've gone I want you to call the police and tell them what you just told me about that girl. Are we clear?'

Another nod of defeat.

As Jessamine left, she could hear Jayden upstairs in the bath playing battleships in the bubbles: 'Pew-pew-pew!'

Thursday 26 January

Present day

Jessamine

Jessamine arrived at the Green Man pub just as they were taking delivery of a load of beer barrels into the cellar. She waited until the last had been dispatched from the truck and approached the man standing half in, half out of the opening in the pavement.

'Can I help?' said the man, signing the delivery note. He handed the clipboard back to the driver.

'I'm looking for someone who works here. Queenie O'Leary?'

The man laughed like he'd just remembered the punchline to a particularly funny joke. 'What do you want with Queenie?'

He knew her. Jitesh had done well.

'I'm looking into the disappearance of a woman from a few months back. There's a chance Queenie might have some information.'

The man lowered one half of the wooden doors back into place. 'Queenie hasn't worked here for years.' He nodded down the road, towards Loughborough Junction. 'You'll find her in the park most days, though I'm not sure how much use she'll be.'

'What do you mean?'

He reached up and lowered the other door so that it was resting on top of his head. 'There's a reason she no longer has a job.' He ducked out of sight and then he was gone.

A five-minute walk down Coldharbour Lane, and she reached a small park, a square of patchy grass, with a path running around its perimeter and up to an old bandstand in the far corner. Aside from a few drunks dotted on benches here and there, the park was empty. She spied an elderly gentleman sitting alone near the bandstand. Unlike his fellow park-goers he was smartly dressed and had two walking sticks placed against his knees. She decided to try him first.

'Excuse me.'

As soon as she opened her mouth he reared up from the bench. Using one of the walking sticks to balance he started swinging the other one towards Jessamine, as though he was trying to smack her in the face.

'Roger! Roger, leave her alone!' One of the men from a nearby bench came up behind him, took hold of the flailing walking stick and gradually pushed it back to the ground. Now mumbling and fussing under his breath, Roger let the other man guide him back to his spot by the bandstand. Once he was settled, her good Samaritan returned to Jessamine, who was making sure to keep her distance.

'He's harmless but when he gets frightened he has a tendency to lash out.'

'Thank you.'

'What did you want anyway?' He took in her coat, bag and shoes. 'You lost?'

'I'm looking for someone. Queenie O'Leary?'

He scanned Jessamine up and down, as though he was trying to decide whether or not to trust her. 'Most days you'll find her over on the bench by the rose garden.' He motioned to a bank of flowerbeds on the opposite side to where they stood. 'She likes to watch the birds.'

Jessamine thanked him for his help and made her way over to the roses. Just as he'd said, a woman was sitting on a bench tossing tiny bits of bread to the sparrows at her feet.

She must have been no more than thirty but she seemed older. Her face was bloated, the skin on her hands dry and sun-thickened.

'Queenie? Queenie O'Leary?'

The woman looked up and blinked. The whites of her eyes were yellow and shot through with veins.

Jessamine sat next to her. Up close she could smell alcohol mixed with urine and sweat.

'I'm not doing anything wrong.' The woman sat up a little straighter. 'I'm allowed to sit here.' Her voice had an addled, sleepy quality. It was a like a slowed-down tape recording, each word stretched wide from vowel to consonant.

'I wanted to ask you a few questions about an old friend of yours.' Jessamine showed her the photograph. 'I think you knew her as Rowena?'

Queenie continued throwing bread to the birds. Jessamine felt the slouch of disappointment. She'd thought that finding Queenie would be the hard part, that after she'd tracked her down it would be a simple matter of asking questions and listening to the answers. She'd never considered the possibility that Queenie might not be able to respond to her. She was scrabbling around for an alternative – maybe she could go back to Erin, ask her for some other names – when Queenie spoke. 'She said they'd come looking for her.'

'When did she tell you this? Have you seen her recently?'

Queenie ran her thumb tenderly against Cassie's cheek in the photograph. 'She gave me some money.'

Cassie had got in touch with Erin, whom she hadn't seen since she was a teenager, and now it seemed she'd also tracked down Queenie.

Queenie picked up the photograph and held it close to her face, as if studying it for detail. Then she placed it back on the bench, upside down.

'She told me what happened to the child, the boy. Someone hurt him.'

'She told you about Matteo?' asked Jessamine, trying to make sense of what she was saying. Maybe Luca was involved, after all. 'Queenie, did she tell you about her son? Was her husband hurting her son?'

'She was scared of what they might do to her. She had to go away.'

Jessamine decided to try a different tack. 'How about this?' she said, showing her Cassie's sketch. 'We think it's a room plan. Any idea why this might have been important to her?'

Queenie looked at the picture and, for a brief moment, her expression changed. There was a new clarity to her gaze. Jessamine felt this wasn't the first time she'd been presented with the drawing. But then the clarity was gone. Her eyes rested slackly on the birds.

'He was hiding something. She knew.' She took a thick crust from her bag and started tearing it into tiny pieces that she scattered at her feet. The birds ventured nearer. 'She said there were racing cars. In the wall. That's what upset her the most.'

Jessamine tried to follow what she was saying but it was becoming more and more nonsensical. She got two twenty-pound notes out of her purse, opened Queenie's free hand, placed them inside and gently closed her fingers around the cash. But Queenie was oblivious, still babbling, still throwing crumbs to the sparrows that hopped and bobbed below.

Jessamine

At five fifty Jessamine was rushing along Shoreditch High Street towards Mai, Hampson & Oakes. She needed to get there before the firm closed at six or she'd have to wait another two weeks to see Miguel. Tomorrow he was flying to São Paulo for a yoga retreat, during which he would be uncontactable.

She was almost at the glass cube that marked the entrance when she heard someone shouting her name. She stopped and turned: Dougie was on the other side of the street. She hadn't seen him since New Year's Eve and considered pretending not to notice him when he started weaving through the traffic to where she stood.

'I thought it was you.'

'How've you been?' She looked at the glass doors, torn between common courtesy and not wanting to miss her chance with Miguel.

'You never replied to my texts.'

On the other hand.

'I'm late for a meeting.' She started to move but he stepped in front of her, blocking the way.

'Did I do something wrong? Did I annoy you?' He searched her face, concerned. 'I thought we had fun.' He seemed genuinely hurt.

'It's not that.'

'Then what?'

She looked at the cut and swoop of his jaw and softened. He was a good-looking man. But then she remembered the plod of their conversation on New Year's Eve. 'It's just not a good time for me right now. I'm sorry.'

Platitude delivered, she said goodbye and went inside.

The receptionist had already turned off her computer and was putting on her coat. After a minute or so of pleading, she took pity on Jessamine, showed her to Miguel's office and left.

He stood up from behind his desk. 'Miss Gooch.'

Sporting a shirt, hacking jacket and a pair of jeans, he was a little less well put together than at their last meeting. There were dirty marks on his cuffs and creases in the underarm of his jacket.

'Thanks for fitting me in at such short notice.'

He held out his hands and shrugged. 'You said you had something you wanted to show me?'

She reached in her bag for the diagram. 'The woman who was calling you, Cassie Scolari. I found this in the back of her diary, I couldn't figure out what it was but a few days ago one of my listeners suggested it might be a room plan.'

She handed it to him and, after studying it for a few moments, his mouth twitched. A whisper of a smile. Keeping hold of the sketch he went over to one of the shelves containing the brown cardboard tubes. He bent low, his fingers dancing across the writing on the white plastic bottoms, selected one and pulled it out with a flourish.

'Let's see.' He popped the white plastic end from the tube, pulled out a sheaf of rolled-up drawings and spread them across his desk. 'I thought so.' He pointed at a drawing in the top right-hand corner. 'Here.'

Jessamine looked at the collection of lines and shapes, trying to understand.

'This is one of my original plans for a very high-profile renovation I did back in 2003.' He placed Cassie's diagram next to the corresponding section. 'This is the second floor. For some reason, your woman sketched this part of it.'

Jessamine felt her pulse quicken. 'Which building?'

'You know it well,' he said, his eyes twinkling. 'Broadcasting House. In 2003 we were the firm charged with renovating and reconfiguring the place. We demolished this clumsy post war-extension and replaced the sloped roof.'

'What?' Jessamine was aghast. 'Why would Cassie be carrying around a sketch of Broadcasting House?'

'That's not the main question here.' Miguel brought forward another drawing from the tube. 'This sketch matches up to my original plans for the building. See? But those rooms were only configured like that for a short time, a few weeks at most. Once the walls were up the top brass came in for a look around and decided it wasn't going to work. We had to change the whole layout at the last minute. Very frustrating.' He pointed to the second version of the architectural plans. Jessamine recognised the dimensions of the studios and meeting rooms she'd frequented for the last eleven years. 'Your missing woman knew what the place looked like before those changes were made, and the only way she could have known that was if she'd somehow had access to the initial plans, which is unlikely, or if she was actually there, in the building, while the work was being done.'

Jessamine did the maths. 'But that means she would have to have been there when she was – what? Thirteen, fourteen?'

'Like I said,' said Miguel, 'that's the question.'

Monday 30 January

Present day

Jessamine

Six thirty a.m., and Jessamine was in a lift with Jitesh, on her way up to the second floor of Broadcasting House. The early start had been her idea. Still on suspension, technically she wasn't allowed to be there. This way Jitesh could sign her in and out while the place was still relatively quiet.

She'd come to take a look at the section of the building Cassie had sketched in her diagram. She already knew it well, having worked in and around this particular floor for years, but today she wanted to try to view it through fresh eyes in case something might help her figure out how Cassie had come to be there as a teenager. Not only that. Leaving Miguel's office last night, she'd remembered something one of the parents had said that day in the playground at Matteo's school. The dad with the two sets of twins. Cassie had gone on a school trip to the BBC earlier in the year, and when she had entered Broadcasting House she had got upset and started acting bizarrely. It was too much of a coincidence. The two had to be connected.

Luca had been brought in for questioning the night before. Marnie had done as Jessamine asked and made a statement about what had happened to her as a teenager and what she believed still to be happening to the young girls in his care. Luca's mother, Matteo's grandmother, had flown over from Rome immediately. Jessamine had found it a small comfort to know that Cassie's son would not end up as she once had, in the care of the state.

As the lift doors opened Jitesh handed her a sheaf of A4. 'The l-l-logs you asked for.'

Miguel had told her that although the BBC had relocated most of their shows during the 2003 renovation, they had managed to keep a few studios in play. He'd also been kind enough to track down the dates when the walls had been in that particular configuration. Curious to know what had been recorded during the time period in which Cassie must have been present, Jessamine had asked Jitesh to search the bookings archive.

She scanned the printouts. It seemed that *In Our Time* and a variety of World Service and pre-recorded Radio 2 specials had continued to operate out of the main building throughout the construction work. Jessamine ran her finger down the page, searching for the dates in question. The log listed the producer and presenter or DJ involved in each show. One name in particular stood out.

'Oh.' Jessamine had been holding the paper up close to her face but now, repulsed, she moved it to arm's length.

'I-I-I know.'

'Him.'

Jitesh nodded.

They crossed the open-plan area and headed for the relevant corridor. The studios and meeting room were empty so Jessamine was able to set about comparing Cassie's diagram against the current layout without bothering anyone.

Miguel had explained how, in the original plans, there had been only one dividing wall between the two studios. The builders had erected the wooden frames and plasterboard accordingly but they had been up for just a few weeks when the project manager decided to tear them down and replace them with a new configuration that accommodated two much smaller studios, a meeting room and a voice-recording booth.

At some point during that time, a fourteen-year-old Cassie had been in the building and sketched the original layout. And now it transpired that in the same period a DJ had been recording a show here, a DJ known to have been a cruel and prolific sexual predator.

She looked again at the two studios. She knew one well, having recorded many of her shows there. It contained the bronze bust of Lord Reith. Cassie had denoted the bust on her diagram with a face. Miguel said that the bust was a hangover from the original building layout, and that although its position in the studio was inconvenient and incongruous they had decided to leave it where it was for fear of damaging its fragile marble plinth.

The X Cassie had marked on her map corresponded to a point on the wall directly behind the bust.

'When I showed Queenie Cassie's map she started talking about a man. She said he was hiding something. That he had done something to upset Cassie.'

Cassie's friend Erin had mentioned the circles they moved in. Had the DJ on that booking log brought Cassie here and abused her on the premises? Was that what Queenie had been referring to? Was that why Cassie had become so distressed when she'd revisited the building years later, as a grown woman?

'W-w-what are you thinking?' asked Jitesh.

Jessamine shoved the booking log into her bag, ready to leave. The building was starting to fill with people. She wanted to go before her presence was noted. 'Honestly, I have no bloody idea.'

2003

Rowena

I spend the afternoon in my room, doing the same thing I've done every day since that night at the birthday party: sipping vodka and texting Millie. She doesn't reply. She never does. I tell myself it's because she's gone back to boarding school.

Leo called yesterday, two weeks after he'd found me elbow-deep in cake at his breakfast bar. He told me that, if he had anything to do with it, he'd never lay eyes on me again, but that someone had asked that I be there tonight. Someone important. He said that, as a favour, he'd agreed to bring me along one last time. Then he wanted me gone for good.

By the time he arrives to pick me up I'm well on my way to being drunk. I stumble into the back of the car, lie flat on the seat and close my eyes. He's never been a big one for conversation on our way to and from places but today there's something deliberate about his silence. It makes the journey into London feel longer than usual. We seem to go across roundabout after roundabout and soon I start to feel sick.

I can feel the vodka sloshing around in my belly. I breathe through my nose and try to distract myself by looking at the mess scattered near my head. There is a copy of Millie's new favourite book, Northern Lights, *an empty water bottle, a tennis ball and the usual scrum of parking tickets, pens and scraps of paper.*

I pick up the Philip Pullman. Millie's name is written inside. In its first week of release she read it twice cover to cover. I notice that the corner of page 240 is folded over. It seems she's reading it for the third time.

I grab a pen and one of the pieces of notepaper sliding around under my head and put them in my pocket. Millie won't reply to my text messages so I'll write her a letter instead. Tonight, in the bathroom at the party. As soon as I get a few minutes to myself. Then, on the way home, once I'm back in the car, I'll hide it in her book. Page 241.

I have no idea what I'm going to write, what I might say to bring her back to me, but I enjoy the thought of her finding the note the next time she picks up the novel. Her smile, at the surprise, at the words I'll leave for her to find.

Thursday 2 February

Present day

Jessamine

For the second time in a week Jessamine clipped a Broadcasting House visitors' pass to her jacket and went to wait by the lifts. Standing next to *The Sower* she looked at the statue's hand, thrust into the pouch of seeds around his waist, and felt for her own pumpkin seeds, now a permanent fixture in the depths of her coat pocket.

The lift dinged open and, taking a breath, she stepped inside. Yesterday, after weeks of waiting, she'd finally got the call she'd been waiting for. The BBC had made a decision about her future at the corporation. HR had asked if she could come in at her earliest convenience. Judging by their tone, the news wasn't good.

Not wanting to catch the eye of any of her fellow passengers she made sure to keep her gaze directed at the floor. She needn't have worried. They were all too busy looking at their phones to waste time gawping at a disgraced radio journalist. She was grateful, and as they began their ascent, she said a small prayer in thanks to Steve Jobs.

A tap on the shoulder.

'W-w-what are you d-doing here?'

Jitesh.

She appraised the ten or so BBC staff surrounding them. They might have been engrossed in their phones but she knew how they worked: any whiff of gossip and their ears would prick up. Jessamine decided to throw caution to the wind. So what if they heard? They'd know her fate soon enough.

'I think I'm about to be fired.'

A ripple travelled through the group. Some opted for a furtive glance. Others were more brazen and abandoned scrolling Twitter in favour of staring at a lamb on the way to slaughter.

Jessamine and Jitesh registered the shift in atmosphere with a shared smile.

They reached the second floor and the doors opened to reveal Giles from HR and Faye, the union rep. Jitesh followed her out. 'M-m-m-maybe I'll see you at the weekend.'

Giles and Faye looked from Jitesh to Jessamine, confused.

'Saturday? I could do with the company. Sarah's on a school trip. I'm going to the Passport Office after I'm done here. Hers has expired. I was supposed to do it ages ago – she's very cross I've left it till the last minute.'

Giles from HR tugged at the lanyard around his neck.

'Sch-school trip?'

'When you're quite ready,' said Giles, guiding Jessamine down the corridor, 'Kimmy is waiting.'

Rowena

We're in the flat in the big square. It's an odd crowd tonight, all fake laughter and jittery hand movements. There's no sign of Queenie or Erin and I don't recognise any of the other girls or boys. Leo said someone asked specially for me but none of the men seem interested.

I slide my finger into my back pocket and feel the paper and pen. I wonder what I should write in my note to Millie. I want to tell her I miss her and ask her if we're still friends.

I'm working my way round the flat, stealing drinks wherever I can, when the celebrity and his brother arrive. This is the second time I've seen them, and as soon as they enter the room the atmosphere changes. It's like the feeling that comes just before a thunderstorm. It makes the hairs on my arms stand on end.

The celebrity is wearing a pale blue polo shirt and white linen trousers, an arrangement of brightly coloured love beads around his neck. The polo shirt is made out of the same soft jersey material used to make Babygros and clings to his arms and upper body. Despite the mild weather, his brother is wearing a woollen coat, its fleece collar a grubby, bobbled white.

Leo approaches them. 'How are you?'

The celebrity has a mouth full of chewing gum. The sound of it against his teeth makes a soft, clacking sound. 'You know. Up and down, round and round, back and forward.'

'Oh,' says Leo, clearly not sure what to make of this.

'More importantly, how are you?' He reaches inside his mouth, removes the gum and starts rolling it around his thumb and forefinger.

'I'm good, I think. Yes, good.'

'Marvellous,' says the celebrity. The chewing gum is now a ball of white. He holds it up close, considers it, and then, with a neat flick of the wrist, he

launches it onto the floor in the corner. He reaches in his pocket for a fresh stick of gum, opens it and pops it into his mouth. I sniff the air. His gum smells of strawberries, sweet and fresh. I like it.

'I've not had the best day, truth be told,' he says. Everyone in the room gathers round. They form a circle and hang on his every word. 'Been recording a new show. For the radio.' His mouth is like a machine-gun, pow-pow-powing his words into our ears. 'Thirty years I've worked for those people. But do they treat me with any respect?' He says each word with such individual emphasis that it's easy to forget it's part of a complete sentence. 'I turn up to do my bit and what do I find? Chaos. The place was a bloody building site.' No one can tell if he's joking, whether they should laugh, if this story is nothing more than the build up to a punchline. 'They're changing the place. Modernising.' He says the last word in disgust. 'Dust everywhere.' He brushes at the knee of his linen trousers as if to rid himself of the dirt still there. 'Time was I had my own trailer. Right outside the front door. My own sofa.' He winks at the girls in the circle. Drops his voice. 'My own bed.' A few laugh. 'Not today. And after everything I've done for them.' There is a new force to his words. 'No. Bloody. Respect.' The circle, who until now had been enjoying this brush with fame, pull back a little. He senses the change in mood and, with a quick shake of his shoulders, his grin is back, his teeth gapped and yellowing. 'So many beautiful ladies here tonight.' He grabs the hand of the girl next to him and kisses it. His mouth lingers against her skin and his tongue darts out, small and pink. He licks her once across the knuckles.

I decide now is the time to write my note. The celebrity being here is the perfect distraction. I go to the bathroom but the door is locked. I plan to try again later and am about to return to the living room when I notice another door, opposite the bathroom. The cupboard. I opened it once by mistake at a previous party and was greeted with a shallow space containing a vacuum cleaner, a mop and an ironing board. More than enough room for me to sit on the floor and compose my letter to Millie in peace. All I need to do is keep the door cracked open and I'll have light by which to write.

I check the entrance to the living room and, once I'm certain no one is looking, I turn the handle. I move to step inside but then I stop. Billy is crouched on the floor next to the vacuum. Playing on his Game Boy, he is wearing a T-shirt, shorts and navy sandals, the front straps decorated with three tiny racing cars, one red, one yellow, one green. His toes are dirty, the underside of his nails caked with grime. He sees me and smiles, as though I've just discovered him after a long game of hide and seek. Before I can ask what he's doing there, he crawls between my legs and scurries away.

I wedge myself into the spot he has just left and pull the door to. Inside the cupboard, it's warm and smells faintly of bleach. Almost immediately I start to yawn, the booze taking its toll. I get the notepaper and pen from my back pocket and try to work out how best to begin. There are words printed in black ink across the top of the paper that I hadn't noticed in the car. Millie's address. I've picked up a piece of headed notepaper. It's no matter. I can tear off the top strip once I'm done. I try out a few opening lines in my head, but they all feel wrong. I swallow another yawn and force myself to concentrate. This letter is important. I need to say something she won't be able to ignore, something that will put our friendship back on track. But before long my eyes start to close. I pass out, slumped against the ironing board, the paper in my lap still blank.

When I wake up I'm confused. At some point the door has clicked shut leaving me in darkness. My mouth is dry and my neck hurts from lying at a funny angle. Then I smell the bleach and I remember. I put the notepaper and pen back into my pocket, open the door and walk into the living room. It's empty. Everyone has gone. Including Leo. How many hours have I been asleep?

I look at the sofa and wonder if it would be okay for me to stay here until morning when I'll walk to Paddington and sneak on the first train back to Oxford. If you jump the barrier and hide in the toilets you can travel without a ticket.

Then I hear it. Voices coming from one of the bedrooms.

I move back towards the hall. I can't make out the words but I recognise the machine-gun delivery.

The other voice replies, high and panicky.

I have no idea what's going on but, whatever it is, it doesn't sound good. I decide it's best not to stay here after all and move towards the door.

The voices stop.

I freeze, and after a few seconds I can hear whispering. Again, I creep towards the door. I'm reaching for the handle when I hear someone behind me.

'Where do you think you're going?'

It's him. The celebrity.

He's no longer wearing his polo shirt. His chest is covered with black hair and dotted with moles, his linen trousers scrunched high around his hips. One of the strands of love beads has broken and the remaining string hangs limp and frayed against his collarbone.

'Home?'

He laughs and looks back towards the bedroom from which he came.

'We can't let a young thing like you go wandering the streets in the dead of night. I'll give you a lift, make sure you get back safe.'

He goes back into the bedroom. There is more whispering and then he reappears, his polo shirt back on. His brother follows behind, wheeling a suitcase. I try to remember if he arrived with one but the evening's edges are blurry, the exact sequence of events confused.

The celebrity starts humming a song. Some theme tune I don't know the name of.

My eyes flick to the suitcase but something tells me I should pretend I haven't noticed it and I look away. 'You don't need to give me a lift. I can take care of myself.'

Too late.

He follows my gaze. Then he turns to me and leans in close.

'No, really,' he says, wagging his finger. Up close I can smell his breath, sweet, like strawberries. 'I insist.'

Jessamine

After it was done Jessamine walked out of the controller's office, feeling lighter than she had in years. In the course of her firing there'd been a few sneery remarks about the podcast, followed by some patronising shit about how they wished her every success as an indie broadcaster. They'd told her that *Potentially Dangerous People* would continue with a new host, a perky and much younger journalist named Camilla Medwynter. Strangely, this hadn't riled her because, for the first time in ages, she felt free.

'I'll see you out,' said Giles from HR, hustling alongside her.

'It's okay,' she said, a new spring to her step. 'I know the way. Besides, it would be nice to say a proper goodbye.'

That was a lie. In truth she wanted to take one last look in and around the studio from Cassie's diagram. The one with the bust of Lord Reith.

Giles stiffened. 'I'm afraid that won't be possible.'

Jessamine pretended not to have heard, and as they approached the studio in question she slowed her pace and peered through the glass, hoping to see something new that would help her understand its significance. A sign on the door said it was out of use until further notice, but two people were inside, a man and a woman. The woman was sitting awkwardly behind the microphone, the man leaning over her shoulder, pointing to various parts of the desk. He seemed to be giving her a demonstration of sorts. A lesson. The woman fumbled with a dial and the man placed his hand around her wrist to guide her. Jessamine came to a stop. They both had their backs to the door but there was something familiar about the man's build, the length and heft of his legs.

Sensing he was being watched, the man turned around. He locked eyes with Jessamine, then took a step back, away from the young woman, as if caught red-handed.

Mick.

Next to him was Camilla Medwynter, her replacement.

A knock and she turned to see Jitesh in the studio next door, waving at her from the other side of the glass. He poked his head into the corridor.

'H-h-how did it g-go?'

Jessamine shrugged. 'As expected.'

Giles from HR coughed. 'When you're quite ready.'

Ignoring him, Jessamine looked beyond Jitesh to a man wrestling with a spill of wires coming out of a wall. 'What's that about?'

'Things keep going wrong with this r-r-r-row.'

'Still?'

'We've isolated it to these th-three studios.' He motioned to the one he was in and the two that flanked it. 'Malcolm thinks there must be something p-putting stress on the electrics. He th-thinks he's found a mass in the services duct. Something big. Maybe a mouse nest.'

Jessamine compared Cassie's diagram to the layout, a thought forming. 'Show me.'

'The duct runs the entire length of this s-side of the building.' He indicated a waist-height point on the wall behind him. 'It comes to a s-s-stop around there.' He pointed at the bust.

'I think you cleared your desk on the day of your suspension,' said Giles, trying to get her moving. 'If you left anything behind, or if we find something hidden away that belongs to you, we'll make sure to send it on.'

'What did you just say?'

'I said if you've left something behind . . .'

But she was no longer listening, her focus now on the section of wall behind the bust of Lord Reith.

'Maybe that's it,' she muttered under her breath.

'Jessamine,' said Giles from HR, 'it's time to leave.'

She slammed her hand against the glass making Mick jump. 'Only one way to find out.' Leaving Mick where he was for a moment, she marched into Jitesh's studio and, ignoring Malcolm's open-mouthed stare, started picking up different tools from the floor and weighing them in her hand.

Settling on a claw hammer and a large wrench she came back out to the corridor and turned to the other studio with Mick and the woman inside.

'Jessamine,' said Faye, 'I know you're feeling angry right now and that those feelings may extend to your old work colleagues but, as your union rep, I strongly advise you not to go in there. The terms of your severance package—'

But it was too late.

Jessamine pushed on the glass door and went in. Mick's face was now white.

'I'm calling security,' said Giles, already holding the phone to his ear.

As Jessamine approached, the wrench now held aloft, Mick took another step away from Camilla, and held up his hands, as though in surrender.

'Jessamine!' shouted Faye. But Jessamine paid no attention: she was too set on the task in hand.

Rowena

I follow them down the corridor and into the lift. We make our way to the underground car park and the celebrity leads me to an emerald car.

'Aston Martin,' he says, stroking the bonnet. 'I call her the Green Goddess. She's my pride and joy.'

He opens the passenger door and I climb in. I've never been inside a car like this before. The seats are soft cream leather, the dashboard polished wood and chrome.

I put on my seatbelt. Through the back window I can see his brother, busy heaving the suitcase into the boot.

All done, he squeezes into the back seat while the celebrity takes his place behind the wheel. Before he pulls away he reaches across and places his hand on my knee. He is wearing a gold watch and the metal is cold on my thigh.

'You got any brothers or sisters?'

I shake my head.

'Count yourself lucky.' He locks eyes with his brother in the rear-view mirror. Shakes his head. 'They can be a right royal pain in the arse.'

I try to smile but my head is aching. I want water and paracetamol and something to settle the churning in my gut.

He guides the car out onto the street and soon we are driving through London. We cross a bridge, its sides picked out in lights. In the distance I can see the bulge of St Paul's and the London Eye, its disc bright against the night sky.

'I need to make a couple of stops,' says the celebrity. 'Won't take long. Then we'll have some fun.'

I feel vodka and bile rise up in my throat and have to work hard not to be sick all over the cream leather.

On the other side of the bridge he pulls up at traffic lights and the brother hops out. He rolls down the window.

'So you'll sort it?' asks the brother, his palm against the car roof.

'Don't I always?' says the celebrity, already pressing the button to close the window.

The lights turn green and we pull away. I turn and watch his brother slide out of view. I realise he has left his suitcase in the boot.

We drive on through the centre of town and soon we're on Regent Street. We cross Oxford Circus and the celebrity pulls into a small side road, outside a building covered with scaffolding. On the pavement next to us is a large sign that reads 'No Parking Any Time: Tow Away Zone' and a CCTV symbol.

'Know where we are?' He nods at the building.

I shake my head.

'That trailer. The one with the sofa. We're sat in the same spot where it used to be.' He clocks the no-parking sign, rolls his eyes. 'I helped make this place what it is today and how do they repay me? By replacing me with a younger model.' He mutters to himself, 'No bloody respect.' He turns to me. 'Know what you do when someone doesn't show you respect?' I shake my head. 'You take it back. You remind yourself who's boss.'

He undoes his seatbelt. 'I need to drop something off.' He laughs bitterly. 'A gift of sorts. You wait here and make sure to take care of the Green Goddess while I'm gone.' He wags his finger in my face. 'Or else!' I can't tell if he's joking. He gets out, goes round to the boot and lifts the suitcase onto the pavement. Then he wheels it over to the entrance, pushes on the doors and disappears inside.

Alone in the car I think of the headed notepaper, still blank in my pocket, my chance to leave a letter for Millie now long gone, along with Leo, back to Oxford. I try to work out what do next. It's nearly three in the morning and I'm stranded in the centre of London without any cash and a tiny amount of credit on my phone. I could call Queenie and ask her to direct me to where she lives in Brixton. Or I could wait here for the celebrity to return.

Two knocks on the glass. I jump, and as I lift myself from the seat I feel how the backs of my legs have stuck to the leather. I look out to see a traffic warden peering in. He mimes rolling down the window. I do as he asks.

'You can't park here.' He points at the sign. 'Any car that does is liable to be clamped or towed.' He nods at a truck on the other side of the road, its engine running, the men in the cab waiting to pounce.

'I'm waiting for someone. He won't be long.'

If the celebrity returns to discover his pride and joy has been towed he'll be furious.

'Tough,' says the traffic warden, already filling in a form. 'You're in the middle of a fire route.'

I look to the brown doors, hoping to see the celebrity returning.

'Please,' I say, remembering the flash of anger in his voice at the party. I don't want to know how it feels to have that anger directed at me. 'He's famous.'

The traffic warden stops writing, holds his pen in the air.

'Let me go and get him.' I undo my seatbelt. 'Two minutes.'

'One minute,' he says, returning the pad and pen to his front pocket. 'If you're not back after that, I don't care if this thing belongs to Frank bloody Sinatra.'

I leap out of the car and run over to the entrance. The doors are heavy, the glass patterned with metal. I push my way inside and find myself in a large reception area, apparently untouched by the building work going on around it. The floor is made out of tiny polished tiles, the reception desk flanked by marble pillars. At the top of each pillar and edged around the ceiling there are boxy black and white lights. There are two security guards. They look at me from behind the desk with suspicion. I approach them with a smile. Mention the celebrity by name. Tell them about the traffic warden.

'Can you get him?'

They share a look. Smirk.

'The old dog.'

They laugh.

'Didn't think he still had it in him.'

They talk as though I cannot hear them, as though I am a creature behind glass at the zoo. I start to worry that they're not going to help but then one presses a buzzer and the barrier opens.

'Get him yourself. Second floor.'

Inside the lift there is plaster dust on the floor. The numbers 3, 4 and 5 on the control panel are covered with cardboard and tape. I hit 2 and soon I'm stepping out into a wide corridor. On one side is a series of doors that lead off into small rooms. On the other there is a mess of open space, beams and exposed wires. The space is divided by wooden frames, yet to be covered with plasterboard, the skeletons of future rooms.

I start to panic. Time is ticking by and this place is huge. I don't know where to begin. The whole floor seems deserted. Then I hear him at the other end of the corridor. He is whistling.

I follow the sound down the corridor and around a corner. The whistling is getting louder.

Then I see him.

I'm about to call out when I stop. He is on the building-site side of the corridor. This section is more complete than the other bits I passed. Some of its walls are already in place. Bunches of electrical wiring spew out of feet-, waist- and shoulder-height holes and I can see a large metal duct disappearing and reappearing behind the section of wall that faces out onto the street. A bronze head on a plinth, covered with protective plastic, is the only other thing of note.

The celebrity is on his knees, busy with something in the cavity between the metal duct and the wall. The suitcase is open on the floor nearby, its lid in the air.

A grunt, and he emerges from the hole and goes over to the suitcase. He bends down, as though to pick something up. As he stands up to his full height I see he's carrying a large object. At first I think it's a duvet, rolled like a sleeping bag, and I wonder why he has gone to such effort to bring something like that all the way up here. Then I see them. Two small feet poking out of the bottom end. The feet are wearing navy sandals, the strap across the front decorated with three racing cars: one red, one yellow, one green.

Billy.

I blink and blink again. Trying to make sense of what I'm seeing.

The celebrity fumbles with him for a second and the top of the duvet falls away, revealing Billy's top half. His arms are at his sides, his face grey. His head lolls back and I see a thick red band around his neck. At first I think it's a ribbon and then I realise: it's his skin.

He is dead.

Who did this? The celebrity? The brother? Both of them?

Frightened he might catch me, I take a step back and continue to watch him from behind a corner on the other side of the corridor.

He covers Billy with the duvet and carries him over to the duct. After lifting a thick bunch of wires out of the way, he slides Billy and the duvet inside. Then he starts fixing the walls back into place.

A rumble. He looks up and there it is again. A low, deep sound that seems to surround us. The whip and snap of the tarpaulin that covers the scaffolding outside.

He continues to shove the duvet and Billy forward, deeper into the duct.

I wonder what will happen when Billy is not returned to his children's home tonight. How long it will take them to raise the alarm? But then I remember everything Queenie said about Billy and us and all the other kids that come to the parties. They choose us because they know we have no one to kick up a fuss on our behalf. They know that we don't matter.

I look around, trying to get my bearings. Standing here now, I'm powerless. But later I can go for help. I can kick up a fuss on Billy's behalf. And when I do I'll need to be sure about where I tell them to look. This place is so big and the building site has left everything so messed up. I need a map.

Keeping one eye on the celebrity, I feel in my pocket for the notepaper and pen I'd planned to use for Millie's letter, flatten it on the wall and then, as best I can, I sketch the rough layout of this section of the building. Taking care to mark how the rooms are divided, the position of the various doorways and the position of the plastic-covered bronze head in relation to everything else, I mark the wall behind which the celebrity is, right at this moment, hiding Billy's body.

X marks the spot.

He wedges a piece of metal across the hole he has just emerged from, stands up and slaps the dust off his hands. Then he zips up the suitcase and, after pausing to stick out his tongue and flick Vs at the bronze head, he continues out into the corridor. He is headed right for me.

I shove the map into my pocket and do the only thing I can think of. I take off at pace, making sure to deliberately crash into him, as though I've only just arrived.

'The Goddess,' I say, my voice shaky. 'They're going to clamp her.'

He is startled but he soon recovers.

'Good girl.' His face softens. 'Coming to get me.' He guides me back towards the lift, pulling the now empty suitcase behind him.

I'm terrified but I try my hardest to act normally. The last thing I want is for him to twig.

In the lobby he strides across the tiled floor, whistling under his breath.

We're almost at the door when one of the security guards calls, 'You there. Stop.'

The celebrity freezes. A flicker of worry. He looks through the doors, to where the warden is waiting by the Aston Martin. I think he's going to ignore them but then he fixes his smile and turns. 'Gentlemen.' He nods politely.

I look at the expression on the faces of both security guards and feel a wave of relief. Somehow they know what he's done, they've seen Billy on their CCTV, and now they're going to confront him. Maybe they've already called the police to come and arrest him. I tune into the noise of the passing traffic outside, straining for the wail of approaching sirens.

'Before you go,' says the guard, coming round from the back of the desk. He seems nervous. I understand. He's about to accuse the celebrity, a powerful public figure, a legend no less, of a serious crime. But then, blushing, he holds out a piece of paper and a pen. 'Can I have your autograph?'

I've felt queasy with booze all night and all night I've managed to keep it down. Not any more. Bracing my hands against my knees, I throw up, all over the tile floor. Booze and bile. Some of it spatters the celebrity's linen trousers. Once my stomach is empty I continue to retch. It's as though my *body wants to turn itself inside out, as though it wants to help me become something else entirely. It's a few minutes before I can pull myself back up to standing. I wipe my mouth on my sleeve, my cheeks wet with tears and sweat. Underfoot I feel a rumble. The first Tube of the day. On its way through the tunnels, somewhere far from here.*

Jessamine

Jessamine barrelled towards Mick and Camilla, and as she got to within striking distance of his head there was a collective intake of breath from Giles, Faye and Jitesh, but then she carried on past him to the bust of Lord Reith. There she stopped and, side-stepping behind the plinth, she pulled out her phone and brought up Cassie's diagram.

'The services duct runs behind the wall here, right?'

Jitesh nodded.

Jessamine looked from the phone to the picture, the picture to the phone, comparing the drawing against her current location. Once she was sure, she placed her ear close to the wall, and began to knock. She soon homed in on a spot around hip level and then, using all her might, she lifted the wrench into the air and smashed it hard against the plasterboard. She peered in close, examining her handiwork. Her first effort had left nothing more than large dent. She tutted. Swinging her arm back she smashed the wrench into the wall but this time she didn't stop to check on her progress. Hitting the wall over and over again, she kept at it until finally a small hole started to appear.

By now Mick and Camilla had retreated to the corridor where they joined Faye, Giles, a bewildered Jitesh and Malcolm.

'Keep going and this will become a matter for the police,' shouted Giles over the banging.

But Jessamine was undeterred. Once she had created a largish hole she switched to the claw hammer, using its curved end to pull at a corner of the plasterboard. Before long she'd exposed the wall cavity behind. She pulled the board free, heaved it off and threw it to the floor. The end section of a large metal services duct was now exposed.

'J-Jessamine,' said Jitesh, approaching her gently. 'W-w-what are you doing?'

She stopped to wipe the sweat from her forehead. 'We know Cassie sketched this place for some reason, right?'

'Right.'

'That it was important to her.'

'Right.'

'We thought it was because something bad happened to her here, when she was a teenager. That maybe this was the location in which she was once abused.'

Inside the wall cavity she leaned across the large metal duct and started bashing the vent that capped off the end of the duct, trying to dislodge it.

'Queenie said Cassie ran away because she knew someone was hiding something.'

A commotion in the corridor. The thump and scuffle of security guards arriving. They stepped inside and two of them approached her warily.

'Put down the hammer, Miss Gooch.'

She looked up and blinked, trying to focus. When she realised who they were she laughed. 'Oh, don't be so ridiculous,' she said, and carried on with what she was doing.

'If you don't put the hammer down we'll have to forcibly restrain you.' They were moving closer to her, but Jessamine wasn't fazed.

'Malcolm's right. There is something pressing on the electrics, something that's been there for over a decade.'

She got down on her knees and reached inside the duct. Above her, the bust of Lord Reith looked on, his forehead high and wide.

'I thought Queenie was talking nonsense. I was wrong. What she was saying, what she was trying to tell me, made complete sense. I just wasn't listening properly.'

The security guards signalled to each other and then they pounced. Taking one leg each they grabbed Jessamine and pulled her away from the wall cavity. But as she emerged from the duct they saw that she had brought something with her. A crumbling roll of fabric. She pulled it into her lap and something brown and withered slipped out and onto the studio carpet. The security guards recoiled in horror.

'Queenie wasn't talking about someone hiding something that had happened, she was talking about *some thing*. A physical thing.' She considered the mummified feet and toes now poking out of the bottom of the fabric, only just identifiable inside a pair of small sandals. 'Whoever "he" was – and, thanks to those production logs, I've got a pretty good idea – Cassie saw him hiding a body.'

2003

Rowena

I make my way along the towpath. To my left is the canal, the water still and black. To my right is the embankment, thick with cow parsley. It has spent all summer growing onto the path and it's impossible to avoid the tickly overhang of its white flowers.

I pick up the pace. I am to meet Leo under Duke's Cut, a bridge a short way from here. In my back jeans pocket is the map I drew marking the location of the body. I'm going to show it to him and he's promised we'll come up with a plan about how best to tell the police. He agrees, it doesn't matter how famous they are, we have to make sure the people responsible for Billy's murder are brought to justice.

I pass a lock. The water level on the other side is much lower. Metal ladders fixed to the wall start to appear at regular intervals. They have the same looped white handles you use to climb down into the deep end at the swimming pool. I guess they're there to help the people on boats come ashore. Ahead is a small bridge. A couple pass underneath and, although they aren't talking loudly, it amplifies their voices and the sound echoes into the air.

I've decided that after this is over I'm done. No more parties, no more men. Most importantly, no more booze. No matter how much it dulls the edges. I've seen what it can do to people, what it's starting to do to Queenie.

I saw her last three nights ago when the celebrity dropped me off outside her Brixton flat. Throwing up like that turned out to be the best thing I could have done. It meant he drove me there without so much as a squeeze of my thigh. It took a while to wake her. I thought it was because it was so late but when she let me inside I saw the stuff on her night table. Empty vodka bottles, old squares of foil, blackened in the middle. That was why I hadn't seen her around these last few weeks. We crawled into her single bed together and while she stroked my hair I told her everything: about the celebrity, about Billy and his racing-car sandals. Just before we fell asleep I made her promise not to breathe a word to anyone, to keep it secret until I could go to the police.

The canal bends round to the right. I follow the curve and then I see it. Duke's Cut. A bulky concrete bridge with a road on top. Its mouth gapes blackly. A car crosses overhead and the splash of its headlights illuminates Leo on a bench below. Facing the opposite direction, he is talking to someone on the phone.

'She's not here yet.' His voice sounds odd. At first, I put it down to the echo. 'No . . . Yes, I know that.' The clouds clear away from the moon and for a brief moment his wrist glints. A bracelet with a nameplate. 'I'll call when it's done.'

I stay where I am, hidden by cow parsley.

The man waiting for me is not Leo.

He finishes the call and I watch as he looks around, searching the gloom. He fiddles with something in his jacket pocket and then he slides the edge of it out into the light. A thick black handle, the hammer poking out of the back like a shark's fin. I recognise it immediately. Sunny has brought his gun.

I rack my brain, trying to understand what is happening. Leo has sent Sunny in his place. He lied. He doesn't care about Billy hidden in the wall: all he cares about is himself, his reputation, his career.

Sunny gets up from the bench and starts prowling beneath the bridge. I search the dark for an escape. I could scramble up the embankment to the road but it is steep and the noise is bound to alert him to my being here. I consider my only other alternative. The canal. A few paces back I passed one of those ladders. Slowly, I retrace my steps and, once Sunny is looking the other way, I grasp hold of the white metal handles, place my foot on the first rung and climb down, into the water.

I submerge my leg all the way up to my calf. It is freezing. I keep going, lowering myself in until only my head and shoulders are left above the surface. Shivering, I keep hold of the ladder and press my body in close to the slimy moss-covered wall. Below the water I can feel the weight of my sodden jeans and trainers and think of my map, ruined in my back pocket.

Above my head I hear footsteps. Sunny.

The ladder is rusted. Some of its bolts have worked their way out of the stone.

He spits.

'Waiting here for hours.'

It sounds like he's directly above me.

'Like his bloody errand boy.'

I pray he doesn't look down. My shivering is violent and I have to squeeze my jaws together to stop my teeth chattering.

He waits a little while longer. It must be only a few minutes but it feels like for ever. My legs and feet are numb.

He spits again and I hear an electronic beep. His phone.

'She's still not here.' A beat. 'Maybe she changed her mind.'

Finally he walks off. I listen to his footsteps getting quieter. Silence. He's gone. Still, I wait a few minutes more before hauling myself out of the canal. I drag myself onto the path and then, water pouring from my clothes, I scramble up the embankment, tearing at the cow parsley, until I reach the road. I look back at the towpath where I've just been. I follow the curve with my eyes, towards the direction Sunny was heading. I blow him kisses, one, two, three for luck, and then I start to run. I'm going to disappear. Somewhere they can't find me. Somewhere he and Leo won't know to look. Not now not ever.

Tuesday 7 February

Present day

Jessamine

It was almost midnight when an exhausted Jessamine got out of an Uber and climbed the five steps to Dougie's block of flats. She checked the text message he'd sent inviting her to dinner back at the start of January, buzzed the corresponding door number and slumped against the wall.

Her last eight hours had been spent at the police station, giving a statement about the afternoon's bizarre sequence of events. As she'd left Paddington Green she'd known that, although she wanted to go home, she was too restless for sleep.

A click and the intercom crackled to life.

'Hello?' His voice was groggy.

'It's me. Jessamine. Can I come up?'

A beat.

'I thought it wasn't a good time,' he said, quoting her platitude back at her.

She cringed. On the way here, in the back of the cab, she'd imagined this exchange differently. In her version, Dougie would be sleepy but intrigued to find her on his doorstep, and then, once he understood her intent, delighted at her spontaneity.

She'd been mistaken. She'd arrived unannounced, uninvited and, worse, she'd woken him up. She was gripped by a terrible thought. Maybe he already had someone there.

'I just . . . it's just.' She took a step back. She was such an idiot. Arrogant too. She'd ignored him for weeks and now, on a whim, she'd decided to look him up. 'Maybe I should go.'

Another beat. She was about to retreat down the steps when she heard a metallic clunk. He'd unlocked the front door.

She went inside, made her way up to the third floor, turned the corner and there he was, shivering in his boxer shorts.

'To what do I owe the pleasure?' he asked, blinking against the light. His hair was flattened on one side, his eyes bruised with sleep. 'Everything okay?'

Everything was far from okay but she'd spent the entire afternoon talking, first to her employers about her termination from the job she'd held for the last eleven years and then to the police.

She had not come here for the conversation.

Earlier, uncertain what time she'd be finished, she'd arranged for Sarah to spend the night at Paris's house. It meant that, if she wanted to, she could stay out all night.

She moved in close until their faces were almost touching and then she reached out her hand and brought his mouth to hers. He tasted of beer and toothpaste. She felt for his chest and smoothed her palm down the ladder of his ribcage. His skin puckered with goosebumps. She dropped her hand lower, feeling for him through his shorts. His breath quickened. He stopped kissing her and held his mouth near to hers so that, for a few moments, they were sharing the same air. Pushing her coat away from her shoulders, he reached inside her shirt and slid his thumb inside her bra. Finding her nipple he circled it slowly, then pulled her inside the flat and kicked the door shut.

Jitesh

Jitesh finished the last of his cornflakes and tried to figure out what yesterday's events meant to the search for Cassie Scolari. Did the body Jessamine found have something to do with the woman's disappearance or were the two things entirely unconnected? He tried to focus but his mind kept drifting, just as it had done yesterday in that police interview room, to a comment Jessamine had made about her daughter, Sarah.

At the time it had jarred, although he didn't know why. Then, when she'd started tearing at the wall with a claw hammer, he'd forgotten about it. But this morning, in bed, he'd remembered and now he was able to pinpoint what had bothered him so.

The day he'd overheard Sarah on the phone she'd talked about getting her passport renewed. She'd said she'd hassle her mum into doing it under the pretence of needing it for a school trip. Sarah was lying to her mother, he was sure of it. But why? Where was she planning to go and with whom? And why did she need to keep the trip a secret from her mum?

Upstairs in his room he closed the curtains and opened the laptop. It took him half an hour to get into Sarah's social media. At first, the contents of her Messenger seemed to suggest she was involved with an older man. But then, as he read the exchanges in more detail, his blood ran cold. It was all so much worse than he'd first thought and, in recent weeks, it seemed things had started to escalate.

He was so immersed in the task at hand that it took him a while to register his father was at the door.

'You have a phone call.'

He checked for his iPhone. It was right there, next to his laptop.

'The landline,' said his father, heading back downstairs.

Jitesh came down to discover the cordless handset on the hall table. He put the phone to his ear.

'H-hello?'

'Jitesh?'

'M-Meera?'

'Hope you don't mind me calling.' She sounded upset, her voice small and quiet. 'I got your number from my dad.'

A flicker of dread. Had something happened with Kishor? 'Are you okay?'

'Not really.'

The dread grew stronger. He'd failed to protect her. He should have told her the truth, explained exactly what she was getting herself into.

'After that night at Kishor's birthday I kept thinking about what you said.' She paused. 'I looked up Shanae's Facebook. Saw the tributes.' Her voice caught in her throat. 'Jitesh, what did he do?'

Relief. Meera was okay. She was distressed because of what she'd learned, not because of something Kishor had done. But his respite was short-lived. Now he had to decide whether or not to admit to his own role in Shanae's demise, to explain how, ultimately, he was responsible for her death.

The day after he'd found the recording of Shanae and Kishor having sex on Kishor's computer he'd approached Shanae in the corridor at school. He'd thought she'd want to know, that she'd report Kishor to the police. He couldn't have been more wrong.

'Why are you telling me this?' Her face was red.

'S-so you c-c-can do something about it.'

A group of boys across from where they stood laughed at some joke that was nothing to do with them and she flinched, suddenly paranoid. 'I don't want to.'

'B-b-but it was wrong. We need to tell a t-t-teacher or the p-police.'

'It's embarrassing enough as it is. Reporting it will make it ten times worse.'

'B-b-but—'

'It's my choice. You have to promise you won't say anything.'

'Sh-Shanae.'

'Promise.'

What else could he do? He promised. He had no idea how much he'd live to regret it.

The next day Shanae wasn't at school. Same on Wednesday. On Thursday he'd come across her in the queue by the common-room vending machine and watched as she fed it some coins and retrieved a packet of crisps. Then she'd just stood there, staring at the packet, as though she wasn't sure what to do with it. When he saw her in the weeks that followed she no longer dragged her fencing kit in her wake.

He'd heard the news the morning of his first A-level exam. One of the other parents from school called his mum. Shanae had killed herself. Pills. No note.

After that his memories were patchy. He must have gone to school, sat his exam and answered all the questions correctly, if his stellar results were anything to go by, but it was all a blank. As were the weeks that followed. It wasn't until his final exam that he seemed to wake up. He'd emerged from the school into the sun and seen Kishor punching the air, triumphant at having finished his last paper. Kishor felt no sadness, no responsibility about what had happened to Shanae. Jitesh felt the oppo-site. If he hadn't alerted her to the existence of the video, if he hadn't promised to keep quiet, she might still be there.

While his friends had gone to celebrate at the pub he had made his excuses and gone home, up to his room. An online tutorial showed him how to fashion a noose from the belt on his dressing-gown. Then he hanged himself from the hook on the back of his bedroom door. His father had found him just in time.

Jitesh's hand went to his neck. The bruising beneath his ears and at the corner of his jaw was long gone. Still, he touched the area gingerly, as if afraid of causing himself pain.

'Jitesh, you still there?' asked Meera.

He'd yet to tell anyone the truth about Shanae and why he'd done what he'd done. Not his parents, not Marty, not anyone. He was too ashamed. It would be a relief to say the words.

'Yes,' he said. 'I-I'm here.'

Jessamine

Jessamine stepped under the shower, closed her eyes and lifted her face to the water. She chose a shampoo from Dougie's random collection of bottles and as she washed her hair she was smiling. Despite everything that the last six months had thrown at her – her break-up with Mick, Tasha's murder, her suspension and then finally, yesterday, being fired from a job she'd loved – here, now, under this shower, she could feel the beginning of something that just might, at a push, be described as happiness.

Yesterday.

She thought again of the crumbling duvet she'd found behind the wall and shuddered. An autopsy would take place later this afternoon but, until then, the general consensus seemed to be that the constant flow of cold air through the services duct had mummified the body over what was almost certainly a period of years. The persistent technical problems in that row of studios had been caused not by mice or dodgy wiring, as was previously thought, but by the corpse collapsing down onto the circuits. The autopsy would also confirm if the person she'd found was male or female but the size of the corpse was unambiguous. Someone had sealed the body of a child inside the walls of Broadcasting House.

She turned, letting the hot water needle at the muscles in her shoulders. Determining the gender of the child was one thing but whether or not they'd ever be able to figure out who the kid was or what had happened to them remained to be seen, especially as Cassie Scolari was the key: she had seemed to know the corpse's location.

The police would want to talk to Jessamine again at some point in the next few days. Meanwhile *Went/Gone* would continue at pace. She'd talked over her plans with Dougie last night in bed. Told him how she planned to drive out to Berkshire today and explore the area in which Cassie's phone had been turned on some thirteen days after she went missing. He'd helped her figure out the best place to park in relation to the coordinates the detective had given her. Although she knew there was likely to be nothing there, other than motorway and a few fields, it was one final thing she wanted to tick off her list.

Jessamine had her head tipped forward, rough-drying her hair with a towel, when she thought she heard her phone. She stopped, trying to isolate the sound, but it was hard to make out anything over the noise of the extractor fan. Was it coming from the flat next door? If it was her phone it was probably Sarah, calling to check in before she left for school. She wrapped the towel around herself and smoothed her hair away from her face. She'd call her back, then go home, change and be on her way to Berkshire.

In the bedroom she saw that Dougie was still asleep, the duvet tangled around his abdomen. He slept naked, and in the dim morning light she could just make out the dark trail of hair that connected his belly button to his groin.

His continued slumber meant it unlikely that the phone she'd heard had been hers. Still, wanting to be sure, she went to her bag and had just reached inside when she felt Dougie's hand on her waist. Drawing himself up to kneeling, he lifted her hair out of the way and kissed the drips of water that remained on her shoulder blades. The search for her phone forgotten, she dropped her bag and turned to him. He had yet to shower but he still smelt fresh, tart. Like pears, new to the bowl. Sliding his hand underneath her towel, he ran his fingers across her hip. She shivered and he dipped his hand lower. Pushing him back onto the bed, she undid her towel and climbed on top of him. Her knees pressed into the mattress and she felt the sheet where he'd been lying, cold against her skin.

Jitesh

Midday on the Commercial Road. Jitesh parked his dad's Ford estate outside Jessamine's building and got out. He buzzed her flat, and while he waited for her to answer he scanned the horizon for parking wardens.

In the end he'd told Meera everything, about Shanae and the events that had followed. She'd listened and then, when he was done, she'd said he had to stop blaming himself, that none of it was his fault. He wasn't convinced, but hearing her say those things had made him feel better, like a weight had been lifted.

Later he'd returned to the contents of Sarah's Messenger and tried to get hold of Jessamine multiple times on the phone. But despite leaving a voicemail and a follow-up text asking her to get in touch as soon as possible she'd yet to reply. In the end he'd decided to come and seek her out in person. What he knew couldn't wait. He had to talk to her now, today. Not least because, reading between the lines of Sarah's last few messages, it seemed something bad was going to happen imminently, something she might regret.

He buzzed the flat again.

No response. Nobody was home.

He checked his watch. Maybe Jessamine wasn't there because she'd had to return to the police station. The detectives were bound to have more questions. If she was in an interview room, she wouldn't have her phone with her.

He could drive to the police station, ask for her at the front desk.

He was just about to go when the door opened and a woman appeared. She was crying, her hand over her mouth. A man had his arm around her shoulders, comforting her. As they passed, the door remained open for a few seconds and he was able to see through the hallway to a commotion in the central courtyard beyond. Curious, he slipped inside and made his way out to the garden. A small crowd had gathered near a brick barbecue. They were pointing at something. He moved closer.

There on the ground, next to a pot of red geraniums, was what looked like a loop of thin white sausages arranged in coils. Then he saw the blood. A paw, bent at a strange angle. It was a dead cat. It looked to have fallen from a great height, the impact exploding its intestines. The creature's ginger fur was soaked with blood but he could just make out a white patch near the hind legs. It took the shape of a love-heart, perfect and symmetrical. Munchie.

He searched the group by the barbecue for Jessamine, and when he didn't see her there, he peered up to her flat on the fifth floor. He expected to see her looking over the side of the balcony, distraught at the sight of her pet prone in the courtyard. But there was no sign of her or Sarah, who was presumably at school.

Footsteps, and he turned to see the man who'd been comforting the crying woman a few minutes earlier. 'Anyone left a Ford estate outside?'

Taking care not to stand in the cat's remains, Jitesh stepped forward.

'Go now,' said the man. 'You're about to get a ticket.'

Jessamine

Jessamine pulled into the lay-by and got out. Dougie had been right. This was as close as she could get by car to where she needed to be. She'd go the rest of the way on foot.

In the corner of the lay-by a cabin was serving sandwiches and tea. A signpost next to it directed ramblers and dog-walkers through a wooden gate and onto a prescribed path across the fields and beyond. Apart from herself, the woman in the cabin and a man trying to wrestle a muddy spaniel into the boot of a Volvo, no one was around.

She checked the map. The message had been sent from Cassie's phone while it was somewhere within a two-square-mile area. The lack of nearby cell towers and the fact it had been turned on for such a short time meant they hadn't been able to narrow it down any more than that. Jessamine had marked the specifics in black Sharpie. The perimeter formed an isosceles triangle on the page and, just as O'Brien's detective friend had said, the M4 cut right across the top of it. Her plan was to walk this perimeter, then explore the inside of the triangle by cutting into and across it at different points. She had no idea what she was looking for. From everything she'd learned about Cassie, the woman had no connection to Berkshire, let alone this obscure patch of its countryside. The police were probably right. Cassie had composed the message just before she'd disappeared, when she had no connection: it had gone into a queue. Then when the phone was turned back on it had connected to 4G and belatedly delivered it to Marnie.

Monitoring her position with the blue GPS dot on her phone, she went through the wooden gate and set off in the direction of the coordinates that correlated to the bottom of the triangle. In a few hundred metres she'd need to deviate from the path, into the fields to her right.

As she walked, she lifted her face towards the light. The early February air was brisk, but the sun was shining and the snow, which had plagued the country all winter, finally gone. She'd only ever driven through this part of England on her way to somewhere else but now she discovered that the Berkshire Downs were beautiful, all rolling chalk hills fringed by trees and swooping fields that were just starting to green. In the far distance, on slightly higher ground, she could see a large manor house that looked grand and old enough to be National Trust, the River Lambourn flowing in front of it. An arched stone bridge provided the only visible crossing.

She yawned. Last night's antics with Dougie were starting to take their toll. Jessamine Gooch: shattered from too much shagging. The notion made her smile. He'd been so different to how he was on their first date. Intelligent, funny. They'd talked for hours. Before she'd left his flat that morning he'd brought her in for one last kiss, and she'd found herself wondering if, against all the odds, he might turn out to be someone with whom she could make a real go of it.

She reached the point at which she needed to leave the path and veered right. After skidding down a muddy incline, she continued for another three hundred metres north and she was there. Somewhere within two square miles of this spot, on Wednesday, 23 November, someone had, most likely unintentionally, sent a WhatsApp from Cassie Scolari's phone.

Walking the perimeter took nearly two hours. She passed the odd copse of trees or hedgerow, but other than that and the background roar of the M4, there was little of any significance. All done, she began to explore the area inside.

Here, she found a few things of more interest. Some of the fields she walked through showed evidence of digging or excavation. To what purpose wasn't clear. The large patches of mud looked to have been recently filled in, the ground around them littered with scraps of plastic orange netting, the soil imprinted with caterpillar treads. She stopped. Going by the blue GPS dot, she was now slap-bang in the middle of the triangle. She looked around, trying to decide where to look next. To her left was a clutch of trees. Approaching its outer edge, hidden among the beech and oak, she came across a small wooden structure on stilts. A hide. Of course. During the hunting season this part of the country was big on partridge and grouse. She climbed up the ladder and found herself in a dark, crudely constructed space. Two rectangular holes offered a view of the field, the perfect vantage point from which to shoot prey.

Jessamine shivered. Out of the sunshine the temperature was brisk. She grabbed a handful of pumpkin seeds from her pocket and chewed them slowly, thinking. The planked floor was damp and mossy in places, the corners rucked with old leaves. Nothing of note. She tried to imagine Cassie inside here or out there, wandering the Downs. But it was all too random. If there was a reason for her having been in this region Jessamine couldn't see it.

She climbed back down the ladder. She'd done what she came to do and now she was going home to see her daughter and have a much-needed early night. Maybe she'd drop Dougie a text, ask him what his plans were for the weekend.

Before making her way back across the fields to her car, she did one final three-sixty turn. Again, her eye caught on the only thing of any real substance: the house in the distance. She checked the map. Sitting on a promontory of sorts, it was a good two to three miles outside the area in which Cassie's phone had been cell-sited. It wasn't marked as National Trust. A private residence then, or a hotel. Walking there would take another thirty to forty minutes. She'd already come all this way. An extra hour wouldn't make much difference.

She set off at a pace. Before long, the ground began to change, becoming boggy and littered with puddles. Her boots and the bottom half of her jeans were soon sodden and spattered with mud. As she neared the bridge she could hear the river, its melt-water rush filling the air like static. She made her way across, and as she reached the apex, she stopped and looked over the low stone wall. The Lambourn had burst its banks. The swollen water foamed dirty and brown.

Up ahead was the manor house and behind it a bank of low hills, hemmed by trees. Its elevated position meant that anyone looking out of one of its many windows would have a spectacular view of the river and Downs beyond. She crossed the bridge and followed the curve of the path up towards the house. When she was close enough she got out her phone, took a picture, then emailed it and its rough coordinates to Jitesh, asking him to see what he could find on the place. Then she sent the same picture to Dougie and made a joke about having gone off the beaten track and asked him to send out the search parties if she didn't make it back before dark.

She crossed the bridge and followed the curve of the path up towards the house. Circling the garden was a ha-ha, a steep turfed ditch that sloped down to a sunken wall. Forming a boundary between the estate's grounds and gardens, it resembled a dry moat and at one time would have been used to deter grazing livestock. A gravel driveway looped round the front lawn and away to the right of the house, along a road thick with trees.

As she got closer she realised the building was older than she'd initially thought, possibly Elizabethan. A brick battlement ran along the point at which the roof joined the house, and beneath it a vast arrangement of latticed casement windows, the entrance marked by a central stone porch. She noticed two cars parked at the side of the house. Hopefully that meant someone was at home.

Inside the porch she rang the doorbell and waited. The front entrance was most definitely a modern addition to the property, consisting of a pair of French windows, the top two thirds of which were glass. Through them she had a clear view of the hallway. A cantilevered wooden staircase circled up past a series of landings, the first accentuated by a huge stained-glass window depicting a family crest.

A woman appeared on the stairs.

'Yes?' she said, as she opened the door. 'Can I help you?'

Sporting a velvet Alice band, a cardigan and a long tartan skirt, she had immaculate white bobbed hair.

'Sorry to trouble you,' said Jessamine, suddenly conscious of the mud on her jeans. 'This might seem odd, but I'm investigating a missing woman. There's a possibility she may have been in or around this area at some point after she disappeared. I wondered if I might show you her picture, see if you recognise her.'

'A missing woman. How awful.' She fished a pair of reading glasses out of her cardigan pocket and placed them on her nose. Jessamine handed her the picture.

She studied it carefully for a few moments, then shook her head. 'Sorry, no. When was it you said she went missing?'

'Last year, November.'

'Ah.' She pursed her lips, apologetic. 'I only joined the house a short time ago. January.'

'When you say "joined", you mean . . .?' Jessamine left the question deliberately unfinished.

'I'm a housekeeper. The family . . .' Not wanting to be indiscreet, she paused. 'They've needed a bit of extra help of late.'

Jessamine thought of the two cars she'd seen parked at the side of the house. 'Is anyone else at home?' she asked, hoping to be invited inside. 'Maybe I could speak with them.'

'I'm afraid now's not a good time,' said the housekeeper. 'If you leave the picture with me I'll be sure to pass it on.'

'My contact details,' said Jessamine, scribbling her name and number at the bottom of the printout. She thanked her for her time and the woman closed the door, but just before it clicked shut Jessamine heard someone shout from upstairs.

'Minty?' The voice was female. 'I need you. Now.'

The door closed and the housekeeper returned up the stairs from which she'd come. Jessamine remained inside the porch for a few moments, thinking. There was something about the voice she'd heard that bothered her. It was like having a stone in her shoe. Tiny but able to cause great discomfort.

The light was starting to dim. She'd need to get a move on if she was going to make it back to her car before dark. She scanned the grounds one last time. In front of her was the lawn and around it the drive, which led onto a road surrounded on either side by dense forest. At the edge of the lawn was the ha-ha, the sheer drop impossible to see from the house, just as the original landscaper had intended. It was grand and beautiful. A Great English Country House. But it told her nothing about what might have happened to Cassie. Time to leave.

Halfway across the drive she realised why the faceless voice had jarred with her. It was the way the woman had said 'I'. She'd brought the sound up slowly from somewhere deep at the back of her throat, like a bucket being drawn from a well. She'd heard it once before when she'd visited the flat on Gloucester Road. The voice belonged to the woman she'd met there, the nurse.

She stopped, trying to assemble her thoughts.

Cassie had sketched the location of the child in Broadcasting House on a piece of headed paper. The address on that paper had led Jessamine to Oxford, the bed-and-breakfast and then to the flat in west London, where she'd encountered a young woman. Now, while she was exploring the area in which someone had switched on Cassie's mobile, she'd come across the same woman.

She was about to turn back to the house, when she saw two figures appear on the horizon. They were too far away for her to make out their faces, but as they got closer Jessamine could see that it was a man and a girl. The man held her by the arm. As soon as she caught sight of Jessamine the girl started shouting.

At first, Jessamine couldn't make out what she was saying over the white noise of the river. But then, as they drew even closer, Jessamine realised she was screaming the same word again and again. It echoed across the Downs, a clarion call.

'Mum!' shouted the girl. 'Mum!'

Friday 11 November

2016

Rowena/Cassie

I'm at my desk working through a pile of invoices when I hear my mobile. The other one, the one I bought for moments like this.

Millie.

I accept the call.

We haven't spoken in years, not since we were kids. Hearing her voice again makes me smile, and for a second I forget the damage I'm about to do. To her, to her family.

'You sound exactly the same!'

'So do you!'

I first contacted her two weeks ago. In the email I told her I wanted to reconnect but also that I wanted to ask a favour. I was thinking of a career change and wanted to pick her dad's brain on how best to go about finding a way into the civil service. I explained that I'd tried and failed to reach him through official channels and wondered if she might be able to provide a shortcut.

I wasn't sure if she'd remember me, let alone agree to pass on my request, but I needn't have worried. She was delighted to be back in touch and said she'd do all she could to help.

Now on the phone she apologises. We'd made tentative plans to meet today for lunch and afterwards she was going to take me to her dad's office in Westminster. She'd call this morning with the details of when and where. But when it got to one o'clock and I had yet to hear anything I assumed she'd had a change of heart. Now, though, she tells me it's because her plans have shifted. At the last minute her father has had to go to the country for the weekend. He'll still see me but I need to come to him.

I tell her I can't. I'm at work. I ask if we can rearrange for another day and search my bag for my diary but it's not there. I must have left it at home. Millie says she'll check but her father is a busy man. She can't guarantee when she can next get me in. I hesitate. I don't want to miss my chance and, besides, I want to get this over and done with.

The celebrity was finally unmasked as a paedophile and rapist five years ago. A number of people came forward with claims about what he'd done to them, and, after investigation, the CPS felt their case had enough merit to go to court. The celebrity's brother was also implicated. But then the celebrity died. A heart attack. His brother followed soon after, cirrhosis of the liver. The subsequent accounts of the pair's reign of abuse were all the more horrific because I knew they were just the tip of the iceberg.

Still, I held back. I had a new name, a new life that I wanted to protect. Going to the police and telling them my story would have meant admitting that the last thirteen years have been a lie. No matter that I did it to protect myself, to keep myself safe from those who might wish me harm. I broke the law, committed fraud. I was terrified that if they knew this they might take Matteo away, like I was taken from my mum.

But then things started to change. After the celebrity's death I saw it on the news, in documentaries. The police were starting to listen. Despite this, I was worried that my claims would be written off as outlandish, the people involved too powerful ever to be brought to account. I'd gone to the police for help before and it hadn't turned out well.

I agree to meet Millie by the underpass next to Embankment Tube in ten minutes. As I hang up, the pay-as-you-go bleeps and a low-power warning appears on the screen. I usually charge it every morning at work – I can't risk leaving it lying around at home somewhere Luca might find it, but what with the prospect of seeing Millie again I'd forgotten. I put on my coat and go to my boss's office. I tell him I've had a call from Matteo's school. He's sick and they need me to pick him up. He wishes Matteo well and says he'll see me tomorrow.

Outside, I start to walk. I feel almost as nervous about seeing Millie again as I do her father.

Leo.

There's no way he'll have bought my made-up reason for wanting to see him. He must know there's more to it, yet he's agreed to a face-to-face. I'm intrigued. By rights, he should be terrified of what I represent, of what I could do. Then again, he thinks I don't know about Sunny and what he sent him to do that night by the canal. As far as he's concerned, I never turned up. Maybe he thinks he can pay me off or that I have no proof, that it's my word against his. Or maybe it's the opposite: maybe he worries that if he kicks this into the long grass it'll antagonise me, make me do something he may come to regret.

I keep walking. Now and then I catch my reflection in a shop window. Plain but smart, no makeup, my hair tied back in a simple ponytail. I've dressed like this on purpose. Nothing like the teenager he used to know.

It was Raf who helped me disappear. After a few weeks' sleeping rough I went to him, desperate, told him I needed a new start, somewhere Sunny couldn't find me. I expected him to talk me down, to tell me I had to come back to the home, to the system, but instead he put me in touch with a friend of his, a man who'd once been in care just like me. Raf said he owed him a favour and got him to sort me out with a new name, National Insurance number, the lot. He made me a few years older too. Sixteen. It meant I could get a job and a place of my own. I'm still careful. You won't find me on social media and I've never been back to Oxford.

I'm passing Coutts when my pay-as-you-go rings. Millie again, checking I'm on my way. As I say goodbye, the phone switches itself off, the battery dead.

I pick up the pace.

At the end of Villiers Street I turn right and head for the underpass. A black Mercedes is idling on the corner. I open the passenger door and peer inside.

'Rowena?' asks the driver.

I recoil. It's odd, being called by my old name.

'Of course it's her, silly. Who else would it be?'

I look to the back seat. There she is. Millie. She gives me a little wave.

I get in and sit next to her. We embrace awkwardly.

'So good to see you.'

'And you.'

She's lost the extra weight she used to carry around the middle and her once ruddy skin is now pale, almost dishwater grey, but she still wears her jumper tied loose around her shoulders, shirt collar up, and she still seems clean, special somehow, in a way I've never figured out how to replicate.

She smiles brightly. 'Shall we go?'

I nod.

Sarah

Sarah had worked so hard to hold back her tears. Now, though, seeing the figure of her mother in the distance was like a needle pressing against the skin of a balloon. All of a sudden everything seemed to pop.

Sarah began to cry.

They walked to the apex of the stone footbridge, to where her Mum stood waiting, and stopped. Below, the river rushed by.

'Sarah?' Her Mum looked from her to the man and then back toward the house from which she had come. She seemed more confused than concerned. 'What are you two doing here together? Has something happened?' She looked Sarah up and down as if checking for some kind of injury.

Sarah tried to find the words. She'd spent so long imagining this moment, fretting about how to explain what had been going on these past months. Now though, it seemed the matter was going to be taken out of her hands.

It had all started this morning.

She'd been eating breakfast at Paris's house when the man had sent her a message. He'd told her he'd been thinking about their situation and that he didn't want them to have to wait any longer. He loved her and she loved him. Now she'd had her passport renewed, he wanted them to go away together, today.

Her first instinct had been no. It was too sudden. Besides, she'd known for a while that although she wanted to continue seeing him she no longer wanted to do as he'd initially suggested and abandon everything for a life together elsewhere. She would miss her home, her school, her friends. Her mum.

After failing to persuade her over the phone, he'd got upset and asked to see her in person.

'Sarah darling, what's the matter?'

'I told him I'd changed my mind.' Sarah tried to breathe through the hic-cupy sobs now racking her body. 'I tried to tell him, but he wouldn't listen.'

The man stared at her mother. It was almost as though he knew her, as though they shared some secret she wasn't party to.

'I don't understand,' said her mum.

Sarah had stolen away after chemistry. She'd only truanted twice before and both times she'd felt sick with nerves. This time was no different. Back at the flat, Munchie had come to greet her, delighted to have company after her night alone. Nuzzling her hand, she'd weaved around her calves, miaowing to be fed. After filling her bowl with cat biscuits and replenishing her water, Sarah had stood up and surveyed the living room, trying to see it through the man's eyes. This would be the first time she'd ever invited him into her home and the prospect of him coming here left her feeling strangely protective of the place. She tried to tidy up but she'd only got as far as fluffing the sofa cushions when the intercom rang.

'He said you're no good,' said Sarah. 'That there are things you haven't told me. About you, about us.'

Inside the flat, even though he was acting strangely, her heart had leaped at the sight of him. Munchie had transferred her affection to this new person and started weaving in and out of his legs, her tail pressed against his jeans. He'd asked her to pack her things. When she'd refused he'd lost his temper. Stormed out. But Munchie was still hover-ing around his ankles, hoping for a stroke. As he opened the front door he stumbled and trod on her tail. Munchie hissed and jumped up onto the walkway's railing to get out of his way. In all the commotion the cat had lost her footing and tumbled five floors to the courtyard below. He'd been distraught. Begged for her forgiveness.

She went to go to her mother but the man grabbed her arm and pulled her to him.

'Let me go.' In the struggle she felt the underarm of her school blazer rip. 'Please, Dad,' she said, the noun still strange on her tongue. 'You're hurting me.'

Rowena/Cassie

Inside the car it's warm and has that artificial pine smell, like it's just been valeted.

I check the time. It's nearly two o'clock. I normally leave at five to pick up Matteo.

'How long do you think we'll be? My son, I'll need to sort out alternative arrangements.'

'Depends. It's an hour or so's drive. If you get the train you should be back around six.'

I compose a WhatsApp to Marnie, one of the school mums, on my regular mobile, asking her to pick up Matteo from after-school club. I tell her I've had to work late, that I'll collect him from her no later than seven. She's always offering to help so I'm sure she won't mind. Then, wanting to conserve power on my only remaining device, I turn off the phone.

The driver pulls away and heads west, out of the city.

'Are we going to the cottage?'

At the mention of her old house Millie shudders. I'm not sure why, she always seemed happy there.

'We've got a place in Berkshire now. We move between it and our London flat.' Her voice falters and she stops to compose herself. 'Mummy's not well. Hasn't been for some time. She's out of it most days, the medication. Still, she prefers to be in Berkshire as much as possible. She likes the space and the fresh air.' She blinks fast, as though she's trying to reset, and when she speaks again she's back to her bright and breezy self. 'How about you? Tell me everything.' She squeezes my knee. 'I've missed you.'

I take her through the simple facts of my life. Luca, Matteo, our house, my job, and then she takes me through hers: caring for her mum, her horses, hunting, a story about a guy she stopped seeing a while back. The exchange complete, we settle into a comfortable silence.

I watch the fields and trees go by. My hands are trembling so I push them down into my lap and try to prepare myself.

It was an interview Leo did on BBC Breakfast at the end of the summer that had decided it. He was on to talk about a new bike-to-work scheme the government were launching, and the hosts were so nice to him and so respectful, but all I could think was that he didn't deserve their respect and that they and the rest of the world needed to know who he really was. Once it was over I went to the bathroom and threw up my cornflakes. On the way into work that morning I came up with a plan.

In the documentaries I'd seen it was clear that, in historic cases like mine, it often came down to your word against theirs. However, it was also clear that any physical evidence was incredibly powerful, and the more victims involved, the harder the case was to dispute. So before I went to the police I decided to do my homework, to make my case as robust as possible.

I figured the location of Billy's body was the least of it. I had a map, after all. Instead, I focused my energies on reconnecting with the girls who used to attend those parties with me in the early noughties. Luca liked to check my mobile-phone bill so, not wanting him to know what I was up to, I bought a pay-as-you-go.

My first port of call was Queenie. She had been the one person I had confided in about what happened that night with the celebrity and then by the canal. I eventually tracked her down to a hostel in Camberwell. Years of drinking and life on and off the streets had left her in a bad way. She remembered who I was and was happy to see me but she was far from coherent, her mind addled from years of alcohol and substance abuse. Not exactly a reliable witness.

I moved on, seeking out as many of the other girls as I could. It was time-consuming and there was more than one occasion on which I lied and called in sick to work so that I could meet someone in person and try to encourage them to talk. Some turned out to be like Queenie, and one was dead. Others were struggling to cope and often found themselves and their kids without any money for food. Luca monitors my bank account so it was hard to get the cash, but I found a way, borrowing from Matteo's after-school-club fees – I'd pay it back once the story came out – and helped when and where I could. Others were on the game. They were the hardest to persuade. But their testimony was important, and I knew that the more of us there were, the stronger our case would be. I followed a few out onto the streets – turns out there's a roaring lunchtime trade in white-van men and bored lorry drivers by the Kent Medway railway arches – and did my best to convince them. That wasn't without its risks. On one occasion I was talking to a woman when the police pulled up. They did us both for soliciting. I tried giving a false name. After that I made sure to meet them only in pubs or cafés.

All of the women I spoke to were reluctant. Some didn't want the families they had now to learn about their past. Others were worried about not being believed, especially the two who had ended up as prostitutes. I told them I had proof. Something that would be impossible to contest. Eventually three women agreed to come with me to the police.

That was when I discovered my trump card, the location of Billy's body, might not be everything I'd once thought. I started to panic.

We continue on the M4 for another half hour or so before the driver pulls off onto a dual carriageway. A little while longer, a few more roundabouts, and we're in open countryside. The light is just starting to fail when we turn into a narrow bumpy lane, lined on either side by trees, which meet overhead, forming a kind of tunnel. It makes it impossible to see where we are or where we're going. Finally, we emerge onto a gravel drive. To the right is a large manor house. The driver guides the car round to the front door and stops. Millie and I get out and he pulls away, heading back towards the tunnel of trees.

Jessamine

'Dad?'

For a moment, the world seemed to stop. Jessamine shook her head, trying to make sense of what was she was seeing and hearing.

'You?'

The man did as Sarah asked and let her go. She ran to Jessamine and pressed her face into her mother's chest. 'I'm sorry. It was just I wanted to see him.'

Jessamine couldn't take her eyes off the man's face. He blinked slowly, like a person who has just bet big on a horse he knows is fixed to win. 'You're Sarah's birth father?'

He took a step forward. Up close she got a waft of his smell. Like pears, new to the bowl.

'I prefer father, but yes.'

'Are you okay?' She studied Sarah for any signs of bruising and then, when that proved fruitless, for any hint of something else he might have done, something that might not have left a mark. 'Has he hurt you?' She tried to focus on her daughter's features – her throat, her wrists – but images from last night kept invading, clouding her ability to think. 'Sarah, has he hurt you?' she asked again.

'Course I haven't,' said the man. 'I love her. I'd do anything for her. To protect her, keep her safe.' He reached out and tucked a strand of Sarah's hair behind her ear. He turned back to Jessamine. 'Shame the same can't be said for you.'

There it was again. His smell. Fresh. Tart.

Familiar.

A few hours earlier, as she'd leaned in to kiss him goodbye, she'd breathed in that same scent and smiled, savouring it and the night they'd just shared.

Dougie.

The man standing before her, her daughter's birth father.

The man was Dougie.

Jitesh

Jitesh guided his dad's car along the narrow country lane, overgrown bramble bushes and low-hanging beech trees at either side. He reached a particularly tight gap and, slowing down, tried not to flinch at the thump-thump-thump of the branches against the doors.

Ahead there was another potential vantage point. Once more he stopped, got out and scanned the horizon.

The bloke from Jessamine's building, the one who'd saved him from a parking ticket, had told him where to go looking. It turned out that the guy had had a conversation with her that morning in the lobby. She'd told him she was driving out to Berkshire for the day. As soon as Jitesh heard that, he'd known exactly where she was headed. The message from Cassie Scolari's phone had been cell-sited to somewhere in the Berkshire Downs. Jessamine must have decided to go and check it out.

He dialled her number, held the phone to his ear and scanned the horizon for any sign of her. Her phone rang once before the automated message kicked in, telling him the person was not available. It had been the same all day, ever since he'd left that voicemail this morning. Either her mailbox was full or something else was going on.

Jessamine had never mentioned her daughter was adopted, but after reading through Sarah's emails it hadn't taken him long to figure out. Her father had killed her mother, after which Sarah had been taken into the care of the state. Since then, Sarah had never had any contact with her birth family.

Her father had tracked her down via Facebook four months ago, and although at first Sarah had shunned his advances, he had managed to persuade her that he wasn't to blame for her birth mother's death. In long, gushing emails he had said she hadn't died because of him but because of a terrible accident. He had been wrongly accused and imprisoned for her murder. Within weeks he had Sarah convinced of his innocence. Once he had her on-side, the nature of the emails changed. He started talking about how badly he wanted to be back living with Sarah, as a family, and had concocted a plan that involved her leaving Jessamine and coming to live with him abroad where they would not be found.

Behind the trees, the sun was starting to set.

Jitesh was about to get back into the car when his phone beeped with an email. It was from Jessamine. She'd sent him a picture of an old house asking if he could look into it when he got a chance. Strange. She was on email but not answering her phone. He clicked on the photo. It was geo-stamped to a point somewhere outside the cell-sited zone. Google Maps had it down as Maugham House, less than two miles from where he now stood. She'd sent the email twenty minutes ago. She might still be there.

He replied, asking her to call him as soon as possible, and got back into the car. After a three-point turn, he drove back up the lane from which he had come. This time, his speed and lack of care meant that the thump-thump-thump of branches colliding with the metalwork was even louder than before, but Jitesh was oblivious, his focus set forward, on the road ahead.

Rowena/Cassie

The car gone, I wait outside the stone porch while Millie fumbles for her key. I shiver. Away from the city it's cold. Heavy snow is forecast for later this evening.

Before she can locate it the door opens and Leo is there.

Since that appearance on BBC Breakfast I've seen him on TV many times and I've trained myself to be okay with it. Now, though, I understand there is a big difference between facing up to him on the screen and being able to handle seeing him in person. I can't look him in the eye, it's too much, so I direct my gaze to a spot just above his eyebrows. His hair is the same crush of curls, brushed back from his forehead, but the blond has been replaced by a silvery grey. The change suits him. I always thought the original colour plus the curls made him look like a giant baby.

'You remember my friend, Rowena?' says Millie.

He nods.

'She has a favour to ask.' She turns to me. 'I need to check on Mummy. Come and find me when you're done.'

She heads upstairs, leaving us alone on the front step.

This is it.

All the time I spent tracking down the other girls from back then I'd thought I could rely on my map, the sketch I'd drawn marking the location of Billy's body. So, when Matteo brought home a letter asking for parents to accompany the kids on a school trip to Broadcasting House, I saw it as nothing more than due diligence, a chance to refresh my memory. But when I got inside the building, two things happened. One, I was left reeling from the memories it brought back, and, two, the layout had changed. The bust of that old guy was still on the second floor but the arrangement of the rooms and walls around it no longer matched my sketch.

It sent me into a tailspin. When we went to the police I wanted there to be no element of doubt. I looked up the name of the architects that had carried out the renovations, found the main guy and contacted him. He'd been away but I kept calling. His assistant said he'd be back on Monday. He's the last piece of the puzzle, him and Leo, and then I'm done. I'm ready.

'Let's go for a walk.' Leo motions inside, towards the back of the house. 'Stretch your legs.'

A different person might feel worried, going somewhere alone with him. But I know he is not a man who likes to get his hands dirty. I follow him down a corridor and out through a small door. We cross the garden and head through a gate in the wall, over to the hills beyond.

Jessamine

Jessamine had questions but, knowing what she did about Sarah's birth father, her instinct was to stay calm and get her away from him to safety.

She began to guide Sarah towards the house but they had taken no more than a few steps when Dougie ran ahead and planted himself in front of them. He held up his hands. *Mea culpa.*

'Look, I'm sorry, okay?' His hands were shaking. He seemed nervous, like he'd figured out his gamble wasn't going to pay off. 'I was just going to follow you around for a bit. I wanted to know more about who the social had got to look after my kid. But then that day in the restaurant I thought, Why not get to know her properly?'

'Come on, Sarah,' said Jessamine. She made another attempt to leave and this time she managed to navigate her way around where he stood without interference. But they'd gone no more than a few steps when he piped up.

'Sarah's a good kid. She thinks she owes you some kind of loyalty.' His voice wavered and then he paused, as if weighing up what to say next. Jessamine kept walking. That seemed to decide it for him. 'I brought her here because I want her to know what kind of a mother you are.' He'd committed to this new tack, still he sounded unsure, but like he was trying not to be.

Sarah stopped. 'Mum, what's he talking about?'

'I had planned on doing this differently.' He raised his voice but there was a strain to his delivery. 'A week or so from now Sarah was going to leave you a note, then we'd get on a plane and we'd be gone. But then this morning you got a call. I looked at the ID. It was a man's name. I thought maybe you were seeing someone else and so I listened to the voicemail but it was from one of your colleagues. I don't know how but he found out about me and Sarah.'

Jessamine remembered thinking she'd heard ringing that morning in Dougie's flat. She reached for her phone.

'I panicked,' said Dougie. 'Deleted the message and then I blocked him.'

'Why are you here?'

'I decided to beat him to the punch. For us to go now, today. I hadn't accounted for Sarah changing her mind. I figured the best way to get her to reconsider was to bring her to you. Once she has all the facts she can decide for herself what she wants to do.'

Jessamine remembered New Year's Eve. How she'd confided in him about what she'd done – what she'd almost done.

'Tell her,' said Dougie. 'You owe her that at least.'

'Please,' she said, feeling sick.

Growing impatient, he turned to address Sarah directly. 'When you were first adopted you were a lot of trouble. Too much trouble, as it turns out. She was going to give you back.'

Sarah looked to Jessamine for reassurance. 'What's he talking about?'

'I struggled, at first. With being a new parent.'

She thought Sarah was going to walk away but instead she took her hand. 'It doesn't change anything, Mum.'

'Did you hear what I said?' Increasingly desperate, he grabbed Sarah's arm. 'You were two years old. Two, and she was going to return you. Like you were a pair of shoes she'd got home from the shop and decided didn't look right.'

'Let go of her,' said Jessamine, trying to pull him off Sarah. For a few moments they struggled together and then, lifting his hand in the air, he slapped her and she fell to the ground.

'I'm your flesh and blood.' He tried again to reach for Sarah, to embrace her, but she recoiled from his touch. 'All I've thought about every day for the last twelve years is you.'

Jessamine had just pulled herself to her feet when behind her she heard a metallic *shunk-shunk* noise. Dougie heard it too. He turned round, trying to locate the source, and his expression went from confusion to fear.

Jessamine followed his gaze. There, at the foot of the bridge, was a woman, a rifle cocked against her shoulder. It was the nurse, the one from Gloucester Road, and her gun was pointed right at him.

Jitesh

Jitesh followed the long driveway to the house and parked next to two other cars. Dusk had fallen and the lawn that stretched in front of the building was cast in a blue-purple light. He got out and was about to go to the front door when he became aware of voices.

He squinted into the gloom. They were coming from somewhere out of sight, beyond the garden, down towards the valley. He crossed the lawn and was about to continue when he saw it. A sudden drop cut into the side of the grass. A few metres deep, it looked like some kind of ditch, one side of which was a sheer vertical wall. From what he could tell it curved along the lawn's entire perimeter. He sat on the ground, then scaled the steep grassy slope to the other side.

The voices were getting louder.

He continued for a few metres more and then he saw them: Jessamine, Sarah and a man. They were standing in the middle of a bridge, below which flowed a river.

Then he saw a fourth figure. A woman. He couldn't see her face but even from that distance it was clear she had a gun. Slowly, she approached where they stood, the rifle pointed at the man's head.

What was going on?

Jitesh's breathing quickened. Retreating towards the ditch, he skidded down its grassy slope until he was out of sight. There he got out his phone and called the police.

Jessamine

The nurse took a few steps towards Dougie. 'I suggest you back away from the girl. Otherwise . . .' She waggled the end of the gun and shrugged as if the consequence of his non-compliance was a matter beyond her control.

Dougie looked to Jessamine for an explanation and, when none was forthcoming, took a step away from Sarah.

'That's better,' said the woman. Satisfied he was no longer a threat she put the safety on and slung the rifle over her shoulder. 'I'm Millie.'

'Yes,' said Jessamine. She was grateful but also cautious. Could this woman, Millie, be trusted? 'I don't know if you remember . . .'

'You came to the flat.'

'I'm looking into the disappearance of Cassie Scolari?'

'Rowena,' said Millie. 'Her name was Rowena.'

Dougie had been sat on the side of the bridge, his head in his hands. Now, making sure to keep his distance, he approached where they stood. 'Is that it?' He directed his question at Sarah. 'Are we done?'

Still huddled into her mother's side, she looked at him with worried eyes.

'I'm sure we can work something out,' said Jessamine, a little too quickly. This was a lie. As soon as they got away from here she planned to report Dougie to social services and the police. Then she'd find a solicitor and apply for a restraining order that would prevent him from coming within a metre of her daughter ever again.

He stared out at the river, crushed.

'I need to get back to Mum,' said Millie. 'Come to the house, get warm.' She nodded at Dougie. 'You, too, as long as you promise to be on your best behaviour.'

Head hung low, he followed the three women back up the path to the house.

'How did you know to come here?' asked Millie, as they walked.

Jessamine registered the slight inference of guilt in her question but, not wanting to scare her off, decided to take a softly-softly approach. 'Thirteen days after she went missing, Cassie sent a WhatsApp to her friend from her mobile. The phone was only turned on for a very short time, but the police were able to cell-site it to an area a few miles from here.'

'A message? That's not possible.' She seemed genuinely perplexed.

'Millie, do you know what happened to her?'

'She said there were others, that lots of women were planning to come forward. I turned on the phone because I wanted to know who they were, to see how much time I had,' she said, still fixated on Cassie's message. Her conversation was with herself. 'It wasn't until I looked through her messages that I clocked she'd changed her name. Cassie. It doesn't suit her at all.'

They'd just reached the drive when in the distance they heard a wailing sound.

Dougie stopped, listening.

Sirens.

'You called the police?'

Jessamine tensed. There was a new bite to his tone. Angry, but also afraid. 'When would I have been able to do that?' she said. 'We've been with you the whole time.'

Dougie seemed to accept her explanation. They continued around the drive, but they had gone no more than a few steps when he came up behind Millie and kick-swiped her legs out from beneath her. As she stumbled he grabbed for the rifle, but she held on to it. They wrestled for a few seconds and then Dougie punched her once, hard, in the teeth. She recoiled in pain and relinquished her grip.

The gun was his.

He took a step back and raised the rifle towards Sarah.

'Please,' said Jessamine, trying to keep her voice calm. 'This isn't necessary.' She grabbed Sarah's hand and held it.

'All I want,' he said, his voice thick with tears, 'all I've ever wanted was to have my daughter back with me, where she belongs.'

He released the safety catch.

'Dougie, you don't need to do this. Whatever you want, we can work something out.'

The sirens were getting louder.

'I'm not going back to prison.' He shook his head, the tears falling freely now. He seemed to have gone into himself, to some reality they weren't part of. 'I can't, I won't.'

'They're not for us. Think,' she said. 'I promise we haven't called the police. We couldn't have.'

He wiped his face on the upper part of his sleeve. His eyes were bloodshot, his eyelashes wet. 'But she could,' he said, nodding at Millie.

'I didn't, truly,' said Millie, her hands up in surrender.

'Please, put the gun down,' said Jessamine. 'I'm begging you.'

'It's very simple,' he said, crying. 'If I can't have her, neither can you.'

He pointed the gun at Sarah's chest and, staring his daughter in the eye, he squeezed the trigger.

Rowena/Cassie

Leo and I have been talking for a while when he hits me. The slap is like a wake-up call. I think of all the times he hurt me. All the times he made me feel small. And then I think about that night by the canal, how he tried to have Sunny kill me, how he didn't care about what they'd done to Billy.

I step forward and, just as he lifts his gaze, I give him a push towards the hole. He is confused more than surprised, and seems to understand what is happening to him only at the last minute. He scrabbles with his feet and hands, but his efforts are too little too late, and as he makes his descent, his head slams against one of the knuckled tree roots and bounces forward, cracking his chin into his chest.

I fall to my knees and peer over the side, expecting to see him on his feet and angry, already trying to brush the dirt from his suit.

He is not moving.

Lying on his back, with his head at a funny angle, his eyes and mouth are open. Ice is starting to curdle the puddles surrounding him. The sky finally decides to release its load. Snowflakes thicken the air. They catch on his eyelashes.

A crackle in the undergrowth. Someone else is here.

'What have you done?'

Millie emerges from the gloom. She must have followed us. How long has she been listening? How much has she heard?

She approaches the hole and then she asks again, louder than before, 'What have you done?'

Jessamine and Jitesh

On instinct, Jessamine jumped in front of her daughter, trying to shield her from the blast. As the bullet tore through her abdomen she was thrown back, onto Sarah. They fell to the ground in a heap.

Sarah scrambled from beneath her mother's weight and cradled her head in her lap.

'No,' she said, crying.

Jessamine lay where she fell, unable to move. The lower half of her body was numb, her top soaked with blood. She breathed in the cordite-seared air and felt Sarah's face come close to hers, her tears dripping down onto her cheek and neck.

She squeezed her hand and kissed it. 'My girl.'

But then Dougie was there, walking towards them. He stood over where they lay on the grass and raised the gun to Sarah's forehead. Crying and jittery, he kept shaking his head and moving the gun away, only to move it back again, as if he was trying to talk himself out of it.

Jessamine put her hand in her coat pocket, scrabbling around for something, anything to protect her daughter, but apart from the usual pile of pumpkin seeds there was nothing.

Millie stepped forward, trying to intervene. But she'd gone no more than a step when he swung the gun round at her. 'Back off.'

Millie did as he said. The sirens were getting closer.

He redirected the gun at Sarah and this time he pressed the muzzle into her cheek. She began to whimper.

'No.' Jessamine tried to push the rifle out of the way with her hand. He placed his boot on the part of her stomach where he'd shot her and pressed down until she released her grip.

'Please,' said Jessamine, almost blacking out from the pain. 'You don't have to do this.'

It was no good. His shoulders were set, his eyes desperate. 'What have I got to lose?'

From his hiding place in the ditch, Jitesh watched the scene unfolding in front of the house with growing horror. He had planned on staying out of sight until the police arrived but now, after seeing Jessamine shot, he knew he had to do something. He had to act.

The man pointed the gun at Sarah's head.

He concentrated on his breathing. Hold for ten, exhale for five. He thought of Shanae and her fluorescent pink and yellow Nikes. Hold for ten, exhale for five. The look on her face when he told her about the video he'd found on Kishor's computer.

Sarah was sobbing, her eyes closed in anticipation of what was to come.

Taking one last breath, he pressed his tongue against the roof of his mouth and brought his teeth together, preparing to shape the word. Then, steadying his hand against the brick, he peered over the edge of the wall.

'Stop!' he shouted, as loudly as he could. The word rang out loud and clear. 'Stop!'

The voice came from nowhere. It caught Dougie off guard and, for a brief moment, he took his focus off Sarah. A flash of blue and red. The police car's lights, making their way through the tunnel of trees. Jessamine did the only thing she could. Bringing a handful of pumpkin seeds out of her pocket, she raised her hand in the air and threw them into Dougie's eyes. He flinched and Millie took her chance. She ploughed into him, head first, and as he toppled towards the grass the rifle went off, the muzzle flash an orange cloud, bright against the black.

Rowena/Cassie

'I lost my temper. He hit me and then . . .' I fumble for my phone. 'We need to call an ambulance.'

Millie uses the toe of her shoe to poke at the handle of one of the discarded tools. 'I thought you were after cash. That you were going to try to blackmail him.' She kicks the tool away. 'I could have lived with that.'

'Millie. Your dad.'

'But the police?' She approaches the hole and, wary of the crumbling sides, takes in the sight of her father unconscious below. A fine layer of snow already covers him. 'Even after everything I told you about my mother?' Gently, as if she's preparing for a plié, she slides the inside of her foot forward, making sure to keep it close to the ground. 'If this were to get out.' A small pile of soil masses, then collapses over the side. It falls like dust. 'The scandal. Her last months would be ruined.'

I stop, trying to recalibrate what she's saying with what I thought I knew to be true. 'Millie, what are you saying?'

'I'm not stupid, Rowena.' She has a strange expression on her face. She looks me up and down. Brushes away the snow that has already collected on her shoulders.

I flinch. I've spent most of my adult life working hard to make sure no one looks at me like that ever again.

'I'm sorry you had to find out like this,' I say, trying to keep my voice steady. 'That's why I wanted to talk to him tonight. To give him a chance to tell you himself.'

'Find out?' She laughs. 'You don't really think I bought all that rubbish about a career change? I know why you wanted to talk to him. I've always known.'

I'm dressed smartly. I have a job and a house and a family. I am a good mother. No one looking at me would ever be able to tell what I was, who I used to be. But there's something about her laugh that makes all this disappear. It disrobes me and leaves me there, nothing more than your regular garden-variety slag.

'I saw you that night. My birthday.'

It's as though she has punched me in the stomach. Suddenly I find it hard to breathe and hunch forward, shrinking in on myself.

It's been thirteen years but I can still remember every detail. How much it hurt, how he pulled and twisted at my hair, yanking my head back and round. Knowing Millie was there, that she'd witnessed it, renews the shame. The thought hits me like a truck. This is why she stopped being my friend.

'I know it's weird for me to feel jealous. Of that. But at the time I thought it meant he loved you more than me.'

Her self-pity gives me strength. I draw on my anger, push back my shoulders, stand up tall. 'Your dad was a predator. It wasn't just me, there were others.'

Her face tells me this is news. That she has no idea about him, about the extent of it.

'What he did, the people he was involved with. Never mind the things he knew were going on and chose to ignore.' I think of that last night in Dolphin Square. How I told Leo what had happened. How he did nothing. 'It was wrong. I hate him.' I think of Billy, still hidden in the walls of Broadcasting House. How, after tonight, hopefully with the architect's help, I'll lead the police to him. How I'll bring to light his murder and the people who covered it up. 'I'd like nothing more than to leave your father here to rot. God knows he deserves it. But that would mean he'd never have to face up to what he did, that he'd never have to answer for his crimes. He needs to live.' I'm back to my full height again, my voice strong and clear. 'We have to call an ambulance.'

Millie steps away from the edge. Finally, I seem to have got through to her.

'I don't have my phone.'

'Use mine.' I hand her my mobile, get down onto the ground and carefully shuffle over to the edge. 'Turn it on, call an ambulance, then go to the house to get help. I'm going to see if he's still breathing.'

She does as I say and sets off back the way she came.

I look down. There is a root branch directly beneath where I'm sitting. It looks sturdy enough to hold my weight. If I use it as a foothold I can make the remainder of the drop to where Leo lies.

I'm about to lower myself down when I feel a whoosh of air near my ear. I turn to see a metal rectangle coming towards me. The shovel makes contact with the side of my skull and the clearing rings with the neat crack of metal against bone. I slump. A small pressure in the middle of my spine. A foot. And I am pushed forward into the hole. I land on top of Leo's body. Thump. Underneath the light covering of snow, he is still warm, his breath tickles my ear.

I black out for a moment but am woken by the wet smack of mud landing on my face. I force my eyes open and see Millie, at the lip of the hole, shovel in hand. Another sod of dirt falls onto my mouth. I can't move. I inhale and the grit joins the air. I gag as the particles hit the back of my throat.

The side of my temple is wet. Blood. I should crawl away but I can't move. The soil is stuck to my eyelashes. Above I hear Millie's quick breaths. See the flash of metal in the moonlight. More mud. It lands, wet and heavy, on my skin.

Friday 6 October

Present day

Jitesh emptied the last of the cardboard boxes onto the shelf and stood back to admire his handiwork. Tea, coffee, and a tin-opener were now lined up against what must have been at least a month's supply of baked beans, dried pasta and tinned tomatoes. Student food.

He looked at his bed. Leaflets advertising Fresher's Week activities were splayed out next to a map detailing the location of the various colleges. Durham was a small university town, just like Cambridge, and Meera's hall of residence was only a five-minute walk from where he now stood. Later, they'd arranged to meet for dinner in hall after which she'd promised to give him a guided tour.

A noise on the stairs and a boy appeared in the doorway, a plastic crate of stuff held against his chest. His new roommate, Christopher.

'H-hi.' Jitesh went to help him with the crate. 'I'm J-J-Jitesh.'

He had been told the name of the person he'd be sharing with in an email a few weeks earlier. It had been hard but he'd resisted the urge to look Christopher up.

Christopher clocked the assortment of Feynman posters Jitesh had already pinned to the wall above his bed. 'You're a fan?'

Jitesh nodded.

Christopher smiled.

Jitesh wondered if this meant that he was also an admirer of the great man. But that question, along with all the other things he wanted to ask, could wait. Christopher would reveal the different parts of himself if and when he was ready, and this was the joy of it: this was how they would become friends.

Jessamine and Sarah navigated their way down the narrow staircase and into the bar. The final two steps jutted out at an odd angle and Jessamine struggled to find her footing. She stumbled and Sarah put out an arm to catch her. As she righted herself, she winced and had to stand still for a few moments until the pain subsided.

It had been eight months since she was shot. Thankfully the bullet had missed her intestine but she had had to have her spleen removed. She was making good progress with her recovery but there were still occasions when she'd misjudge leaning or twisting and experience an intense ripping sensation inside her abdomen. Her surgeon had told her it would stop eventually: it was just a matter of time.

Millie had told her that her surgeon had said the same thing. She had caught the bullet Dougie had intended for Sarah. Now in HMP Downview, awaiting trial, Jessamine had visited her on a number of occasions and found her to be in unusually high spirits. Prison, she said, was very like boarding school, in its own way.

Sarah waited until she was sure her mother was okay and then, linking arms, helped her up the final two steps. They emerged into the cavernous room and Jessamine was suddenly aware of all eyes on her.

Tonight was the launch of *Went/Gone* on Radio 4. The BBC had licensed it from her and to celebrate they were hosting a small party to which the press and some of her friends had been invited. Her fee for the podcast hadn't been huge, but Jessamine had divided it equally between two trust funds, one for Matteo and one for Tasha's baby girl, now out of the neonatal unit and thriving.

Meanwhile, interest in herself as an indie broadcaster continued to grow. In the last week she'd been contacted by three major brands offering significant sponsorship for her next series. She'd yet to decide whether or not to take any of them up, but if and when she did the sums in question would be more than enough to provide for her and Sarah for at least the year to come.

Jessamine spotted O'Brien handing a drink to a woman with red hair, and Ellen Griksaitis chatting to Jackie from the domestic-violence helpline. Ellen looked up and waved. Dougie was now back in prison, awaiting trial for the attempted murder of Millie, Sarah and Jessamine. Ellen had been key in helping them get in place a restraining order that would forbid him to contact Sarah or Jessamine ever again.

Jessamine thought often of Rowena, the girl Cassie used to be, of Queenie and Billy Huggett, the boy whose body she'd discovered inside the walls of Broadcasting House. Cassie and Billy had both been in care.

It wasn't lost on her that, were it not for Sarah's adoption, theirs was a life that could easily have been hers.

While Sarah went over to say hello to Ellen, Jessamine collected the large box she'd had delivered to the venue earlier that day, and approached O'Brien and his friend.

'Jessie, this is Susan,' he said, introducing the woman with red hair. 'My fiancée.'

Jessamine offered her congratulations and, once she had admired Susan's diamond ring, she handed him the box.

'Charles, Susan.' She presented it to them with a flourish. 'This is for you. An engagement present.'

He tore off the gift wrap and studied the diagram on the outside, confused.

'It's a toaster, egg poacher and a Teasmade all in one.' She'd tried to choose something akin to the many ridiculous multi-purpose presents he'd given her over the years.

He laughed.

The investigation into the murder of Billy Huggett was ongoing – the autopsy had revealed a fractured hyoid bone, an injury commonly associated with strangulation – but with Cassie, the only apparent witness, now dead, it seemed unlikely the police would ever be able to identify the culprit. O'Brien, though, was of the same opinion as Jessamine. Hiding the body in the walls of Broadcasting House, the very heart of the BBC, suggested the person had had some kind of grievance against the institution. The celebrity, later unmasked as a paedophile, was known to have felt under-appreciated by the BBC in his later years and had been at work in the building during the window of time Billy had been placed there. This, combined with the arrogance the celebrity had shown throughout his life – in his pursuit of his victims and his subsequent dealings with the police – suggested he considered himself untouchable. Jessamine and O'Brien were in no doubt that he was their man.

The room was now at capacity. Donna, the BBC publicist, gave Jessamine a wave, beckoning her to the microphone where she was to give a speech about the podcast and thank everyone for coming.

En route to Donna, Jessamine stopped where Ellen and Sarah were chatting at the bar. Bringing Sarah in for a hug, she pressed her face into her daughter's hair. She smelt of hairspray and shampoo but there, underneath the raspberry and vanilla, she could smell something else too, loamy and familiar. Sarah's scalp, sweeter than any shampoo. As she breathed deep, she was hit by the almost painful rush of feeling she'd experienced many times before. Now, though, she found she had the word to describe it. The word was love.

Went/Gone: **Episode 6**

Early evening, Friday, 11 November 2016, the heart of the Berkshire Downs. In a wooded copse half a mile's walk from her parents' Elizabethan manor house Millie Wiles looks down to where her father, Leo, and her childhood friend, Rowena, lie unconscious in a hole twenty feet deep. As the snow starts to fall, she picks up a shovel and covers their bodies with two inches of earth. The snow will do the rest, hiding them for months to come. Afterwards, Millie returns to the house and sends a number of texts and emails from her father's phone to colleagues, saying he has decided to take compassionate leave of absence to care for his sick wife and that, for the foreseeable future, he will be uncontactable.

My name is Jessamine Gooch and you are listening to *Went/Gone*. If you've listened to every episode so far then you'll know that what began as a podcast into the investigation of a missing woman named Cassie Scolari turned out to be the story of what happened to a teenage girl named Rowena Garbutt, more than fourteen years earlier. Now, in this, the last instalment in a series that has been all about questions, we bring you some answers.

Acknowledgements

Sophie Orme, my whip-smart bobby-dazzler of an editor.

Kate Parkin, Jennie Rothwell and all at Bonnier Zaffre.

Mary Griksaitis, for lending me her expertise on the care system and adoption process. Mary is an incredible woman and over the years has helped many children like Rowena.

Steve Roche, for helping me with the beginnings of this book and for always being there whenever I need guidance on police matters.

Sarjoo Patel, for introducing me to the wonder that is Neasden Temple.

Naomi Kelt, for her insight into those who volunteer at the Domestic Violence Helpline. I have taken liberties with the ways in which the helpline operates but, sadly, the lack of refuge places for women and children is not a fiction. If you would like to donate then please go to www.refuge.org.uk

Helen Oakwater. I was first alerted to the issues surrounding adopted children and social media thanks to Helen's excellent book *Bubble Wrapped Children: How Social Networking Is Transforming the Face of 21st Century Adoption*.

Luke Genower, my development partner-in-crime, brain-stormer of sticky plot points, first reader and, most importantly, my friend.

CPL Productions. My work family. Charlie, Amanda, Trish, Arabella, Danielle, Murray, Janet, Heather, Abigail, Jess, Dawn, Arshdeep and Alex.

But, as always, thanks above all to Alan and Dorothy. My world.

If you enjoyed *The Dangerous Kind*, why not join Deborah O'Connor's Readers' Club by visiting www.bit.ly/DeborahOConnor?

Dear Reader,

I first heard the term Potentially Dangerous People while researching a TV programme I was working on. The concept fascinated me. There were all these people out there who had never committed a single crime but who the police felt certain would one day go on to commit an offence that would cause serious physical or psychological harm. I wrote it down in a notebook and forgot all about it. Then the Rotherham child sexual exploitation scandal happened, closely followed by Operation Yewtree and many other horrific cases of historic sexual abuse. Watching the news I was struck by how ubiquitous the abuse was, stretching as it did across time, culture and class. The dangerous kind, it seemed, were everywhere. Even more terrifying, they tended to hide in plain sight. Stumbling across that note I'd made all those years earlier, I decided I wanted to write a novel about these monsters, more importantly I wanted to write about the incredibly courageous people who stand up to them.

If you would like to hear more about my books, you can visit **www.bit.ly/DeborahOConnor** where you can become part of my readers' club. It only takes a few moments to sign up, there are no catches or costs.

Bonnier Zaffre will keep your data private and confidential, and it will never be passed on to a third party. We won't spam you with loads of emails, just get in touch now and again with news about my books, and you can unsubscribe any time you want.

And if you would like to get involved in a wider conversation about my books, please do review *The Dangerous Kind* on Amazon, on GoodReads, on any other e-store, on your own blog and social media accounts, or talk about it with friends, family or reader groups. Sharing your thoughts helps other readers, and I always enjoy hearing about what people experience from my writing.

Thank you again for reading *The Dangerous Kind*.

All the best,

Deborah

Want to read
NEW BOOKS
before anyone else?

Like getting
FREE BOOKS?

Enjoy sharing your
OPINIONS?

Discover

READERS FIRST

Read. Love. Share.

Sign up today to win your first free book:
readersfirst.co.uk

For Terms and Conditions see readersfirst.co.uk/pages/terms-of-service